# THE LUMINOUS DEAD

# THE
# LUMINOUS
## DEAD

A NOVEL

## CAITLIN STARLING

HARPER Voyager
*An Imprint of* HarperCollins*Publishers*

THE LUMINOUS DEAD. Copyright © 2019 by Caitlin Starling. All rights reserved. Printed in the United States of America. No part of this book may be used or reproduced in any manner whatsoever without written permission except in the case of brief quotations embodied in critical articles and reviews. For information, address HarperCollins Publishers, 195 Broadway, New York, NY 10007.

HarperCollins books may be purchased for educational, business, or sales promotional use. For information, please email the Special Markets Department at SPsales@harpercollins .com.

Harper Voyager and design are trademarks of HarperCollins Publishers LLC.

FIRST EDITION

*Designed by Paula Szafranski*
*Frontispiece image © Brandon B / Shutterstock*
*Maps designed by Mike Hall*

Library of Congress Cataloging-in-Publication Data has been applied for.

ISBN 978-0-06-284690-7

23 24 25 26 27  LBC  11 10 9 8 7

*For my mother*

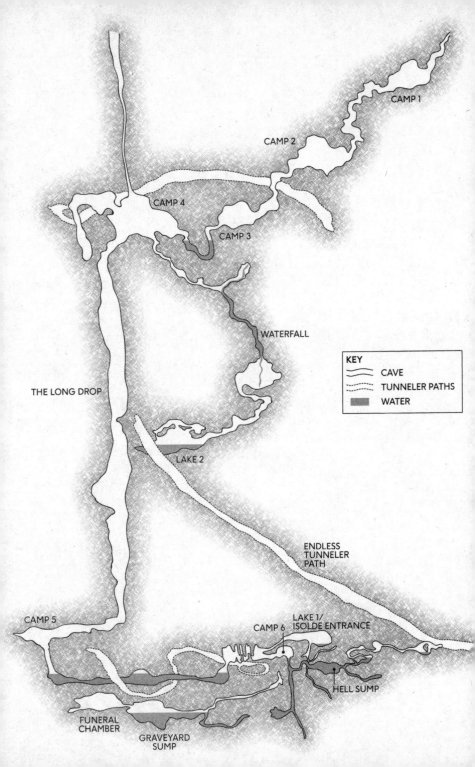

CAMP 1

CAMP 2

CAMP 4

CAMP 3

WATERFALL

KEY

CAVE

TUNNELER PATHS

WATER

THE LONG DROP

LAKE 2

ENDLESS
TUNNELER
PATH

CAMP 5

LAKE 1/
ISOLDE ENTRANCE

CAMP 6

HELL SUMP

FUNERAL
CHAMBER

GRAVEYARD
SUMP

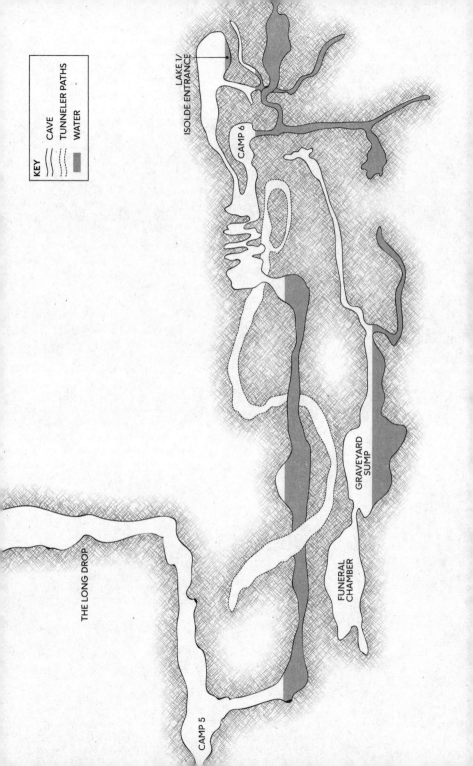

KEY
CAVE
TUNNELER PATHS
WATER

LAKE 1/
ISOLDE ENTRANCE

CAMP 6

THE LONG DROP

FUNERAL
CHAMBER

GRAVEYARD
SUMP

CAMP 5

# THE LUMINOUS DEAD

# CHAPTER ONE

She'd never gone this deep.

Gyre wriggled her armored body another centimeter into the crevice, then eased her bag of gear after her. The plating on the back of her calf scraped over the stone, and she winced at the noise. Nobody had warned her that the opening to the lower cave system was so small—or empty. To be fair, she hadn't gotten a lot of warning or preparation. She'd been too eager to get below the surface to question if there should have been more than the limited orientation she'd received.

Still, when she'd signed up for the expedition, she had assumed three things:

One, that there would be a team assisting her, monitoring the readings from her suit from afar, pulling up maps for her when possible, and keeping her company in the dwindling light as she left the surface.

Two, that she would enter through a giant borehole into

a mining camp, and would stage in that camp before pressing deeper into the ground.

And three, that the amount of money she was being offered would be directly related to the sophistication of the expedition.

And yet here she was, alone in a tiny crevice in an unknown site, her helmet speakers silent.

"Caver here," she said for the fifth time. "Would appreciate contact, base."

For the fifth time, there was no response. The only sounds were her breathing inside her helmet, the soft pulsing of the alert system displayed in front of her face, and the groan of her suit against rock as she contorted her spine and pressed through another few centimeters.

Gyre paused, leaning against the curved crevice wall. Maybe she should go back. Maybe her suit was malfunctioning. At the hospital where she had been fitted into it, she had gone through the regular check and double check of all systems, including communications transmission. Everything had been fine then, and her year of helping other cavers into similar suits told her that all systems were go. But she didn't have a death wish, and going any farther without comms was suicide. Her eyes flicked over the readouts inside her suit again.

Everything was normal.

"Beginning to suspect suit is shot," she said anyway, addressing the emptiness. "Preparing to abort."

The speakers in her helmet finally came to life. "Negative. Do not abort. Caver, continue." The voice sounded female, clipped and authoritative. More important, it sounded real—not a computerized response.

*Well, that got a reaction.* Gyre's lips twisted into a bitter approximation of a smile. "Roger," she muttered, and shuffled another few centimeters.

The crevice widened abruptly about half a meter farther in, and Gyre stumbled out, reflexively moving to dust herself off. But carbon polymer just scraped over carbon polymer, a frustrating reminder that for the next several weeks—or even months—she wouldn't be able to feel her own skin. She shook her head.

*Rookie.*

The suit was her new skin, filled with sensors and support functions, dampening her heat and strengthening her already powerful muscles with an articulated exoskeleton designed to keep climbing as natural as possible. She wouldn't even remove her helmet to eat or sleep. Her large intestine had been rerouted to collect waste for easy removal and a feeding tube had been implanted through her abdominal wall ten days ago. A port on the outside of her suit would connect to nutrition canisters. All liquid waste would be recycled by the suit. All solid waste would be compacted and cooled to ambient temperature, then either carried with her or stored in caches to be retrieved on her trip out. Everything was painstakingly, extensively designed to protect her from . . . *elements* in the cave.

And, all the while, her handlers would be monitoring her vitals and surveying her surroundings for her. It was Gyre's job to move and climb and explore; it was her handlers' job to document.

"Caver, continue," repeated the woman from before.

Gyre scowled, then straightened up and looked around the cavern. Her suit used a combination of infrared and sonar pulses to generate readings on the surrounding topography, which was reconstructed into what looked like a well-lit but colorless scene on the screen in front of her. In an emergency, the reconstruction could be turned off and a normal light turned on, but it wasn't advisable to have a lamp burning, giving off heat, attracting attention down in the cold darkness of the caves.

There was a reason, after all, that cavers could demand enough money that they'd be able to get off-world after only two jobs, maybe three.

Too many cavers didn't make it that long.

Just one of the many reasons Gyre was going to do it in one.

"Continuing," she acknowledged, but paused first to drink in the space. The ceiling was high and vaulted, the ground even and dry. Far off, she thought she could hear water. The surface had been in a near-constant drought since she was a child, but most of the deep caves in this area still had water flowing through them, and would periodically flood from harsh, sudden storms that destroyed settlements and washed away topsoil and structures on the surface. This was the first time she'd personally set foot in a chamber this deep.

It was beautiful.

It was also unnerving.

She made her way to a marker blinking on her HUD, clambering down a wide natural staircase, a duffel full of equipment and food slung over her shoulder.

"Where's the mine, base?" she asked as she slid over one of the larger drops and landed in a haze of dust. "Is this new ground, or just a new entrance?"

Base was, of course, silent.

Maybe this was normal. She'd never heard of taciturn support teams from the senior cavers she'd talked to, but she also hadn't been allowed in the topside command rooms. The problem was that *if* this was normal, the team would expect her to know that.

*They* didn't know this was her first time down.

Gyre came to the edge of another, larger drop. Like the five she'd descended to get down to the initial crevice, this one had an anchor at the top, and a fresh, high-quality rope leading down. There had been other cavers here, and recently.

"Base, requesting a topside search," she said, considering the rope. "Confirm that there are no other cavers ahead of me. I'm seeing signs of—"

"There is no mine, and no other cavers," the woman said. "Equipment was put in and caches established in anticipation of your descent."

*Okay.* No mine wasn't ideal, but not unheard of; her boss must just be looking for deposits in new ground, sending people in one after the other. It wasn't common these days, with most of the land already picked over, but in a true expedition like that, pre-stocked caches were a good idea. Given the pay rate on this mission and the sophistication of her equipment, this was clearly a high-end pursuit, and yet—

And yet so far she could only be sure of one person in the support room, and the techs who had helped calibrate her suit hadn't been chatty or worn the logo of any of the major mining concerns. She'd known from the beginning that this was an individual-run expedition, and at the time, money and the quality of the equipment had eclipsed all other considerations. They'd been worth falsifying her credentials here and there to make her look proven. They'd been worth hiring a surgeon to redirect her bowels for a month—something she really couldn't afford, but the payout from this job would more than cover it—just so that she'd have the appropriate scars when the expedition's doctors cut her open.

But now that she was underground, she was beginning to wonder if she had made a giant mistake.

Of course, there could still be five or ten techs. Maybe they were all shy. Maybe the woman with the mic was territorial and a total idiot. It was possible.

If that was the case, she just had to keep going until shift change.

In the meantime, she reassured herself that expeditions were always top-heavy. They could afford to be, *had* to be. They were standing on a veritable mint deep below the surface of Cassandra-V, the only thing keeping the colony halfway viable, and decades of mining had taught them a few things.

Like the fact that early teams that went down to establish mines or take samples ended up dead. Ninety percent failure rate. Big groups, small groups, solo explorers . . . it didn't matter. Something always killed them.

Something always killed them, until somebody got smart enough or desperate enough to try wearing a drysuit down, alone, into a cave. Even now, nobody was sure if it was because it blocked heat rising from the body, or smell, or something else, but one person, in an enclosed suit, could survive. One person, though, needed help keeping watch while they slept, and the suits became more and more elaborate to provide for longer and longer survey missions. Now missions had at least five or ten techs topside. She'd seen it firsthand, working support on two medium-sized operations. A year ago, she'd helped her first caver into a similar suit—a hotshot guy with two expeditions already under his belt—and it hadn't been nearly as elaborate and high-tech as this one. This was top-of-the-line and must have demanded an even larger crew.

So where were they?

The sensible thing would be to call off the mission and walk back out, while she still could. But she'd sacrificed too much to get here, this deep, with this much money on the line.

She didn't want to go through it all again. Next time, her embellished work history might not stand up to scrutiny. And if she was wrong, if there *was* a team, and she walked out? Nobody wanted to hire a caver who would breach contract. Not when there were so many others waiting to be picked.

*Not when there are a hundred other kids as desperate as I am.*

Gyre rolled her shoulders back to center herself, then clipped into the rope at hip level, attaching the duffel to her suit. It was the first of several she'd be ferrying in that day, the rest stacked and waiting for her on the other side of the narrow crevice she'd entered through. She reached behind her to the hump of hard carbon seated across her shoulders. All her equipment was slotted into the suit itself, and the storage space on her back protruded almost like a satchel. As she ghosted her fingers over the release sensors, her HUD displayed what was stored there. Her rappel rack was within easy reach, and she released it from its slot, then hitched it to the front of her suit and threaded the rope through its bars. Once it was secure, she glanced over the edge again.

Her readout display blinked as it measured the distance down with a few sonar pulses: 70 meters. In normal light, the bottom would've been pitch black, but her HUD's reconstruction showed it in full detail as if it were only a few meters away. She crouched to check the anchor, even though she'd already practiced this hundreds of times since signing on to this project.

Nothing about cave exploration should be done on autopilot.

Everything looked fine. She'd been trained—or rather, she'd taught herself—to place her own anchors every time, but the other, shorter drops she'd already done *had* been anchored correctly.

Base had confirmed this one had been placed for her.

"Caver, continue," her handler said, her voice flat. Emotionless.

Gyre straightened, checked her device one last time, then stepped off the edge.

# CHAPTER TWO

Her first camp was just shy of a quarter kilometer from the entrance slot, and five hundred or so meters below the surface. Just as her handler had said, she'd found a cache waiting for her, but additional fresh supplies would still be necessary. Even with high-density, compact nutritional canisters, she'd need more than the few stashed here if she was going to stay under for longer than a month, and then make the climb back out.

She spent two days making three trips back to the surface to retrieve gear. The topside base said nothing else after the beginning of her second trip. At first, Gyre was relieved; the woman on the other side of her comm line, so far her only contact, was abrasive and cold. Her silence left Gyre to make her own decisions. It was comforting for a few hours, as if this job were just like all her solo practice runs. But then the overbearing quiet became too much. Five hundred meters of stone separated her from human contact, and she felt it in her bones. She'd never been under for more than a day on her own before—one of the many small details she hadn't exactly been forthright about when signing on.

So she murmured and sang to herself, trying to distract her itching nerves, the sound never leaving the confines of her helmet as she settled into camp at the end of the second day. It was a quick task. No fire, no sleeping bag, no cooking. Instead, she patrolled the perimeter, administered her meal for the night, then tried to get comfortable.

The suit had some limited internal padding and support; it served as a moving sleeping roll as well as armor and structural enhancement. But that was like saying a metal stool was furniture, and therefore equivalent to a bed. She positioned herself as comfortably as she could, locked her armor in place to lessen the load on her muscles, and powered down the visuals in her helmet.

"Going to sleep, base. You got my back?" she asked the black emptiness.

"Affirmative."

The same woman. She'd been there—probably—the whole time. No shift change.

No team.

*Fantastic.*

"Does base have a name?" Gyre asked, trying to ignore the alarms going off in her head.

Nothing.

Trying to keep her voice light, she said, "Does base care to tell me why an expedition this expensive isn't giving me a full crew?" It was a risky move; if her handler got angry, Gyre would be screwed.

"You are adequately supported," the woman said.

"But it's just you, right?"

Silence. Then: "Yes."

"That wasn't in my contract."

"Your contract," the woman said firmly, "promised *adequate support*."

Gyre twitched, jaw clenching. She breathed through her nose, counting up to ten. "This is highly unusual," she said. "I'd feel more comfortable if I knew you had relief up there."

The handler said nothing.

Which left Gyre facing the same choice as before: be smart and leave, or stay and make it work.

She shouldn't risk staying. But she *couldn't* risk leaving.

"Does base have some music she can pipe in, or a book I can read?" she asked grudgingly.

"Go to sleep, caver," her handler replied. "I will keep watch."

*Yeah*, Gyre thought, scowling, *until you pass out yourself because you've got no relief up there.*

But biology won out over her better judgment. She was exhausted, muscles sore and mind foggy, and it wasn't long before her thoughts began to drift. Back when she'd started exploring the slot canyons and pseudocaves near her home ten years ago, she'd just been a twelve-year-old girl expertly avoiding her house and her dad. The pseudocaves, which could almost reach the depth she was at now, didn't require suits. They had the usual risks: cave-ins, flash floods, falls, lack of food. Some of them were wickedly difficult to navigate, demanding top-tier skill. But two or three people could go down for the day without a suit, or with just an old-fashioned simple drysuit with no intestinal rearrangement and no catheters if they were really worried. Nothing would come out of the blackness and kill them. But the pseudocaves also didn't have minerals. They were economically useless, and usually empty.

So she'd played in them, first for fun, then to build the skills she'd need to sign on with a true cave expedition and earn enough money to get herself off the planet.

She still remembered, vividly, the day she'd nearly broken her legs on a fall. She'd been just shy of her thirteenth birthday and had been descending in pitch darkness, her headlamp extinguished by the spray of an early rains waterfall now dominating far more of the cavern than it usually did. She'd been too arrogant that day to abort, or switch to a different lamp, so certain she could navigate the rest of the descent by touch and memory.

And she'd been able to, until about six or seven meters above the bottom—close enough to not be in life-threatening danger, but far enough to cause a problem if something went wrong. The roaring of the waterfall had gotten louder, and she'd assumed that was because she was getting closer to the bottom. She hadn't realized that the recent rains had knocked free a bit of stone and the waterfall had changed trajectory just enough that as she lowered herself another meter—too fast, much too fast—she was caught in the thundering torrent. She'd lost her grip on her rappel rack and slid down the rope, pushed by the force of the water, unable to arrest.

But then she slammed to a halt, feet not more than half a meter from the ground, her rack caught on a knot that shouldn't have been there, was only there because she'd screwed up packing her gear. Without it, she would have hit the ground, twisted her ankles or broken her legs. She spluttered, her hands finally gripping the metal and squeezing tight, obsessively, as her heart pounded. Water continued pouring over her, soaking her to the core. She'd been giddy on the adrenaline; she'd survived her first brush with death.

By the time she'd made it back to the surface, everything but her hair was dry. Her manic energy had faded, as had her excitement; she'd been left with a bruised chest where her harness had jerked her to a halt, and exhausted, trembling muscles. She'd limped back to town, to her house in the western reach by the cliffs, and collapsed in her kitchen, close to hypothermic and with the aftereffects of adrenaline still twisting up her insides. Her dad hadn't been home.

With nobody else to talk to, she'd stared up at the photo of her mother hanging on the kitchen wall. *Your fault*, she'd thought, over and over again. Her mother had made her into this. *Your fault*, she'd thought.

*Your fault.*

Gyre twitched, then swore, eyes shooting open. Her HUD was on full brightness, and her heart was pounding, just like it had back in that waterfall. White noise blared in her ears. Her suit unlocked a second later, and she scrambled to right herself, to get up on her feet.

But there was no red flashing readout on her HUD, and as she came to full wakefulness, the noise lessened and her screen dimmed to normal levels.

"Good morning, caver," said her handler. "Time to get to work."

Gyre cursed.

"Your goal for today," the woman continued, ignoring Gyre's invective, "is to reach Camp Two. I've adjusted your HUD to show the way. Each trip with your supplies is estimated to take roughly three hours. Return trip will take two. Your schedule allows three days for this segment."

It was the most she'd said all together, but Gyre didn't

care. She pressed her hands to her chest, willing her heart to slow down. "Screw you," she hissed.

"Walking is the most expeditious way to work off the epinephrine injection, caver."

*Epinephrine injection—* "That's supposed to be for emergencies only!"

Her HUD flashed. Text began scrolling across it, quickly, until it stopped on an excerpt that read:

THE CAVER AGREES TO SURRENDER BODILY AUTONOMY TO THE EXPEDITION TEAM FOR THE DURATION OF THE EXPEDITION PERIOD, IN ORDER TO FACILITATE THE SMOOTH OPERATION OF THE EXPEDITION AND TO PROTECT THE CAVER'S WELL-BEING. AT THE EXPEDITION TEAM'S DISCRETION, THE EXPEDITION TEAM MAY PERFORM THE FOLLOWING, NONEXCLUSIVE TASKS:

ADMINISTRATION OF CERTAIN HORMONES AND NEUROTRANSMITTERS, INCLUDING BUT NOT LIMITED TO ADRENALINE, DOPAMINE, AND MELATONIN.

ADMINISTRATION OF CERTAIN PHARMACEUTICALS, INCLUDING BUT NOT LIMITED TO ANTIBIOTICS, OPIOID PAINKILLERS . . .

And then it scrolled again, until it reached her signature.

"'In order to facilitate the smooth operation,'" Gyre repeated through gritted teeth.

"Caver, please prepare for your first trip to Camp Two."

Gyre hesitated a moment longer in opposition, then began securing the first duffel.

She'd made her decision. She was doing this for the money, for her mother. A power-tripping, asshole handler working without backup didn't change that.

It just meant she'd have to stay on her toes and get good at swallowing her anger.

⌄

The contract had been more or less standard. No matter how many times she thought up a new biting retort to her once-more taciturn handler, she couldn't move past that fact. Caving was lucrative, but ultimately a horrible job, and one you could only do for a few years at most before you were too injured to keep going, or you couldn't take the isolation and the strain anymore, or the cave just straight up killed you. The smart ones cashed out early, with both their paycheck and their health. But there was always the allure of bigger, more lucrative, more dangerous jobs. The temptation was what dragged them all in; it didn't let them go easily.

Most cavers were young these days, under twenty-five, a few even younger than she was. They'd all grown up on this colony where every job was wretched, where general life expectancy was low by the standards of other, more "civilized," well-supported worlds. Backbreaking labor and low pay were the general rule. If you had the skill for it, then why wouldn't you trade a little bit of bodily autonomy for enough money to feed your family or to start a new life?

Why wouldn't you accept a single handler, if you'd already lied to get this far, if the money on offer was so good, you'd only need to do one job?

Trade-offs. Always trade-offs.

So instead of voicing all the biting comments bubbling up inside her, Gyre attempted a different approach during her second trip to Camp Two, her muscles burning and her thoughts buzzing in the dark.

"Base, that still you?"

15

Nothing. She ignored it.

"Because if it is, I hope you get some sleep soon. With what they're paying me, they can afford some shift relief. I don't want you falling asleep right when a Tunneler jumps me."

She hoped that made the woman smile. Or frown. Honestly, she just hoped it made the woman react.

She maneuvered herself along a narrow ledge, belly pressed to the cavern wall.

"But if it is just you, we should get to know each other," she continued, working the articulated toes of her suit into a better hold and levering herself and her pack along the line she was clipped to. "You got a name?"

Still nothing. Gyre tamped down the flare of irritation.

"Moller didn't tell me much about you when he hired me." Moller was the expedition owner. She'd met him twice: once at her interview, and once in the hospital where she'd been given a full examination and gone under for surgery, waking up properly rearranged for her suit. He'd been less sleazy than the other expedition owners she'd talked to. Off-worlder, with enough holdings elsewhere that he wasn't overly invested in the colony. That worked better for her; he didn't want an indentured servant—he wanted a *caver*. She couldn't say the same about most other male owners. She'd counted herself lucky.

Now, though, she was starting to suspect she'd been played. She'd been lulled by how kind he looked. Good clothing, a soft voice. Salt-and-pepper hair. And yet he'd stuck her with a single handler—why? Why increase the odds of failure so much? Some sort of arcane tax-evasion scheme? Or maybe he got off on watching a woman flail in the darkness, struggling to survive.

No, that didn't add up; he'd spent the money on the technology and her paycheck, if not the topside staff. Nobody would pay this much just to watch her die.

Right?

"Actually," she said, her curiosity turning genuine and a little desperate, "he didn't tell me anything about you. Didn't mention that I wouldn't have a whole team. He talked about the high-tech suit but didn't mention that this wasn't an existing cave system. Is he always like that?"

"Often," the handler replied at last.

Gyre shuddered, a surge of endorphins cascading through her at the fear and relief triggered by hearing that voice. Her handler was still there. She clipped into the next anchor as she transferred to a new, descending line. Just a few meters down to the next platform.

"Is he there with you?"

"No, he's not," she said. "He doesn't stay long."

"Is that normal?" Gyre asked as she rappelled down in a few quick, easy bounces. "I got the sense that he wasn't personally invested, but it's a lot of money."

"It's not his money."

Her handler sounded as if she were standing right next to her, and Gyre thought she sounded amused, like Gyre had just told a half-decent joke. A joke Gyre wasn't getting.

"Rich dad?" Gyre hazarded.

"Rich employer."

Gyre frowned, hefting her supply bag and moving along the rim of an old breakdown while skirting the boulders. "Most expedition owners don't like working for anybody but themselves, in my experience," Gyre said, leaving off that *her experience* was limited to assisting on two expeditions and listening to a lot of shit-talking in bars.

She looked around. It was another short descent to Camp

Two, but there was a nice wide, flat stone nearby, and she set down her duffel and hopped onto it, settling in for a break. "So, who's he got holding his purse strings?"

The other side of the line went silent again, and Gyre frowned. She'd felt like she was getting somewhere with the woman, at last—and talking about Moller hadn't seemed too risky. Gossiping about the boss had always seemed like a constant of the human condition.

Gyre stretched out on her back as she waited for a response. Her gear bump propped her up, and she bent her legs at the knees before triggering the armor lockup, creating a hard couch for her to rest on. She groaned as her muscles relaxed those first few millimeters.

Gyre was just considering a short nap when her HUD blinked—activity on the comm line. She took a deep, anticipatory breath.

"Mr. Moller," her handler said without preamble, "is my employ*ee*. As are you."

The breath came out as a confused whine, and she quickly muted her side of the comm as she spluttered and unlocked her armor, sitting up.

*Oh.*

She'd never considered that option.

"Caver?"

"Here," she said after unmuting herself. "And it's Gyre. Call me Gyre. Miss Boss."

"Em is fine," the woman said, and there was that hint of amusement again. "Now: get up."

"I've been making decent time—ahead of schedule," Gyre protested.

Something on the left side of her HUD began to glow, and Gyre turned her head until it was centered. It wasn't a goal marker, and it wasn't directly on the path to Camp Two. Curiosity outweighed her annoyance, and she stood, then reached for the duffel.

"You can leave that," Em said.

Gyre frowned, her hand dropping back to her side. "What's the marker for?"

"Something I think you'll appreciate, based on your file," she said.

Gyre imagined the woman sitting at her station. Was she finely dressed? In pajamas? She didn't sound much older than Gyre herself. Her voice wasn't scratchy or squeaky; instead, it had a low, smooth richness. It was the kind of voice that would've turned Gyre's head in a bar.

Off-world accented, too. Educated.

Gyre hesitated a moment longer, that marker burning on her screen, before giving in. The climbs hadn't been hard the last two days, but they'd been constant, and she hadn't explored nearly as much as she'd wanted to. She hopped down from the rock she'd been lying on and made for the glowing marker.

It led her to one of the cavern walls and faded in intensity as she neared. The image on her screen shifted, its colors adjusting to something closer to what she'd see if she had a proper light.

On the wall was a small growth of a pale white plant with substantial, translucent stalks. They were topped by what looked like tiny glowing flowers, and she crouched down to get a better look. The never-ending dry season up top meant that most of the local flora were tough, spiky, hard-rinded. Flowers were rare, and rarely attractive.

This, though—this looked like what she'd seen in pictures and vids from the garden colonies.

Em had been right. Gyre could feel herself smiling in wonder. *This* was what had kept her going down farther and farther into those pseudocaves, far beyond avoiding her dad, well before she'd ever thought of leaving Cassandra-V.

Back then, she'd wanted to see something special. She'd wanted to be strong enough, clever enough, to make it to places others had only ever dreamed of. Somewhere along the line, it had gotten twisted, focused entirely on success and money and getting off-world, but that initial impulse was still alive inside her.

"What does it grow on?" she asked. "It's just stone down here."

"It's a fungus. Similar growths are all over this system, especially lower down. There are creatures that live in the water in the cavern and sometimes they wash up and die," Em replied. "Up here, sometimes insects fly in. And when the rains come, they wash in soil and everything that's in the soil. This one's been there for several months, though, so it'll probably drain its host soon and die."

"So it'll be gone by the time I come back up this way?"

Em hesitated before saying, "Possibly."

*Possibly*—because she thought Gyre might bail soon, or because she was a perfectionist and hadn't done the math? Gyre didn't intend on bailing, so she leaned in closer and reached out to touch it.

"I wouldn't advise that," Em said. "I don't have data on any interaction between its spores and your suit."

"Can I take a picture?" she asked, frozen in place.

"I've taken it already."

Her smile fell. Maybe Mr. Moller wasn't a voyeur, but Em certainly enjoyed controlling her suit from her seat on high. Most expeditions, from what she'd learned from veterans, left their cavers to their own devices except in cases of emergencies—like the adrenaline injection should have been. Even if the contracts allowed it, those weren't usually used to rouse cavers in the morning when their handlers were ready for them to start moving.

"Right," Gyre said, straightening up. "Well, thanks."

Em didn't respond, probably tapping at the feeds of various metrics coming off her suit, or maybe reading a novel. Gyre didn't care. Whatever connection they had started to make had already been severed. She stalked over to her duffel and hefted it, then headed off for Camp Two.

# CHAPTER THREE

It took several trips over the course of two days to haul all the required gear to Camp Two. The climb was long, but relatively easy, barely providing a challenge now that she'd gotten used to moving in the suit and managing the duffels. On the third day, at Em's direction, she didn't push out from Camp Two. There was no explanation. She simply woke up naturally, with no input from Em, and when she reached for the first gear duffel, Em interrupted her with a curt, "No hauling today."

And that was it.

It was probably just a rest day. She was ahead of schedule, and prolonged expeditions were taxing on the body, even with the support of the suit. A good handler would have taken Gyre's input on it or explained her logic, but they'd already established Em was far from a good handler.

It didn't make the change of routine any easier to take.

Her mind rushed through scenarios. And she fixated on one in particular:

Maybe something was wrong with her suit and Em was working on a fix.

Her stomach twisted as she inserted her nutritional canister for the morning, and she tried to ignore her imagination telling her the cannula had been jarred. More likely, really, was that a small crack somewhere in her suit was venting heat. Death by infection or by Tunneler—both stirred up a keen edge of fear in her gut.

She paced, refusing to allow the air surrounding her to warm up.

But nothing changed. Em's side of the comm line was still silent, and her readings remained green and stable.

After the first hour, the fear began to feel hollow and useless. Exhausting. And as crazy as she was, Em would have said if Gyre was in danger. Even *she* couldn't be so callous.

Probably.

Gyre shoved those thoughts—and the fear—aside and began to explore the space around Camp Two, desperate to keep herself occupied.

There were towering stalagmites in this section of the cave, and when she adjusted her sound pickup, she could hear the faint dripping of water farther out. Her camp was set atop a large plateau, surrounded on two sides by tumbling breakdown boulders, one by a sheer drop, and the last by an easy slope that led up to Camp One. She pointed herself off the other three sides until her sonar readings built up a better picture of the cave, sinking into the vastness of the chamber, the humbling mass of natural architecture rising up around her.

Then she called up the marker for Camp Three.

Nothing came up.

"Em? Have you loaded in the route to Camp Three?"

"You're not going to Camp Three yet," Em replied. Well, she was there, at least. Not sleeping. Not out having some fancy lunch with an investor.

*Not leaving me here to die.*

Gyre wasn't sure if she was relieved or annoyed.

"I'm not sitting on my ass all day," Gyre said. The constant, unyielding presence of her suit made that physically impossible. If she'd had a bed, a chair, even a vid to pass the time with, it would've been a different story. But with nothing but her suit—no comforts, no distractions—there was no way she was just going to sit around patiently until bedtime. "I'm going to go take samples and scans. You *are* going to try to sell this route to a mining company, right?"

"Sure."

Em sounded distracted, noncommittal. Gyre's skin prickled in a mix of frustration and unease that was becoming too familiar, like a pinch in a bad pair of boots, rubbing a blister into her flesh.

*If you're not going to sell it, what the hell am I doing down here?*

She opened her mouth to press Em on the topic, then stopped herself. She was still close enough to the surface that an extraction was possible. If she pushed too hard, if she pissed off Em, then Em could pull the plug. Em might have been a bad handler, but she was also the purse, the director, the dictator.

But there was no way to fund an expedition like this—even without a full surface crew—without at least *intending* to survey the mining prospects and sell them to the highest bidder. That was the whole point. That was where the money flowed from. Nobody spent so much capital on exploration for curiosity's sake. So where was her paycheck going to come from?

24

The thought of this all being for nothing—of coming topside to find the whole mission had gone bankrupt—made her face burn. Just her luck. She'd been a fool to hope, to believe, that this job wasn't some kind of scam.

Still, even then, the best way out was through. Finish the job, and then be able to talk up a real, legitimate expedition, trade on having actual experience under her belt.

*As long as Em doesn't get me killed.*

Gyre tried to calm herself by clambering along the breakdown pile. Her long limbs came in handy as she slipped over large, rounded boulders, digging her fingers into the tiny pitted holds on the surface. The carbon plating on the palms of her gloves was textured and never slick from sweat, while inside her skin was coated with a reactive, body-temperature gel, giving her a superior grip that still felt almost natural.

She dropped down to another boulder, then began sidling along the face of the rock she'd just dropped from, making her way over to another part of the descent. She pressed herself flat against the rock, unable to look down to where she balanced on her toes on a thin ledge. She felt her way along, shuffling step by step, dogged by thoughts of coming topside to nothing. If Em's company folded—

Her foot slipped.

She skidded down the too-smooth face of the boulder, reaching for the ledge. Her fingers caught once, twice, but didn't hold, and she couldn't find purchase with her toes or knees, either. Her suit screeched across the rock, and then abruptly stopped making noise.

She was falling through the open air.

Gyre twisted, trying to protect herself, but her hip struck a rock and spun her. Her back hit next, and while the shielding and stabilization of the suit kept her spine from snapping,

25

it didn't stop the pain of the impact. She shouted, then rolled, sliding off another boulder. A low, grinding noise filled the air, coming from above her, and she swore, jamming her fingers into a crack, fighting to keep her grip. She dragged herself hard to her right just as one of the boulders above her came loose with a roar and tumbled down several meters.

It would have killed her.

"Caver!"

Her vitals were no doubt flashing on Em's screen now, though her own screen had gone perfectly clear, allowing her an unobscured range of vision. Gyre pulled herself up with a groan, then began checking over her armor. A few surface scratches, nothing structural. She leaned back, letting the relief rush through her as her screen returned to normal.

"Gyre!" Em didn't sound worried, Gyre reflected.

Just mad.

"I'm fine, thanks for asking," she bit out. She kept her eyes closed a moment longer, then sat up and surveyed the chamber from her new position.

There was something below her, on the next flat surface. Something white. Past the breakdown pile. She frowned: there was something white, and the readout seemed impossible.

Then it disappeared.

She blinked rapidly. It didn't come back.

"Gyre, go back to Camp Two." Em's voice was booming, harsh. Authoritative. Definitely not worried for her health.

Gyre ignored her, sliding carefully down another few boulders, closer to the flat expanse. She toggled through modes on her HUD. Nothing. Whatever she'd seen was gone.

*Gone.*

That wasn't—that couldn't have—

"Caver, that was an order."

"I saw something," she responded, speaking half to herself.

"Your sensor readings were jarred from the fall," Em said. "I've reset them. There is nothing down there. I repeat, return to Camp Two."

*Fuck off*, Gyre thought, anger flooding through her. No more going along without question. She dropped the last half meter to the flat expanse. Then, her heart still racing, she turned off her reconstruction view and switched on her headlamp.

The cave looked remarkably similar. The difference between real sight and the reconstruction was minimal, except that she'd lost some of her field of view and subtle pieces of information about her surroundings. The colors she could see—a dirty pale gray for the stone, with various iridescent whorls of inclusions, and the surrounding, oppressive dark—those were different. But the lines were the same. The features, the same. Nothing had changed.

Except for the body at her feet.

She stared down at the wreckage. The suit had been half crushed. The mask was off, revealing pits where eyes had been, and tight, dried skin stretched over a prominent, masculine chin. The caver's chest had been split open, and filamentous white fungus grew from the hole. His legs disappeared below a boulder that had tumbled from the pile, much like the one that had almost killed Gyre.

Bile rose in the back of her throat, and she turned away.

*That* had been what she'd seen on her HUD. The white, the strange readings that suggested high concentrations of carbon ahead of her—

And Em had hidden it.

Her stomach spasmed, and she turned away, bracing herself on the nearest boulder. She squeezed her eyes shut, fighting the urge to vomit.

"Gyre?"

Cavers died all the time. Cavers on established routes died all the time. She had just narrowly avoided the same fate that had killed that man.

There was nothing *strange* about finding a dead caver.

There was nothing strange about finding a dead caver—but there was something strange about the owner of the expedition manipulating her reconstruction display, hiding things from her, injecting her with adrenaline just to get her moving in the morning.

Paying her way too much.

"Gyre? Gyre, respond."

"What the fuck do you want?" she rasped.

"Gyre, get back to Camp Two."

"Fuck you."

This wasn't worth it. No matter how much she needed to get off-world, this wasn't worth it. There would be other expeditions, other options. Em could try to blacklist her for failing to finish the expedition, but Gyre had been lying around obstacles for so long, she'd find a way to get past that. Gyre cursed again and began dragging herself back up the breakdown pile, refusing to turn her reconstructed view back on.

She'd go back to Camp Two. And then she'd just keep going back to Camp One.

"I don't appreciate being lied to," she hissed at Em as she hauled herself up. She skirted the boulder she'd displaced, giving the entire section a wide berth.

"I didn't want to disturb you."

"The hell you didn't!" Gyre spat, surmounting the lip of Camp Two. She straightened, then grabbed up one of the duffels, searching through it for a meal canister. She found one and jammed it into its port. It was supposed to be a careful, slow process. She didn't care, and triggered a fast release, wincing as the paste flooded her gut, her stomach twisting and heaving at the intrusion. She choked down bile again. She was uncomfortably full, the fresh meal too soon after her morning feeding, but she didn't intend to stop moving until she was out. She needed the calories.

Em stayed quiet the whole time.

Fed, she cast the canister aside. It bounced down the pile of boulders as she took off toward Camp One, calling up the HUD marker, waiting for it to appear over the circle of light cast by her headlamp.

It didn't come.

"I'm done!" Gyre shouted. "I'm done! This expedition is over."

Em said nothing, and the HUD marker still didn't appear.

"Marker!"

Nothing.

Gyre's blood boiled, her muscles trembling with the urge to strike out, to hit Em somehow. She bent double, fighting to remain in control of herself. "Em," she whispered. "Em, pull up the marker."

Nothing.

She closed her eyes, taking another long, slow breath, then tried to straighten up.

Her suit refused to move.

"Em, what are you doing?"

Gyre tried to move her fingers—just her *fingers*!—but nothing happened. Then she tried to kick, balling up her thigh muscles and lashing out as hard as she could. The suit didn't even groan.

Her headlamp turned off.

She'd never felt claustrophobic in her life, not even the

night she'd spent trapped in a slot cavern. But now she could feel herself trembling. Her thoughts raced.

"Em," she whispered. "Don't do this."

"We should talk," Em said.

"Unlock my suit."

"Not yet."

"Em, this is a safety hazard. What if a Tunneler—or something else—what if there's a cave-in—"

"Nothing on my readings suggests any of that."

"And I'm supposed to *believe you*?"

Em didn't respond for a moment, then huffed into her microphone. It was the single greatest expression of emotion Gyre had heard out of her, and it added to her panic.

"Em, unlock my suit. Please."

"I don't want you heading back to Camp One," Em said. "The caches I have set up in here will, in addition to what's in your duffels, last you at least two months, but that's without any accidents or emergencies. Any unnecessary doubling back might mean you don't reach our goal."

"*Our* goal? And what goal is that? I don't recall being briefed on *our goal* before you dropped me down here!"

"Calm down, Gyre. Your heart rate and blood pressure are getting dangerously high. I would prefer not to administer anxiolytics."

"Then tell me what your *goal* is. Because if it's mineral veins, I guarantee you we've passed at least two or three already."

"I don't need to explain myself to a caver who lied about her experience."

The words took a moment to register. *She knows.* Yet instead of being worried, Gyre felt relieved—and angry. No more dancing around the truth. Her lips drew back in a snarl. "Even more reason for you to let me leave, then."

"Even more reason for you to *calm down*. I'm willing to keep you on this job and *not* sue you for false representation."

Gyre stopped struggling, going very still. *Fuck.* A black mark was bad enough. Being sued would mean she'd lose what little she had, too. She'd be publicly dragged through hell in the courts, and then nobody would ever trust her after that, even the lowest-paying climbs. She'd never be able to get away from it.

Never get away from *here*.

She closed her eyes against the flare of rage and hopelessness in her chest.

"I don't need you to trust me, Gyre," Em said. "I need you to climb. And that, at least, you can do, based on what I *was* able to verify about you."

"Actually," Gyre snapped, "you do need me to trust you. Because if I don't, I don't want to be down here. I'm not dying because of you." Her breathing was fast and ragged in the close blackness of her suit. She knew Em was watching it on her readouts, knew Em could see everything about her.

It made her want to tear the suit right off.

"I'm—sorry about the adrenaline," Em said at last, the words clearly awkward in her mouth.

She turned the headlamp back on.

"Thanks," Gyre spat. The light took the edge off her panic, but not her anger. "Apology not accepted."

Her comm line crackled with Em's frustrated growl. Gyre hoped she was tearing out her hair at the thought of losing the contract, of having to start all over again.

"I don't enjoy sending people down there," Em said at last.

Gyre snorted. "Then what's it about?"

"I need somebody to get deep into this cave system," Em said slowly, as if picking every word with care. "It's a hard trek, harder than most expeditions, and much longer, with less support. It's more dangerous by definition. So I need, if not your trust, then your permission to intervene on your behalf. More than the average expedition."

Gyre looked up at the vault above her, trying to think of how to respond to that. Em's threat still echoed in her head, a knife at her back prodding her onward. Forcing her to agree, to trust Em, to rely on her.

She didn't have much of a choice, did she?

"I'd feel a lot more comfortable knowing what I was trying to find down there," Gyre said.

"And I'd feel a lot more comfortable if you concentrated on the cave. Treat it as an exploration mission. If everything goes well, you'll see things nobody else has ever seen."

Gyre refused to take the bait. Em was mimicking, almost exactly, one of the personality and motivation questions she'd answered when she signed up for this job. It was underhanded, a distraction.

Like so much of what she did.

"If it's so hard, you should have briefed me before I came in. Walked me through the challenges."

"I don't know all of them."

"But you know this part. The caches, the anchors—"

"I've done this before," Em said, "unlike you. I know what I'm doing. I'll also note you didn't ask for a briefing."

Gyre hadn't asked because she hadn't thought to, had assumed it would happen *to* her eventually, and then it had been too late. Maybe, if she'd actually had the experience she'd claimed to—

No. This was not about her. It was about Em, about this cave, about how she'd *done this before*. Gyre swallowed. This wasn't just her.

"So the body I saw?"

"Was from a failed attempt four months ago, at the start of this season."

"What was his name?"

Em didn't respond.

"Em, unlock my suit and tell me his name so that I can— give him a funeral. Or something."

Em inhaled sharply at that, and the suit released.

Gyre dropped to her knees in relief, relishing the feeling of her suit sagging with her. She flexed each of her fingers and twisted around in place. It was like she could breathe again. Then she stood and went over to the lip of the plateau, staring down toward the body.

*She's done this before.*

"What was his name?" she asked again.

More silence. Then Em cleared her throat. "I would have to pull up his contract."

Her heart sank, twisted around in her chest. "You don't even remember."

"We weren't on a first-name basis," Em replied softly. To her credit, it didn't sound like a threat, or a promise that Gyre was special.

Gyre was fairly certain that she wasn't special at all.

She was fairly certain she was just another body.

"When this is all over," Em said, her voice gentler than it had ever been, "I'll get you off-world. To one of your favorite garden worlds. That's on top of your pay."

Gyre closed her eyes, pressing her hands to her helmet. For just a moment, she could picture it. Broad foliage, gentle rains, a different life. But it wasn't enough. She wished she could rub at her eyes. Her fingers slid over the screen and the bump of her lamp, and with a sickening drop she realized

33

that her headlamp would've been giving off heat and visible light for—what? Ten minutes? Fifteen? She shut it off and finally restored the reconstruction.

The body didn't change. It was a small gesture, and no doubt calculated, but it was effective.

*Trust me*, it said. She shouldn't, couldn't, and yet . . . and yet she had no other choice.

"We should get moving," Gyre said, grimacing. "Before something follows the heat off my lamp."

"The funeral—"

"I'll do it on my way out," she said, grabbing up a duffel, not pausing to wonder why Em cared. "And I don't have a favorite garden world."

"Your file—"

"My mother went to one of the garden worlds. That's it. That's just where I start looking."

Em didn't respond.

"Marker to Camp Three," Gyre said, her voice hard.

"You'll—you're actually going forward?" Em asked, and she had the decency to sound shocked.

"You aren't giving me much of a choice," Gyre said. "But the way I see it, you *do* need me to perform well. You need me to engage. So here are some ground rules: You don't take control of my suit unless it's an emergency. You don't inject me with anything unless it's an emergency or I beg you to. If you do either of those things again just because it fits your agenda or schedule, I'm opening my helmet and letting the Tunneler come for me and your mission is scrubbed. I get that you need control down here, but you hired me for a reason."

"Yes—you were willing to take a less-documented job," Em said. "You were willing to lie to get it."

"For that pay, almost anybody would. I'm sure you know that better than I do."

Em didn't respond.

"You don't take control of my suit, and you don't *lie* to me. I'll check. I expect access to my headlamp whenever I want it, so I can make sure that we're looking at the same things. I can't do my part if I can't trust what I see. If me getting through this is so important to you, then you need to trust me. And in return, I don't need your help getting to a garden world. What I do need is your help tracking down my mother." With as much money as Em had poured into Gyre's suit, it should be easy enough for her. Easier, at least, than it would be for Gyre. "Agreed?"

"Agreed." Em cleared her throat. "Camp Three marker on."

"Proceeding."

# CHAPTER FOUR

She reached Camp Three after a long day's hike and was relieved to find that it had zero dead bodies. She checked, toggling off her display and turning on her lamp, pacing the nook that Em had led her to. All she found were a few small, slow-moving, translucent-bodied bugs that ducked away from her light when she came close. After maybe a half hour of watching the whisper-thin, ghostlike things, she lost interest and began to explore. Out of all the crevices within easy walking distance of camp, only one turned into a small tunnel. She wandered down from the nook and peered in. Em said nothing. She'd returned to her earlier reticence, most of her interactions limited to markers that appeared on Gyre's screen and readouts she now shared with Gyre directly instead of parsing into speech.

With no response from Em, Gyre explored further. She followed the winding, narrow tunnel that was barely tall enough to walk upright in, her light bouncing off the walls and casting eerie shadows. The walls themselves were studded with murky, crystalline outgrowths, and she paused at one of them, wondering if she should take a sample. She was peering at the refraction of her headlamp's glow in its cloudy interior when she heard it.

The dripping of water.

In a great rush, she became aware of how dry her mouth was and how her skin prickled inside of her suit, covered in a thin layer of old sweat and dead skin beneath the layer of feedback film that clung to her and allowed her suit to respond to and assist her in climbing. The suit "cleansed" internally every twelve hours or so, using body-temperature water recycled from her urine and introduced through her nutrient canisters, but it was a whisper of a sensation in the film, easily forgotten. The thirst, though . . . some of the water was available for sipping, but she hated drinking it, knowing where it had come from, and so even as her body remained hydrated from the intrusion of the feeding tube into her stomach, her throat itched. Since the last time she'd heard water at Camp One, five days ago, she'd learned to ignore the thirst, learned to ignore the feeding tube, the constant press of the suit on her flesh, the inability to touch her own skin.

But the sound of water brought it all back.

She left the wall to follow the sound. Should she let Em know? No, Em already knew if she was by her machines, and if she wasn't, Gyre couldn't reach her. She continued around a bend and down a steep but short drop-off.

Her lamp glittered off the surface of a small pond. The liquid—she realized with a jolt that she shouldn't simply assume it was water—filled the end of the narrow tunnel up to where Gyre stood, and she edged closer to it, then crouched.

She reached out her hand. "Unknown liquid, sample," she murmured. Nothing happened. Had the function been jarred in her fall? Her suit had shown no abnormalities, so it was more likely that she was misremembering the verbal command. "Sample, liquid," she tried, and this time a tube snaked out from her ring finger's armor. She touched it to the liquid and it sucked in a bead.

Her readout flashed. *Water.* High in certain minerals, but its pH was close to neutral. It wouldn't degrade her suit.

She shuffled forward, the water sliding over her boots.

There was no current, no ebb and flow, not even a coolness through the polymer of her suit, but just seeing herself touch water was soothing. She hadn't seen more than a dry creek bed in years, and water in the settlements was strictly rationed, most of it going to the mining concerns, industry, and agriculture. Oh, if she could only wriggle out of her suit, go for a short swim—

"Not good," Em said.

Gyre froze, startled. "Excuse me?"

"This passage shouldn't be flooded this time of year," Em said, her voice clipped and slightly distant. "That means the other dives will be harder than usual, and longer. I might have to reroute around a few sumps, too." Gyre thought she could hear Em's fingers typing. "Normally, you wouldn't be diving so soon."

Gyre frowned. *Diving.*

Em noticed her silence. "Your file does say that you have diving experience."

"*Swimming* experience," Gyre said, her face heating with embarrassment. Diving was an occasional issue in caves, but training for it was difficult, to say the least. She'd prioritized building strength and climbing skills, not trying to chase down pools she couldn't afford to work in and equipment she couldn't afford to rent. It had seemed like a small lie to tell, after padding her professional caving history.

*Diving.*

And she did know how to swim . . . for the most part. But it had been years. Years since her dad had made enough money and had enough jobs that they had traveled to the cities where there were pools for her to swim in. And she'd never been *good*. Her mother had, apparently, taken her swimming when she was a baby, relying on her natural instincts to teach her the basics. She could stay afloat, get to safety, but . . .

But she wasn't a *swimmer*. Those didn't exist on Cassandra-V. There just wasn't a need, and not enough money for it to be a hobby. She'd thought it would be fine.

Now she wasn't as sure. What if *this* was what ended their little dance?

"In your suit, swimming and diving should be mostly equivalent," Em replied at last. "Head back to Camp Three, and I'll pull up a map for you. I need to rerun some numbers. Some of the caches might be flooded. I'll need to check when they were put in, see what I stored everything in."

"Right."

Em wasn't pulling her out.

Gyre eyed the water a moment longer, then turned and heaved herself over the rise back to the main tunnel. The glimmer of her headlamp on the crystals prickled at her nerves, and she shut it down and keyed up the display. Everything was going to be fine. It was going to be *fine*.

It didn't feel fine.

She hated feeling like this, uncertain and worried. It made her want to flee—or fight. The glimmering had dimmed but hadn't disappeared entirely, due to a textural overlay the

39

computer provided to indicate composition. With a strangled swear, she lashed out, slamming her armored fist into one of the larger outcrops.

The noise was louder than she'd been expecting, booming out through the enclosed space. The crystals cracked, sprinkling her armor with fine, glittering dust. She took a deep breath.

She was fine.

She made her way back through the passage and over to the nook, carved out of the stone wall of the cavern. She maneuvered herself into a sitting position against the wall, then locked the bottom half of her suit and relaxed into it, looking out at the space before her.

It was smaller than the Camp Two cavern. She'd always liked closer spaces more. The huge vaults were impressive, but they left her feeling almost as exposed as she felt topside. Cassandra-V was a population-overflow planet, a raw materials colony, and it had never attracted the best of people. Nobody moved there because they wanted to. The few good people—the empathetic people, the people who cared about social order—tended to die young and idealistic deaths, leave planet as soon as they could, or grow old and cynical, sand-whipped and exhausted by the weight of believing the other colonists could be better than human. Everybody did what they had to do to survive. She'd heard stories about how the main spaceport cities had children begging for any amount of coin, with their limbs broken or amputated just to evoke pity. After a kind, misguided soul tried to help, a block later they'd be mugged for all they had left.

On the surface, open spaces just meant more directions for people to come at you. Nobody had your back, and humans were nasty, sad creatures. Her mother counted. Em counted double. And she was risking everything because . . .

"Here," Em said, interrupting her thoughts. A map glowed to life on the inside of her helmet, then appeared to project out slightly in front of her for easier viewing. The 3-D model rotated slowly, then condensed into a more legible cross section. "Here's where we are now." A blue light pulsed, roughly a quarter of the way down into the caves—vertically.

There was still a lot of horizontal distance to traverse too, with winding dips and rises, a very long vertical shaft, several more caverns connected by a long passage, and then a deep, bowing tunnel.

Green light began to fill in from the bottom, drowning the deepest tunnels. "This," Em said, "is where the water usually is this time of year—its lowest point. Perfect for descent. This section"—the U-shaped tunnel near the end of the system, where the detail of the map became much rougher, as if she didn't have enough data to fill it in—"is always flooded. There's no way around that, but the section is generally navigable. Given the level of water we just saw," she continued, the main flood rising up, "we can expect several more tunnels to be flooded. Either that, or something's changed."

"Tunneler?" Gyre asked, grimacing.

Em considered. "Possibly," she said at last. "But nobody else has access to this system. They do move on their own, but usually not through existing caves. Still . . . if it came close, and weakened a passage that then filled with water . . ."

"Just a natural disaster," Gyre said, shaking her head. "Like a fucking earthquake."

"In this case, yes."

"So what? I just swim through?"

"Exactly. Your suit is already equipped for it. It's got a rebreather and can fill air sacs to counteract the weight of the suit itself. The bags you've carried this far will have several spools of diving line that we'll load into your suit once you've finished hauling gear—you'll hook that to the walls every so often so that you'll be able to find your way back, if, for some reason, you get lost and I can't help."

"Sounds great," she muttered. "And does the suit help with the swimming?"

"Aside from some fins you can extend, no. No motors or other direct help. Inefficient. I tried that."

Gyre wished she could tug at her hair or scrub at her face. Something. Anything. "Just how many times *have* you tried?"

She didn't expect a response. On the other end of the line, Em huffed out a breath. It was loud, like she was leaning forward over the microphone, maybe putting her head in her hands, raking her fingers across her scalp. Another exhale.

Then she cleared her throat.

"Thirty-five, not including you."

*Thirty—*

Gyre couldn't stop herself from looking back toward the path to Camp Two. That body had been fresh. How many more had there been? Thirty-five expeditions would have taken *years*.

Thirty-five expeditions, and Em was still sending people back down?

Doubting she'd get an answer but needing to try, Gyre asked, "You still haven't found whatever it is you're looking for?"

"No," Em said, sighing. Again, her breathing was loud. Gyre could picture her fisting her hair, scrunching up her brow. "No, I haven't."

"Then how do you know it's down here at all?"

"Because before I started sending expeditions, I—went

42

down there myself. All I need is somebody to get as far as I got, that first time."

Gyre frowned. "You were a caver?" Em had sounded strange when she said *I*, a slight hesitation that made Gyre uneasy.

"Back when we still went down in teams, yes. As a team, we could make it down. But—"

"But Tunnelers," Gyre said softly.

Em cleared her throat again. "Yes. 'Like a fucking earthquake.'"

The words hung in the air, as if they were outside her helmet altogether, hovering like a living thing just in front of her. Em had been down here, with a team. Teams didn't make it. Teams never made it when they went deep. Hers couldn't have.

But Em had made it.

Gyre looked back toward Camp Two again, wishing she could see through the walls, see the dead man in his broken suit. Em had done an abrupt one-eighty at the mention of a funeral, and . . .

Her shoulders hunched up and she leaned forward, mirroring Em's imagined posture, resting her helmet in her hands.

"Do you want me to pull them out?" she asked softly.

Em didn't respond.

"I've done rescue descents before in the bigger pseudo-caves, you know. I told Moller that. That wasn't a lie."

"I know," Em murmured. "But no. It's too dangerous. And there are—too many."

"How big was your team?"

"Five people. Including me." Her breathing filled up all the space in Gyre's suit, but instead of letting her float, it weighed her down.

Gyre was shaking now.

*This is too big. This is too dangerous.*

Even if she'd been able to stop the trembling, she knew Em could see the spike in her heart rate. Yet Em said nothing. Gyre couldn't figure out if she loved her or hated her for that, loved her or hated her for finally—*finally*, so many days in—being halfway honest about something.

"One out of five," she said at last, trying her best to sound brave and flippant, "aren't the best odds I've faced." She couldn't get the next words out of her mouth.

*But they're not the worst.*

The tech had improved since then. Em had mapped out most of the route and set up caches. And Gyre—despite her lack of credentials—was very, very good at climbing, had worked toward this moment all her life.

But she couldn't say the words, couldn't be brave and flippant for them both. Death was too thick in the air between them, the bodies—seen and unseen—following close behind.

If there was one blessing, it was that while her head and chest hurt, she still had enough self-control that there was no burning prickle of tears in her eyes.

Em said nothing.

She had to get up and leave. This sudden turn to honesty made Gyre suspect that Em wouldn't follow through on her threat of litigation. She might not even try to stop her. But instead of standing, Gyre remained frozen, dreading the climb back. She faced possible death if she continued, but that was no different from what waited for her if she ran. Here, she was prepared. Here, she could rely on herself. Up there? Up there, she'd have to find another way to earn enough money to survive, and the options she had left to her were poisonous. Manual labor, servitude, desperate crime. Or she could take other caving tours, more mundane tours, and have to survive two or three instead of just this one.

And even after this job, there was still one last gamble before her: finding her mother at all in the wide expanse of systems beyond Cassandra-V, without the considerable resources Em clearly had.

"But they're not the worst odds I've faced," she finally whispered.

*I'm screwed.*

# CHAPTER FIVE

The next four days were spent ferrying equipment and inventorying caches. Em didn't say much, and Gyre did her best to enjoy the reprieve. The cave system *was* beautiful. The vaulted ceilings, the narrow crevices she eased herself through, the crystals and fungal growths on the walls—they all combined with the calm quiet of being deep underground to present a magical illusion that she was somewhere safe.

She'd always been fine with the weight of thousands of tons of stone above her head.

Still, every time she stopped at Two to load up, she couldn't ignore the body. It made the weight harder to bear a little more each time. She almost asked Em to hide him again, but couldn't bring herself to make the request.

This cave killed people. It was best to remember that.

On the fourth day, once she finished ferrying the equipment, she turned down the draw distance of her display and sat with just herself in a dim circle of light.

*Thirty-five.*

She was just one more caver after nearly three dozen others had come down here and failed to find whatever it was Em was looking for. That number had haunted her through all the days of climbing. Her one comfort had been that Em, for all her lies, was very good at the mechanical part of handling. Gyre's computers did what they needed to, and Em drew her attention to details she needed, otherwise allowing her to work. It made sense; Em had been down here before, knew the challenges, knew what Gyre would be feeling, thinking, wanting.

It made Gyre want to believe, in turn, that the others had failed through their own faults. That she could succeed where the others hadn't. She could make peace with this. She was trapped, yes, but there were worse fates on offer back on the surface—and this might still pay off.

Caves were always a means to an end for her first, but they'd also been more than that. They'd been where she was safe, where she was independent from a neglectful father and a wasteland world, where she could excel. Em's history aside, this job provided her with a better suit than she'd ever thought she'd have a chance to wear. The cave itself was challenging and beautiful. And Em wanted her to go deep, deeper than anybody had been able to manage on their own.

She'd heard somewhere that pride came before the fall. But she wasn't going to fall.

She was going to *climb*.

⌄

Birdsong filtered into her awareness, and Gyre stirred, shifting in the unlocked portions of her suit. She frowned, furrowing her

47

brow against the nonsensical sound. It remained, grew slightly louder, then plateaued. Birdsong. Birds she'd never heard. She cracked open one eye, scowling.

It was just the cave. It was just Camp Three. She hadn't been magically whisked to her mother's garden world.

"Is that a better alternative to the adrenaline?" Em asked, her voice only slightly louder than the now-looping track of birdcalls.

"Yeah," Gyre grunted, loosening her suit and rolling onto her side. She pushed herself through a number of stretches on autopilot, then rummaged in her pack for a nutritional canister. As she screwed it into the side port of her suit, she yawned.

"I'm glad," Em said, as the sludge made its way into Gyre's stomach. "I could also try music. What do you like?"

Gyre shrugged, then waited to see if Em could read that expression from her command post.

"I'll download a few sample tracks to your suit, then," Em said, her own response unreadable. Response to silence or to her shrug? It didn't matter, Gyre decided.

She screwed up her face at the still-alien sensation of the sludge coating her guts. She worked her jaw as if she were chewing and then swallowed. Sometimes it helped.

"Are you ready to try the dive today?" Em asked.

She was being solicitous again. Gyre wondered at the stark contrast with her usual harshness, at whether it was instinctual or forced. She swallowed her phantom meal again. "Yeah," she said.

"All your vitals are good," Em said. "So I'll clear it."

"You'll *clear* it?" Gyre laughed sharply, incredulously. "Right. What would you do otherwise, lock my suit? Take me to court?"

Em didn't respond at first, then huffed a sigh. "No, I'd ask you nicely to take a break."

"Had to think about that."

"There were less-nice ways of phrasing it."

"Oh, feel free. I've heard worse."

"I'm sure." Em's voice had gone quickly from tight and frustrated to grudgingly amused, and Gyre found herself smiling.

The banter was . . . nice. Especially after the silence of the four days before.

Her readout blinked purple on the bottom right edge: CANISTER DEPLETED. She keyed the port closed, then unscrewed the spent canister and stored it with the rest of the cache. As she went through the full-suit check, swapping out the nearly drained onboard battery with a fresh one and inventorying every spot where she'd scraped against the wall or fallen down the breakdown pile at Camp Two for further damage, she hummed to herself.

"You sound happy," Em said. "Good dreams?"

She stopped humming. "Don't remember."

No dreams to speak of, which was a good thing. She was especially glad there hadn't been a return to the nightmares she'd had the previous three nights while ferrying gear, where she'd seen herself drowning again and again, or being caught, the servos of her suit dead and her muscles exhausted, to starve in some rocky crevice beneath the water.

She didn't voice those concerns. Instead, she went over to the gear duffels. "You said I'd need to change my load-out?"

"Yes. Get the smaller duffel. Take one of the small spools and load it into the secondary line compartment."

She fished it out, then paused when it glimmered in her reconstruction. "It's different?"

"It will show up on your sensors in everything but the worst silt-out."

*Silt-outs.* She'd read about those, heard other cavers talk about them. If she kicked against the bottom, or any horizontal shelves, she'd start a cascade of muck that would make it physically impossible to see, and that would seriously limit what her sonar and other sensors could do. She'd be blind.

She tamped down her panic at the thought.

"Right."

"I have a full map of this flooded section, but with the out-of-season wetness, something might have changed," Em said. Gyre did her best to pay attention as she cinched up the bags.

"What about the gear? These don't look waterproof."

Em sighed. "The fabric is water-resistant, but no, the seals aren't waterproof. Later in the season, I send people in with dry bags for this sump, but the cache at Camp Four has some too for the sump between Four and Five. We'll use those to carry the extra batteries over from Three."

"Sounds tedious."

"It is."

*Great.* More time down here. More trips through the sump. Gyre tried not to groan as she made herself start moving toward the crystal passageway, with just one last look around.

"Before we get that far, though, you'll need to swim it the first time," Em continued. "The main things to keep in mind are to obviously stay away from the bottom, and attach the line as you go. You don't need to get all the way through the passage on the first try. You can treat it as a training run."

"I'd rather just get it over with."

"Wait until you're down there to decide. With where the water level is on this side, I estimate that this flooded section is probably just over a hundred meters. Doable in one push, but long enough to be disorienting."

She waited for Gyre to protest, but Gyre said nothing.

"Regardless of how many dives you do to cross it, it's long enough that you should run a line."

"Yeah? What's the usual cutoff?"

"Sixty or so meters before you use a line at all. More if you come across branching paths and aren't sure which is which. With the line, you'll peg it to the wall every fifty meters or less, as needed."

"And I've got enough for this?"

"Yes, the spool you loaded in will get you through the whole way. There's also more stashed farther on. So: attach it to the rock right before you go under. That way the line won't disturb anything."

Gyre had reached the edge of the water, and she crouched down, looking at it. The suit's rebreather would keep her safe, and she likely wouldn't even feel the change in temperature. It should be *easier* than free swimming.

But a lot of people had died in this cave.

*Not me*, she thought, repeating it over and over like a promise until she felt her nerves settle.

"Ready," Gyre said.

"Here, first," Em said, and brought up the 3-D model of the section of flooded cave, which appeared to hover a half a meter or so in front of Gyre. A movement of her hand made it turn. She squinted at it, noting its shape—a basic U-bend—and its length, and hoped that any other important features would magically stand out to her. It remained just a model.

"Ready," she said again.

"Continue," Em replied. "Wade on in."

"The silt—"

"No choice. The sump doesn't get deep enough to jump into until after the wall in front of you. Walk slowly. Lift up and step down cleanly. No dragging your feet."

"Right." Gyre reached out her leg as far as she could without losing her balance, then put it down carefully. The silt that Em had mentioned was slick and Gyre stiffened as her foot threatened to slip out from under her. Once she was stable, she straightened, and brought her other leg into the water. She couldn't feel it, couldn't tell where it was lapping against her knees. She took another step, looking down the whole time, wishing she could see the eddies of silt rising and spiraling around her calves. Instead, her display showed a blank blue sheet, marking the surface of the water, an adjustment no doubt designed to help diving.

She moved forward.

This time, the water came up to her thighs. A glance up showed her that the wall was less than a meter ahead of her, but the model had shown a sharp drop-off nearly in line with it. She adjusted her display until she could see below the surface.

There. It didn't exactly yawn open beneath her, but it definitely looked more like a swimming pool and less like a bathtub.

She crouched and settled her palm against the stone below her, beneath the water, hand bent back to trigger the drill to drop down below her wrist. Once she was sure the positioning was where she wanted it, she blew sharply to the bottom left of her helmet. The drill whirred to life, cutting into the rock like it was thick mud instead of stone. Silt bloomed up around it, clouding the water and obscuring her hand. She kept working by touch.

When it reached optimal depth, it stopped, placed an anchor bolt, then withdrew. The drill retracted and flattened against her arm once more. The silt settled. She fished the line from its spool opening along her flank and hooked in, then looked down.

That was a lot of water. A lot of open, drowning water, with no way to get to air between here and her end point. She would have to trust the suit, trust Em. Trust herself to learn fast.

She could do this.

Gyre stepped out beyond the drop-off and sank beneath the surface.

Em adjusted the buoyancy of the suit for her; her descent slowed just shy of the bottom, which looked like it had a much deeper deposit of muck than the entry pool. Her chest burned as she slowly rotated to horizontal, and she tried to open her mouth, exhale. Her instinctual lizard-brain screamed at her that she would drown if she did, even without the feeling of water on her skin, even with the way her helmet made her surroundings look like air.

Maybe that was it. Maybe her lizard-brain thought she was in space. Outer atmosphere. She deliberately opened her mouth wide, and when nothing rushed in but air—recycled, tinny air but air all the same—her lungs gasped and adjusted, and she could breathe again.

"Your $O_2$ stats dropped."

"Just making a wish," she murmured, her lips still half closed against her pointless fear. It seemed wrong to speak, down in the water. You couldn't speak underwater even if you could somehow breathe. Sound would be muffled by the fluid and the shroud of silt hanging film-like around her. If she turned off her display, her headlamp would only illuminate a meter or two in any direction. She shook herself in her suit, wiggling her fingers, then slowly began kicking her legs. From the toes of her boots, small fins extended, making each kick a little more fluid, more powerful.

The line spooled out behind her, smooth and slow, and Gyre practiced keeping herself equidistant from the tunnel walls, hovering between floor and ceiling. The tunnel continued to arc downward, but even without her kicking, she sank in modulated bursts.

"Stop that," she said, stilling. "I want to be in control of this." She was adapting quickly, her nerves giving way to the actions, and she needed the training wheels off. She needed to know that she could do this herself.

"It's more exact this way," Em replied.

"As long as your computers spit out the correct math."

"That *is* what they're designed to do."

"Em."

There was silence on the other end of the line, followed by a faint beep. "Right. You're set to stay at neutral buoyancy even while moving. If you need help—"

"I'll *say*," Gyre said, and resumed her descent.

She'd been warned about this—ground teams who thought that the suit readouts told them everything. But suit readouts were just numbers and models. The people doing the interpreting were still *people*, and their own personalities and particular brands of screwed-up informed how they interpreted those numbers. Em could see where she was on a map, and could read her adrenaline levels, her blood pressure, her suit's buoyancy, but she couldn't read Gyre's independence or need for autonomy.

Or her love of tight, claustrophobic spaces.

If she turned her display off, she would be floating in a vast expanse of nothing—terrifying, horrifying nothing, beyond the glare of her light. But with the display on, she could see how close the walls were. The tunnel itself was barely three meters tall, with almost a quarter of its bottom covered up in silt. The walls were even closer together. As she approached an upward spiral that would've taken fancy linework and scrambling if it had been dry, she simply rotated her body and pushed *up*, feeling the ghost of the sensation of a nearby object that just barely didn't brush her suit.

She didn't need a practice run at all. It was like she'd been in water all her life.

"Gyre. Line," Em said, breaking her reverie.

"Fuck off," she spat reflexively.

"Anchor your line or abort," Em replied, with what sounded like an exasperated sigh. "Do this safely or not at all, please."

*Please.*

Gyre frowned and slowed, reaching out for a side wall. "Should I go back? To before the spiral?"

"Best practice says yes, but just wrap it here and move on." Em sighed again, this time without trying to hide it. It was followed by a yawn. "You're going too fast."

"Turns out I like this. It's therapeutic. Lucky you," she said, bracing herself by stretching out across a narrow part of the tunnel, catching her toes on one stone wall. "I could use the drill, too, yeah?" she asked, her hand hovering by where the line emerged from the suit.

"A hard anchor isn't needed here and would disturb too much silt. Usually, I'd have you use silt screws, but those aren't currently stocked in your suit," she said, no note of apology or embarrassment in her voice. Instead, she yawned again. "See that outcrop to your left? Wrap your line three times around it."

Gyre frowned as she kicked gently and drifted over to the knob of protruding rock, not yet worn down by the passage of water. She looped the line around as advised, then tugged at it. It held.

"Tired?"

"Caffeine drip," Em replied.

"Bad choice," Gyre said. "You'll still crash eventually. When do you sleep, anyway? When I'm asleep? Who watches the computers?" The loop of line blinked green in her HUD, signaling that Em's computers had also confirmed it was secure. She pushed up and off her ledge.

"I do."

"Don't tell me," Gyre said, grimacing. "You're some sort of cybernetic hybrid who's actually *plugged in* to her monitoring computers."

"Not a bad idea," Em said. "You're coming to the end of your first bit of line."

"Already?"

"You were in a bit of a zone through the descent. Didn't want to interrupt. You're picking this up quickly."

"It's one of my better traits. Besides, small tunnels are my favorite."

"Mr. Moller did note that on your intake," Em agreed.

"So how do you do it?" she said, once again slowing as she prepared to swap to a new spool. "How can you watch me all the time?"

"I try to sleep when you do, when possible. You're not the only one with an adrenaline shunt into your system. Given certain inputs from your sensors, the computer will wake me up immediately."

"And today? I just woke up. Shouldn't you have slept recently?"

"Something came up. I'll be fine. Once you're through or you're done for the day, I'll crash for a bit."

Gyre finished combining the line, thinking, frowning, chewing at her lip. "You really need a better system," she said finally, as she began ascending again. "If you want to keep running these excursions, anyway. And you need to stop lying."

"It won't get me better people," Em said. "I have tried that, you know. I was completely up-front at the start. But it turns out desperate people do a better job. I guess we . . . sense something the same in each other."

"I'm not seeing many similarities, from where I'm sitting."

"Anchor on the right wall, Gyre."

She dutifully stopped and braced herself, looping the line three times around a smaller protrusion. "I'm just saying," she said, "you should train your guy to watch the screens while you sleep or something. It's not going to cost you that much more, proportionally." Anchored, she pushed off again, kicking up.

"Different people have different priorities. I prefer to be the only one steering things."

"And when things go wrong?"

"It has never been *my* failure in leadership or analysis when a caver dies, if that's what you're asking. You're approaching the surface."

She wanted to press Em further, but she could see the end of the sump, and she was caught up in relief and the urge to get out of the water and onto solid rock again. Gyre began swimming in earnest, legs pumping. Em didn't speak again until Gyre broke the surface of the sump.

"Good. Now put an anchor on the wall above the waterline. Tie it instead of clipping, then cut the excess." Gyre set to work as Em talked, activating the bolt drill again. "When you're ready, turn right. There's your best exit. You'll have to climb, though. Usually you'd have an inflatable raft here to make a small camp on the water, but those are stashed farther in at this point in the season. That'll make the climb harder to start. Since you're here, though, I want you to take at least one run at it. Make progress for when you pick up again tomorrow."

On the other end of the line, Em cleared her throat. "Before you start," she added, voice a little softer, "I have to say: You've covered a lot of ground today, especially given that you had to learn a new skill. You're doing well."

Gyre glanced up, ignoring the dig on her experience and the uncomfortable kindness. "Let's just get it over with. There's a ledge over there I can brace myself on to get started. Turn up my buoyancy?"

The sacs in her suit inflated slowly, and soon it took effort to push down. A few long reaches and she hauled herself up and out of the water, and safely over the edge. From there, she stood and wriggled, adjusting to the feel of a buoyant suit in normal atmosphere and gravity. The sacs deflated, but only partway, insurance against any falls over open water.

When she was settled, she braced a hand on the wall and finally asked, "So whose failure was it?" She inspected the wall before her and tested a few initial handholds distractedly. "Are you going to tell me all those cavers just couldn't hack it? Or is a computer failure on your end not *your* failure?"

"I could give you a list. I'd rather you stay focused on what you're doing, however."

"I'd like to be focused too, and that means knowing the risks of the job. You don't think I'm going to end up paranoid? Obsessed? Distracted?"

*I'm halfway there already*, she almost said, but shook her head and made herself pay attention to the climb.

"No, you're not the type. You're a mastiff, not a neurotic lapdog."

Gyre snorted. "Fascinating comparison," she muttered. She looked around for old anchors and found none, so she hauled herself up the stone one body length. "Climbing," she added belatedly.

"Climb on," Em said. After a second, she added, "I meant it as a compliment."

The muscles between her shoulders bunched in irritation. She wasn't sure what she'd really expected from Em—it wasn't ever going to be a satisfying answer. Gyre ran her fingers along the stone, searching for a good crack for her main anchor. Her display lit up with helpful suggestions from Em, which she only glanced at, trusting her instincts more than whatever algorithm Em was using. If Em was going to be asleep on the job, she couldn't let her natural skills get rusty. She couldn't relax into the suit's support.

She felt a surge of vindication, hot in her belly, as she wedged the first cam into what her visor color-coded a "third-tier" crack and watched as it blinked once, twice, then flipped to "optimal."

Grinning, she added another cam and a nut, then tied onto the anchor and tested it with her weight. It held.

"Good find," Em said.

*Huh*—she hadn't expected the woman to acknowledge her success. Gyre checked and double-checked the anchor and her belay and adjusted the feed of her rope.

And then she began climbing.

# CHAPTER SIX

"Gyre."

"Don't say a *word*."

Em didn't say anything, but by the sound in Gyre's helmet, she did bring her fist down on her desk. Gyre fought the urge to snap, or to find something to throw.

Except there *was* nothing. Absolutely nothing.

Her muscles burned and her head ached, and where there should have been a cache with more batteries for her suit, more nutritional canisters, more gear, there was nothing. The cache wasn't just empty: it was gone.

It didn't make sense.

"We need to push forward," Em said softly.

"Like hell *we* do," Gyre spat. "That climb took four pitches, Em. *Four.*" Four pitches that took upward of twelve hours, clipping in to an anchor on each one, going back down to retrieve the gear that she could, then climbing back up and drawing up her line to reuse it. Em had told her to stop, to rest for the day suspended on her line, or to go back to Camp Three to rest and resupply, but the cache should've been right at the top. She should have been able to sleep, then use the top line she'd attached at the summit of the climb to ferry gear the next day. It should have made everything that much easier, that much faster.

But the cache wasn't *here*.

She was exhausted. She'd thought she was numb. But numb implied no feeling. And Gyre definitely felt something.

*Anger.*

"If this cache is . . . *gone*—" Em was saying, her voice pained.

"How could it be gone, Em? *How?* Nobody knows about this cave, right? And last I heard, Tunnelers don't *eat caches.*"

"Stranger things have happened," Em muttered. She sounded vulnerable. Almost hopeful.

That didn't make sense. Nothing about this mission made sense. Gyre shook her head. "Maybe you made a mistake. Forgot to leave something here. Sent me down the wrong tunnel."

"No. The last caver in before you, Eli, he stocked this. Just like you, he hauled gear, he filled it. And even if he hadn't, I've had caches in there last *years.*"

Gyre sank down to her knees with a strangled curse. She pressed her hands to her helmet, wishing she could rip the thing off and dig her fingers into her hair, could massage at her skin, could press against her eyes until her bone-deep exhaustion and anger and fear melted out of her.

"Press forward, Gyre," Em said, her voice softening. "I know you're tired. I know you're hungry. But your suit can only run on the batteries you're carrying for another six days, and the next cache is two, maybe three away. If there's another sump, or a tunnel collapse, we'll need that three-day buffer."

"And I suppose going back is out of the question? Going to Camp Three, or—or a cache we bypassed?"

"We didn't bypass any caches."

"I don't believe you," she snapped. "I've known you for over a week now, and if I've learned one thing, it's that you're a control freak. You may not have any *human* backup up there with you, but you can lock this suit up with a button, you use adrenaline injections to wake people up, you modify my sight readout—*you have other caches* for when things go wrong."

That seemed to strike a chord. When Em spoke, her voice was back to normal, alert and affronted instead of pained and distracted. "Are you implying that I *engineered* this?"

"I'm going back to Camp Three," Gyre said. "Restocking."

"You can't carry more than you already are, and you can't pull batteries through the sump outside your suit without shorting them. *Keep moving.*"

"Fuck you."

She sat down, hoping it pissed Em off. But as she waited for Em's next salvo, her panic ebbed until she could face the problem more clearly. This was bad, but it could be worse. Em was right; the faster she got to Camp Five, the better.

Em was just wrong on the particulars. Getting to Five fast meant resting now, not pushing forward. A few hours wasn't going to make a difference to her battery levels, but it *was* going to impact how safely she could climb.

"I'll sleep here," she muttered, and pushed herself up.

"A happy medium," Em said, bitterness tingeing her voice. She sighed, perhaps rubbed at her temples in frustration. Gyre staggered over to a niche in the wall that she could see the rest of the cavern from, and hunkered down inside of it, wishing hard for a bed of some kind, or a hot meal. Instead, she methodically began setting up her next feeding.

"This has never happened before," Em murmured. "I'm sorry."

Gyre grunted.

"You—you did that climb faster than anybody else I've ever hired," Em said.

"I don't want your flattery right now."

"Did you learn from your parents?"

She snorted. "No."

"So this really is just to get the money to find your mother, then? Not the continuation of some—family adventuring tradition?"

Gyre shifted, grimacing as her cannula protested. She shook her head, her lips threatening to curl into a smile. "Been telling yourself stories?"

"I didn't think you'd appreciate it if I looked her up. Without your direct say-so, anyway. Would you like me to start?"

She hadn't planned on taking advantage of Em's resources now, here, before she was out and had more bargaining power, but why not? "Yeah," she said.

"What was her name?"

"Peregrine. Peregrine Price."

"Do you have any other information on her?"

"No. Not even an ID number or what colony she was originally from." *No connection at all, other than our genetics.*

"That's fine." There was no pity in her voice, and Gyre was glad. "Anything else?"

"Like?"

"What did she look like?"

"Like me. Light brown skin, freckles, red hair. Brown

63

eyes. Tall. She dyed her hair blond the last few years she was here, though. Maybe she still does."

"What was her job?"

Gyre opened her mouth to respond, then hesitated, staring out at the rock wall of the niche. She closed her mouth, licked her lips. "I . . . barely remember," she said after a moment. "She left a long time ago."

"I see," Em murmured. "How old were you?"

"It was a long time ago," Gyre repeated.

Em didn't respond, and Gyre sank into the silence like she would have a soft foam bed. It was reassuring, that Em now felt bad enough that Gyre could shut her up with a few clipped words. If it took being an ornery smart-ass, dragging every order of hers through a wringer out loud so Em could hear it . . .

Her stomach cramps eased as her body adjusted to the flow of paste and began to soak up the calories. The fog in her head began to clear. Her muscles ached, but they relaxed somewhat, trusting in the suit to support them.

Em finding her mother was everything she could have wanted. It would be a blessing. It would make everything easier. Cheaper. She needed to cooperate.

"I think she was a teacher," Gyre said at last. "Or—a nanny? I remember being jealous of her, when I was very young. She was always around other people's kids. But that stopped when I was maybe five. I guess fewer people were having kids by then, and most were sending them away if they could." She licked her lips again, then nudged the toggle on her wrist that extended a drinking straw. Most of her hydration was taken care of directly by the suit and her meals, but sometimes she needed to wet her throat. She took a long pull of the filtered water, then leaned her head back against her helmet, looking up at nothingness. "For the next few years I barely saw her, even before she left. I've talked about it with my dad. He won't tell me what she was doing."

"Do you have any theories?" Em asked. The gentleness was gone, replaced by concentration. It was gratifying. Was she already plugging data points into her computer?

"The usual. That she was—involved in drug manufacturing or strike breaking or something else nasty. Something that meant she had to leave." Gyre closed her eyes, squirming into a comfortable-enough position and locking her suit so she could go full-body limp in it. "Sometimes I thought that she fell in love with some rich man, that he took her away from her miserable life on this miserable planet. But that's . . ."

"Not miserable enough for Cassandra Five?"

"Exactly," Gyre said with a short, huffed laugh. "You almost sound like a native now."

"How do you know she went to a garden world?"

"Wouldn't you, after this?" Gyre asked.

Em was quiet.

"She left a note behind," Gyre said. "It was short. Just said, *I'm going somewhere green. Follow me when you can. Love, Peregrine.*"

Gyre could faintly hear the rustle of fabric as Em shifted on the other end of the line. "The note was for your father," she said. "Not you. Otherwise she would have signed it 'Mom.'"

"Probably," Gyre said, shrugging with a bitter smile. *And you'd think a mother would have at least mentioned her child.*

"Strange, though, that she wouldn't give a place if she meant for him to follow."

"I've always thought she didn't know where she was going," Gyre said. "Or maybe she meant it as a challenge. I don't know. The letter pisses me off, either way. If she wanted us to

65

follow her, she should have given us something more. Money, a plan, or just the damn tickets to go with her. Instead, we got three sentences." The corner of her mouth twitched as her feeding finished, and she grudgingly unlocked one arm of the suit and fiddled with the canister lock, twisting until it released. The suit had already sealed at the port site, and the canister sealed itself as soon as it was exposed to air. The scent of waste or food—even the nasty, lab-built sludge in the container—was another Tunneler-attraction theory, though it was one that didn't make any sense to her. Nobody had ever seen one eating, and the caches *usually* survived just fine.

Still, better safe than dead.

"Why do you want to find her?" Em asked.

"Because she's my mother," Gyre said.

"But she left you. And you've said you don't think she had a good reason."

"I never said that."

"Okay, let me rephrase: all the reasons you've told me have been good for *her*, but they haven't taken you or your father into account at all. And before you tell me that your father wasn't a good reason to stay anyway, and she made the right decision abandoning you—"

"I never said—"

"I have *some* experience with reading people, Gyre, and I know that twisted-up mess is part of the story." Em didn't sound like she was smiling, or self-satisfied. She sounded tired, and that pain had crept back into her voice. Was she familiar with the feelings herself? The thought made Gyre uncomfortable, desperate to be understood and angry that Em could see through her, all at once. "Before you tell me all of that," Em continued after a moment, "just tell me what you want when you find her again."

"I want . . . answers," Gyre said. "I want to hear it from *her*. And maybe I want to punch her, I don't know. I don't know what I want to do."

Em hummed softly. "Losing people is hard," she said. There was an odd roughness to her voice that made Gyre shift in her suit, that went beyond how Em talked about the other dead cavers. "Sometimes you just need to see them again, to be sure it's really over."

She was talking about her team.

And she wasn't wrong. But beyond that, Gyre wanted proof that her mother was healthy and happy, so Gyre could hate her for it. If she found her mother, and her mother was half dead in some hole, with the only green in her life the blanket she'd bought for a narrow cot . . .

Hating her for leaving wouldn't feel so good.

"You should get to sleep," Em said after a moment. "I'll wake you up in six hours, if you last that long. Do you want any assistance?"

Gyre looked at the flat expanse of floor where the cache should have been, and shuddered. "No. If somebody took it—"

"Nobody took it."

"If somebody took it," Gyre repeated, her skin crawling at the base of her neck, "then I don't want to be drugged when they come back."

Em was quiet for a long stretch, and then she sighed. "Understood. I'll wake you up in six."

Gyre didn't respond, instead surveying the cavern one last time, concentrating on the unmoving walls and the towering vault above her. It felt too open in here, but everything remained steady. Her sonar detected no sounds beyond her own.

She was alone, at least.

Slowly, she settled into something like sleep, thoughts

drifting and turning hazy. Her display darkened, then went black, and she was too far gone to feel panic at being trapped inside her suit, relying only on Em to keep watch. Her eyes closed.

∨

Gyre frowned at the time readout in her helmet. It had only been two hours since she'd begun drifting off, and she groaned, unlocking her suit and trying a different position. It didn't help; despite the long day, her mind refused to completely quiet. Grudgingly, she stood up and stretched.

Em didn't greet her over her comm.

Panic spiked through her, and she scanned the cavern. *Alone.* She was alone. Em had said that she would try to sleep when Gyre went down for the night, but here? Now? With the cache missing?

Not to mention, Em had been down here before; she knew the risks better than most topside teams. And she still worked solo. Why? If she was so desperate to get somebody down here safely, she should be using every advantage her money could buy. It didn't make sense, and it smelled rotten.

And where the hell was the cache?

She increased the field of view on her helmet's simulation until she had the equivalent of a fully lit room. A shaft stretched away overhead, and the stone floor was level for a few meters before gently dropping off down to her right. Lichen grew here, too, a soft texture restricted to the crevices.

Gyre craned her head back and stared up the shaft. A shaft like that could lead up to the surface, or to nowhere at all, and even her sonar reconstruction couldn't map high enough up it to tell her. There was a tiny stream of water coming down one side, dripping from the edge once every thirty seconds or so;

could rains have flooded this entire part of the cave, washing away the cache? Maybe . . . but there hadn't been any rains in the last few months, as far as Gyre knew. And even *if* there had somehow been a flash storm strong enough to flood this room, there would have been other signs. Trash washed in from a nearby settlement, lingering puddles, lusher plant growth up the walls than half-dead lichen. There was nothing.

So that ruled out flooding.

Gyre was just about to turn away from the shaft when she made out a faint, familiar bump in the rock.

*That's a bolt*, she thought, quickly followed by, *No, can't be.* The simulation her helmet provided didn't allow for the glint of light on metal, so maybe it was just a small stone wedged in a crevice. She squinted and moved closer to that edge of the shaft, but it was so far above her that she couldn't hope to reach it without an actual climb.

Still, if it *was* a bolt, then there were probably others farther up the shaft. Em probably already knew about the shaft, in that case. So why hadn't she mentioned it? If it went up to the surface, or even close, it could cut this initial staging time in half.

Maybe it wasn't that simple. Or maybe Em didn't know about it at all.

Maybe *this* was why the cache was missing.

The thought made her skin crawl, and she looked over her shoulder, surveying the perimeter of the chamber. Nothing. But that didn't stop the sudden feeling that she was being watched. If somebody else was in the cave, and Em didn't know about them . . .

Gyre began pacing the limits of the camp. There were no signs that anybody had been there recently, but that didn't mean anything; a caver in a suit didn't leave much trace, by design. What *did* stand out was the lack of rope attached to the

69

bolt in the shaft. If somebody else had come down that way and taken the cache, they'd left the way they came and taken their line with them.

But that didn't mean they couldn't come back.

Gyre circled around toward the slope leading away from the direction of the sump, wrapping her arms around herself. Down that way was the path to the next cache. She paused at the foot of the slope, then turned, looking up at the shaft again.

Then she looked lower, and right in front of her was a small shelf created by water and weak stone, half the width of the tunnel leading farther away. It was easy to miss on the way down, easy to step over. But something about it was off—even in the simulation, the colors didn't quite seem right. She moved closer, crouching down, holding her breath.

Under the stone ledge was a climbing suit.

Gyre's heart stopped, then began to hammer frantically in her chest once more. *Another caver.* She dropped to her knees and grabbed the caver's ankles. The suit was rigid, forming braces over two badly broken legs. Her hands shook as she hauled the corpse out, and then she laughed, helplessly, as she saw the same logo on the breast of the suit that she wore on her own.

*Not* an intruder, then. Not whoever stole the cache. The simulation couldn't see through the helmet's mask, but then again, Gyre didn't want to.

This was another caver who Em had left to die.

She could see, clearly, what must have happened: the climber had come down the shaft. Maybe one of the bolts had failed, or maybe it was simply climber error, but either way, they'd fallen. They'd broken their body and their suit.

There was no choice but to await death. With starvation

and shock beating at them, even with all the drugs Em could pump into them, they wouldn't have been able to ascend the shaft again, or clear the sump and make it out the way Gyre had come.

And then what? Em had removed the line, and abandoned the shaft?

But that *still* didn't explain the missing cache.

Gyre sat beside the body, at a loss of what to do. Finally, she shook her head and tucked the body back under the stone lip, then returned to where she'd slept. She sat down, dimming the view in her helmet. She called up readouts and skimmed through them: current depth, current external temperature, her body temperature, her blood-sugar levels.

She was paging through the inventories of the caches she'd already passed when she noticed a new file, separate from the ones she'd flipped through over the last several days. It was a larger file, and when she opened it, she could see it was neatly subdivided based on a code that appeared to contain the date, among other identifiers. She opened one.

It was the dossier of a young man, complete with the same records she'd just been viewing of herself: biometrics, cache levels, location in the cave system. It was dated two years ago, and, while the narrative was terse, it described his first week and a half in the cave in exacting detail.

He'd made it as far as the sump, full by that point in the season, but something had gone wrong. His suit had malfunctioned, according to the notes. Its filter canisters had failed less than fifteen minutes into the dive, and he'd drowned, panicking and opening his helmet when he realized he wasn't getting any more air.

According to the notes, his body had been retrieved on a cache resupply at the start of the next season.

This was it. The list of Em's failures. Gyre's throat closed up as she stared at the thirty-five files.

How many? How *many* cavers had died before her? How many of the thirty-five had made it out?

Had *any*?

She skimmed through the other dossiers and found the one for the man at Camp Two. *Adrian Purcell.* He'd likely be retrieved at the start of next season, she thought. And the caver here? Had they been from the start of this season too, or was retrieving them too difficult, too dangerous? Obviously something or somebody restocked the caches, but was it equipped to pull bodies through numerous sumps, and up and down the ascents and drops she'd found?

*If I die down here, will she even try to get me out?*

"Em?" she asked.

No response. She was still away from her console.

Gyre kept one eye on the rest of the cavern as she read through the dossiers. There were still at least two sumps ahead of her, depending on the path Em wanted her to take, and nobody had made it past the last. Two more caches were supposed to be between her and that last camp. Five to six cavers made an attempt every year, and only eight had survived in seven years. It was a horrific number. Twenty-seven dead, in total.

Twenty-seven dead out of thirty-five.

She was going to be sick.

Gyre staggered to her feet, leaning on the nearby wall and taking deep breaths. She closed her eyes against the files still open on her screen. *Twenty-seven out of thirty-five.* Fuck, she was going to die, just like the rest of them. And Em hadn't seen fit to tell her any of this, not after Gyre had found Adrian's corpse in Camp Two, not after she'd told Gyre about her own team.

Because she'd known she would turn back. Known she would panic. Panicked cavers made mistakes, rushed their tie-ins, died. *It would have been dangerous to tell me*, she thought, then slammed her hand against the stone hard enough to jar her arm, because *why* was she making excuses for the woman?

The nausea faded, replaced with anger, with fear.

Slowly, she opened her eyes again and then sat back down, staring at the file. Em had left this for her as a stopgap against the paranoia she'd felt during her dive, a peace offering, but it could be more than that. If she was going to survive this, if she had any hope at all, she needed every scrap of information she could glean.

She'd need it as a defense against Em.

As Gyre read through the files again, she learned the name of each caver before her—and forgot half of them again just as quickly as she moved between each record. Some had died from equipment malfunction, some from human error, some from horrible luck. Some had turned and run—the smarter, smaller portion. Only five had made it down to what was marked as the final camp. Two had survived that, turned and fled.

The other three had died, two with their spines broken, one simply losing contact with Em's computer as he was swept away.

The climber under the ledge was named Jennie Mercer. She'd been the second to try the shaft entrance. The first attempt had gone well enough, though there had been a close call on the way in with what Em suspected was the nearby passing of a Tunneler. That caver had turned back of their own accord.

Jennie had been bold, and fast, almost as quick with the routes as Gyre. She'd been rappelling down, clipping in to bolts the previous caver had left as she went. When she ran out of rope, she should have attached the fresh line to her original one. Instead, she'd decided to make the last bolt she'd passed her new anchor bolt, tied into it and off the old rope, and continued down from there.

She was taking a rest not attached to anything else for just a moment—stupid, *stupid,* she should have known better— hanging close to the bottom of the shaft, maybe nine or ten meters from the cavern floor, when her anchor bolt came loose from the stone. Apparently, there had been out-of-season rains earlier that year. Water had collected just above the bolt, and it had gotten into the crevice formed when the bolt was driven in. It hadn't been done right, or the material had been faulty.

Whatever the reason, the bolt had given way and Jennie had fallen. Her legs had been smashed to pulp. Gyre could feel the panic, imagine the pain and terror. Unable to walk, barely able to think, the cavern dome stretching too far above her, leaving her unprotected and vulnerable, Jennie had done what Gyre would have.

She'd crawled under the shelf and waited for the end.

That could have been her, ten years ago. She could remember the feeling of falling, the darkness, the rush of water. She could see it happening to her here, just like the others. Adrian, Jennie, all the dossiers spread out before her.

*Two more sumps. Nobody's made it past the last one.*

Yet, even after so many deaths, Gyre wanted to believe Em had a plan. She wanted to believe Em had picked Gyre for a reason, that she wasn't just meat for the grinder. She wanted to believe that Em had seen through Gyre's lies and her short professional history and trusted what Gyre always had, that she was good, very good.

But that would be naïve. Em hadn't even explained why

74

she was down here, beyond vague mentions of her dead team. Everything was extrapolation spackled with hope and desperation.

It was those two things that drove her now. But she had to keep her guard up. To evaluate Em's every move. To stay alive. To get paid and to take advantage of all Em's resources in the process.

And to take down Em when this was all over, so that there would never be another Jennie Mercer, dying in terror, abandoned by the woman she'd thought she could trust.

$$\vee$$

"Good morning," Em said. She sounded well rested, less blasted out and hollow than Gyre felt. "I see you found the new material I downloaded to your suit."

Gyre chose her words carefully. If she was going to beat Em at her own game, she had to be as smart, as incisive, as subtle. "I didn't think you'd really have a list." She paused. "I found Jennie last night. Jennie Mercer?"

Em was silent for a moment, and Gyre supposed she must be calling up the dossier on her end—a thought that immediately disgusted her. *Can't you even remember the people you killed?* "I see," Em said after another few heartbeats. "How do you feel about it?"

"It would be difficult to get her body out," Gyre said, getting to her feet. Her anger roiled patiently.

"The easiest way is probably back up the way she came," Em agreed, her voice carefully controlled.

"But you'd have to redrill all your bolts," Gyre supplied. "If that one failed, then others could as well."

"Exactly. The way you came in is more difficult, but there's less risk of equipment failure that I can't see coming."

75

Just what she'd expected Em to say. Gyre shook her head, and considered plugging in another nutritional canister, but her stomach immediately protested the idea. Instead, she began stretching. Her muscles were sore, stiff, and under-rested. She shouldn't have pushed so hard on the previous day's climb, and she should have slept longer the night before.

She needed to be at the top of her game. No mistakes.

"There are a lot of failures in those dossiers," she said after a minute as she slowly leaned back, reaching for the wall with her hands to brace herself and stretching out her lower back. What she said was a statement, but what she wanted to do was ask, *What are you going to do about it, Em?*

"I know."

"Twenty-seven out of thirty-five."

"Sometimes I feel like the job is cursed."

"You could say that," she said, wanting to shout it instead. "You could always have another handler, you know. So you could get enough sleep."

"I already told— No, Gyre, I've tried that. It's . . . hard to keep the mission's focus that way. You've already passed substantial ore deposits, and when other handlers see that, they start fighting with me to end the mission. Once ore is found, the risk of continuing farther is outweighed by the existing success. That leads to varying messages to the caver, which can lead to mistakes."

Gyre scowled as she straightened up, then stretched forward, wiggling her hips to loosen up her pelvis. "I know. I read about what happened to Agnes Boyle." Em inhaled sharply. "But that's a lot of people, Em. And a lot of years without success. At some point, you have to admit that you don't know how to beat this."

"I know it's too many," she confessed, her voice softer.

"Too many failures, too many deaths. You asked if I felt computer errors were my fault."

Gyre canted her head, frowning.

"Of *course* I feel like they're my fault," Em said, "and every gear malfunction, too. I just—can only do it better the next time. Even the times it's been pure climber error, I wonder if maybe I just picked the wrong person. I wonder if I should have known better. So I go back and refine my screening tools."

"'Screening tools'! As if these errors are just defects on an assembly line. People are *dying*!" Gyre said. "Maybe you should try a different *way*, Em."

"I do! Every time! I've tried every entrance, picked cavers with different backgrounds, enhanced the equipment I send in. Sometimes it helps, sometimes it doesn't, but I'm getting *closer*."

"I'm glad *you're* getting closer. But what about us? The last four cavers before me died, Em! That's not *closer*."

Em made a strangled sound. "I know it doesn't seem like it, but—"

"No. Don't give me that shit," Gyre said. "Just tell me—what's different this time?"

Silence. Then: "Your physical strength is in the top tier of cavers I've sent down. You're younger than most by a few years as well. You don't have a family waiting for you. And then there are the variables that are less directly related to success: Your psych tests suggested that you do this for the rush, and for your pride, not just for money. You don't have any previous expedition experience and you were willing to lie about it, but you weren't very good at it. You're still good at the job, despite that. They could all have no effect, or they could make you better or worse suited to the job. In each aspect, you're not different from all the previous attempts, but combined you are."

"Em, that sounds—"

"Weak, I know. But things are changing. Evolving."

"You're sharing information with me," Gyre said.

"Exactly."

Gyre grimaced. "And you've agreed to my requests. I'm sure that's different too. Think that will be enough?" *It has to be*, she left unsaid. *Because I'm not dying here, not for you. Because I need you to keep talking, keep giving me the whole picture.* The more she knew, the safer she'd be—and the more she could guard against Em sabotaging the mission, inadvertently or otherwise. The more she knew, the greater her chance to get back topside.

The more she knew, the more she could use against Em when the time came.

And who knew? Maybe with enough information, she'd learn something that meant she didn't have to go the full distance for her paycheck. It felt like the better choice than standing here in the dark, no cache in sight.

Em said nothing at first, leaving Gyre to stew in her thoughts. Then she sighed. "Up until yesterday, I thought that would be enough. But now a cache is missing, and I checked the logs. It was restocked three weeks and five days ago." Her exhale shivered over her microphone, long and slow. "I still think you knowing all this will make a difference, but . . . Too many variables are changing."

Too many variables. *Me—I'm one of those variables. That's all I am to her.* Shaking her head, Gyre eyed the rest of the chamber again. She still had the uneasy feeling that she wasn't alone, and was certain somebody—not a flood, not a Tunneler—had moved that cache.

Nothing else made sense.

But neither did turning back. No, she needed to keep going, take the risk for the better reward.

Push just a little more and find a way to win this.

"I'm not going back," she said.

"I'm glad." Em didn't sound happy, though. She sounded desperate.

"Who does the restocking?" Gyre asked.

"You, mostly. Especially for the deeper caches—it's why you ferry the gear. It's for yourself, and for the next attempts. Sometimes I can get somebody to hire on just to stock the first two caches, but it's rare."

"So you need me. You need me to keep going, as far as I can."

"I do."

She had to get moving, or the fear would eat her alive.

"If you can get back to sleep," Em said, "you still have two hours on the clock."

"I'd rather conserve the battery charge. Marker to Camp Five."

"Gyre, you should reestablish Four as best you can, haul gear—"

"Let's get this over and done with, Em. You wanted me to press on last night, and whatever happened here, it's not a good spot for a cache anymore." *It's not safe.* "I'll stage from the next camp. And whatever else happens, maybe you should start considering this climb the last one.

"Ever."

Em was silent.

"Marker on."

For just a moment, there was nothing. Then the marker flared to life.

Gyre started walking.

# CHAPTER SEVEN

Camp Five was two days away, down a very steep drop.

Gyre worked efficiently and methodically through the morning, locating each bolt that Em flagged on her screen and carefully testing it before hooking in. Occasionally, she opted to put in a new bolt rather than trust an old one, or to load a cam or two into a good crack in the wall, and she watched as Em flagged the ones she passed over as unsafe. A few Gyre decided to trust, but not completely; she added more cams nearby as a safeguard.

Her stock of gear dwindled, but it was better to be safe with such a long fall below her.

It wasn't sheer cliffside for all of it, but it was too steep of an incline to stand easily on. She rappelled down it slowly until, finally, she passed over its edge and perched above the void, fingers clawed tight against the stone. Her heart pounded as she navigated to the first of several ledges Em had called out for her. There, she found a stable position facing out into the gap and locked the bottom half of her suit, standing with three quarters of her feet on solid rock. She set up her midday nutritional canister as she did her best not to look down.

Instead, she looked out across the space in front of her. It was more open here than it had been above, where in a few spots it had narrowed to a slit barely large enough for a human to pass through. Here, the other wall was a good fifteen meters away, and the expanded pocket continued down for quite a while. Lichen clung to the roof the sudden flare had created, and as she waited for the canister to finish unloading and worked her fingers in her suit's gloves, she momentarily turned off her simulation screen and looked up in the darkness to the pale glow. They looked like stars.

She turned her reconstruction back on when a few pinpricks began to look more like watchful eyes. Nothing was there, nothing but lichen. She tamped down the irrational fear. Better to spend her energy on the rational ones: the climbs, Em, her resources.

Herself.

Her body was still exhausted from the day before, and the lack of sleep was beginning to make her sluggish, but the ledge she was on was too narrow to sleep on. The suit would continue to hold her upright if she needed it, but the display and route showed a much larger ledge not too far below her. Her canister depleted and stored away, Gyre unlocked the legs of her suit.

She pitched forward.

"Shit!" she shouted as she lost her footing on the narrow ledge and swung out into the gap, her line too long to help hold her in place. She twisted desperately on the rope, trying to get back around to facing the wall, but her momentum brought her smashing into it before she could turn. Her arm struck the ledge and pain exploded up through her shoulder and neck, knocking her breath from her lungs. She gasped for air as she scrabbled for a handhold, but the fingers of her right hand were clumsy, fumbling, half numb. Her left hand caught hold of the edge at last and she was able to dig her toes in to stop herself from swinging out again.

"Gyre? Gyre, are you okay?"

Her chestplate scraped against the cliffside as she clung close to it.

"*Gyre!*"

Em's voice was distant over the rush of blood in her ears, and the throbbing pain in her arm. She forced herself to pause for a moment and wiggle the fingers on her right hand. They all responded.

"Gyre, I'm not showing a bone break. Gyre, can you hear me?"

"Yeah," she grunted. "Just—give me a moment."

"I can shunt in pain medicine—"

"No," Gyre gasped. "Absolutely not. I need to get down to that next ledge. I need my head for that." She licked at her lips and took stock. She was holding on to the edge of the thin ledge, her feet planted strongly in the stone below it. Her line was taut now. Why hadn't she shortened it up while she was resting? Jennie had made almost the same mistake, and it had killed her. Gyre knew better. This was what she was good at; this was her *life*.

How could she have screwed up?

*Em.* Maybe she should have been better than that, but Em had cost her sleep, had made her paranoid enough to push on instead of staging thoroughly for this climb.

Her head spun, but her right arm was beginning to hurt less. Not enough, but at least it wasn't getting worse.

Must have just smacked a nerve. Better than the alternative. Gyre moved her right hand, toggling the retraction of her line. Slowly, she walked herself back up to where she'd started.

Feet back on solid ground, she considered her options. Her arm still throbbed and would probably be useless for at least half an hour. But the larger ledge below her was big enough to lie down on, and was recessed slightly into the wall. Softer stone must have been there, once, and dissolved before the rest of the cliffside. If she could just get down there . . .

But to do that, she'd either need to trust the old bolts or go through the painstaking process of finding new cracks or driving pitons. It could take over half an hour, if she was clipping in at reliably safe distances and favoring her arm.

Or she could fudge the safety parameters again, and rappel down with less security. It was within range of her current rope.

"I'm going to descend," she said.

"Gyre, return to Camp Four. Use your ascender." Em still sounded on edge, panicked, and for a moment, Gyre hated that reaction even more than she hated Em. Em had put her in this position; if somebody should be panicking, it was Gyre.

After reading all those dossiers, Gyre could almost understand, though. Em didn't want to lose another one.

*No—she doesn't want to* restart.

And that only made it worse. Em wasn't afraid of *Gyre* dying; she was afraid of wasting the money. Of finding a new victim.

She made herself count her breaths, up to ten inhales, then ten again. Finally, she said, "I can't climb up with my arm like this." She kept her words slow, her tone steady. "Even with the ascender, it's not safe."

"Then keep your rope short and lock your suit. You need rest."

"I'm not going to get it dangling from a rope. I'm going to descend," Gyre said.

Em was silent for a moment, and then Gyre's helmet screen brightened in the lower left corner. She looked to it, and found a dark-skinned, very tired woman not much older than she was looking back at her.

She was too young to have been down here with a team.

She'd lied.

Again.

But before Gyre could protest, before she could even really get angry, Em said, "If you fall, I can't get your body out." Her voice was soft, her mouth moving in time with the words. Gyre's heart stopped mid-beat. "Please do this safely, Gyre."

The face disappeared.

This had been different—easier—without a face to the voice. Without knowing how similar they were. She'd already known Em was a liar, but to know that she couldn't be older than her twenties? And to see how she was so *scared* and exhausted and *human*—

She took a deep breath and looked up, forcing her mind to clear. They could talk it through later—if there *was* a later. If Em had enough experience to get her out.

Oh fuck. What if *Em* had lied about her experience, just like Gyre had?

"Gyre?"

She was fucked. But she couldn't think about what that meant until she was off the side of the cliff. She ignored Em—

and the persistent throb in her arm—and thought through her next steps. Before she could do anything else, she had to get off the side of this cliff. She had enough rope. The anchor above her had to be treated as compromised now, after taking her fall. Even if she could have climbed up to check and reinforce it, it was better to just put in a new anchor.

She moved to the edge of the ledge most in line with the platform below. After locking her suit legs again, she surveyed the stone in front of her. There were no good cracks for cams, but she needed to conserve bolts. She thought it over a moment and then cleared her throat.

"Suggestions?" she asked, her face burning with embarrassment and anger.

Em turned on the analytic overlay. "Didn't want to distract you," she said, her voice tight.

"Just checking my work." Gyre managed a smile, as if it would reassure either of them. She didn't want to admit that she didn't trust her brain one hundred percent at the moment, given the earlier fall. That she had to trust Em more than she trusted herself, even knowing that Em must have blatantly lied about her own experience. So she picked the spot Em had marked as the best combination of within reach and sturdy. She placed her left palm against the stone, then paused.

"Is something wrong?" Em asked.

"We've been putting in a lot of bolts," Gyre said, glancing down the drop-off. "If it is vibration through the rock that calls them—"

"A lot more mining operations would have already been wiped out. It's safe."

That all made sense, and she'd even believed it herself for a long, long time. Just because Em had lied about her experience didn't mean she was incompetent. Her help until now proved that. The quality of her suit proved that. The other dead cavers—

*Get out of your head, Gyre.* "Right. But we could also run out, couldn't we?" she said. She hated being this rattled.

"Your gear levels look good."

*Right.* She needed to trust Em. Just for now, until she got control of herself again.

She started up the drill, and it slipped the bolt into the new hole almost before she registered that the drilling had stopped. She took a moment to test the bolt from all angles until she was certain it was wedged in firmly. It took her weight as she sat down hard toward the ledge.

"Descending," she said.

"Descend," Em replied, and Gyre walked herself out against the wall. She waited a handful of breaths clinging to the wall like a spider, then began walking herself down the cliffside, fingers poised to trigger the rappel rack. This model, hooked into the chest of her suit, was far more reliable than the one she'd nearly broken her legs with when she was younger. Still, she kept all her attention on it and the passage of stone beneath her feet. Nothing else mattered, until she was finally almost level with the new ledge.

The ledge wasn't directly below where she'd placed the bolt, though, and so she needed to pause to add a cam before she could crawl her way across to solid ground again. Her right hand was still half numb, and she fumbled to work the cam into the nearest serviceable crevice. By the time she'd clipped in, her endurance was almost gone, arrested by the uselessness of her arm and the ebbing tide of adrenaline in her system.

"Can you look at this for me?" Gyre asked, grimacing.

There was no change in her display, but after a moment, Em said, "You're good. Climb on, Gyre."

Gyre sagged in relief, the cam taking her weight easily. So close—just a little farther, and then she could rest. She traversed the last few meters to the ledge, her good arm trembling, her toes feeling clumsy against the rock. Once she was safely over the protrusion, she dropped down, released and anchored her line, and then sat down heavily.

"This is new," Em said.

*Leave me alone*, Gyre thought first, before she pushed down her exhaustion again and frowned, looking around. "What's new?"

"This tunnel."

*Tunnel?* Gyre twisted sharply, looking over her shoulder to the depression in the rock. What she'd expected to be a maybe meter-deep indentation went back much farther. A short ways in, the ground became level and oddly smooth.

"It's new?" she repeated numbly.

"It wasn't here last time." Gyre could hear fast typing on the other end of the comm. "And it's too big to be a natural formation."

"And too deep to be from another mine?" Gyre asked.

"And too far away from other concerns," Em agreed.

"Shit," she whispered.

"Tunneler."

"No." Gyre leaned her head back against the wall, staring up at the underside of the ledge above. "*No.*" Tunnelers were one of the few disasters her skill couldn't prevent.

"It doesn't mean you're in danger," Em said. "It's probably long gone, or we would have heard it today, or yesterday. And that, combined with other information your suit's been sending me, supports my theory that the flooding between Camps Three and Four is the result of a Tunneler-caused change in the layout of the caverns, not off-season flooding. It should mean Camp Five is still manageable.

"In any case, you need to rest. Now that I know you have this much room here, this is going to be a way point between Camps Three and Five, for gear ferrying."

"No," Gyre said, the sharp syllable bitten off before she could stop herself. Gear ferrying would add at least a week, going back and forth through the sump, then up that pitch, then all the way down here. It would give her more time to prod at Em's story, find what she needed to protect herself, but she wasn't sure she could manage it. Seeing the same passages over and over, climbing past where she'd fallen today, hauling gear through the unsettling Camp Four cavern. She was tired and she was angry and she just wanted to keep going.

Besides, Em didn't want her stocking caches just for herself. She sat up straighter and glared at the impersonal display inside her helmet. "I meant what I said at Camp Four," Gyre said. "I'm not ferrying gear. This is your last expedition."

Em didn't say anything for a moment, before stating, "Your contract requires you to transport the supplies. Gyre, it's for your own safety. Running out of food or power down there would be—"

"Are the other caches depleted? Or gone?"

"I—I don't know. Maybe," she conceded. "But even if they're not, you should only go forward with the best I can offer you. That means as many supplies as you can carry. The Camp Five cache is the second to last one I have on this route, with a long dive between there and Camp Six, and it might . . . take longer from there."

"From there to your mysterious goal?" she asked. While

she talked, she eyed the tunnel warily. It seemed more stable the farther away from the ledge she got, but if Em was wrong . . .

*Focus.* The tunnel didn't matter. What mattered was that Em still sounded worried, maybe even contrite. Gyre had to strike, drive the wedge in and pry loose a few more secrets.

She sat up straight and addressed the tunnel as if Em were sitting just inside it. "You lied about your team."

"I did."

"I don't suppose I could make a case that your own false-hoods have undermined the expedition," she said, and was vindicated by a sharp, shuddering breath on the other end of the line.

"I want you to look me in the eye," Gyre said, her voice low and harsh, "and tell me why you lied about the team. About what you've *killed twenty-seven people* for. Cameras on, boss."

Em remained silent, long enough that Gyre began to grind her teeth. Her shoulders were back and straight despite the lingering pain, despite her exhaustion. If Em was looking at her stats, she wanted Em to see how very serious she was.

"All right," Em said.

*Yes.* Relief flooded through her and she tucked herself more fully into the mouth of the tunnel, away from the cliff face. She even smiled, a vicious little thing.

At first, nothing changed. Then Em's face appeared in the lower left corner of her helmet.

For a moment, Gyre couldn't think. There Em was again, in full, living color, so different from the flat tones the reconstruction used to help her understand depth and material. It was surreal, mesmerizing to see another person, to see *her.* She searched Em's face for any sign of incompetence, but instead, she only saw a focused, hyperaware woman. A *beautiful* woman, at that. It didn't seem possible, and her mouth gaped open for a few heartbeats. But then her frustration punched through, and Gyre managed a thin, bitter smile. "Well?"

Em's eyes darted from side to side, too ashamed or panicked to meet Gyre's gaze. She had dark circles under her eyes that looked like they had been there long before Gyre had entered the cave. Her hair was thick, pure black, haloing around her face in a mess of tight curls. Her skin was darker than Gyre's, a rich, warm brown without freckles or moles. She was stunning, even in her exhaustion, even though her full, doll-like lips were chapped and torn from chewing at them. She pursed them as she thought about what to say next, the motion deepening the small cleft in her chin.

"There was still a team," Em said at last. "Before they knew the Tunnelers were a real thing. I didn't lie about that."

"Whose team?" Gyre pushed.

"My parents'," Em said tightly, "but it—feels like mine. That's why I said . . . it doesn't matter. I was six when they went down. My father was an experienced climber; my mother was just getting started."

Em's gaze finally settled on one point, hopefully where Gyre's image or statistics floated on her screen. After only a moment, though, Em's eyes lost focus, making the illusion of her presence all the less convincing, all the more unnatural. "They were hired by one of the original mining concerns and sent down there. They reported all the ore closer to the surface, but the company wanted more. Wanted to tell their shareholders how rich of a plot it was. So they kept going down. Past where you are now. They went through a—an extensive sump, and . . . you know what? I'll just upload the videos for you. You can see for yourself."

That didn't sound good.

"The important thing," Em said, "is that they didn't all come back up. That's the long and short of it."

It also didn't add up to anything at all.

Gyre scowled. "So you want me to—what? Get the bodies out?"

Em shook her head. "Too dangerous," she said. "I just want to give them a funeral. And formally map everything they found. I just want it to not be in vain."

Her mouth dropped open, disbelieving.

*That's* it?

Gyre thought back to the dossiers, of the horrible ways all of those other cavers had died. She had almost understood it when it was Em who had survived this cave and lost her team. She could have understood other reasons—a huge mineral deposit deep in the cave, say, or even a way in to sabotage another concern. She could have understood a lot of things.

She didn't understand *this.*

"How can you think this is worth it?" she asked in disbelief.

"That's my father down there, with three other good people."

"You've killed *twenty-seven* other people trying to get to a bunch of corpses! And in seven years you haven't gotten close *once*! And you think that's something I can accept because those corpses belonged to *good people*?"

"This is why I don't tell people."

"You mean this is why you lead people to their graves. You have no idea what you're doing. And more importantly, you have no *idea* what it's like down here."

Em's lip curled in anger, a muscle jumping in her throat and fracturing the illusion of a beautiful, sad girl. Her gaze focused again, and she stared directly into the camera. "I never lied about how dangerous this mission is. I'm paying more than enough money. My reasons are just that: *mine*. You all knew you were risking death. You all did the math for yourselves. I just let your decision-making stay objective. Nobody needs to think about my personal motivations when theirs are all that should matter. *And*, for the record, I grew up running topside missions. My mother founded Arasgain Technologies, which developed the suit you're wearing. *I* pushed the development of all the new models in the last nine years. This is my life, Gyre, and I am very, very good at what I do."

*Arasgain Technologies.* Arasgain was—the best. It was small, brilliant, and independent of all the mining concerns. The logo on her suit had had no small part in getting her to sign up. And Em was saying it was her, all her.

Maybe so, but that didn't make Em infallible.

Gyre shook her head again. "You're a real piece of work, you know?"

"I'm aware," Em growled. "My mother got a lot of money for that mission and she used it to start this company. She wanted to say goodbye to my father and the others, too, and now I'm doing what she couldn't finish. I'm going to do what she wasn't able to. And I inherited everything, so in the meantime, I'm using most of the money to keep developing tech to keep you cavers safe, just like she did. What I want to do with the rest of my money and my time is my business. How is that any different from you chasing the fantasy of your mother?"

Her heart jumped at that, twisted into a tight little ball. "Shut up. I'm not killing anybody to get there."

"You're still sacrificing everything for a ghost."

"What are you sacrificing? Your hoard of money you didn't even earn?"

"My entire life, Gyre! This is all it's been for years now,"

Em hissed. "I barely sleep, I barely eat, I just try to keep people like you alive, and you all keep dying!" Her face had gone stormy and dark, her brow shining with beaded sweat. She was shaking.

Gyre stared back, unflinching, uncaring if the helmet had its own camera feed. "This is fucked," she said slowly, as calmly as she could. "You're a goddamn murderer, Em. There's no excuse, no reason that anybody else would ever accept. You're not trying to get money; you're not trying to save people. All you're doing is trying to change somebody else's past. Living in somebody else's pain."

Em's face flushed with fury. "So what, then—are you going to turn around now? You didn't turn back when you found out how many were dead, when you thought it was my team that had died down there. That I'd been down there. What's different?"

*What's different?* Knowing Em was ignoring reality to try to save people who didn't need saving. Knowing that Em could never succeed, that this would never end. Knowing that Em didn't see how pointless and horrific this was.

"I'm leaving," Gyre said, and stood up.

Em's eyes deadened, and she sat back in her seat. Her face slackened into blankness, calm control. "Sit back down, Gyre. Think this through. You can't win against me in court."

"I don't care."

"I can make sure you're blacklisted from other caving jobs."

"I'll take the risk."

"It's unsafe for you to climb back up without rest," she said, as if she cared. "Sit down, sleep, climb out in the morning."

"Fuck you! I told you that you don't get to control me anymore." Gyre reached for her rope, ready to clip in.

"Gyre, look at me. No matter what you think of me, I don't want you to die. I didn't want *any* of you to die."

Gyre paused, obeying despite herself. She looked at Em, young and twisted and proud. The blankness had fractured slightly, and Em had leaned forward, manufacturing an innocent, worried look for her. She looked like she was in pain, like she was afraid. Like she was sorry.

If Gyre hadn't known how good a liar she could be . . .

The lines of Em's face began to blur. Gyre took a step back, unsteadily, then sank down to one knee as her body quickly became leaden. She searched her display but there was no alert, no explanation as to what Em had injected her with. "What have you done?" she asked, reaching out to stabilize herself against the ground. "What are you doing to me?"

"You need to rest," Em said.

She sagged, spreading out along the ground as whatever sedative Em had pumped into her system took hold of her. She felt her suit lock once she was down, her right arm pulling into a safe, restorative position.

"You're a fucking monster," she managed.

"I'm aware," Em said, and then her face disappeared from view.

# CHAPTER EIGHT

Gyre woke up disoriented. Her thoughts were sluggish, her vision blurred. Her mouth tasted like death and her stomach ached. She tried to move, and couldn't. Her heart stammered in her chest. She jerked against whatever was holding her—it didn't budge.

The panic took over before she could think. She couldn't even ball her hands into fists, couldn't turn her head, and she knew—she *knew*—that she was being watched. She remembered eyes in the darkness, or had it been a broken suit mask?

No, wait. That had been a dream. She'd had a nightmare about Jennie Mercer following her down, her suit locked into an unnatural shape as she staggered into the tunnel.

Her suit.

She nearly vomited. *She drugged me.*

*Again.*

Fury riding just under her skin, Gyre unlocked her suit

and sat up. She pulled up her reconstruction to full draw distance, which simulated a brightly lit cavern. There were no eyes in the darkness, no ghosts there to terrify her. Her fear faded as she took stock of her state. Her right arm was feeling better, but it was stiff. She stretched it, rotating the joints, and then locked the arm of her suit with it tucked up by her chest, as if it were in a sling. The change in position seemed to help.

Another hour to warm up, and she'd be good to climb. Climb to Camp Four, swim the dive again . . . if she pushed, she could get halfway to Camp Two before she needed to sleep again. Two days, three tops, and she'd be out.

If she'd just turned back at Camp Two, or at Four, she'd already be back in the sun. Fuck, what had she been thinking? *Get the money*, that was what she'd been thinking. Find a way to blackmail or bully Em into paying her, and then leave as soon as she'd accomplished that.

But that had been based on Em being rational. This wasn't rational. This was madness.

She had never been down here. She had killed twenty-seven people chasing nothing. She'd just been a voice in their ears, the promise of coming topside once more.

Whispering them to their deaths.

Gyre paused, then checked the feed of documents Em had shared to her suit. There were the videos, like she'd said. Gyre scrolled through them with a flick of her eyes, until she found the one with the earliest chronological date.

It didn't matter. She had already decided to turn back, and as soon as she was out of this cave, she'd be free of this nightmare, of Em's ghosts.

And yet . . .

She wanted to see them, see normal people, see somebody

who wasn't *Em*. Wanted to see who could be so important that their deaths could break a little girl and rebuild her into . . . whatever her handler was.

She activated the first video.

Four people sat around a small campfire. Gyre frowned at the open flame, before she remembered Em saying that their team had been one of the first. This must have been back when they were treating these expeditions like recreational spelunking on other planets. They all were wearing topside clothing, heavy enough to ward off the pervasive chill, a few with harnesses still on. Their packs sat nearby. They were laughing.

It was a strange sound to hear, down in the caves. It made her heart ache, her skin itch. One week down, and she was already coming close to tears over hearing laughter, over seeing faces. Other cavers talked about this, but she had been so sure she wouldn't care.

She cared.

There was one woman and three men. They ranged in age from a boy maybe Gyre's age to a man that she guessed was in his late forties, and they all looked excited. Tired, after a long day's climb, but excited. It was strange, seeing the cave lit only by the fire and a few headlamps still on and propped nearby, but if she had to guess, they were at Camp Two. She could see the talus pile behind the older guy.

"No, what I'm *saying* is that—what if there's, like, an entire underground city down here? Wouldn't that be cool?" said the youngest of them, the one who couldn't have been more than a year or two older than Gyre. He had long dark hair pulled back into a low braid, and his skin was a dark russet from a combination of heritage and long sun exposure.

"Yeah, and what if there's buried treasure?" replied the

woman, who Gyre judged to be in her mid-thirties or so, with broad cheekbones and a wicked grin. When she turned, Gyre thought she could see a tattoo peeking out above the neck of her shirt and curling up behind her ear, along her shaved scalp, but maybe that was a comm cord. Em's mother?

Then a voice very similar to Em's came from directly behind the camera. "That would be the find of a century. Not the treasure—a city. We haven't found traces of another sentient race in—"

"And what if there are *traps*?" the kid cut in. "Like those old movies—traps to keep grave robbers out!"

"So now it's a tomb?" the older guy said, and shook his head, reaching out with a gloved hand to pull a can out of the fire. *Real food*—her mouth watered.

"I mean, if it's a city, they have to have dead people too, right?"

"Unless it's full of enlightened immortals," almost-Em supplied. The third man, who hadn't spoken yet, cracked a smile as she continued speaking. "If we're going to go full drama vid."

"I like buried treasure more," said the man with the can. He was tall, stringy, with close-cropped dirt-brown hair.

"Ore's buried treasure enough," the third man said. He had a smooth voice with a rich, lilting accent. He smiled again, his teeth flashing against his nearly black skin. "With what we've found so far, we're going to be rich."

The camera shifted, Em's mother turning it around to face herself. She looked like she was in her mid-twenties, maybe the same age Em was now, and looked eager and happy, foreign expressions on her daughter's face. She was pale-skinned, her blond hair curling gently against her cheeks, and her green eyes glittered. She had the same small notch in her chin as her daughter. "You hear that? Laurent says we're all going to be rich."

"We're the dream team!" the kid shouted. "And when we find our ancient city—"

He was cut off by a low rumble. The woman's expression froze, her gaze going past the camera. "Is that—"

"It's too early in the season for rain," Laurent said, and Gyre could hear some of the others standing up.

"A drill? Maybe another company is trying to horn in—" the kid started.

"Doesn't make sense, Halian," the stringy man snapped. "What are they going to do, destabilize the caves and then hope they can still get the ore out safely? I—"

"Both of you, shut up," the woman with the shaved head said. Em's mother's expression had changed to alert trepidation, her lips slightly parted, the camera forgotten.

The low rumble had stopped, but it took another minute of pained silence before she murmured, "Maybe it's nothing."

"Yeah," Halian said. "Yeah. Nothing."

One of the other men grunted.

Em's mother looked back at the camera at last, and managed a small smile. "Dream team, signing off."

The video ended.

# CHAPTER NINE

Gyre realized she had one hand resting lightly on her throat, and slowly lowered it. Her heart was hammering in her chest. That rumble—it must have been a Tunneler. She eyed the rest of the videos warily.

*Em's seen these.*

It wasn't enough to change anything. But it did make everything click, a heavy weight settling into her bones. Now Gyre could begin to see how a girl could grow up in the shadow of this, knowing the tragedy so intimately that she was warped into a monster, determined to finish what her mother had started by any means necessary. If Em had grown up watching these videos, knowing that her mom had gotten out but her dad hadn't—

Gyre could see it. She'd thought her obsession with chasing her own mother was bad enough. This . . . this would have been all-consuming.

It didn't matter. It didn't justify the deaths. Understanding Em didn't mean she wanted to help her, wanted to risk her *life* for her. And beyond that pointless understanding, the videos didn't change anything. They weren't proof Em had breached the contract. They weren't proof she'd broken any laws. It wasn't a way to get out and take the money anyway. It was just . . . tragedy. So what if she felt pain for the other woman? Caring about the emotional damage of some alienated millionaire wasn't what she'd signed up for.

"You're awake," Em said, and her voice was enough to bring her anger roaring back to full flame.

"You drugged me."

"I did. You were behaving erratically."

Gyre clenched her jaw hard enough that she could hear her teeth creak. *Erratically?*

"I wanted to give you some time to think. And," Em said, quickly, before Gyre could get a word in, "I have something to offer you."

"I won't believe anything that comes out of your mouth," Gyre said, and stood up. Her head spun, and she reached out and braced herself against the wall.

"I have an amendment to your contract," Em said. "Please sit down and hear me out. And I suggest a nutritional canister."

"Fuck your suggestions." Even if it was a good one. All she could think about was what Em had just said. *An amendment.* A way out? Gyre sat down slowly, scowling. "Keep talking."

Em's voice was level and measured as she said, "It memorializes my previous offer, that I will use my personal resources to locate your mother. And that if you continue on to Camp Five, I will also relinquish my rights to sue you for falsifying your professional background, and I will not provide negative references to future potential employers. In the event the cache at Camp Five is also missing and it is unsafe for you to continue, the expedition will end and I will pull you out per the terms of your employment agreement."

Gyre's chest burned and she realized she'd stopped breathing. "And why should I trust that the amendment will be valid? I don't imagine you're going to summon a witness."

"No," Em admitted, having the decency to sound embarrassed. "You're correct. But I have something better."

Gyre's brows rose. "Better."

"Yes. I've loaded the amendment into your suit, and I'm currently recording this conversation both from your suit and from my desk. The two feeds are being uploaded and stored in a black box—neither of us can get in to hear them until the date specified in the amendment, and they cannot be copied or altered. It is legally admissible evidence. If I try to nullify the contract, you'll have my words to use against me."

Gyre was shaking. *There has to be a catch.* But the only catch was that Em could be lying about the recording. Yet, as she watched, Em began displaying the upload feed, as well as specifications for the black box. Gyre wrapped her arms around herself, but the suit's resistance was hard and the movement didn't give her any comfort.

This was it.

"All I have to do," Gyre said slowly, "is get to Camp Five."

It wasn't a way out, but it was the start of one. Freedom. All she had to do was finish this one descent, and then she could leave. She might not get any money—Em had been careful to make no promises—but she'd be free to try again on a more normal expedition, only a little worse for wear.

But this was Em. Em closed her eyes and inhaled deeply before saying, "Yes. Just one more day. And then you can turn back. Or . . . or you can go on."

*Not happening.* With that recording ready to protect her from Em's retaliation, there was no reason to stay.

With that recording—

Gyre sat up straighter, then slouched again, trying not to look too alert. She hoped Em was too busy waiting for a response to notice her heart rate jump again as she realized, *If I can keep the recording running, I'll have her.*

She fought down the urge to fiddle with her interface. She'd need to wait until Em was asleep, away from her desk. But then . . . then, if she could figure out how to turn it on . . .

Gyre thought of the team in the video, Jennie's broken suit, Adrian Purcell at Camp Two. Not only could she black-mail Em into paying her, she could get vengeance for all of them.

"What about sedation? I want it off the table."

"No," Em said. "You're down here, you're my responsibility."

Gyre hissed through her teeth. She wanted Em out of her body, *now*. But it wasn't worth losing the opportunity over, and she put aside that particular grievance for later.

"Let's sign the amendment, then." The words were out of her mouth before she could second-guess herself. "Camp Five it is."

Em laughed weakly in relief. Gyre read through the amendment, which was written in plain language so that she felt comfortable giving her assent and hearing Em do the same. The document left her view, and she made to stand up again.

"Eat," Em said, reiterating her previous suggestion.

"I want to conserve what I have." Her hand went instinctively to the compartment where her remaining rations were stored, while her gaze flicked to her battery readout. Em had knocked her out for over ten hours, leaving her that much closer to swapping to her one backup.

"It should only be one more push to Camp Five."

"And if that cache *is* gone?"

"You'll still have enough food to get back to Camp Three at normal activity levels. I'll try again with somebody else once I've restocked everything."

Gyre scowled but said nothing. What *could* she say? Em clearly didn't care that Gyre objected to the mission. *Try again.* The thought of Em sending another parade of people down here to die turned her stomach. She'd have to get the recording up and running before she got to Five, then.

"Your arm isn't incapacitated. How is it feeling?"

"Stiff. Guessing it's bruised. I'll be able to climb today."

Em answered with silence again.

Gyre crouched down and set up her feeding. She held herself up on her knees, her left hand braced against the wall, and turned to look down the tunnel.

"Did you do any scans on it? Down there, I mean?"

"Some. I am, of course, limited by where your suit is. Everything seems settled. The Tunneler passed a while ago. You were safe."

Gyre sucked on her straw in an attempt to ease the rough cracking of her throat. "Anything interesting happen while I was out?"

"I made you a roast dinner," Em deadpanned.

Gyre snorted. "Fuck you."

"I'm . . . I am sorry, about the sedation," Em said. "I really did think it was in your best interest."

"To shut me up?"

"No, to make you sleep. You didn't, at Camp Four. If you'd fallen again trying to climb out—"

"You swore to me. You agreed."

"I know. And I broke my word."

"Well, I know better than to take you at it, now, don't I?" Em said nothing.

"You can't control everything. Not my mind, not my decisions."

"I know," Em said. "I know." But it didn't mean she wouldn't do it again.

Gyre hated this. She hated this part, this vulnerability. Knowing that she couldn't trust Em. But that had been true from day one.

She just needed to keep going.

Em cleared her throat, then said, "My suggestion is that you reach Camp Five today and rest there, take a day to think about if you want to keep going. If you do, then you head back here with a portion of the cache. The ascender should make that relatively easy, just a few hours to get up. Then you can stage the gear hauling between Camp Three, here, and Five as anticipated."

"And after that, if I do keep going"—*if I need the time to catch you in more of your lies,* she thought—"Camp Six is the last?"

"It is."

"How many of your cavers made it that far?" She knew the answer from the dossiers. Five. Did Em still remember?

"Five," she said. "It's the last sump that's been the biggest problem."

"That's the one that those—what, three or four died in?"

It was three.

"Yes. That's the one. It's claimed three of mine." Em's voice trembled on the last word, then firmed up again as she continued, "The one before it is substantially more straight-forward."

She'd remembered. She couldn't remember the names, but she could remember the numbers. She wasn't a complete monster.

Just very close.

"The rest turned back," Em noted quietly. "They didn't all die."

Gyre bit down her response; she needed Em to lower her guard, not keep fighting her. She stared down the tunnel as she waited for the feeding to finish, wriggling her hips every so often as if it would help the cramping, crawling sensation in her gut. When Em's parents had come down here, they'd been able to eat real food, scratch their itches, massage their cramped muscles. They'd been able to sit around a camp-fire together, reach out and touch one another. She was jeal-ous until she reflected on her fall the day before. That could have broken Laurent's arm, without the protective carapace around it, and it certainly wouldn't have healed as quickly as it had.

Suited or suitless, they all seemed to suffer and die the same. Nobody should be down here.

Canister spent and stowed, Gyre straightened up, her eyes still on the tunnel.

"It should be stable, if you want to explore. It seems to go down in the direction of Camp Five. It may be an easier path."

The cliff was the simpler, known path, but Gyre didn't like the idea of leaving the tunnel unexplored behind her. "I'll take a quick look," she said, stepping across the jumbled

106

rock at the threshold into the smooth portion of the tunnel. It branched off to either side, ascending sharply on the right, arching down to her left in a gentle slope that looked more walkable. She went left, hugging the wall as she edged along.

The floor was smooth, with a slight dip in the center, and the entire opening was a flattened oval, wide along the top and bottom, sharply curved at the walls.

The shape of a Tunneler?

She walked for about ten minutes before she saw the sudden drop-off, the sharp curve down where the Tunneler had changed course. She eased herself close to the corner, where the ground was buckled, almost wrinkled, pushed out into the open air of the tunnel when the creature had left it in its wake. She crouched, one hand on a ridge that jutted out over the shaft, peering down.

It seemed to go on forever.

"Is this still lining up with Camp Five?" she asked.

"I think so, but not directly. Better to go the original route," Em replied. Then she inhaled sharply. "That buckling—"

"When it went down, it must have pushed some stone back behind it. Like dust on a road."

"It's going the wrong way for that."

Gyre frowned. Em was right. If the Tunneler had been going down, *behind* it would have been up. It would have created a fence, not a shelf.

"So it was coming up." Gyre stood, then turned, looking back the way she'd come. "And it kept going—"

"Toward Camp Four," Em said. "Whatever attracted it must have been there. And recent."

"The cache?" Gyre said, her voice suddenly weak. But there had been no sign of a Tunneler breaking into Camp Four, near the cache or otherwise. The cache hadn't attracted it. That left . . . "Whoever took the cache. That's what you're thinking, right?"

"Somebody is *in my cave*," Em whispered.

"*Was.* *Was.* Gyre had to believe that, or she'd turn tail and run, amendment or not. Because no matter what Em thought, right now it was *Gyre's* cave, and she didn't want to share it with anyone.

So it *had* to be *was.*

"We didn't see any trace of them. They have to be gone by now. Maybe the Tunneler—"

"If there's another entrance now, I need to find it." Em's voice had gone cold. Mechanical.

Gyre didn't need this. She didn't need Em to be distracted, and she certainly didn't need to give her own imagination any fuel. Her skin was already beginning to prickle with the feeling of being watched once more. "No. Camp Five first." *I need to get this turned around.* She couldn't get dragged into this; she had to get *out.* But she also needed a better excuse than fear, something Em would listen to in her obsession. "I can't—I can't stage from here without more gear," she stammered out, "and I can't haul from Three easily without those dry bags—that's why we kept pushing forward to begin with." Gyre shook her head and began walking up the incline. "Camp Five marker," she said. "Put it up."

Em muttered to herself, but the Camp Five marker appeared on her screen. Gyre took one last glance over her shoulder at the jagged ledge. Then she sped up to a trot, taking the gentle path up to the cliffside much faster than she had come down.

The moment she stepped out of the smooth tunnel and back onto the rougher rock of the ledge, she shuddered in relief.

She went out onto the ledge again and looked up at her leads from the day before. With the gear hauling—or the potential need for a fast escape—it would be best to leave them there for now even though it reduced how much line she had left. She toggled her next—and last—spool into place inside her suit.

"Is this enough to get me down?"

"Yes," Em said. "There's more at Five."

Gyre nodded, her lips pursed in thought. Even if Em was wrong, Gyre could always climb back up, make for Three again in a pinch. She'd have to keep an eye on it though, be ready to bail. There was no way she was going to try to out-climb the rope.

She hooked herself into the line from the day before and made her way out to the original bolt, checking her cams as she went. Everything looked sturdy. She shouldn't have needed Em to tell her that much. Once she had transferred to the vertical length of her old rope, she began to descend once more, hand over hand and step by step.

⌄

Half an hour in, her right arm felt almost normal again, and the work was easier. The lingering effects of the sedative had worn off, leaving her head clearer than it had been since before the sump at Camp Three. She increased her pace. Again, a few of the bolts had to be replaced, and again, Em's overlaid calculations seemed correct. They worked together with a few words exchanged every ten to fifteen minutes. Em sounded distracted, and still angry.

Gyre itched to dig into her suit's workings and find the recorder, but she kept herself only to the climb. She was losing precious time to prod at Em's defenses, but she couldn't risk Em seeing her fussing with it.

Then Em said, "I need to look into something. Wait for me when you get to the bottom."

Her line closed.

Gyre swore loudly and thumped her fist into the rock wall. Her suit scraped against the stone, and the impact jarred yesterday's injury. She sucked in deep breaths through her clenched teeth, then let go of the wall, hanging for a moment in her harness while she gestured angrily toward the surface.

"Yeah, just leave me down here during a climb. *Great* handling!"

There was no response, and as Gyre's pounding heart quieted, she realized that, hanging there in the dark, she was entirely . . . Alone.

*Unless the cache thief is still here*, her nerves whispered. She pushed the thought away. Better to be alone on the side of a sheer drop than on the side of a sheer drop with another climber somewhere else on the wall.

She situated her toes back into holds on the wall and resumed her bouncing glide down toward her next bolt. Every time her rope nudged against an outcropping, or her spool released unevenly, her throat tightened. She could *see* the other climber up at the tunnel ledge, grabbing her rope, hauling it up hand over hand—or unfastening it, and letting her plummet. She swallowed a surge of panicked bile and looked down. There was still so far to go, longer if she did it safely enough to guard against company. And the climb back up would take—

No, she couldn't spook herself like this. The chances of the other climber still being alive were slim to none.

*If there even* is *another climber*, she reminded herself.

No, the thing to think about was how, if Em was still gone

110

by the time she reached the base of this wall, she'd have time. Time to set up her trap, time to ensure she could get out safely. Cache thief or no.

Camp Five's marker burned steadily at the bottom of her screen. *Oh*, she thought. *Em didn't toggle it off before she left.*

That said something—that she was *surprised* that Em hadn't screwed her over in her anger. That it seemed reasonable that she would have turned off the marker to strand her where she wanted her. Gyre laughed, helplessly, at how quickly things had gone from almost okay to nightmarish.

If Em had ever wanted Gyre to trust her, she'd given up on the ledge. That cold look of hers when Gyre had told her to screw herself over administering the sedative—Gyre knew that look on a deep, intimate level. That was the look of somebody resigned to being the monster they knew they were. The self-awareness was no comfort, didn't imply that Em wanted to or could be brought back to reality.

All it meant was that she needed to get the recording going. If Em had given up on being trusted outside the bounds of a formal contract amendment, there was no telling how much further she'd go.

She clipped into another bolt. The process was automatic now, the route easy enough, just long. Too much time for her mind to wander, to go all analytical on herself. She'd turned to caving as a way to escape all this thinking. And now this cave was forcing her to live inside her own head, and for the first time she could remember, she hated not being able to see the sky.

She kept climbing, and Em's line remained closed. The ground grew closer, and her rope was long enough. After what felt like days, but her HUD said had only been four and a half hours, she reached the end. Gyre let out a sigh of relief as she settled her weight onto her feet again. Solid ground after half a day's descent felt like some kind of magic, and once her rope was secured and she had cut herself free of it, conserving the last length, she knelt and set up her feeding.

After that, she had real work to do.

# CHAPTER TEN

The ration canister was spent and the recording was running.

Gyre paced, glancing at the comm line. Em was still gone, and the longer she was gone, the less Gyre could sit still. When Em returned, there was a strong chance she'd see the recording running. Gyre hadn't found a way to hide it. And what then? Would she voluntarily scuttle the expedition? Would she reveal that the original recording had been a ploy? Or maybe, maybe, she'd miss it, overlook it in the sea of information streaming from Gyre's suit to her computers.

Camp Five wasn't far off. Gyre could feel its presence like a rope tied around her ankle, tugging her farther into the cave. And like a noose tied around her neck.

She could still feel the phantom sensation of impossible eyes bearing down on her from before.

She managed to wait for the better part of an hour, pacing in tighter and tighter circles, her battery charge dwindling, until at last she came to the conclusion that it was pointless to sit and wait. Better to know if the supplies were there, better to know if she needed to turn back now to get to Three on her backup battery, better to know if she was going to have the time to pull what she needed out of Em.

Gyre turned her attention to the marker to Camp Five, calling up the three-dimensional map Em had shown her before.

There were no hard climbs in between her and it, no meandering paths that meant the straight shot to the marker wasn't so straight after all. The camp itself was situated at the rim of another steep drop-off, and if she was understanding the key correctly, the drop-off was filled with water, another sump like the one she'd passed through two days ago.

Or was it three? Planetary time was losing meaning down here. Whether the sun had risen and set two or three times made no difference to the rhythm of the climb. She'd slept twice since the sump, and that was all she knew, and all that mattered.

At any rate, she didn't have to swim it today—hopefully never would. The time she spent hauling gear should be all she needed before she could turn back. Committed, she began picking her way through the cavern. She wriggled her toes in her boots, the film encasing her flesh shifting with her, slimy and unavoidable. Her throat tightened but she kept moving, willing her body to acclimate again, forget the weight of her suit, the unnatural hole in her abdomen.

The sensation faded. So far, a walk was all she needed to banish that awareness.

*And if Em asks, that's exactly what I'm doing.*

The cavern and tunnels she passed through were much the same as the ones above the first sump. The stones weren't worn smooth by water, and she supposed that even though the first sump was much closer to the surface than these, and even though the water levels rose in both at the same time, the upper sump got its water through a slightly different mechanism, which meant that the area between the two didn't flood. Otherwise, she'd be underwater now, she supposed. What would it be like to explore an entirely underwater cave system? To know that if one single thing went wrong with her suit, she could drown?

Just thinking about it made the suit feel even more restrictive, and she had to stop and remind herself that wasn't the case.

She'd gotten lucky, in a sense. With all the lies she'd told to get here, she could have been handed something she *couldn't* handle—climbs that were beyond her ability, teams that expected her to be half scientist, half explorer, an entirely submerged expedition. Instead, all she had to deal with was her now-absent, lying handler and an impossible death curse.

She shook her head to clear her thoughts and turned sideways to navigate along a ledge that was less than a meter wide. Strictly speaking, she should have clipped in, but she didn't want to use up the last of her rope. The fall off the side wasn't too bad, an uneven rocky slope but one that ended only a meter or so below her. She'd just be careful.

As she reached the midway point, she glanced behind her. Something moved.

Her heart rate quickened as she clawed her hands into the stone behind her, the rock face crumbling slightly at the pressure. Holding her breath, she stared out into the distance.

Nothing.

Nobody had followed her down the cliff face. She groaned. She *had* to get herself together; there were no other cavers here, and nothing but bugs, fungus, and Tunnelers could live this far below the surface. Of those, she only had to fear the Tunnelers, and she'd have heard it if one was close. She was safe. If she kept jumping at shadows, she was going to screw up.

*And I'm* not *going to screw up.*

*Just a little farther . . .*

She hugged the wall as she traversed, then took a moment when she reached the other side to stretch, placing her hands at the small of her back just below her equipment hump. She looked around the passageway, which widened out like a horizontal funnel in front of her. Camp Five was at the end of this space, not far away at all. She couldn't see the sump from here, but she could see protrusions along the floor, growing denser the closer to camp they came.

Crouching, she toggled through the views her HUD gave her. The reconstruction just showed strange, lumpen shapes, but as she switched to her headlamp, she could see that they were glowing faintly, the same bioluminescence of the fungus up near Camp Two. These growths had no delicate flowers, though. They were uneven bulges along the ground, reminiscent of fleshy tumors, and she grimaced as she began picking her way between them. She vastly preferred the caves she'd explored when she was younger. They weren't as deep or as wet, and so they were just—empty.

Bone-dry and dead.

As she approached the Camp Five marker, she could see the drop-off, but it was difficult to pay attention to. The fungal growths were getting bigger and closer together now, and she struggled to find safe areas to step. By the time she could see her first glimpses of water down below, she had given up on avoiding them, and instead began taking the most direct route to the lip of the almost circular hole. A fleshy bulb squelched beneath her boot, and then deflated in a sudden burst, biolu-minescent dust—no, spores—erupting from it and coating the ankle of her other leg with a fine, glowing mist.

*Hope my air filters can handle that*, she thought. Reflex-ively, she glanced over her shoulder up the wide, gently sloping field, back to the narrow ledge she'd come from.

In the low light, she could barely see anything. She toggled back to her full reconstruction view, half expecting to see a figure at the end of the tunnel.

There was nobody there.

*What the hell is wrong with me?*

She smothered a helpless, relieved, embarrassed laugh. Her, jumping at shadows. Afraid of monsters in the dark, just because the monster in her ear was away from her desk. Turn-ing back, she squared her shoulders and crossed the rest of the ground to the rim of the cenote as quickly and authoritatively as she could. The reconstruction barely showed the spores, but Gyre could see the readouts in the corner of her screen going wild with new feedback as the powder coated the lower half of her suit and floated on the air up around her head. No alerts flashed up in front of her, but she couldn't resist the urge to hold her breath, only sucking in a deep gasp of air when her chest began to burn.

*These are probably always here*, she reassured herself. *Em knows about them. It's safe. It's safe. It's . . .*

*Where the fuck is Em?*

She reached the rim, then scanned along its circumference for the cache, a box of rafts Em had said would be there. She found it bolted to a nearby shelf of stone, under a hollowed-out feature, not tall enough to stand up in and barely tall enough to crouch below. She reached in and tried to drag it out, but it refused to move. She searched out the release button and pressed it. A compartment opened, revealing a line of tight, compressed packages, and nothing else.

Hm.

She took one package out and closed the box, then stood up and checked the label, embossed into the plastic housing so that it would show up on her feed. It was indeed a raft, and she walked back to the rim of the sump with it, wading through more ankle-high fungal growths. The spores hadn't let up, despite the path she'd trampled. She ignored them. Coming to the edge, she peered over it. The level of the water was only four meters or so below her, and there, about halfway around the wall, was an anchor attached to two sturdy lines. The rest of the cache? Submerged—why? She glanced at the mushrooms again, wary. Batteries and canisters went directly into her suit. Maybe there was a contamination risk.

The thought made her shiver. She hadn't wanted to go down into the sump, but the longer she stood up here, exposed to both the spores and . . . whatever else there might be, the better the water sounded.

There were a few bolts in the stone leading down, but she'd have to put in new line, and check the safety of each anchor. She only had a limited amount of rope left, though she guessed more was stashed in the cases in the sump. It was the safest option, to take the old route down, but the thought didn't appeal to her, not least because for the first time in her life she was sick to death of climbing. Gyre considered the situation for a moment longer, then looked at the water. It was a clear fall, and her reconstruction was showing the pool extending much farther below her, based on previous scans of the area.

She opened the raft packet and thumbed the button at its top, then waited as it inflated. As soon as it was sturdy and sealed, she tossed it over the lip of the cenote, backed up a few steps, then took a running start and leaped into the air. For a few breathless moments she was weightless, and she tucked her limbs in against her chest, fighting off the panic that flared inside her. Then she hit the water, sending a huge plume upward, and sank down as her suit switched effortlessly over to diving mode. The sudden change in state left her almost euphoric, and she broke the surface half smiling, swimming over to the raft. A few minutes' work was all it took to secure it to the wall with a short line, to account for some rise and fall of the water level, and then she clambered onto it and began hauling up the boxes.

They broke the surface, and she held her breath as she checked them over. Still sealed. A few quick movements and she had one of them open, and she sagged with relief as she saw fresh nutrition canisters and batteries, the latter wreathed in a soft glow. The second had line and bolts. She quickly began reloading her stashes, exchanging the scrap of line left over from the Long Drop for fresh spools, wishing her hands would stop shaking.

She was safe.

*Safe.*

The thought reverberated through her, the first time she'd felt anything better than uneasy and exhausted in days.

This wasn't the best place to haul gear to and from, and she wasn't sure she was prepared to make that ascent two, three, maybe even four times, but that argument could wait until Em came back.

What mattered was that the cache was here; nobody had snuck in and taken it. The cache was here, and she would have enough time to record Em's lies. The cache was here, and she could . . . rest, bobbing gently on the surface of this small, sunken lake. She looked out at the water, its surface smoothing out now that she wasn't disrupting it.

As she glanced over the readouts on her screen, now settling in the absence of the spores, her gaze dropped to where the videos were stored. Was there any point to watching the other ones? Maybe the last—that way she could see what was coming, just in case she had to go all the way to the final camp. Or was there a video of the sump attempts? She scanned through the list, right hand fiddling in the air as if it were controlling the motion. Finally, she opened the last video, dated several months after the others.

It was time to see how the cave had killed its explorers before Em had decided to help.

# CHAPTER ELEVEN

Em's mother looked directly at the camera, but she was unfocused, listless. Her hair was long and unkempt, hanging in lank tendrils around a thin, worn face. The circles under her eyes were dark and swollen and her lips were cracked. There was no trace of the exuberance Gyre had seen in her in the first video.

"Isolde Arasgain, age twenty-six by Earth reckoning," said a woman's voice from off camera. "Formal debrief after Oxsua Mining expedition seventeen, second attempt on location at 40.3719, -82.3983, outside of Hebron Township on colony Cassandra Five. Local date June thirty-third, galactic year twenty-two thirty-two."

A shadow shifted on the table in front of Isolde as the interviewer moved away from the camera. She didn't come into shot.

"Expedition seventeen consisted of five adults: Halian

Foster, Laurent Okeke, Yao Hanmei, Julian Flores, and Isolde Arasgain. Ms. Arasgain is the only member of the expedition to return as of this date. The other four members are reported dead."

Isolde's brow furrowed in pain, but then slackened into exhaustion.

"Ms. Arasgain, please state for the record your relationship with Laurent Okeke."

"Married. Father of my child," she responded, her voice clipped.

"How old is your child?"

"She's six."

"That's a fun age," the interviewer said.

Isolde's expression didn't change.

The interviewer waited a moment longer, then cleared her throat and said, "Please state for the record how long it has been since you emerged from the site outside of Hebron."

"A month, give or take," Isolde muttered.

"Please speak up and give as exact a number as you can."

"Thirty-two days," Isolde said, her gaze flicking to what Gyre thought was the interviewer. "Give or take."

"Thank you. Ms. Arasgain, please describe in your own words why this debriefing has been put off for this long."

"I've been in treatment for severe dehydration and shock, as well as five broken bones," she said, then gestured to her left arm. It was in a sling, Gyre realized. She said nothing for a moment, then sighed and looked away. "As well as psychiatric review for—post-traumatic stress disorder."

"Caused by?"

"Do I really have to spell it out?"

"For the record, Ms. Arasgain."

Isolde scowled and then shoved her hair out of her face with one shaking hand. "Caused by the deaths of my team. Including Laurent."

"Please describe for the record what led to the deaths of Mr. Foster, Mr. Okeke, Ms. Yao, and Mr.—"

"I don't want to talk about this."

"Ms. Arasgain, we went through this—"

"Turn off the damn recorder," Isolde snapped.

The image lingered for a moment. Then it cut to Isolde in different clothing, her hair scraped back into a bun, sitting in the same room.

"Resuming debriefing," the interviewer said. "Ms. Arasgain, please describe for the record what happened leading up to your evacuation from expedition seventeen."

Isolde didn't look much happier this time around, but she looked more in control of herself. Her gaze was focused. "Our team encountered a large sump, the second we had needed to traverse since we'd begun exploring the site. Underground scans had indicated pockets of water, so we had brought in diving equipment, but the second sump appeared to be much larger than the first, which had been more or less a straight shot through a tube. We contacted mission control and they requested that we go ahead and begin mapping the new sump, to see if there was an accessible way through.

"The sump was larger, but relatively easy to navigate. Not as simple as the first sump, but nothing—concerning. Wide passages, no currents. It took us seven days to find a passage through to a chamber not reachable on foot, mapping as we went and taking precautions to avoid equipment damage. We also found several exits onto pools that were within walking distance of our camp. On the tenth day, we began ferrying the team and our waterproof equipment through the sump to the new chamber. Lau—Mr. Okeke's rebreather began to malfunction, but we were carrying $O_2$ tanks. We got him through the sump."

Isolde stared directly at the camera as she spoke, her hands clasped tightly in front of her. She had her arms drawn in tight against her sides, protectively, and her voice was almost robotic. "We decided to stop and repair Mr. Okeke's rebreather at that point."

"Were you carrying any extras?"

"Yes, two."

"Who made the decision to fix the malfunctioning equipment?"

Isolde's gaze darted to the interviewer. "We all did," she said, frowning. "It looked like it could be fixed. No reason to take one of our emergency replacements out of commission when we didn't know what else was ahead."

"Ms. Arasgain, I'm not questioning your judgment," the interviewer said, her voice softening.

"Like hell you're not. I know Oxsua thinks that if it can prove it was—was—*human error*," she snarled, "then they can get out of making this right, but—"

"Isolde," the interviewer said firmly. "That's not going to happen. I've told you, the families of your team will be compensated—"

"What about the bodies?"

"By your own account, we can't get them back."

Isolde said nothing for a long moment, then in a sudden explosion of movement, she unclasped her hands and slammed her fists into the table. Then she shoved her hands into her hair, clawing at her scalp, and took several deep breaths.

The interviewer didn't turn off the camera.

"So you stayed to fix the rebreather," the interviewer said after nearly a minute had passed.

"Yes," Isolde replied, her shoulders sagging. "Hanmei was familiar with the—the equipment. She'd done the most cave diving out of any of us. Her last job had been on Tullius Twelve, on another Oxsua job."

"Was this your first Oxsua job?"

"No. My third."

"Had your previous jobs been on Cassandra Five?"

"The one before had, but it hadn't gone very deep—we didn't find an entrance into the lower caverns. The first one was back home, on Yulo Prime."

The diversion made Isolde relax somewhat, and she sat back in her chair, looking up at the ceiling.

"Was Ms. Yao able to fix the rebreather?"

"Yes, though she insisted on using it herself instead of letting Laurent use it again." She'd abandoned any pretense of formality, her eyes going distant, her mouth tightening. "Said that if it went bad, she'd take responsibility." Her voice hitched on the last word.

"How long were you in camp on the other side of the sump?"

"Three days, maybe four, while she worked on it," Isolde said.

"What did you do next?"

"We decided to explore further. We had about half of our gear through the sump, but we didn't want to spend time ferrying the rest until we were sure we wanted to keep going."

"Your map showed three exits from the chamber reachable without going through other sumps. Is that right?"

"I . . . Yes, that's right. We started with the north one."

"At what point did the tremors begin?"

"Weeks before that," Isolde said. "Though they weren't as bad."

"And after the sump?"

Isolde shook her head, tapping her fingers on the table. Her sling was gone now, Gyre noted. How far apart had these been filmed?

"I . . . I don't remember. Maybe four days after we got through the sump. Sometime around when we started exploring."

"Please describe them."

"Like an earthquake, I guess. Or the vibrations of loud machinery. It was . . . It was really low, infrasonic maybe. Made your heart—wiggle. Shiver, I guess." She hunched up in her seat again, pulling one leg up onto the chair. She was wearing loose, nondescript clothing. Hospital issue? "Like strong bass. Up earlier in the cave we'd been able to hear it, like a rumbling sound, but down there we felt it."

"And did you see anything?"

"Not at first."

"How often did you hear—or feel—the noise?"

"A lot. I don't remember."

"Was it constant?"

"By the time the tunnels came down, yeah. It was."

"You're jumping ahead," the interviewer said.

Isolde swore softly but didn't do anything more than wrap her arms around herself and look away. Gyre watched as minutes ticked by in silence, the interviewer not pressing this time. At last, Isolde shrugged and said, "I guess we'd feel it . . . maybe once every few hours at first. But by the end of that week, when we'd turned back from the last tunnel—the one to the northeast, that led up and around; it dead-ended in a drop-off and breakdown pile, leading to a sump pit that we were planning to explore the next day—when we started coming back, Ha—Mr. Foster, Ms. Yao, and me—by then it was getting close to constant."

"Did it get louder?"

"Are you asking if that *thing* got closer to us? Yes. It did. Obviously, it did."

"But did the noise get louder?"

"Yeah, I guess so. It got stronger. The night before, I woke up with my chest seizing up. Halian had a coughing fit. Sorry. Mr. Foster."

"Refer to them however you're comfortable with."

"Right."

"What happened on the day of the event?"

"The *event*," she said bitterly.

The interviewer once again said nothing.

Finally, Isolde said, "We were climbing back down toward the camp. There was a tight passage. I'd gone through, and so had Hanmei, and we'd been hearing—feeling—the tremors all day. Halian was halfway through when the rock just—"

She shook her head, biting at her lip and staring off into the distance.

"Halian's spine was broken instantly. We couldn't see his—his—anything but his legs. I don't—he died. The gap collapsed with him in it, the rock flowed down like it was water. One minute we could see him and the next there was smooth rock where the tunnel had been, and his legs were on the ground."

"Let's take a break," the interviewer said.

"No, let's *not* take a break," Isolde said, her expression darkening. She glared at the interviewer. "You *knew*, didn't you?"

"I don't know what you're referring to, Ms. Arasgain."

"You knew something was down there. That's why all

of us were from off-planet. The locals already knew, didn't they?"

"Let me send for a nurse, Mrs. Arasgain. You're clearly distressed."

"What, don't want it on the record? Well, that's too fucking ba—"

The screen went blank.

$$\vee$$

The visual feed clicked on again. Isolde was standing, her back to the camera, her shoulders hunched forward.

"Are you ready to continue?" the interviewer said.

"Might as well get it over with. Where did we leave off?"

"Mr. Foster," the interviewer provided.

Isolde nodded slowly, then turned around and went back to her seat. This section looked like it was the same day as the previous one, though Isolde's eyes were red-rimmed, and her lower lip was swollen from being chewed on. "So . . . yeah. He—we saw him die. Hanmei and I booked it back to the others. I don't—do you need to know what we talked about?"

"Just what you decided to do is fine."

"We decided to get the hell out of there," Isolde said. Her voice was raspy, her throat shot from crying or screaming or both. "Left the gear, suited up to dive. Everybody could feel the tremors by that point, and we could all see the sump was doing—*something*, but we had to get out. I guess we panicked. I mean, up until then, some of us still thought the collapses and tunnels other teams were finding were boreholes from drills that got there before us, or—or—lava tubes, even though it didn't make sense. But down there, we knew it couldn't be either of those things. Hanmei and I saw it happen, and we *knew* that it was something else, and it hadn't gone away. So it was maybe five hours after Halian had—that we tried the sump. Hanmei had been up late the night before, and the climb back had been rough. We should've waited. We should have . . ."

As she trailed off, she ran her hands along the edge of the table. Her cuticles were ragged, bleeding in places. "So we went into the sump," she said. "There'd been a collapse, or a—a shift, and there were currents that hadn't been there before, *strong* currents. We almost lost Laurent again; it was like a riptide. Only thing that saved him was that it sucked him to a crevice that narrowed too fast for him to get lodged in. I got him out. But my back was to the others, and there was silt everywhere—we'd lost half our lines, and it was all we could do to get ourselves back to the surface, back where we'd come from."

"You mean the camp with the three tunnels out."

"Yeah."

"How long did the attempt on the sump take?"

"I don't . . . An hour? Maybe half that. Or twice that. I don't know. Laurent and I got out around the same time. Julian was already there; he'd broken—I don't know, three ribs in the current. His shoulder, too."

"And at what point did you realize Ms. Yao wasn't there?"

"Immediately. First fucking thing."

"Did you attempt to find her?"

Rage passed over Isolde's face, followed by pain. She whispered, "No."

"Did any other member of the team attempt—"

"No. Laurent was freaking out, and Julian couldn't swim anymore. We just—we decided she'd made it to the other side. We had to believe she'd made it to the other side, or that she was still down there trying, that she'd be okay."

"What did the team do instead?"

"Lost our shit," Isolde said, her elbows on the table, her hands fisted in her hair. "Yelled at each other. Julian thought he was going to die, that we wouldn't be able to carry him out with his injuries. Laurent was spooked. He'd almost died twice in that sump."

"And you?"

"I just sat there mostly. How do you . . . What do you say? When you've lost two people in one day? When you don't know if you'll make it out, but you have your six-year-old daughter waiting for you to come home? Nothing would have helped."

"When did you make your next attempt on the sump?"

"Maybe a day later," she said. "Julian wasn't doing so well, and he was just babbling day and night about how we were going to die, about how Laurent should've kept his rebreather because Hanmei was the best swimmer out of all of us, and how we needed her."

"Mr. Flores didn't believe Ms. Yao had made it to the other side?"

"He thought she would've sent us a message. But our receivers were all screwed up, probably from the collapses and everything. We hadn't heard from anybody since the first cave-in."

"So Julian was upset."

"Upset? Of course he was upset. I mean, wouldn't you be? And he was in so much pain, but Laurent wouldn't let him take any of the stronger drugs because if he passed out and there was another collapse—anyway, I needed to get away from it. I offered to try the sump on my own. Laurent insisted he go too, said it wasn't safe otherwise. I thought maybe the silt would've settled, and the currents maybe would have sorted themselves out, but he wouldn't listen to me."

"Did he go with you?"

"No. We had an argument at the edge of the sump about it. I told him that one of us had to make it out, for Emogene. I finally promised that I'd just go and attach new line, and I'd come back after the first spool. It was going to take at least six. That way, I'd definitely come back, and we'd have a better sense of what was happening."

"Why didn't the team approach it this way on the first attempt?"

"We didn't know the lines had broken. We were racing to get out. When we realized what had happened, I put some line in, and Hanmei did too, and we tried two different paths, but everything was so chaotic. I don't know. Hanmei went first, Julian following her. Laurent was with me; that's why I went after him when he got swept away. Julian said that Hanmei signaled for him to go back when he was injured—a current smacked him into a jagged outcropping that hadn't been there before, ripped his suit open too—"

"I understand. What happened on your second attempt?"

"I went in by myself, and I put in anchors, all hard anchors, twice as often as I needed to, took out the old ones to make sure I didn't get confused. I was down there for maybe—maybe four hours that day."

"On one spool?"

"No, I started on the second. Checked in with Julian and Laurent. I didn't—I didn't see any sign of Hanmei at that point, didn't see much of anything. Then, on my second line, I hit an unexpected current and lost my grip. It took me maybe an hour to find my way back to the line. I thought—I thought I was going to die. I was blind, and everything was dark and loud, and I could hear those tremors still; they were beating on my eardrums."

"But you found the line."

"Yeah. Somehow, I found the line."

"That's very lucky."

Isolde shook her head. "I got back out, and Laurent wasn't there. I went back to camp. He was kneeling over Julian's body."

"Was Mr. Flores dead at that point?"

"Yeah. He was. He'd overdosed on the pain medication we had with us."

"Do you believe it was deliberate?"

"He took all of it. Yeah, I think it was deliberate."

"Do you have any reason to think that Mr. Okeke . . . helped? Or caused it?"

"*No,*" Isolde snapped, "and I don't think that matters, even if he did. Julian—he'd done it while Laurent was waiting for me to surface again, while I was lost. Laurent thought he'd lost both of us. When I found him, he was screaming."

"I . . . understand. Isolde—"

"We were still feeling the tremors," she said, ignoring the interviewer's attempts at comfort. "We both knew we had to get out soon. We were afraid the rest of the cavern would collapse. So I left Laurent and I kept laying line. When I got to the last spool, I told him to pack up and follow me out. I got—I got to the end, somehow. I almost lost the line another four times, and I couldn't find an exit at first—I panicked—but I got out. I hauled myself out at one of the other openings we'd found way back at the beginning. I barely recognized that section, but I knew it reconnected with the path we'd taken down and . . ."

"And did you find Ms. Yao?"

"No. I never saw her body."

"Did Mr. Okeke join you?"

"No," she said.

"Did you go back for him?"

"I waited. I waited for two days. But on the first day, the

tremors got loud again. When they got quieter, I tried going back. The currents were different. The lines—the lines had gone."

"And at that point what did you do?"

"I told you, I waited. I waited until I started worrying that I'd run out of food on the return climb. So I left the heavier gear there, and I loaded up with food, and I . . . I left."

"When did you reestablish contact with the Oxsua surface team?"

"Two days later, past the other sump—that one hadn't changed. I was climbing up the—the long fall, the one that's almost a kilometer straight down. I told them what happened. A team met me halfway to the surface a few days after that."

"Did anything else of note occur during that period?"

"I broke my collarbone, my arm, on a fall. A couple ribs, too. Kept—kept hearing the tremors. But nobody else died. I didn't die."

"Did you ever see what caused the tremors?"

"No."

"Had any other part of the cave system changed?"

"I don't know. Surface crew told me that they were getting different readings, so I guess something did. Are we done here?"

"I . . . Yes, I think we have everything we need. Thank you, Ms. Arasgain. Your compensation should be available by the end of the week. Oxsua Mining does apologize for the unforeseen risks of your expedition."

Isolde looked up at the interviewer, then at the camera. She managed a thin, brittle mockery of a smile before the recording ended.

# CHAPTER TWELVE

Gyre shut down the video, numb, her breathing loud in the confines of her suit.

She'd heard of people dying in collapses caused by near misses with Tunnelers, or getting swallowed in a direct pass, but to think of Halian, crushed, cut in half because of that thing . . .

In the Tunneler path she'd walked through, some of the stone had been removed, but some of it had been compressed, smoothed out, shoved into a smaller space than it should have been. If a Tunneler had passed by and there had been a gap for the stone to go into—

She couldn't think about it. This was no established mine, where controlled cave-ins sealed off the main chambers and somehow created a buffer wide enough to keep Tunnelers from sensing human activity. But compared to Isolde's team, she was as safe as if she were back on the surface. For all Em's faults, she'd taken every precaution. Gyre's suit vented no heat save for the little generated by her headlamp. Her nutritional canisters gave off no scent.

She was safe.

Her hand hung in the air as she tried to bring herself to close the video, the list of all the rest. But she craved them too. If she went back to the earlier videos, she could see them laughing, see them smiling. Shake the emptiness inside her.

But then she thought of the look on Isolde's face as she'd gone over exactly how every member of that team had died, including her husband—how dead she'd looked as she talked about her child—

She couldn't watch another one of those. Em had watched all of them, over and over again. She was sure of it. They were all Em had left.

They're why twenty-seven cavers had died.

Gyre stood up to stretch, the raft rocking beneath her, supply box at her side nudging against her shin. Still no sign of Em. Whatever she was looking into had taken her well over six hours now. *She's probably asleep*, Gyre thought, then looked around the cenote. She needed a task, something to occupy her and shake off her nerves. Pursing her lips, she knelt down on the edge of the raft and placed her hand just above the water. "Sample, liquid," she murmured, and watched the tube emerge from above her ring finger, watched the bead of liquid it retrieved pass up into her suit.

WATER. POTABLE. NEUTRAL ACIDITY. CANDIDATE FOR
REPLACEMENT OF RECIRCULATION.

"Yeah, let's do that," she said, then fumbled for another minute to find the option to start the process. It required her to stick her arm down into the pool, and so she flattened out on her stomach, both arms hanging over the side. Chin propped on the edge of the raft, she peered down into the depths, thinking about the coming dive. Both Em and Isolde had said this one was simple, straightforward. Just long. She'd managed the first sump easily enough, but that was *before*. Before she knew Hanmei had drowned in a sump, and so had several of Em's cavers, and the thought of diving again made her skin crawl.

She glanced up at the rim of the pool. Chances were good that Em would be back, but she had to consider the possibility that she'd be on her own for the foreseeable future. Something might have happened to Em, or maybe she'd just given up and fled, now that her cave was compromised, now that one of her precious human sacrifices knew the truth of what was going on here. Now that Gyre knew she was being led by a woman who'd never been down here herself, who was chasing ghosts just like she was chasing her own mother. Em had at least been right about that part. They were the same.

If she didn't hear from Em soon, she decided, she'd rest and then stage her return climb to the surface. Maybe it was better that way—if she could prove that Em had abandoned the expedition, couldn't she countersue? There must be some avenue there, some option. Evidence of what Em had done was optimal, but stubbornness could only take her so far.

And she didn't want to stay down here a second longer than she had to if it turned out she *wasn't* the only person in this cave.

Lying prone, unable to see anything but the water below her, Gyre grew uneasy. She could feel eyes burning into her back, and she couldn't force the fear away entirely this time. Fear twisted in her belly, helped along by Isolde's stricken description of the Tunneler, of what it could do, and of the helplessness she'd felt down here.

Gyre had thought she never felt helpless below the surface, but now she could see that it was an act. Bravado. Necessary, too, because now that it was wavering, she couldn't think straight. Her neck prickled again, and this time she jerked her head up as much as she could, trying to see above the lip of the hole.

*Something's there.*

She stared for ten seconds, thirty—but, as ever, there was nothing. Her back screamed at her unnatural posture, and she grudgingly lowered down to the raft, arms still stuck below the surface as her old waste water was removed from the suit and fresh new water was brought in. She could barely feel it, a coolness spreading across the film that covered her skin. But when she took a sip of water, it was cold and clear and tasted like minerals. She took another sip, then another, then froze.

This time she could *hear* something from above the rim.

It was faint, a bare whisper, a distant popping that sounded like the fungal growths releasing more spores into the air. She looked up, squinting. Was the luminescent rain of powder growing thicker? She couldn't tell for sure with the reconstruction on, and she craned her neck, fighting through the pain, searching from the far rim of the pool to just above her.

Isolde stared back down at her.

The shock of seeing another person, another face, stabbed through her. It was so much more real, so much closer than a face in a video. She scrambled to stop the exchange of water, the interface forcing her to look away for just a second. She was on her feet in another gasping, desperate breath, the raft rocking dangerously beneath her. The open battery cache almost slid into the water. She looked back up, rushing to the stone wall, ready to climb.

There was no one there.

Gyre stood, shaking, fingers clawing into the rock. Had it just been an afterimage from the videos? It would only take a few minutes to climb back up and search the cavern if she did it without anchors, but the longer she stood there, the raft bobbing and pitching beneath her feet from the waves she'd created, the more her shock turned to fear. Nobody was down here. Nobody *could* be down here. Em had been certain.

But there was the missing cache, still unaccounted for.

*Something took it.* Someone *took it.*

She made herself crouch and fumble the battery box closed, before pushing it off into the water, where it would be safe. Her eyes never left the rim, scanning for any hint of life.

It couldn't be Isolde. Isolde was dead. Em had said that both her parents were dead. Gyre, her eyes still riveted on the spot along the rim where she'd seen the impossible face, searched for any kind of dossier on Isolde Arasgain. "Come on, Em. Come on." There, a small obituary. Scanning the article, Gyre read that Isolde Arasgain was last seen nine years ago near the entry point for this cave. No sign of her, body or otherwise, had ever been seen again.

*She didn't die.*

*She's down here.*

But she had to be dead by now. She *had* to be. Nobody could survive down here for almost a decade, not through the season changes that made parts of this cave impassable, not without a suit that could use the food in the caches, not while Em was sending down caver after caver searching.

Searching for . . .

"Oh no, Em," she said, her throat tight. "Don't tell me I'm

here to find her. Don't tell me you're hoping it was her who took the cache."

Even as she said it, though, Gyre knew she would've hoped for the same thing. It was impossible, but what else could Em cling to? Sure, Gyre believed that Em wanted to say goodbye to her dad, too, but that couldn't justify so many deaths, not even for Em. But if Isolde had simply left Em nine years ago, and walked back into this cave . . .

She watched the rim for another minute, her heart pounding, but Isolde's face didn't appear again. Swallowing thickly, Gyre keyed her external speaker. "Isolde? Anybody?"

Her voice echoed across the chamber. Her vision blurred from staring too hard without blinking. She closed her eyes, then cracked them open again immediately.

Nothing.

Hands shaking, she turned off the reconstruction. Maybe—maybe Em was back at her computer. Maybe Em had hidden the face. But in the darkness, the room lit only by the glow of mushrooms up around the rim, a faint, rocking layer of spores on the surface of the water, and her small headlamp, she was still alone. Her light barely reached the rim, but there were no faces, no hulking, lurking shadows. She turned her reconstruction back on. The brightly lit, desaturated shapes were familiar and welcome.

She could see five easy spots to place anchors. She could still climb up, see for herself that there was nobody else there. Or she could trust it, sleep here, wait for Em. But what if she was wrong—or right? That it wasn't Isolde, but that some*thing* was down here, with her, waiting?

She needed to dive. It would be safer below the water. She pulled up her map; Camp Six was just through the large tunnel below the surface. The sump was longer than the first one had been, like Em had said it would be, and more convoluted than the simple U-bend she'd already faced, but there were no true branch points, and no tight squeezes. Em wouldn't have let her swim it on her own, or press on without a rest, but Gyre couldn't sit here without looking back at the lip of the cliff every twenty seconds. She sure as hell wasn't going to be able to sleep.

She needed to move. She always went forward. She'd get through this sump, and then she'd be safe from—whatever it was. Isolde, an afterimage, or something else. Then she could regroup.

It would take her one step closer to the final test of the cave, but she had to risk it.

She checked her line and underwater anchor reserves, then plunged into the sump without giving herself time to argue.

$$\vee\!\!\vee$$

Gyre swam. She swam for hours, at times clinging to her brightly lit reconstruction and at times turning it off in a panic, afraid that she was looking at a lie. They always matched, though, and she always retreated back to the reconstruction. She methodically drove her anchors, laid her line, and checked her readouts, afraid of seeing movement in the water behind her. But as time passed, and everything remained the same, she began wondering if she'd seen anything at all.

Except she'd heard the fungus bursting; she'd seen the spores thicken. Surely something had caused that. Which meant something had moved up there—or she was going mad.

*Which is worse?*

She swam through the tunnel, its widenings and narrowings, maneuvering around jutting rock and old stalactites that were slowly eroding as time crept on. There were small living things in the water, little fish and crawling arthropods, and they all scattered as she came close. These were the things that fed the fungus up by Camp Five, and they in turn fed on things so small she couldn't see them.

The sump had one bell in it, a pocket where there was air, and she marked it on her line, just in case. A plastic arrow that gleamed red on her reconstruction, pointing up. Then she moved on, the path turning slowly upward.

Finally, she broke the surface of the water. She anchored her line and cut herself free, then hauled herself onto the stone bank. There was no hard climb here, just a wide shoreline. The chamber she'd emerged into was full of rocky outgrowths, from both the sloping ceiling and the ground, forming an overlapping toothed maw, a complex pattern flattened into chaos by her colorless reconstruction. It made her uneasy, but she pushed through the feeling, changing her visual filters to restore some shadow, some sense of depth.

She paced around one of the nearby stalagmites, which had a base over a meter across. Another set of filaments grew here, a lichen instead of the fleshy masses behind her, no doubt nourished by the dripping water and the yearly flooding she expected came from the sump.

Her readout indicated that the lichen was emitting trace amounts of light, so she powered down her simulator. The light was faint, but there. It was different from the white fungus flowers of the upper chambers and the globular masses by Camp Five, casting a more ghostly blue glow from where it extended fanlike protrusions.

The lichen was beautiful, but she found she didn't care at all. The wonder from the first encounter with the flowers was gone, replaced with leaden dread.

She checked her line to Em. Still closed. Just a little farther, then. Camp Six, and she'd be calm enough to settle down for the night.

Turning her head, she saw more of the glow farther down the chamber, growing incrementally brighter. She turned the simulation back on and made her way toward it, stretching her legs out as she went. She was tired, bone tired, and her head swam as she moved. The optical illusions and impossible geometry of the outcroppings danced and twined together in front of her, no matter how she fussed with her settings. She shook her head to try to untangle it all, then paused to change the simulation again, this time to show an approximation of the room as if she had her lamp on. It was harder to pull off, but a welcome alternative to actually turning her light on where somebody—anybody—might see it. In the more realistic colors and shadows, the space once more resolved into something comprehensible. The artificial light source in her reconstruction mixed with the overlay of the lichen's luminescence made everything appear delicate. The lichen covered every surface around her, shimmering, and grew stronger toward the left-hand side of the cavern. Her marker for Camp Six was almost obliterated by the pulsing glow.

She could hear the movement of water from ahead, and as she stepped around a column formed by two outcroppings meeting, she saw its source: a stream flowed down a nearby wall, and from there through a channel in the ground. The channel grew wider as it went. Gyre followed it, picking her way across it in places on islands of rock that hadn't been worn away yet, until she stood at the banks of a small underground lake, its surface still except for where the small, trickling flow met it. The banks were short cliffs of scalloped stone, striated with what appeared to be different colors or compositions. Out farther in the water, a few outcroppings of the same layered rock pushed up from the depths, delicate pillars that looked as if they could topple at any moment. And all along the uneven walls and vaulted ceiling, the blue lichen cast its light. The water was clear and calm, and beneath the surface lichen glowed, lighting up the lake. The whole space amplified it.

Gyre's shoulders sagged in a minor surrender. She powered down the reconstruction entirely and found she could still see. The space was beautiful, not unsettling like Camp Five or the maw behind her, and she laughed helplessly. She'd just been spooked. Spooked and tired, because she wasn't taking reasonable, human breaks. The glow of the lichen was enchanting, once she could see it divorced from the fungal tumors at Camp Five, and she felt her heart rate slow, her muscles relax. She let the beauty overwhelm the horror for a long while, then pulled back into herself and checked her map.

Camp Six was close by, but the way was blocked by a wall. She would have to go back and around. This lake appeared to connect to the sump, but Em had left a note.

ENTRANCE TO SUMP IMPASSABLE. STAGE FROM
SECONDARY ROOM.

Gyre's stomach curdled, and she turned away, trying to stave off the rising bile in her throat. This was it. This was the hell sump that had killed Hanmei. Had killed Laurent. Had they originally entered from this bank? Isolde had said that the old entrance had been closed off, that she'd needed to find another way out.

This whole cave was cursed. She couldn't ever let herself forget it, not for a second.

She retreated back to the room of the outcroppings, away from the glow, and switched to her reconstruction once more.

She found a narrow spot with few approaches to tuck herself into. She hunkered down there, drawing her knees to her chest.

*At least five bodies are in that sump.* Em's divers, Laurent, and Hanmei. Beyond that, several more of Em's sacrifices had turned back at their first encounter with it. Had any been able to establish a line that held, or did it keep moving? Did it shift every time? It had taken seven days for Isolde's team to map it—how long would *she* need to be down there? Gyre's mind raced through the possibilities, conjuring images of herself being wedged into tight crevices, unable to free herself, waiting until her battery ran out of power—or of the crevice closing on her in a snap, flowing around her as the Tunneler passed nearby.

All of that could have happened as she swam to Camp Six, she realized.

She shouldn't have moved forward on her own.

She swore and scanned through the other files Em had sent to her suit, desperate for a distraction for her fevered thoughts. She found music, and put it on random, sagging in relief as lazy singing filled her helmet. Off-world music, but unobjectionable. Simple. A sad love song. She'd take it.

Eventually, she stretched out onto her back, or as much onto her back as the suit allowed. She stared up at the stalactites above her and at the uneven ceiling. In places it was no higher than the ceiling of a room, but in others it shot up into uneven shafts that terminated several meters in the air. Gyre's fingers itched, as if she needed to be climbing again despite her exhaustion. It had taken Isolde two days after she'd struck out from the sump to get halfway up the long cliff. If she started now—

Em's line clicked open.

"I've found your mother."

# CHAPTER THIRTEEN

Gyre shot upright. "*Em?* What—where have you—"

"Your mother. She's alive, remarried with three children, on a garden world as you expected. She's still going by Peregrine, and there were no outstanding warrants for her arrest, so I believe you can put to rest the theory that she ran off-world with a cartel."

Gyre shut off the music and blinked rapidly, not entirely comprehending. Her thoughts whirled between Isolde in that interview room, the sump, and the idea that her mother—*her mother*—had been found, had been found *alive* and with a new family and—and she'd seen Isolde at Camp Five and *this* was what had isolated Gyre for the last nine hours?

And then she snuck a small glance at the indicator light at the bottom left of her screen. The recorder was still on.

"She's on an artificial garden world in the Viarsian system," Em continued as if nothing was wrong. She must not have noticed it yet. Gyre trembled with relief and hunkered down a little in her suit. "I'll get you a first-class ticket once you're above surface again," Em said. "As part of your compensation. I've prepared another contract amendment."

Guilt washed over her. Should she say something, admit to the recording? No—no sense in risking it.

She cleared her throat. "I—*Em*."

"As circumstances have changed drastically since your engagement, if you would like to turn back upon reaching the sump, you will receive both the ticket and prorated compensation."

"*Em*." No, she *had* to turn off the recording now, before Em saw, before Em realized Gyre had betrayed her. Em was offering up everything Gyre wanted on a golden platter.

Yet Gyre hesitated, thinking of Adrian Purcell, crushed and abandoned at Camp Two. Jennie Mercer lying broken and cold up at Camp Four. The faceless cavers who would follow after her.

No . . . not everything.

She stared at the indicator light.

"I know you watched the last video," Em said, still unaware, still totally consumed with her side of the conversation. For the first time, Gyre realized Em's voice was tight, her words clipped. Mechanical, like Isolde's had been in that video. "So you understand now. How dangerous this is. How . . . sick I am."

Gyre clenched her jaw and looked around the room. Em was right. She *was* sick. She'd left Gyre on her own, in the dark, suffering.

She'd led more down here to die before her.

But Gyre could understand now, her thoughts swinging wildly, pulled in a thousand directions at once.

*Mom. Alive.*

She swore, and looked back up at the ceiling, as if she could see Em that way. "Yeah, I understand."

"Will you be turning back? I assume so, even though you're already almost at Camp Six despite my instructions."

*Yes. No.* She clenched her fists and resisted the urge to look at the recording indicator again. "I need some time." She needed to think, and her mind wasn't cooperating with her just now. She babbled out, "And I wanted to see the sump. Might as well know what I have to work with before making a choice."

She had the money, had her mother. She didn't have enough to stop Em from doing this again. She had a deadly sump dive ahead of her.

*I saw your mother at Camp Five.*

What if she told Em about that part? It would compromise her, perhaps trigger some reiteration of her earlier confession on the ledge of the Long Drop. But Gyre could see how that might play out, with Em incapable of abandoning the impossibility that her mother was still alive, stranding Gyre down here to keep searching. Or worse, sending down more cavers despite any actions Gyre took against her back on the surface, too desperate and wild with grief to care about the consequences.

And besides—with how long Gyre had been going without proper rest, the chances of it just being an afterimage from the video, caused by frayed emotion, were too high. Right now, the recording had only captured a few half-spoken words at the sump. It didn't tell the whole story. It barely told *any* story. But if she described the encounter on the recording it would count against her own reliability.

Em was quiet, waiting. Gyre fought the urge to cradle her

aching head in her hands. Instead, she looked back toward the marker for Camp Six, then called up a map. It was a longer walk than to the shore of the cavern lake, but there wasn't a noticeable change in altitude. Easy enough.

"I told you to stay put," Em said at last.

"You also left me for nine hours."

"Then you should have slept."

"Camp Five was within walking distance," Gyre said, scowling. "I walked there. The cache is in place."

"Then you should have waited for me there. Taken advantage of having a break from me."

"That wasn't a break. That was a divorce. You left me in midair."

"You were fine. You're one of the best climbers I've worked with," Em said. "And I—" Her voice broke and she went quiet for a moment, just breathing. When she spoke again, she sounded calmer. "You didn't want to go that far to begin with—I don't understand." Worry crept into her voice, past the careful blankness.

Gyre's face heated. "I—" She hesitated, unsure of what lie to tell. "Those mushrooms creeped me out, I guess," she muttered.

"Mushrooms?"

A small shock rippled through her. Em knew about the mushrooms, right? "Yeah," Gyre said slowly. "They were blanketing the floor. Really nasty. They exploded with spores. I didn't want to test the suit's scrubbers on it."

"That's concerning—cavers have encountered various fungi down there, but the last person to reach Camp Five didn't find anything like that." The soft tapping of keys came from Em's line.

Another shudder of unease clenched Gyre's ribs tight. "Then why was the Five cache underwater, if not for the mushrooms?"

"The spaces around Five and Six flood regularly. I don't want the boxes . . . moving. At Six, I've got a good niche to put them in, but at Five the one good spot only fits the raft box. It makes more sense to sink the rest to the bottom of that sump. There's no current, and less of a chance of it moving. The sump here is too . . . active. It's safer up here, even if the niche gives way."

She could hear her heart pounding in her ears. "Makes sense, I guess."

Em cleared her throat. "Your suit stored metrics from the spores. I'll review them in a bit. But, Gyre, diving on your own, without resting first, through a section you'd never encountered before? You could have died." She let out a shaky breath. "Very easily."

"I'm not going to die," Gyre said, her voice stony. "I know what I'm doing."

Em didn't respond, no doubt wondering just how much Gyre really knew.

She wondered herself.

Her skin crawled like a thousand of the translucent insects from Camp Three had gotten inside her suit. She looked around, nervously, the overlapping maw of stone penning her in. She had to move. She set off, and was halfway across the space when Em spoke again. "My mother should have gone back for him. For my father."

*Focus. Focus on her.* "Based on what she said?" Gyre asked, approaching the passage that would lead to the camp. "No. *She* would have died."

"Well, she died anyway, didn't she?"

That almost caught her up short. *Did she?*

*Yes. She must have.*

*Right?*

"Gyre?"

She had stopped walking, and started moving forward again, hoping Em hadn't seen the spike in her adrenaline, couldn't see how tense she was. The passage was through an awkward gap, not exactly tight but hard to brace herself in, with large, smooth, round protrusions. It was like wriggling into the belly of some beast, but Em didn't express any concern. Gyre tried not to think about Halian as she ducked through the opening.

"If it helps," Gyre said, clambering over another outcropping, the exertion stilling the shaking in her bones, "I would have done everything she did. She got out. That's all that matters."

Em made a strangled, angry sound, and Gyre winced.

"I mean, that's why you're here. She came back, she built her company. Nothing she could have done would have changed any of it, except—except for not walking back here to die in this cave. Not leaving you behind."

"Stop talking, Gyre."

*No.* She needed this shred of interaction, whatever it was. This distraction. Gyre frowned, pushing herself over a final ledge and down onto a small drop-off, where the room widened again. "How many people have you actually talked to about this?" she pushed.

"Enough."

"Yeah, but I'm the first one who's come down here with you, right?"

*I'm the only one who's understood.*

"That's right. But you know as well as I do, if she'd gone back for my father and died, you wouldn't be down there. I'd just be in therapy somewhere. It would have been better for everybody."

She was right, but Gyre couldn't find any response to it. She didn't have the energy to. She'd never been the comforter, the gentle one, and now, spooked by the cave, unsure of what she was perceiving, and knowing that her mother had just started a new life on a nicer planet, a life that required money and safety as prerequisites, she didn't want to be either.

But she needed the distraction. She needed Em to keep talking, or she'd tear herself apart.

*Breathe, breathe.* She didn't *need* Em.

Gyre crossed her arms over her chest as she looked around the room. There, by the far western wall, was a small pool of water—likely the sump. A thin layer of water crept over the surrounding floor, not more than a few millimeters deep and not expanding across the entire cavern.

Tucked on the northern wall, on a small rise—

"Cache is here," Gyre said, and made for it. *Now let's just hope it's fully stocked.* She wasn't sure she could bring herself to haul through Camp Five.

But she had to, didn't she? To buy time? Her head hurt.

"Levels should be good," Em said, responding to the new jump in Gyre's heart rate. "Are you seeing any signs of— tampering? Was Five okay?"

"Five was fine. Can't see on this one yet." She increased her pace to a jog, only slowing when she could make out the orderly shape of the storage containers. "Yeah, I think it's okay."

Em let out a deep sigh. "Good. Good. Check the batteries, though, make sure they still have full charge."

"Way ahead of you, boss," Gyre said. "I swapped out at the last cache. These boxes and the ones at Camp Five are a lot sturdier than the earlier ones."

"I don't always use them. They're bulky, hard to move. But I feel safer leaving them on the harder-to-reach camps, since they might not see another person for—years. And they're completely watertight, in case of flooding. The earlier caches don't need to be. Camps in the middle, like Three, get a lighter option to split the difference."

*Smart*, Gyre thought as she opened the box, letting herself sink into the familiar cadence of Em's voice. *You've got this all figured out. So why have you been failing for years?* Everything inside glowed faintly and looked fine, and she picked up a battery, letting her suit run diagnostics on it via the cameras and sensors installed on its surface.

"Good to go, though since you picked up a fresh set at Five, you should leave them in for now to conserve."

"Right," Gyre said. Part of her never wanted to leave sight of the cache again, in case whoever had taken the cache at Camp Four was still wandering through the caves, could somehow make the swim from Camp Five.

But who could it really be, down here? *Isolde, wandering the caves for nine years—*

She needed to stop thinking like that. It was physically impossible that she'd survived a week, much less the better part of a decade.

"Your heart rate jumped. Again. You've been erratic since I came back," Em said. "Is something wrong?"

"Just spooked," Gyre said, swallowing thickly, closing the case and going to check the other boxes of gear. All of that seemed fine too. "Long day. You were gone for a while. What was that about?"

"Finding your mother. It seemed important. For both of us."

"And? That wouldn't have taken a day and all your attention. And it wouldn't have made you change my contract. I know you."

Em sighed. "I was calling my contacts at the local mining concerns."

"What did they say?"

"Nobody's sent a caver down here. I own this opportunity, and they all know it. But my contacts could still be wrong—since they all know I own it, whoever came down here would have to be careful about who in their organization knew they were trying something. Whoever called the Tunneler, whatever happened to the cache . . ."

"It could just be some local kid dreaming of making it rich," Gyre supplied, though her heart felt like lead at the news. *Or it could be your mother.* "You don't exactly have the same presence as the other concerns, and this doesn't look like an established site."

Em laughed at that. Gyre managed a grim, thin smile as she settled down against the wall by the cache.

"Is that the sump over there?" she asked, jerking her chin toward the small pool.

"Yes. It's not the easiest way in, but it's the only one now."

"Your parents went in through the lake, right?"

Em sighed. "Of course you explored."

"You already knew that," Gyre countered, exhaustion flooding her now that she was off her feet again. She fought against it, unwilling to close her eyes. *Pay attention.* "Be honest with me. I know my suit pings my location."

*Be honest with me. Have you seen the recording running?*

"I didn't know, actually. I didn't check."

"Didn't think to, or didn't want to?"

"I'm not appreciating the interrogation," Em said, her tone warning—but not detached, nor outright angry.

*Baby steps toward being a person*, Gyre thought. Then: *I don't need her to be a person.*

But she wanted her to be.

Grimacing at her own weakness, Gyre shifted in place, trying to get comfortable. She hated this suit. She'd thought she'd been prepared, doing day jaunts in older models she'd been able to rent, but a day wasn't a week. A catheter was still a catheter, but it wasn't a resection of her bowel, a cannula in her gut. Most of the time, she could ignore the bigger indignities—a testament to the suit's design, to the surgeon's skill—but then there were moments like now. What she needed was to feel safe and to have a minimum of things needing her attention. She needed to clear her head, plan, think. Instead, when she went to comfort herself, soothe away the tension enough that she could hear her own thoughts, all she could think about was how she couldn't rub her eyes, or even touch her fingers together.

She would have given anything to rip the whole thing off her.

*And even if I turn back tomorrow, it's still the better part of a week*, she thought, and groaned out loud.

"Is something the matter?"

*Everything.*

"I'd give anything for a hot shower," she said instead. "And a beer."

Em chuckled. "I can only imagine. I've been in those suits a few times, but just for a day or two maximum. Testing it out to make sure changes I made . . ."

"Weren't going to immediately kill whoever you suited up? Thanks for the quality control."

Gyre realized the banter was relaxing her, and felt sick. This was the woman who had let twenty-seven people die. She was a mass murderer—or a serial killer. The distinction wasn't exactly clear to Gyre.

But this was also the woman who, so far, hadn't shown any inadequacies that should have led to so many people dying in so many different ways. This was also the woman who, confronted with her own behavior . . . apologized.

Who amended Gyre's contract, who offered Gyre everything she had wanted for as long as she could remember, and who was willing to give up if Gyre wanted to take it and run.

*Not give up*, she reminded herself. *Try again with somebody who doesn't know what she's done.*

It felt hollow, just now. She wanted to believe Em cared, if only until she felt a little stronger, if only until she knew what she was going to do next.

"If it would help," Em said, her voice soft, barely intruding on her thoughts, "I can pass cooled water through your suit when you go into the sump, or into the lake. That can mimic the sensation of actually bathing."

"I said a hot shower," she said.

"I don't think you'd like the feeling of warm water in your suit, given where it could be coming from."

Gyre made a face, then laughed. "Yeah, cold bath it is. If it's like the fluid-exchange feature, it feels pretty nice."

Pause. "When did you do that?" Em asked.

"Camp Five."

"Even with the spores?"

Her stomach twisted.

*The spores.*

Fuck. She hadn't even thought . . . but she was on the other side. She was fine. Right? *I'm fine. I'm fine?* Except she'd been spiraling for hours, afraid, jumping at shadows. *I'm—*

Gyre took a second. "I don't think it was a full recirculation, I got distracted. You're . . . going to run those tests, right?"

"I've got them running on another machine as we speak. I'll have answers in about an hour. Gyre, you should have told me you had more exposure than just breathing recirculated air in that chamber."

"I didn't stay long."

"No, you did a several-hours-long dive while possibly impaired."

"Maybe they messed with my judgment." *Maybe they made me see something in the dark.*

"Don't do it again. Wait for me next time."

She snorted to cover her shame and fear. "Planning on abandoning me again?"

*Please don't.*

"No," Em said, and Gyre sagged with relief. "But that was so reckless, I can't even—if I'd known, I would have been terrified."

Terrified. For *her.*

Gyre tried not to react, but her thoughts immediately went back to the Long Drop, how her fall had triggered something in Em, changed something. After her fall, Em had wanted Gyre to see her. To understand. She'd been afraid of . . . what?

Of starting over. Or . . . of losing her?

The thought cleared away the grasping chaos of her panic. Em sighed. "Anyway, in the meantime, if you do want that bath, I recommend the lake, for obvious reasons."

"The currents."

"Mm-hm. It's mostly quiet in the lake these days—much safer."

"Right." *As safe as anything down here.*

"And recirculating your entire water supply might be the best course of action. If anything, it could clear out any remaining spores. You know, I had one caver try to swim the sump with me running cool water through the suit. Thought it would help him handle the environment better."

Gyre bent her head. "I can guess how that turned out."

"He actually survived," Em said softly. "But he bailed after the first encounter with the currents. Barely got out. I . . . couldn't blame him. He'd given me enough information for the next push, so I pulled him out. Paid him the agreed-on wage."

"You—what?"

"I'm not a complete monster," Em replied. Her face appeared in the lower corner of Gyre's screen, still young, still beautiful. Her hair was pulled back into a large bun at the top of her head, and she looked a little better rested, and more than a little worried. Gyre could see more of Isolde's features in her now, including that particular set to her jaw that spoke of deep exhaustion, relentless determination, and inherited pain. Traumatic memories, passed down from mother to daughter. "You're not the only person I've offered full pay for a half-finished job," she said.

"Nice to see you again," Gyre said. It came out sounding more vulnerable than she'd intended.

Em quirked a brow.

"What makes you decide I need to see your face?"

"I thought it was polite, now that we're having actual conversations."

"Is that what this is?"

"Isn't it?" Em managed a smile and idly fiddled with a curl that had come loose from her bun. Gyre felt an immediate pang of envy—what she wouldn't give to touch her own hair. "But to the point: everybody that comes back up gets paid, even if it's a fraction of the full arrangement. Everybody who dies . . . their family gets paid. In full."

"It's not in the contract."

"I know," Em said. "People do *read* their contracts sometimes. It—"

"Changes how people behave," Gyre supplied.

"Exactly."

Still a monstrous manipulation—how many of her cavers would have turned back instead of pushing onward? Gyre had come this far to protect herself, after all, and she *knew* that she should get out. The others hadn't had that luxury.

But it was difficult to feel the horror when she could see the humanity and the pain in Em's face. She thought she was doing good. She thought she had no choice except to let them die, but she could at least make it better after.

Monstrous. Human.

Understandable.

"Your mom really made that much off Oxsua?"

Em visibly flinched at the name. "She made enough. Invested most of it. Built up the company with some of it, kept generating wealth with the rest. I inherited it all. And since then, a couple of my cavers have asked for other jobs, and I've given them lower-paying ones, but scouting actual plots. Sold the rights, invested again. Half the tech I've invested in are things I use here, and you can see how advanced it's gotten. I'm on the front lines, I guess."

"If you weren't so obsessed, you'd be famous. Your company already makes the best tech. If you ran standard expeditions, everybody would want a job with you."

A job, Gyre reflected, that even in a normal cave system would still have what would be an unacceptable mortality rate on other planets, in other industries. The caves were soaked in death, just not . . . not like this.

"Yeah." Em shrugged. "I know. But I don't like putting people down there. Not for profit."

Gyre swallowed, trying not to feel sympathy. "You've got a way higher failure rate than most surveying missions," she pointed out. "The others aren't *safe*, but the risks are obvious, and with the money people earn from them, they make better lives. Get off-world. Most of them survive, even if they don't get out intact."

"And your point is?"

"That companies like Oxsua serve a purpose. That you're not better than them."

"Eventually, they'll leave, you know."

Gyre snorted. "Yeah. We all know. Eventually, they'll find the limit of what they can do without Tunnelers killing them all, then they'll move planet. We all *know*. But it's not like there's anything we can do about it. And it's not like you're helping us prepare for that any more than they are."

"I'm not saying I am." Em had leaned forward slightly, had her elbows on her desk and her hands folded before her, her chin resting on her knuckles. "I'm saying I'm not doing this for the money. I'm doing this because I have to. And at least, for every suit and scanner I help perfect by field-testing this way, even if my caver dies, ten, twenty, maybe more will survive, will get the chance to use the system like my mother did. When I pack up, maybe it'll turn out that my net impact was nothing. I know that lives aren't some finite value, I know that better than anybody, and ten don't outweigh one, just like my mother and father don't outweigh the—the twenty-seven people I've led to their deaths since. There just isn't math for that. Can't be." She looked upward, brow furrowing with a hint of pain, then continued.

"But at least the people who get involved in my mess know that this is a very dangerous mission, and at least the people who wear my tech outside this cave can feel a little more sure they're bringing home the money they make themselves, and not as a crematory box."

Em fell silent then, looking uncomfortable now that all the words had poured out of her. Gyre found herself trembling slightly, trying to parse everything. That calculus was as raw as Isolde's pain in that exit interview, and Gyre couldn't fight the feeling of Em's grief being a living thing, as inexorable as a Tunneler but with a beating heart, a pulse that throbbed and curdled in the vein.

"I'm not a complete monster," Em said once more, her voice quiet. "Just most of one."

"Drama queen," Gyre shot back, but the words felt hollow. She understood Em—more than she wanted to.

And with that understanding came the revelation:

She wanted to *help* her.

*Fuck.*

Em shook her head but didn't cut the feed. Instead, she left it up as she turned her attention to another screen, and Gyre could hear the faint clicking of her typing, watched her lift her hand every so often to manipulate the display. Gyre stretched her arms above her, then nestled herself against the battery and canister boxes, watching the play of light on Em's face. It was soothing, watching somebody else work instead of working herself. Watching, instead of being watched.

"You passed your neurological test," Em said after a moment. "And so far, the results are coming back that your suit is undamaged. It'll take longer to get results on if the spores affected your air scrubbers."

"Neurological test?"

"Even if the exposure was impairing your judgment back at Five, you sound like you're back to normal now. On edge, but I can't blame you for that."

Gyre grimaced. That meant—that meant all her panic this side of the sump had been just her. Her racing thoughts, her wild swings of emotion, her eruptions of panic—all her. "Yeah. Guess not. Glad to hear I'm not dying."

She sat with that thought a moment, turning it over. She'd been so focused on Em, she'd forgotten that the cave was dangerous outside of her handler. She'd let it get into her head. She couldn't let that happen again.

She took a deep breath. "So . . . you really found my mom?"

"Yes," Em said with a glance at the camera. "Here, I'll send what I found. You can look at it whenever you like."

*Now, now, now, now*—but she hesitated, looking at the file. If Em knew she'd seen Isolde, Em wouldn't have been able to guide her out safely.

If Gyre knew about her mother, could she keep it together enough to climb out?

"Not yet," she said, getting back up. Her feet took her, unthinking, to the sump entrance. It looked like a puddle from afar, but as she grew closer, she could see how deep it was. Still, it would be a tight entrance. Her skin pebbled into goose bumps.

*You don't have to go in there.* Gyre had a sinking sensation that even Em would say that much, if she asked. Em, worried about the spores, worried about her falling, sitting up there and watching that video of her mother, of all the other cavers dying—

*She did that to them*, she reminded herself, but it rang hollow now. Em had set the stage, had invited in the players. She had set a goal that meant longer expeditions, but those weren't any more dangerous for her withholding of information. Adrian Purcell had died from a freak rock collapse. Jennie Mercer had died because of bad caving practice and nature-damaged equipment. Who could Gyre truly blame? *Em, Em,* Em was the only person *to* blame, but it didn't feel right.

Em was an experienced handler. So far, she hadn't led Gyre astray in any physically dangerous way outside of the incident on the Long Drop. This expedition shouldn't be killing this many people.

*This cave is cursed.*

Beneath her feet, the sump roiled, ready to strip her lines and bash her against rock. But Isolde had made it out. It was manageable. It was doable.

Why couldn't anyone *do* it?

"Gyre?"

"Just thinking," she murmured. Reluctantly, she turned her attention away from the sump and back to her readouts. The recorder indicator was still green, still steady. A black box up on the surface was storing all of this. If she took it before a court, what would they find?

Nothing illegal. Nothing beyond the bounds of the contract. They'd get context, an explanation, and an unanswerable question. Who was at fault? Was Em a murderer, or just irresponsibly obsessed?

Would a court even try to stop her?

Never.

She turned and made for the maw cavern.

"Where are you going?" The words were bare of any accusation or anger, and a glance at the corner of her screen showed Em still working away, expression alert but placid.

"To take that bath you suggested." To clear her head. To get it back on straight.

Because right now, right here, she was considering diving into that sump and finishing this herself, the way Em wanted her to. Finish the story, witness the dead, and then climb back out. If not for Em's sake, then for Jennie's. For all the cavers who had come before her, who would come after.

Gyre levered herself up and over the barrier leading out of Camp Six, hissing as her sore, swollen muscles protested, then wove her way between the pillars toward the lake, up and down the shelflike sheets of stone that remained from the passage of floods. Em turned on a secondary marker for her, but Gyre knew where she was going already. She'd always had a sixth sense about the layout of caves—would it extend to the sump? Was Em right to trust her with diving, despite her lack of training? Could she handle the currents, make the right split-second decisions? She wasn't a strong swimmer. Em knew that. Em should tell her to stop.

Em had brought her this far.

Knowing Em, she'd already tried experienced cave divers—people as good as Hanmei. She'd probably tried every combination of skills she could find, searching for the one that would be right. The problem, as far as Gyre could see it—aside from this being a suicide mission to begin with—was that half of any success was luck. She'd always believed that. It scared a lot of people, and sometimes it made her angry, because of course she wanted to control her fate. But it was true. Luck had seen her born on this godforsaken rock, chance had led to her mother running away, pure providence had kept her from snapping her legs as a kid.

Luck might let her finish this, for good.

She passed into the luminous cavern again and dimmed her display to nearly true colors. She felt a pang of nerves, but it quickly subsided to the general level of unease she'd almost grown used to. Whatever phantom eyes she felt on her back, she could push away with the knowledge that Em was at her computer. Em was watching for her. Seeing Isolde at Camp Five—that had been chemical, a distortion created where the spores and her nerves and that video had met.

Whatever had taken the missing cache, the others were fine.

Everything was going to be *fine*.

She approached what looked like an easy, gentle entrance to the water, and dipped her toes in.

There was a few-second lag, but then Em tapped a key somewhere, and cool water ran over her foot. It wasn't quite specific enough to mimic the feeling of dangling just her toes in the water, but it was a thoughtful, attentive touch. Gyre bit back a surprised sob of sudden relief and looked at Em's image.

Em was engrossed by her readouts, leaning forward slightly. She had no idea what that tiny gesture meant to her.

Gyre watched her for a moment, transfixed by the gentle curve of her cheek, the slight parting of her lips, before she realized her heart was fluttering in her chest. Her pulse was quickening, and she hated it. It wasn't fair. Not only was she—stupidly—considering *helping* the other woman, even after everything that had passed between them, but Em was just her type. She was smart and driven and beautiful, and so unreachable that she could've been halfway across the galaxy. Gyre wondered, just for a moment, if Em would have noticed her topside in any other situation. But no other situation mattered. There was only the cave, and this fucked-up tether between them, making them both desperate for contact, making her dream of something easier.

Gyre took a few steps into the lake, and her other foot was awash in water—or, well, the recycled solution of water and several other components that the cleaning mechanisms in the suit used. It didn't really feel like standing in a pool, but it felt better than nothing, and was stronger and more controlled than the diffusion she'd felt from changing the water out. She wiggled her toes, imagining the crusted sweat being washed away, the film resettling into an invisible skin.

The lichen below the surface crunched under her boots as she waded farther in, illuminating the depths. Out toward the center, the lake grew noticeably deeper, but even here, it would quickly rise to over waist height. Gyre walked in to her knees, then jumped out, remembering the relief at Camp Five from diving in, before it had all gone wrong.

"Hold your breath," Em said, and she hit the water.

Her entire suit was flooded, though Em graciously left her head for last, giving her enough time to close her eyes and puff out her cheeks. She wriggled the muscles of her face and shook her head, enjoying the flood over her scalp, between the tight knots of her hair. The sensation of cool water was bliss, and she floated herself back up to the surface, rolling onto her back. Em drained some of the water in her suit, and Gyre inhaled sharply and opened her eyes.

She relaxed.

The ceiling was beautiful. It almost looked like a night sky, with the trails of faint light from distant lichen, and the shadows between stalactites and other formations creating a rich, roiling heaven.

"How is it?" Em asked.

"Better than I expected," Gyre said.

"I can always pipe in some light music, too," Em said, finally glancing at the camera again with a quick smile. Those smiles weren't getting any stronger, but they were coming more readily, softening Em's jagged edges.

Gyre shook her head, the water in her suit sloshing and shifting her hair slightly. "No. Just like this. This is fine."

# CHAPTER FOURTEEN

She slept heavily that night.

When she woke, Em's camera feed was off, but her comm line was open. It was comforting, to know she'd been watched over while she slept. Em had remained visible on her helmet's screen until Gyre had drifted off the night before, working in silence, and the odd companionship had made things . . . easier.

It shouldn't have, but Gyre had been too tired to feel guilt, either for enjoying the other woman's presence or for the recording indicator that had remained, unchanged, throughout the night.

As she plugged in her morning canister, she considered the indicator.

"Good morning," Em said, interrupting her thoughts.

"Hey," Gyre said. She made herself smile, lean back on her heels. "Have you slept yet?"

"Briefly, yes."

*Now or never.* "I've been thinking."

"The new amendment," Em said, and it popped up on her screen before Gyre could protest. "It's here. I wouldn't have withheld it from you the other . . . last night, but I wanted you to feel rested and alert when you signed it."

*Turn back, turn back. Be selfish. You've always been selfish; don't stop now.*

"I don't want to sign it," she said. It didn't *feel* right.

Em let out an involuntary sound, like a hitched breath, but it wasn't clear if it was a whimper or a gasp. "I . . . I . . . *What?*"

"I don't want to sign it," she repeated, her shoulders drawing up toward her ears. Her gut filled with nutritional paste. She felt sick. "Look, I've come this far. Right? There's just this last push?"

"Yes," Em said. She sounded desperately confused, desperately hopeful. Like she was edging up on a skittish beast.

"Then I might as well continue, right?"

"It's dangerous." Em swallowed audibly. "You read the dossiers. Saw the video. You're saying you're willing to risk that, even though you don't have to?"

But she *did* have to. It was the only way to stop Em from doing this again, the only way that would work for good. Finish the mission and get it all on record as insurance. Everything wrapped up in a neat little bow.

Gyre swallowed, looking skyward, to the vault of stone above her. "What does my personality inventory say about me?"

Em tapped a few keys. The document sprung up in front of her, replacing the contract. "That you're strongheaded," she said. "That your willingness to lie about your professional history wasn't to cover a lack of skill, but to let you jump over entry-level risk. That you have few connections outside yourself, and that your only goals relate to your own success." She paused. Then: "Not to your own enrichment."

Yeah. That sounded about right.

"That's why, then," Gyre said. "I'm a stubborn bitch who knows best. That work for you?"

Em hesitated, and Gyre waited for her to try to argue, to try to dissuade her. She had so much ammunition she could use. She could list every danger, or even invoke the contract to close the expedition out.

But she didn't. Instead, she said, "I understand. We'll continue."

Gyre unhooked the used canister. "Is there any equipment at Camp Three that isn't also at Five or here?"

"No. There's just more of it," Em said.

"Hauling that gear sounds like a stupid idea, then," she said, standing. "If the goal is just to get to the chamber on the other side of the sump—" She paused when Em snorted, no doubt at *just*. "If it is," she continued after a moment, reaching the battery box and crouching to unlatch it, "then there's no point in trekking between Three and Five that many times. It'll just increase ration consumption and battery usage, *and* increase the chance for injury. If we'd been able to go between Three and Four as planned, it would make more sense, but with the Long Drop *and* the first sump, *and* the climb between them . . ."

"I can see the logic in it. But for the next caver—"

"You haven't been listening—there won't *be* another caver," she said. She closed the case and stood. "I've come this far, and I don't intend to die for you."

Em let out another shaky breath.

"So are we good to go today? Take a first stab at it?"

"I should be rested enough, yes. And your biometrics look

good." She hesitated. "If you'd like to have more time to think it over—"

Gyre cut her off. "How much sleep did you get?"

"I managed five hours."

"In the last how many?"

"That's . . . difficult to answer. When I'm manning the systems up here, I usually sleep for only ninety minutes at a time. Just enough time for REM sleep, and I do it every several hours as necessary. This was one of my longer rests."

"Sounds miserable."

"Less miserable than living in a suit for several weeks," she pointed out.

Gyre snorted.

"Are *you* ready, then?"

She looked over at the sump entrance. *Last chance. She'll still let you leave.*

*Probably.*

"Yeah," she said. She felt good. Surprisingly good. Like she'd slept for days instead of hours. She stood and stretched, finding only the stiffness that came from sleeping in a suit. "I mean, assuming those tests you ran on the spores came back fine?"

"I would have woken you up if there was a problem. You're clear; there was no trace of anything in your system. Looks like we were worried for nothing."

"Glad to hear it," Gyre said. She crouched again and swapped her battery; the level on her current one had looked lower than she liked, no doubt because of the tests the suit had been running on her blood and body while she slept. Besides, it was best to go in fresh.

Best to go in clear-headed.

"No drugs," she said as she stood up and stretched. "No adrenaline, no nothing."

"If you get into a situation where—"

"Have you actually experienced what it feels like to have that stuff dumped into your system without your say-so? It's going to fuck with me, not help me. I'll go slow today. We shouldn't even get into a situation where it *might* be necessary."

Em didn't respond, clearly not pleased with the idea. Gyre ignored her in turn and began opening the supply boxes, separating everything into organized piles.

"There's an anchor by the pool edge," Em said. "Check the integrity of it, but you should be able to go from there."

"Can I take extra spools of diving line?" Gyre said, tapping one of them.

"Yes, but you only have space in your suit for two. I have an array of lengths and sizes. Not all of them slot easily into your suit—they're from earlier expeditions—but they should be fairly easy to carry. My suggestion is to stock your suit, then take one or two handhelds, and use those up first."

Gyre reloaded the slots on her suit with the appropriate spools before looking through the other options. There was a small handheld spool, easy to manage; she set that aside as well.

"There are also silt screws, for if you can't find a good place to attach a line. General practice is to do what you did in the first sump, looping the line around formations to keep it steady, but that might not always be possible. These handle the muck better than climbing bolts, and are faster and easier to place, since they don't need to take your whole weight. Swap out your climbing bolts to the ones in the cache. Your main bolt drill will work with both."

"Can I take both kinds?" Gyre asked, hesitating. "In case there's dry climbing, or there's too much muck and no outcroppings?"

Em thought it over. "Usually I'd tell you not to split them given your limited carrying capacity, but there should be a small pod in your equipment hump filled with cold-light sticks."

"The techs topside mentioned them. Said they were experimental?"

"Not in design, but in effect. I don't have data on how things . . . react to them."

She didn't need to say what "things."

*Tunnelers.*

Gyre nodded and then reached back, running her hand over the various compartments until her screen showed she was above the right one.

"They're for an emergency situation where your headlamp and reconstruction no longer work. A suit breach." Em's voice was uneasy at the thought, and Gyre tried not to picture that scenario. "But that's unlikely," Em said quickly, "and trading them for more equipment to *prevent* a suit breach is a solid alternative. Move the extra climbing bolts to the small pod, and load the bigger space with the silt screws. I don't want you running out, and you'll still have to manually swap back, but it should give you the best of both worlds."

"Small price to pay," Gyre said, opening the compartment catch and thumbing out all the plastic sticks inside. She tucked them into the gear box she'd taken the silt screws out of, then began moving the old bolts over, going slowly and taking inventory as she went.

She was left with twenty extra once she'd packed the small space. Grudgingly, she put them away.

Closing the pod on her back and starting the fiddlier work of emptying her bolt drill's storage chamber and swapping over to the silt screws, she glanced at the pool again. "I shouldn't trust the old anchors in there, right?"

"They may not lead in the right direction anymore," Em confirmed grimly. "There may also be existing line in there, so go slow, and make sure to add those directional markers consistently. I'll do my best to record where you are on them from what I can see on my camera, but there's always a chance I'll miss something, and have an—incorrect calculation of how far you are from safety."

Gyre shivered. That had almost killed one of the other cavers on a dive, she remembered.

*Turn back, turn back.*

She ignored it, forcing down the fear and her selfishness, ignoring that they were the reasonable things to feel now.

She continued inventorying and kitting out. Her adrenaline was up, but not in a helpful way; she was shaking slightly, and nervous of having her back to the pool. Em needed an experienced diver, not—*her*. Her earlier bravado was once again beginning to fail, leaving her uneasy and vulnerable.

Maybe she *should* haul gear. Take another day.

No—waiting would make it worse. If she was nervous now, how would she feel after a day of just thinking about it? Her options were to do this now or bail, and she was already in it. She was diving today.

"One last thing," Em said. She sounded hesitant, almost apologetic.

Gyre stiffened. "Yeah?"

"In case you're trapped, and cut off from me, there are . . . kill switches built into the suit. In case there's no way out."

Trapped in her suit, starving or suffocating, crushed half

to death. The images came to mind far too readily, and she forced herself to focus on packing up the unused gear. "Won't need them."

"Hopefully not. But if you *do*—"

"This isn't the time, Em."

"It's the only time."

Her HUD shifted, flowing through a sequence of menus slowly enough that she could have tracked how to do it. She did her best to ignore it. The image settled on dosage information of various drugs.

"Stop," Gyre said.

"No. Look. You have options. I recommend an overdose of morphine, but both sedatives will also work if they're above these volumes." The numbers flared yellow, throbbed. "Any less and it won't definitely kill you, or it might make you suffer needlessly. There's also a way to suffocate yourself. You could just turn off the exchanger fans, but I recommend coming here"—the screen shifted again and Gyre tried to turn away, but of course it followed her, hovering just in front of her eyes—"and using this command to make the suit shunt the helium it uses for your buoyancy sacs into your suit proper. It will displace the air and make for a much easier death."

"Stop telling me how to die," Gyre hissed, her hackles raising at how easily Em could discuss this. Like it *was* just hitting a switch.

"I need to know that you know. Things can go wrong in there. Things *do* go wrong."

Gyre growled, then shut down the option menus, clearing her field of view. "Fine. I saw it. I understand. Let's just get this started."

Em didn't respond. Gyre took that as agreement.

They ran down a checklist of gear one more time, and then she approached the pool. She found the original anchor at the lip of the pool, and tested it while Em ran confirming diagnostics. It was still strong, so she attached the start of her first short handheld reel to it.

"No water in the suit this time," she said.

"No water," Em agreed.

"Diving," she said.

"Dive," Em called back, unable to hide the tightness in her voice.

Gyre glanced skyward one more time, then slipped into the pool. She sank quickly, the water covering her head, and she kept desperate hold of the line as she turned and oriented herself toward the first passage. Her suit adjusted automatically, extending her small diving fins, switching from air exchange to her rebreather without so much as a shiver.

The sonar reconstruction she looked out on was clear close to her, but quickly became hazy the farther away she looked. Even though the reconstruction had changed to bright, artificial daylight colors for ease of use, she felt closed in and, almost immediately, lost. It was one thing to embrace tight spaces, but another for there to be no clear way out. Her heart pounded as she looked around. The stone surrounding her protruded and fell away in odd formations, tunnels leading in three or four directions off the shaft she was in, and in the distance she could see overlays of what she assumed were currents, different-colored explosions of lines mapping water flow that wavered and disappeared every so often as her sensors couldn't locate them. Flashes of white danced across her screen, old line flapping through the maelstrom.

"Sorry for the chaos. It's the silt," Em said. "I've improved the sonar capabilities of the suit over the last few years, but it's harder to change the laws of physics. The silt bounces sound back and confuses the sensors."

"I get it," Gyre said, her suit's buoyancy returning to neutral as she came in line with a passage that branched off directly ahead of her. That odd weightless feeling was almost worse than sinking. She turned herself slightly, but it took a forceful motion, one that immediately made part of her view shudder as her turning upset the silt flowing around her.

She closed her eyes tightly for a moment, then opened them wide as she realized she could be moving without even feeling it. She was right where she'd left herself, but she clung to the wall all the same. Apparently, her panic at Camp Five had made things seem a lot easier than they really were.

Or maybe they were that easy. Maybe she was just letting herself get spooked. She rolled her shoulders, trying to relax.

"Drive a second anchor bolt here," Em said. "A hard one, not looping it on anything. That way, if the line were to break up at the surface for any reason, you'd still know this is the exit."

*For any reason.* "God damn it, Em," she muttered, but prepared to drive the bolt.

"What?"

"Nothing," she said, then flinched as the sound wave from the drill made everything ripple and shift. She ran her line through the anchor as she waited for it to still, tying it off securely like she had up at the surface. *Just in case. Just in case the cache stealer comes back and takes my gear and I need to pump myself full of drugs instead of dying a slow—*

Why would Em say something like that? It didn't do either of them any good. Muscles tense, she used the bolt as a leverage point to turn herself back to the cave.

"Which tunnel am I going down?"

"The one straight ahead of you. The side branches on your left narrow too much to pass through. The one on your right—that's the one the caver who went in before you—"

"Eli," Gyre supplied, the dossier vivid in her memory.

"Eli," Em repeated, then cleared her throat. "That's the one Eli was swept down. I don't know where it goes, but it's not worth the risk."

Gyre swallowed and oriented herself toward the tunnel ahead. She couldn't argue with Em's logic. "Swimming forward."

"Swim on," Em said.

Gyre wished she could have pushed off the wall, but she couldn't risk more silt skewing the reconstruction. Just the motion of her arms and legs as she crept forward disturbed her sight, and her head began to ache at the constantly changing landscape. Her line unspooled behind her, smoothly.

Then the fin on her left foot hit it on a downward kick, and she lost her grip on the reel. She swore and twisted, but the effect on the silt erased the reel from sight. She dove toward where it should have been, hand outstretched, hoping, hoping—

Her fingers caught line, and she followed it, hand over hand, trying not to unspool any more line than she'd already lost. She went down, and down, and—

"Gyre," Em snapped. "*Gyre.*"

"If I don't catch it, it will keep—"

"Follow the line back to your anchor," Em said. "Tie on a new line. Reel in the old one."

Gyre was gasping from the sudden fear and exertion, and it took a moment to process what Em had said. And her tone of voice—had she been shouting her name, and Gyre hadn't even heard her? Her heart was pounding in her ears loud enough that it was possible. She swallowed down her panic and then carefully turned, following the line back in the other direction.

She reached the anchor in a few minutes and took a moment there to close her eyes and calm down. Then she clipped in and began pulling in the unspooled line, gathering it up in her hands as she floated. It felt like it took an eternity, but at last she had the reel in hand.

At least it had been a short line.

Instead of hooking in a new line, Gyre unclipped and followed the old one up. Surfacing, she gasped as if she'd been holding her breath. Her sight stabilized, and she tossed the reel and tangled coil of line toward the camp cache, then held herself on the rim of the sump, just breathing.

"*Shit,*" Gyre said.

"We can be done for the day."

"Hold on," she said. "I'm just—just freaked out."

"That's an especially valid reason for resting. More than."

"I want to lay more line than that."

"This is the easy part," Em said softly.

"*I know,*" Gyre snapped. Then she stopped, shook her head, and took a long, deep breath, holding it in her belly for a moment. She let it out slowly, and turned to look back down at the sump. "Let me try it without the sonar reconstruction."

"No."

"My head is already pounding and I was only down there for—what, fifteen minutes? Twenty? The way that it represents the uncertainty with the silt—I can't *think*."

"Then maybe you should just pull back!"

Gyre's breath hissed out of her angrily. "Let me try it with a headlamp," she said slowly. "Just until the next anchor."

"I've already tried it that way; it doesn't work. If you go

178

down there, you go down there with everything I can give you."

"Em, what you're giving me isn't *useful*. I'm going back under, and I'm going to—"

"Hold on," Em muttered.

Gyre hauled herself from the sump and sloshed out of the standing water over to where the extra spools of line were, her lips curled into something bordering on a snarl. She had a fresh spool and was halfway back to the sump when Em spoke again.

"There," Em said. "Go under. Try that."

Gyre reached the pool and stepped into the darkness, letting herself sink down. Her suit's lamp switched on, and the reconstruction was no longer bright like daylight. Instead, it was overlaid on what she could see naturally, the shifting of the computer readouts hidden somewhat by the silt and darkness. The overlay gave her more information, and made the currents visible, but she could match it up with real landmarks now, hazy though they were.

Because the cavern was filled with roiling silt.

She'd known it, but seeing it as the dark, murky hellscape it was . . .

Gyre took a deep breath. "That should work," she said. "Much better. Less overwhelming."

"Let me know if at any time you want the reconstruction to be clearer."

"Got it. Following the line down to anchor two now."

"Swim on."

Gyre followed the line down to the anchor. She attached the spool to her wrist, in case she dropped it again, then clipped the line onto the bolt. Carefully, she swam forward, keeping an eye on how she held the reel and how her body moved in relation to it. What had been easy on her first dive, and so far down her priority list on her second, was now all-important. Once she was comfortable, and not much farther out than she'd been when she lost the first reel, she turned her attention back to the space in front of her.

This section of the sump was narrowing quickly and dipping down. For a moment, it looked like there was only a solid wall in front of her. But a few kicks forward made the image resolve itself. Down, and then up again; that should do it.

"Still forward, right?" Gyre said. "Not straight down into that pit back there, where I lost the spool?"

"Forward."

She angled herself down only as far as the forward path led, and toward the nearest side wall of it. There, before the path turned upward once more, she paused to drill in another anchor. The bolt drill made the silt shift and seethe, blurring and darkening her readout for a moment, and pushed her back even as she kicked against it, until the bit caught and dragged her closer to the wall as it cut in.

The drill stilled and the silt settled. She pulled her wrist away, then hooked her line through the new anchor and set a plastic marker on it.

"All right, I'm going down and around this outcropping," she said.

"Go slowly. Look here," Em said, and the colored lines marking a current flow brightened. There were two different colors. "On your side is a pushing current. The suction-return current to stabilize the chamber you're in is on the other side. Both are weak here, but they'll grow stronger in this passage. The last time it was mapped, it was very narrow."

"Which side should I take, then?"

"I recommend the pushing one; you're less likely to lose control on it, but take it at an angle and tack back and forth. Stay away from the suction. There's no telling where it could take you. Or turn back for the day."

Gyre swallowed, hoping to loosen her dry throat. She refused to consider Em's second option. If she got out of the sump again, she'd turn tail and run.

Em waited a moment, then continued, "On the way back, you'll take the other side. We'll lay line for that when the time comes, on a different reel. Are you ready?"

"Yeah," she said. "I think so."

"Take your time," Em said.

Gyre nodded inside her helmet. After watching the swirling colored lines for a moment, she turned back to her rope and checked the distance markers. They were painted on, outside of the reconstruction, but they'd been visible even without light input, which Gyre supposed meant they were made of acoustically distinct materials. *Smart.*

She was distracting herself to avoid what came next. She chewed at her lip and checked her reel, made sure she had a good grip on it.

"If it would help, I can brighten the colors on the pulling current," Em said. "Make it a Do Not Cross situation."

"Yeah, that would help."

The suction grew more vibrant on her screen, until her brain saw it as a solid wall. *Better.* She'd still have to be careful and controlled, but it was a lot easier to avoid smashing into something that looked impassable.

And if things got bad . . .

*I'll just stop swimming.* The current should push her back to here. She'd have to protect her head and as much of the suit as possible in case she scraped along or banged into the rock walls, but the current would lead back here, and then she could plan her next move.

"All right, starting," Gyre said, and began swimming at an angle into the narrow gap, toward the brightly colored wall. The effect of the current was light at first, a nudge against her leading shoulder. But by the time she drew close to the wall marking the shift in the current, she was having to kick harder, could feel the pressure of the water like a weight on her head and shoulders.

"Turn," Em said as Gyre was already beginning to reorient herself. She was mostly through the slot now, and turned sharply up, her body curving around the edge of the outcropping. As she turned back toward the other wall of the passage, her left hand connected with the bottom of the slot, and her readout went dark as a plume of silt rushed past her, dislodged by the light touch.

She hesitated, and the current started to push her back down the passage. Panicking, she kicked again; more silt, but she launched from the bottom and up against the stream. She made her way to the ghostly outline of the far wall that her readout had shown before the silt obstructed everything, swimming hard, her hand outstretched.

The current grew stronger, and her muscles burned with the effort. Her hand found rock, and she grasped at it, but her fingers slipped off the surface worn smooth by the powerful, continuous flow of water, the thin layer of silt or whatever else covered the rock in the face of the current slick and unforgiving. Gyre gritted her teeth, kicking hard just to stay in contact with the wall.

"Gyre—"

"I'm thinking," she snapped.

"Listen—go toward the back of the passage. Turn ninety degrees to your right, instead of the entire way around. The slot's opened up enough that there should be some distance there."

*Right.* She tried to turn, but the break in her momentum let the current take control of her. With a shout, she surged forward, her shoulder brushing the rock as she turned, her foot catching and slipping on the wall but giving her just enough force to shoot back toward that end of the passage. Her body screamed at her as she powered her way forward, but her readout began to clear, her blindness dissipating into the same roiling, dark, murky hellscape as before.

She reached the back of the passage. The suction current grew brilliant on her screen again.

It was less than ten centimeters from her.

# CHAPTER FIFTEEN

Em swore, and Gyre wished she could mute the feed. She needed to think. She was barely clinging to the rock, like a lamprey hanging on desperately by just its mouth. She grappled for a hold in the stone, and her fingers found a small crack not yet worn smooth. She clawed her fingertips into it and locked that part of her suit, effectively clamping her on the rock for the time being. She then curled up, bringing her feet to rest against the wall nearby. Craning her head back as far as it could go, she looked around and took stock.

Em was now, blessedly, silent.

Her sense of direction was horribly skewed by the changes in angle, but she was fairly certain she was looking *up*, and to the left of where she'd entered. The passage was definitely getting bigger, which meant that the current should lessen the farther from the slot she was. If she pushed off and swam like hell for where the passage began bending back on itself again, the current would be broken. She could rest there.

Probably.

But she definitely couldn't stay here; the suit's grip on the crack wasn't perfect, and eventually the current would knock her free. Driving a new anchor was out of the question, with the force of the current pushing so hard on her. Any action now was better than dangling, feeling her grip slip millimeter by millimeter. Carefully, she aligned herself toward that probable bend and shimmied a few centimeters farther from the suction. Then she pushed off and put everything she had into swimming hard and fast against the current, her body as heavy as lead from the pressure against it. Her muscles screamed, her head ached, and her lungs burned, but she crawled bit by bit through the water until, suddenly, there was no resistance, and she shot through the water to her target.

Gyre slowed as she reached the apex of the curve in the passage. There were handholds here, and she wrapped her fingers around one, panting. The rebreather built into her suit was working on overdrive, barely able to keep up with her oxygen needs. She could hear it straining over the roar of blood in her ears, her cheeks tight and heavy from her exertion.

*If those scrubbers fail—*

On the other end of the line, Em sighed in relief.

"That enough for the day?" Gyre got out.

"Almost," Em said. "Although . . ."

Gyre's blood spiked with familiar anger at Em's single-mindedness, before fading again as she realized Em was right. *It will always be that bad, getting through.* The line would barely help at this point. In fact—

"How do I lay the line? With all those turns?"

"I . . . it's almost impossible to do it properly," Em said.

185

"With that current. Just leave slack in it, and put directional markers on it."

"Does this point work as an anchor?"

"That point will lead you to the correct side of the opening, so yes. Just leave enough slack that you can hold on to it while working back and forth."

"Right," Gyre said. She looked at her reel, where the line was taut. Caught on something, or just not enough of it? She'd almost forgotten it was in her hand during the swim. If she'd dropped it, she might not have noticed that, either. The thought terrified her.

She manually unspooled another several meters, then drilled the new bolt. Slowly, her muscles stopped burning, and her heart rate returned to normal. Almost in concert, her mind stopped racing too, and she was able to consider what to do next.

Going back now would mean she hadn't accomplished anything, apart from scaring herself. She looked around the bend.

There were multiple paths from here, it looked like: the bubble of a chamber bent off in different directions, and the whole room was a mess of current lines, though none as strong as the ones she'd just come through.

"You should place the anchor for your return trip before you do anything else," Em said. "Connect it with a jump line."

Gyre pulled her attention back to her anchor and finished tying off to it. "What?"

"You should have a short—very short—spool located just below where your third ration canister is stored. Release it," Em said.

One hand on the reel and anchor, she twisted, reaching

186

back and fumbling for the release. The smaller reel came free into her hand, and she attached the line, a different color and diameter, to the anchor.

"So your goal is to swim across this neck of the passage, to right before where the pushing current that will lead back is."

"Why not come out the way I came in, since we know where the current leads?"

"Too little control. That current . . . two divers have died on that specific swim. Where the tunnel does its sharp bend up, the current slams divers into that shelf."

*Good thing I didn't let go*, she thought. Then: *I'm as far as any of them ever made it.*

She wasn't sure if she was savagely proud or overwhelmingly scared. It was all running together.

Gyre pushed away from the wall, using the exertion to quell the shaking that threatened to consume her. It was blessedly free of silt, thanks to the current and the bolt drill. She swam carefully around the marked edge of the current's range. Reaching the other side, she focused on placing the bolt instead of the effort ahead of her just to get out safely.

She was glad Em hadn't given her all the excruciating details beforehand, glad she hadn't scoured the dossiers anew before diving in. She knew she would have overthought it, fixating on the shelf and not on her own direct survival. There was only so much the mind could parse at once.

Em . . . had gotten her through that passage.

Bolt in, she attached just the short reel.

"You can cut this line," Em said. "Store the rest."

"Got it," she replied, and obeyed. Then she followed the line back to her original anchor and took in the excess slack in her main reel. After a second's thought, she attached the diving line that came directly from her suit to the original line, then cut it and stored the spool. That way, she couldn't risk dropping it if she was overwhelmed again.

"Do you think you can take a break? You're in a neutral section, right now. It's the safest place, if you need to rest. You could even sleep here, if you tied into a safe part of the wall."

Gyre looked down at her dangling, floating legs. Sleep, where one malfunction could kill her in a matter of seconds? *Fuck no.* "Tell me what you know about the next part," she said.

"Not much. It's . . . the farthest anybody's gotten."

The words sent a shiver through Gyre, a heady mixture of panic and pride.

"Do you have any of those tunnels mapped yet?"

"A few. But things change."

"Give me one of the unmapped ones, then."

A marker appeared at the entrance to one of them, that headed back in the direction that she thought was the sump opening. A quick check on the map Em was building up confirmed it. It had no currents around it, but also seemed unlikely to be helpful. She kept herself from demanding another tunnel. An easy swim would be good right now.

She took it slow, putting in anchors as she navigated the edge of the cavern toward the chosen tunnel. She saw other bolts in the walls with scraps of line between them, and ignored them, as if they were ghosts sent to waylay her. She spent the next hour mapping the tunnel, which quickly turned out to be a dead end, but she and Em both knew it was a good opportunity for her to rest without feeling impotent. Or trapped. Em didn't speak much. Gyre supposed it was out of fear, and out of readiness for everything to end, just like it always did when people got this far.

She didn't feel like talking either.

Leaving the tunnel, she left her line in but studded it with markers that she and Em agreed would mean "nothing this way" for if she needed to double back. She moved slowly, pausing to let the scanners do their work in constructing the chamber from multiple angles. Her muscles appreciated the break, though they would have appreciated a massage more. Still, her brain was catching up with her weightlessness, and the disorientation of moving in three dimensions so freely was fading.

Surveying the rest of the chamber, she mentally checked off four of the tunnels as—probably, unless something had shifted—already mapped. That left only a few new options, two of which were across the chamber from where she was. Both led down, and started from a short, common branch.

"I'm going to lay line to the path I'm looking at," she said. "All right."

Em was growing more and more nervous. Gyre wished she had the bravado left to tell her to buck the fuck up, but the words felt ashen on her tongue. Em's worry was adding to her own stress, her own nerves. If they weren't careful, they'd start spiraling into full panic together.

Gyre began the methodical work of swimming closer, moving along the bottom of the chamber. She could feel the currents plucking and pushing at her back as she went, but they were all weak here, and she lessened her buoyancy until she had the strong tendency to sink.

It took fifteen minutes to reach the short branch, laying line as she went. Looking in, she could see the markers for strong currents, and she hesitated. Everything was a mess through there, and it wasn't much bigger than two people. No room to tack back and forth like she had on the way in. "Do you think that they'll cancel each other out on me, with enough weight?" she asked.

"It's—possible," Em said. "Definitely possible. But you can turn back for the day. Or try one of the low-probability passages."

"No, I want to see," Gyre said. The truth was, she didn't want to see. She was tired, and it was daunting, knowing that the currents could shift and the tunnel could lead anywhere—or nowhere. That she could get stuck. But she also didn't trust herself to get back in the water the next day. And she wanted to get a closer look at the tunnels; the floors seemed to wave back and forth in the current. It wasn't silt. Algae? It was the first sign of life she'd seen in this sump. After placing her anchor at the mouth of the branch, she swam in slowly, drawing close enough to get a better look.

The floor was covered in small, branching things that looked deep, translucent brown on her readout. She passed her hand over a patch, and they reacted, pulling back.

"Some kind of algae. Keep moving."

"It's the first we've seen, though," Gyre said. "Shouldn't it have been in the stiller parts?"

"Possibly. I—huh."

"Huh?"

"You're not in water anymore."

"Uh. I'm pretty sure I am."

"You're—you're in water, but it's not freshwater anymore. Or salt water. There's a host of other chemicals you don't usually see down there. The suit isn't equipped to read them all, but it might be what the algae's living off of, and why we're just seeing it now."

Gyre frowned. "I don't get it. It was just water when your parents were down here, right?"

"Yes. Which could mean this passage doesn't go anywhere,

and is just eroding some mineral bed further in. Either way, Gyre, your suit isn't rated for it. You need to turn back."

"Are there any negative effects from it?"

"Right now? Not yet. But without more data, and without bringing up a sample to the surface so my lab can analyze it, I can't predict—"

"Em, we both know this is one of the only sections you haven't tried yet. I'll have to go through it at some point." *I either go in now, or not at all.*

She couldn't make that decision for herself, not when she was in the same water as three dead cavers, as Hanmei. As Laurent.

Gyre waited for Em to do her calculations, not sure what conclusion she wanted her handler to land on. The suit wasn't showing any signs of failure; if it was an immediate death sentence, they'd have warning signs by now. But Em had seemed nervous about risking Gyre's life, ever since she returned at Camp Six.

If Em could decide Gyre's safety was more important than an answer, what did that mean?

"You're willing to continue?" Em asked, keeping her voice studiedly neutral.

It was a coward's answer, but clear enough. Em was still Em. "Just tell me if my suit starts degrading," she said. "I'll pull out immediately. I do want to be able to get out of here, after all."

"Right," Em said tightly.

Gyre nodded, then managed a smile as much for herself as for Em. "Hey—we could be close to the end. Yeah?"

"Yeah."

"Trust me. I've never died on a mission yet."

Em snorted. "You've never *been* on an actual mission."

"Yeah, but I also haven't died on one."

Gyre's smile strengthened, and she kicked up slightly to bring herself closer to the branch point. Neither option looked easier than the other. Both were just as tight, and the currents were already tugging at her suit.

"Flip a coin?" she asked.

"Gyre."

"Heads is the left branch."

Silence. Then the soft clink of a coin on the table. "You're going right," Em said.

Gyre nodded and turned that way. She headed for the pushing side of the current, though it was only as wide as two-thirds the width of her body. She did her best to narrow down her profile, swimming mostly with her legs, arms pressed out before her. She made it several meters up the passage, the current tearing at her, before she couldn't bear the pressure on the crown of her head. There was no handhold for her to cling to, but the passage was straight. No risk of a ledge smashing her brains out if she let go.

So she let go.

The current pushed her back toward the algae foyer. "Let's try the other one," Em said. Gyre opened her mouth to agree, swimming toward the left branch.

Then the suction current from behind her caught her up in it.

Before she could react, she was in the right-hand tunnel again, the water pulling her backward, faster and faster.

She shouted, twisting, trying to spread herself out and catch the pushing current again. "Em, I need weight!" she said, and she could feel her suit grow heavier, but the current was only growing stronger. A few meters in, the ejecting current ceased to exist, leaving only the inexorable drag. She jerked her arms and legs in as the passage hooked to one side, curling into a ball and covering her head as she struck the wall, rolling and bouncing along it. Pain blossomed in her shoulder and back, and then she was free of the rock again, just long enough for her to lift her head.

"Gyre!" Em shouted. "Shelf!"

She was rocketing toward one, where the passage hooked up suddenly and fanned out into a thin vent. "Buoyancy!"

"Won't help! Get ready!"

On instinct, she kicked with the current and angled herself up, and when the turn came, she flowed with the water around the shelf, chest scraping over the rock and slowing her progress—but her suit wasn't breached. She felt her line catch on the overhang, tug, and snap away. She shot through the vent.

The current lessened.

Her head spun, and she fought down the bile trying to rise in her stomach. Her body was shaking, and all she could hear was the pounding of her pulse in her ears. She couldn't see anything, and she thrashed, scrubbing her hands over her helmet. "Em? *Em?*"

She couldn't hear her own voice. Blind, she twisted in nothingness. She reached out in every direction and felt nothing except the light buffeting off the current behind her.

*I have to stay put.* No. *I have to get to air.* No. *I have to—I have to—*

She was going to die.

# CHAPTER SIXTEEN

Gyre cried out, a wordless howl, and she kicked, swimming hard in whatever direction she was pointed in. Em had been right all along. Everybody died. This entire project was *cursed*, and even though she'd thought she was in control, that she'd been smart and known her fears and judged the risk and made her own choices, she'd been wrong. She was going to die. She was going to—

Her hand spasmed, reached out without a conscious thought. Her fingers brushed rock.

It was jagged, broken, and she clung to it, urged on by the motors of her suit. *Em.* Em was controlling her suit. The connection hadn't been broken, and she shuddered, hauling herself close to the wall and closing her eyes. *Deep breaths*, she told herself, and the pounding in her head began to lessen. If Em could control her suit, could see this rock wall, then that meant it couldn't be the sensors. Maybe it was only the display.

Which meant the headlamp should still work. She lifted her head to toggle the light, then realized she could see without it.

"Gyre!"

Em's voice was clear and loud in her ears. Gyre bit back a sob of relief. "I'm here," she whispered.

"Thank god," Em said, then exhaled shakily. "The anxiolytics must be taking effect."

"What?"

"You panicked," she said. "You wouldn't stop screaming, and then you went quiet and stopped moving. I was afraid that . . . that . . . well."

"The comm line, it cut out," Gyre said, shaking her head and frowning. "The display, too. The suit—"

"Your suit is fine," Em said. "A few abrasions, but no damage to speak of. You were lucky."

"The comm line," Gyre repeated.

"It never closed," Em said gently.

Gyre twisted in the water, staring around her. There was no roiling silt here to obscure the reconstruction, and no currents to speak of except for a gentle fan behind her, the one that she had felt at her back. Her display was bright and clear. Gyre's frown deepened. Her thoughts felt foggy. The medication?

But all the drugs in the world could only dull the throbbing, aching truth.

"I . . . I can't swim back out," she said. *I'm going to die.*

Em appeared in the corner of her display, features drawn, expression hollow. Empty. Gyre knew what was coming. *No,* Em would say. *No, you can't. End of the line. Do you want to suffocate or be sedated?*

But she said nothing, only frowned, canted her head, her shoulders shifting as she typed. "You may not have to," she said at last. "Turn around."

Gyre stared, unmoving.

"Do it," Em said.

Slowly, Gyre twisted, her hand still clasped to the outcrop of stone Em had guided her to.

She was perched on the edge of a jagged opening, filled with cracked stone and giant, tumbled boulders that the water had yet to take the edge off of. It was maybe a meter wide at its narrowest point, and on the other side the walls appeared to be smooth.

Curved.

Gyre pushed off and kicked for the passage. It was exactly the same as the tunnel on the Long Drop, an oblong resting on its side in cross section, and there, a few meters up from the gap in the wall, her display shimmered at the water's surface. "This is—"

"Tunneler," Em confirmed.

Heart in her throat, Gyre broke the surface of the water, then dragged herself onto the smooth, sloped floor. The incline was almost too steep to lie on, but not quite, and she rolled onto her back, panting and staring at the arched ceiling.

*Tunneler.*

She was too numb, too exhausted, to be afraid.

Too numb to hope.

But maybe all she had to do was climb.

>>

She drifted in and out of consciousness, carried away on the wave of anxiolytics Em slowly weaned her off of. On Em's suggestion, she fumbled through the setup of a feeding, drifted as the paste pulsed into her. From time to time, she could hear Em's breathing. She didn't know if that was intentional or not, but it was alternately comforting and intensely irritating.

When she stirred and flexed one hand, Em cleared her throat. The video feed was off once more, an illusion of some sort of privacy.

"I'm awake," Gyre mumbled, and unscrewed the now-spent canister.

"Good. I have a plan."

*Climb.* That was the plan. Gyre groaned, closing her eyes.

"There's a strong chance this route is connected to the path up to the Long Drop," Em said. "However, even if it is the same tunnel, it may not be passable the whole way up. There's no way to know if this is the most recent trail it's left in the area, or if it's crossed it again and caused a collapse."

"That's reassuring," Gyre said, bitterness tingeing her voice. Em still sounded so calm. Analytical. Cold, like usual. There was no trace of the vulnerability she'd shown at Camp Six.

Well, Gyre had failed, hadn't she? That sump should have taken her to that last chamber, and instead, she'd fucked up and ended up who knew where. If she'd just put in a stronger anchor before she started swimming against those currents . . .

Gyre made herself roll over, then pushed up onto her hands and knees. It took every inch of her willpower. Her body ached, and the drugs had left her irritated and foggy now that they were mostly out of her system. Without them, she was teetering on the edge of panic again, but she refused to ask for another dose. Refused to descend back into that numbness. Instead, she let the anger of Em breaking her promise about injecting her at all take over.

It was amazing what being angry at someone for saving your life could do to clear your head.

"I'm sorry," Em said. "I hope it takes you home too, but I've lost too many people down there. I have to be practical. That's my job."

"*Practical,*" Gyre parroted back, lips curling into a snarl. "You've already written me off, haven't you?"

"No. Of course not."

"Why didn't you just throw the kill switch when I ended up here? When I lost my chance?"

She hoped that made Em flinch.

"Because I'm not a *murderer*, Gyre," Em said, her voice tight and high now. "Because you're still alive, and as long as that's the case, I'm going to do everything in my power to get you through this."

"You put me *in* this, Em! So drop the act." Gyre balled one hand into a fist and slammed it into the smooth rock below her. "Can't you just be scared for *one* minute?"

"I'm terrified!" Em shot back, and there it was; the stress turned into anger, turned into something honest. "But as far as I see it, I have two options: one, break down and stop being able to help you, or two, *be a fucking professional.*"

God, that was refreshing.

"I suppose one of us has to be," Gyre said after a beat, and smiled.

Em replied with a wordless, strangled shout, followed by audible, heavy breathing. Finally, she composed herself enough to say, "I know that you are under unimaginable stress. I know that you thought you were going to die. I'm sorry. I thought you might die too. But you didn't."

Gyre exhaled shakily and then shook her head. "Okay," she muttered. *I'm sorry.* She wanted to take Em by the shoulders, shake her, demand that she apologize specifically for every selfish decision that had brought Gyre here. Except Em had given her a way out yesterday. Except maybe none of this would have happened if Gyre had just hauled gear, talked to Em, stopped her that way. Except it had been Gyre who had looked at Jennie Mercer, looked at Isolde on that tape, and decided that she *owed* something to people she had never met, people who had never been her responsibility.

And now here she was, facing death, and she'd never get to set this right.

Her face burned.

"Don't be afraid," Em said. "If I'm right, it's just a long walk. You can do this."

"Shut up," Gyre whispered, and shoved herself upright.

She staggered, unsteady on her rubbery legs, and stared up the smooth tunnel.

"You can rest more," Em pointed out. "Sleep, if you need to."

"It's just a long walk," Gyre replied, then took a step. It was like moving a fifty-kilo weight.

"Use a line."

"I don't need one." The slope was steep but manageable, smooth but not glasslike. Her next step was a little easier, then the next a little more.

*You know how to do this.*

She sucked in a deep breath, her ribs spreading with it, pressing into the suit carapace. *You know how to do this; you're built for this.* One step followed the next, and soon she'd remembered the rhythm, the strain on her chest and her legs, the bob of her head and the sink of her hips. She didn't need a line.

Em was quiet for a long time after that, and the only sound was Gyre's breathing echoing in her helmet. The path ahead of her curved ever so slightly to the left for the first kilometer, then back to the right after that. Aside from that curve and the incline that kept her calves burning with effort, each step was the same as the last. The composition of the rock around her barely changed. It was all tightly compacted, unnatural, as if the walls had been coated with a sealant. The Tunneler, when it swam through stone, must push the rock out of its path into what little space there was between each molecule, each atom. And from that tight compaction came a faint glimmer, the rock compressed into a refractive matrix.

It lost any magic it held after the first hour.

Her head felt full of plastic stuffing the longer she walked without something new to see. She cycled through display options, from full brightness to a sickly pink overlay showing porosity—all homogeneous, all unchanging, all the same disgusting color—to just her headlamp. That last setting brought her nerves back in full force, the first time since washing up on the shore of the tunnel that she'd remembered that sensation in Camp Five of being watched, of that paranoia when Em was still checking her blood for signs of intoxication.

She switched back to full brightness quickly.

When her shins began to scream from the constant slope, Gyre stopped walking. She stared back at the empty passage below her, curving gently to one side until the walls seemed to merge into each other in her reconstruction. Should she eat again? How long had it been since she'd eaten at the bottom of the slope? How much should she conserve her now-limited supplies? Should she keep moving? Her head ached.

Em began to hum, instead of offering any useful input.

Gyre clenched her jaw and began walking again.

Her throat was dry, and she sipped at her straw, eyeing her display. With terrain so easy to traverse and so unchanging, maybe she could split her attention, find a distraction from the way her thoughts refused to flow in order, from the way the skin along her spine crawled from seemingly nothing. But her only options were videos of the team and the dossier on her mother. Just her mother's name was enough to make her chest contract, and she closed the viewer.

*Later. I'll look at it later.*

*Once I'm safe again.*

Em continued to hum, and said nothing.

Another hour crawled by as she continued walking to no-where, her thoughts turning murky and thick. *I'll just be even farther from her when I die, is all.*

The terrain remained unchanged, step by step. She barely looked anymore, barely saw at all, her eyes unfocused. Slowly, though, she began to notice small whisper-thin dots, fragments shifting along the right edge of her vision, and she turned, slowed.

Small specks glided past her, barely more than a ripple on the ground until she turned her full attention on them. They were the same density as the surrounding stone, or close to it, and her reconstruction couldn't always differentiate them. At first there were only a few, and then more, and then a great wave of skittering motion. Gyre took a step back, toward the curved wall, fixated on them. Insects, all of them, some kind of tiny bug, and all going down, down, down, back the way she'd come. Her heart quickened. Her throat closed up. She hadn't seen any sign of motile life since Camp Five with its tiny fish and crabs, and there could be nothing for them here. Nothing to eat, nothing to find. There wasn't even lichen growing on the walls.

Yet they flooded past her, crawling over her boots.

Em said nothing, only hummed.

The flow began to thin, and then they were gone.

Gyre swallowed and started to walk again. She thought of asking Em if she had seen them, but she was too afraid to know the answer. If they had been real, wouldn't Em have reacted? But if they weren't, wouldn't Gyre's sudden pause have worried her? Wouldn't Em have comforted her? And instead, it was just that droning. Not a song, not music, just an unending, rhythmless tune.

"Stop humming," Gyre snapped, when she couldn't stand it anymore.

"I'm not," Em said.

"You've been humming for the last two hours." Gyre shook her head, frustrated, then froze.

There was no humming.

But there was a ringing in her ears, soft and barely noticeable. It sounded a lot like Em's humming, but not quite as real as the other woman's sigh at the other end of the line. Gyre couldn't help but drink up that sound.

"Probably a stress hallucination," Em said.

"A hallucination," Gyre repeated. She slowed, then stopped, leaning against one of the walls. She stared up at the stretch of tunnel before her, no different from the one behind. "No. I'm not hallucinating." Not the sound—she hadn't hallucinated the sound. The bugs, maybe, but not the sound. She couldn't be hallucinating it *all*.

"A response to the environment, maybe. Tinnitus, in the absence of other input."

"I *heard* you. The whole time. Why weren't you talking to me? Keeping me occupied? If it's a response to the environment—"

"This is normal, for what it's worth," Em responded, her voice carefully controlled to be comforting, gentle. "Given your circumstances."

"Do you mean the isolation, the lack of food, or the certainty of death?" Gyre pictured Isolde's face hovering in the darkness, then glanced over her shoulder, half expecting to see something—different. But there was only the unchanging, gentle slope. The same curved walls. "There's nothing normal about this, Em!"

Em said nothing.

Gyre scowled and turned her attention back to the path.

"Have you heard or seen anything else?"

*Your mother.* Gyre forced the thought away. It had been the spores, hadn't it? Except . . . Em had said that there had been no trace of any contamination in her suit. No indication that it had ever affected her at all.

Gyre swallowed thickly. "Shut up."

"I need to know, for your safety."

"My *safety.* Good one. No—I'm fine. There's not much we can do if I'm not, anyway, right?" The back of her neck prickled; Gyre ignored it. The bugs had gone down, back to the sump, and for a moment it was like she wanted to follow them. Like they were drawing her back, plucking at her skin, her nerves.

"Medication," Em suggested. "A longer rest."

"I don't want to sleep in here. And I definitely don't want you dosing me anymore."

Em turned on the video feed again and met Gyre's eyes. She was exhausted herself, unwashed, her curls picked apart into frizz. "No drugs. But sleep—I'll keep watch for you," she said. How she sounded so confident, so in control, despite how destroyed she looked, Gyre couldn't make sense of.

*Because I'm hallucinating?*

"At the very least, you should eat," Em said.

Gyre shook her head. "I need to conserve rations. Walking isn't hard."

"But the sump was, and stress is." Em shifted, her shoulder rising as if she were lifting a hand. Then she stopped, hesitated, grimaced, and lowered it again. What had she been about to do? Introduce more drugs? Force Gyre to sit down? Or maybe Gyre was just imagining the gesture.

Whatever it was, she hadn't done it, Gyre reminded herself.

"Please," Em said. "Please, for me?"

*For her.*

Gyre wanted to laugh, to shout. To cry. The tears were already there, waiting. "I don't want to do anything for you right now," she whispered, but she sank to her knees all the same. The last thing she wanted was to serve at Em's will, but at the same time, it was such an easy win. Follow the command, feed her growling, taut stomach. If she followed every command Em laid out, wouldn't it take her out of here?

Possibly not. But food was food. And she wasn't ready to die yet.

"Gyre," Em said softly.

"I know," she said. "Stress. Sorry." She loosened a canister from its slot. Two down, but she still had enough to last her the better part of a week, and Em was right. She'd need her strength. "Stop being so nice," Gyre added.

Em's lips tightened into a thin line, and she looked away. "I can do that," she said after a moment. "But I—"

"I don't want your guilt," Gyre said. *You caring is why I made the decision to go on.* "Just—just treat this like it's part of the expedition."

"I thought you wanted me to be afraid. Or to be talking to you."

"I don't know what I want you to be! Just not . . . not this." She groaned and let her head fall back against the wall, then fumbled with the port at her side. Started her meal. Shuddered. "I don't know."

"I almost lost you," Em murmured.

"You still might."

Em's expression was stricken as Gyre looked at the little picture of her in the corner of her screen. She winced. Turned off the video feed.

She didn't want to be feeling any of this.

*Think about the pseudocave*, she told herself. *Think about the first time you almost died.* She'd been terrified then, too, but she'd been giddy. Pumped up on adrenaline, excited to fight. It hadn't lasted her all the way out, but it had gotten her up, kept her moving long enough. If she could just grasp on to that again . . .

"I'm not going to die," Gyre murmured.

And then she sat back and waited for her feeding to finish.

# CHAPTER SEVENTEEN

She walked for five more hours, the incline staying shallow enough that there were only two occasions where she put bolts in to scale sudden pitches, too smooth to climb without a rope. Still, by the end of the day, she was exhausted and weak, brain fried by the constant evenness of her environment. It was as if she could feel the thrum of a Tunneler on some back channel of her brain, an echo off the stone it had bored through as it passed. Without input, her brain seemed bent on creating its own stimulation. There were no more skittering insects, but she had songs stuck in her head that sounded like they came from far away, and the movement of her hand at the edge of her display became a distant figure more than once. It wasn't constant, but it was relentless.

And then the feeling of being watched came back.

It had been a prickle, a crawling in the back of her mind just after the bugs had passed her, making their way down to the sump. Now it was a bone-deep dread, a sickness in her stomach. It strengthened in waves, and the more she fought it, the stronger it grew. She felt it like a presence, like a tug at her center, like she was forgetting something she shouldn't be. If she just turned around, she would see them: Isolde, or some other stranger—perhaps Hanmei, waterlogged, or Jennie, legs broken into impossible angles—waiting for her. It didn't matter that there were no hiding places in this passage, that it was impossible for anybody to have followed her. Down here, she could imagine them emerging from the blankness of the walls, as phantom-thin as the insects.

She clamped down with as much willpower as she could muster, refusing to let herself look over her shoulder or signal to Em in any way that she was losing her grip on reality.

Maybe something in her suit *was* breaking down. Maybe Em had been wrong about Camp Five's spores, and they'd gotten through the suit's filtration. Just because they hadn't been in her bloodstream by the time Em had checked didn't mean they hadn't done irreparable damage. She could see it now, scans of her brain marked by great black holes where the spores had eaten away at her. Or maybe the chemicals in that final, horrible sump had started some slow rotting of the suit itself. She tried to remember if Em had gone into detail about the tests she'd run. *Had* she tested Gyre's blood? She couldn't remember the feeling of blood being taken, but would she have even noticed? Em had said she was clear, that she was fine, but ... *Can I trust what she said?*

*Can I trust that she even said it?*

Gyre pictured the commands that would take her to the medical readouts in her suit. She could look at the log, look at how much of each drug was left, look at test results—if Em had run them. If she hadn't scrubbed them.

But she was too afraid to look. If Em had run the tests, if it hadn't been the spores, then Gyre had seen Isolde, and that meant that Gyre could be sensing something *real*. Something impossible, following just behind her.

She made camp after seven hours of mindless walking. Em had tried starting conversations several times over the course of the day, but Gyre had only grunted in reply, too nervous that her unease and growing panic would seep into anything she said, too afraid that what she was hearing wasn't Em at all. It had made the climb feel like an eternity.

"It looks like there's a change up ahead," Em said as Gyre sat back, her head against the rock, staring at nothing and wondering if she wanted to use up one of her remaining meals.

Real? Not real? She didn't lose anything for looking, she decided. Heart thudding in her chest, Gyre turned her head toward whatever it was Em was seeing. Her reconstruction showed only the curved walls of the tunnel. She hesitated a moment, then took a leap, desperate for interaction. "Don't see it," she said.

"It's not clear enough for the computer to shunt it to you," Em said. "Lots of uncertainty. Can you get closer?"

A new terror bubbled up into her throat, threatening to choke her as she staggered to her feet and took two lurching steps up the passage. *Not clear enough for the computer to shunt it to you.* How often did that happen? She'd thought about Em deliberately hiding things from her, but not about the computer algorithms making sure she never saw *confusing* things. If the computer knew another person couldn't be down there, would it hide movements? Signs?

Computers didn't work like that, she reminded herself. Not clear enough meant that it was far away, or at a weird angle. There wasn't anything lurking just at the limits of her sonar.

There couldn't be.

"There's a branch-off," Em said, interrupting her thoughts. "It could lead back into the main system."

"Or nowhere." Gyre straddled a deep crack in the rock, then stopped, staring down.

It was the first change in the tunnel all day.

The reconstruction expanded, mapping out all the gaps and dips and uneven patches of stone until, finally, she reached a jagged gap in the rock. It was a drop through the bottom left of the tunnel, out into a large cavern. Much of the floor below appeared to be covered in water, but across the cavern there looked like there were a few accessible banks. Large, divot-topped, tiered pillars stretched toward the ceiling from the water.

Gyre braced her hands on either side of the opening, staring. She knew those pillars. She knew that water. It called to her, and she nearly fell to her knees.

"Is that—"

"It's not the lake by Camp Six," Em said.

Her heart fell and frustrated tears welled up behind her eyes with fierce pressure. She fought it down. *Wrong, wrong, this is all wrong.*

"But I might know where you are now," Em continued cautiously. "I'll need you to go down there for a better look, though. If it's where I think you are, I can get you back to the surface. And there should be older caches nearby."

The surface.

She could barely think, picturing the sun, the cracked soil, her tiny cot. *The surface.* If she climbed down there, if she made her way back up to the cave entrance, it would all be over. Screw Jennie and the others, screw trying to fix this. Screw whoever came down next—that had never been her responsibility.

*She* was the only responsibility she'd ever had.

Gyre backed away from the crack in the stone. "Should I eat, then?" she rasped. Her voice sounded strained, barely human. She cleared her throat. "Before I rappel down there?" She didn't like the thought of using one of her few remaining rations, not so soon after having two others, but the less she ate, the weaker she'd get. She couldn't be weak. And Em's answer should give her a good idea of how safe Em thought she really was. Hold off, and Em was worried. Go ahead, and everything would be fine.

"I think so," Em said.

*Everything will be fine.*

Gyre settled down heavily, gut uncramping at Em's permission. When she reached for her ration, she realized her hand was shaking. She could feel herself swaying on a thin tightrope, clinging to the assumption that she wouldn't die, while understanding that she almost certainly would. Too much confidence, and the balance would fall apart. Too much cynicism and she'd give up.

But that cynicism felt so good, so right, so inevitable. She was fucked, and she wanted to languish in it.

Her eyes went back to the crack. *Or*, she thought. *Or we keep pushing, and I fall apart later.*

That was what the Gyre from before the sump would have done. What *she* would have done.

She seated the canister into the port on her side, then let her head drop forward into her hands. The sludge pushed through the cannula and into her gut, and as it flowed, she became aware of every centimeter of her skin covered by the barely there whisper of sticky, body-warm gel. The electrodes coming from her flesh, her scalp; the unrelenting structure of the suit polymers and machines; the distance between her cheeks and her palms. She fought the urge to take her helmet off or rip the canister from her side. Each feeding was getting harder to bear, half because of fear and hunger, half because of this growing physical irritation. She couldn't tell if it was only in her head, or if something was beginning to go wrong. Her skin itched. Her joints hurt.

She wanted to be done.

"Gyre."

"Don't want to talk," she muttered.

Her video feed blinked on, and Gyre stared at it, too tired to turn it off. Em looked pristine. She'd changed her clothing at some point, and her hair was pulled back neatly at the nape of her neck. "You've gone past stressed. You sound terrified."

"I'm trying to ignore that," Gyre said, scowling. Em couldn't know. If Em knew, she'd give up on her, write her off—as good as dead, another failure.

"I've seen this before, once the shock starts to fade. Once you start to feel trapped."

"I *am* trapped!"

Nothing.

"I don't need to be psychoanalyzed," Gyre muttered. "I need to get out of this *stupid* suit, I need to see the fucking *sun*."

Em rested her chin on her fist, gazing at the screen that Gyre assumed had her face on it. Maybe it didn't. Maybe it was just a bland readout of her hormone levels. Cortisol high. Adrenaline high. Was there even a camera inside her helmet, or was she just a static headshot in a dossier?

"I need you to concentrate on only the next step in front of you," Em said. "I'll manage your resources; I'll keep you going. I'm going to get you out of there—myself, if I have to."

Em, climbing down into this hellhole. The thought was perversely pleasing.

"If down there is where you think it is," Gyre said, "how bad is the climb out?" Em was right. If she focused on the next steps, one at a time, they'd be manageable. Tasks she knew she could do. One foot in front of the other. She rubbed at the surface of her helmet, wishing she could massage her temples through the polymer.

Em hesitated, then conceded, "Bad. Part of it is through an active waterfall. There's also only one cache you're going to be able to reach easily. It's half empty, and has been sitting there a long time. Not everything will be usable. But it's still rations, a few batteries, more line."

Gyre grimaced. "Will it even still *be* there?"

"Unless there's been more Tunneler activity that I don't know about, it should be."

Or unless it was stolen like the other one.

"This route, it rejoins the route I took?"

"Yes. Near Camp Four."

No resources she could count on, then, if this cache that was on the way was as depleted as Em was saying. She groaned, sat back, stretched out her spine. But at least it would cut off the ascent up the Long Drop. It could be worse. "And then the dive to Camp Three."

"Yes."

"And it's worth it? Instead of just going forward?"

"I still don't know if this tunnel leads to that ledge. And if you refuse to sleep in here, things could—deteriorate."

Gyre winced. *Deteriorate.* Em could tell, could see what was happening to her. If Gyre could just trust her, rely on her, lean a little bit into . . . what? Em wasn't here to put a hand on her shoulder, to hold her tight. She was just a voice in her helmet.

A current of drugs in her arm.

Was Em beginning to feed her anxiety meds again, to counteract her irrationality? If she focused, would she feel the fog creeping in at the edge of her thoughts, just enough to make her reliable again?

Gyre hesitated, then toggled the medical interface. Nothing was active. There was the counter for the anxiolytics, and a log showing one dose used, dated to the sump. Adrenaline, one dose. Sedatives . . .

Three.

Gyre stared.

*Three* doses. One on its own, then two in succession. She checked the log on the double dose; it had been spread out over more than sixteen hours. And there were other logs too—blood samples taken, tests run, all in the same time frame. At Camp Six.

She'd felt like she'd slept for days because she *had*.

Her stomach lurched, spasming against the feeding tube. Em hadn't said she was sedating her. Em hadn't said she'd been out for over a day, unprotected and vulnerable. Em had told her everything had been fine.

But everything hadn't been fine. Em had broken her promise—again. Gyre should never have trusted her.

Should she trust her *now*?

"Gyre?" Em murmured. "Feeding's done."

"Right," she said, shivering. "Better get climbing." Gyre tried to sound cheerful as she unhooked the canister, but even she could tell it sounded brittle and wrong. She stared down at her hands, at the metal tube that had held a terrifyingly high portion of all the food left to her. Had she taken this one from Camp Five's cache?

Had the seal protected it from the spores?

"You can rest before the descent," Em said, her voice so soft, so gentle.

Gyre jerked forward, a whole-body response to the idea, then covered the involuntary twitch by rolling up to her knees, putting away the spent ration. "Absolutely not," she said. "I'm not sleeping up here." *I'm not letting you sedate me again.* Her legs quivered as she stood up, but her hands didn't shake as she began putting in bolts. The stone was already fractured, so she put in multiple anchors, silently thanking herself for insisting on taking them with her.

If she hadn't swapped the climbing anchors into her suit, what would she have done? The silt screws couldn't take her weight. More proof that all she needed to do was trust her instincts; they'd brought her this far.

Everything seemed stable, but she didn't want to risk a fall from this height, even—perhaps especially—into water. She had no idea what currents were lurking beneath that lake, though she could certainly hope for none, since Em had said this didn't lead back to the sump.

*If* Em was right. If the computers were right.

Once the anchors were in and her ropes were set up, she checked her attachments to the line. One hand twitched, threatening to descend into full-blown tremors, but as she stared at it, it firmed up. If she was lucky, it would just be an adrenaline-pumping free-air descent—enough to ground her in her body again—then a brief swim, and hopefully an easy walk up to dry land. Then she could try to sleep.

She hoped she hadn't used up all her luck surviving the sump.

She hoped she'd been hallucinating at Camp Five. She hoped Em had gotten the spores out of her system. Because beyond everything else, she hoped she wasn't really being followed. A few quick tugs, or a blade, and the ropes—

She hoped, she hoped, she hoped, *she hoped*.

*No.* Gyre steadied herself, forcing away the thoughts, then began walking backward down the edge of the hole. From there, she swung out into the open air, fingers gripping vice-like around the bars of her rappel device.

Her equipment held. She sighed in relief, and heard an echoing exhale on Em's line. "Nervous?" Gyre asked, chancing a glance at the screen, her old bravado rearing up reflexively and snugging tight around her like a crusted bandage.

"Watch your hands," Em said.

Gyre's smirk faded. She concentrated on working her rappel device, easing her fingers apart by degrees, making sure the rope was feeding through smoothly. She could see the approach of the water from the corner of her eye, the surface rendered a placid, unmoving dark blue to set it apart from the surrounding stone. The wrongness resting in her gut eased. This was familiar, this was good. Hanging from the rope, she could think straight again. The pull of gravity, tugging her down, felt strong, and right.

Get to the ground, climb back out. She'd done this before.

She toggled through the display options reflexively, learning the cavern, memorizing the layout. The last known depth of the pool was only a meter where she was headed, so there shouldn't be any swimming needed. Good—her legs burned too much to be useful in the water. The composition of the rock here was similar to Camp Four. And her headlamp showed a blue luminescence beneath the surface of the water, familiar and comforting.

Her headlamp also showed a figure standing in the water. The figure sank below the surface.

"Em?" she whispered.

There were no ripples, no sign that anything had been there. But she'd seen it, the darkened outline of shoulders, of a head, disappearing into the surrounding gloom. Her heart stuttered in her chest, and she closed one hand around the rope in reflexive fear. There—again. It was just a flash, a shadow in the glow. It looked like a body, floating just below the surface of the water. Moving. Impossible.

*No. No, no, no.* "Em!" she shouted, fumbling and turning the reconstruction back on. The cavern was bathed in analytical gray light, every feature marked out, every object unmoving. The surface of the water was once again rendered in flat blue, impenetrable. She tried the other settings.

Nothing.

"What is it?"

There was nothing out of the ordinary. Everything around her was static. Erased? Had the computer removed the "confusing" input? Or was whoever it was too far below the surface for the sonar to find?

Or was it another figment? Was she contaminated, her mind already twisting into knots?

"Did you see that?" she asked, turning her head from side to side, searching.

"Did I see what?"

"The—the reconstruction feed, it records, right? Even if it's not displayed? Can you—"

"Yes, but it will take a minute to pull up. Gyre, what's going on?" Her voice had gone from tired and distracted to alert, sharp.

"I saw somebody," Gyre whispered.

Em said nothing.

"Em, there's somebody down there. I saw them, in the

216

water. Out in the deeper part of the lake. It was a person; it was definitely a person." Her panic was growing, taking physical form in her chest, sitting on her and pressing down with all its weight. She wrapped both arms around the rope, hugging tight to it, eyes fixed on the ground below.

"You turned off the reconstruction."

"I know. My headlamp—"

Em shook her head, the motion drawing Gyre's attention through her panic. "Breathe, Gyre. Your lamp doesn't reach that far. It's probably just the nerves and exhaustion, combined with the darkness."

"I saw it against the glow! There's somebody there!"

"The human brain projects stimuli where there are none, when it's overworked or deprived."

"What, like your humming?" Gyre snapped.

"Exactly like the humming. It's a known phenomenon. Under stress, people hear things, or sometimes see darting shadows. Sensory deprivation chambers induce very realistic hallucinations of flashing lights and presences. It usually happens in places that would be distressing. Like this. There could even be infrasonic noise, maybe from the Tunneler, making you uneasy. It's fixable."

Fixable. Fixable, unless all her *food* was contaminated—how had she missed that until now? "My feeding—it's from Camp Five—"

"It's fine," Em said. "You're fine."

"Was I *fine* when you had me sedated at Camp Six?" Gyre asked, her voice cracking.

Em didn't respond.

"I saw. I saw the logs," Gyre hissed, hoping she was ashamed. Hoping it hurt.

"It was a safety precaution," Em said, voice strangled at

first. But when she spoke again, she'd regained her footing, her tone firm. *Arrogant.* She leaned in toward the camera. "I've run every diagnostic I can. I checked all your food. You were fine. You *are* fine, just under too much pressure."

Gyre's lip curled. If it wasn't the spores, then it was *her.* *Crazy,* Em was saying. *Unreliable.* "Em—"

"I already checked," Em said firmly. "Your sonar didn't pick up any trace of a living thing down there. There are no other concerns with people mapping this cave system, or anywhere within at least sixty kilometers. You're alone."

"And the cache at Camp Four? I didn't hallucinate *that.*"

"No, you didn't," Em admitted. "But whoever or whatever moved it couldn't have used those supplies without one of my suits. They couldn't have made it this far. It's impossible. You're alone, Gyre. You're seeing things."

"And why should I believe that? From you?" Gyre growled, one hand releasing from the rope, fingers scrambling over the outside of her helmet as if she could shut out Em's voice by covering her ears, or take the whole fucking thing off. Her skin crawled beneath the feedback film. "If there's somebody else down here—"

"There's *not!*"

"—you'd hide them in the name of *caver management*; you'd keep me blind to them until the second they came up behind me if you thought it'd save your precious, insane mission—"

"Gyre, you're spiraling. I'll give you another injection of anxiolytics. It'll help."

"The fuck you will," Gyre snarled. She sucked in air, desperate to quell her shaking, then puffed out her breath to cycle through the options displayed inside her helmet. She needed to shut Em out long enough for her to get down to the ground, check the whole chamber. She needed Em *out* of her suit, her display, her head. It was like Em lived there now, deep in the recesses, in the folds and valleys of gray matter, a voice riding shotgun in her brain. Maybe it hadn't been stress, back in the tunnel. Maybe when she'd felt that sick sensation that she was being watched, it was because she could hear Em's breathing, the faint sound of her shifting at her desk. Em, always there but not there, necessary but ultimately useless, so useless. Worse than useless.

*Dangerous.*

"Gyre, what are you doing?" Em asked. Her fear was just a small note over careful, flat affect, but it was growing stronger. Her eyes had widened, her cheeks paled. Good. Let her be afraid, not for Gyre, but for herself. Let her marinate in it, even if it was only the fear of failure, of having to start over again, of having to live with that guilt added to the pile.

If Gyre was going to die down here, let Em feel it. Let it break her.

Gyre closed the comm line, and then reopened it to a different frequency. She couldn't lock communications closed altogether, but she could leave Em behind, and commit herself to a nonexistent line, a ghost channel. Silence expanded around her, only broken by the heaving of her breast. The lower corner of her display was replaced by the cave.

"What now?" she asked the emptiness, then laughed, sitting down heavily. "Lock my suit, drug me—but you're on your own now, just like I am."

Nothing answered her.

She waited for retaliation, for the fuzzying of the world from antianxiety drugs, or maybe a sedative, for her suit to lock up, securing her on the rope, for Em to find a way around the communications block. But nothing happened. Slowly, she cycled through her display options, illuminating the motion-less cavern and the pool below in varied colors and textures until, finally, she switched back to her headlamp.

There had been nothing, no signs of movement, but she had to be sure. She didn't want the smallest chance of interference.

She opened her faceplate, getting rid of the HUD entirely. The air was cool. Real.

She could feel the cave on her flesh.

All her training screamed for her to close her helmet again, to stop venting heat, to restore the integrity of the suit that was the only thing keeping her safe and alive down here, but she couldn't do it. For the first time in weeks, she could feel the real world, curling against her cheek, filling her lungs.

For the first time in a long time, she could trust everything she was perceiving.

The water waited below her, the faint, ghostly glow beck-oning. A meter deep. She could stand in a meter, could see the bottom.

Gyre began descending again, her fingers clumsy on the rappel rack. She went slowly, craning her head in every direc-tion, pausing every few meters to check for movement. Nothing shifted. Nothing changed as she slid down the line, as her feet broke the surface of the water, as she sank in up to her hips. As she fumbled to unclip herself, her heart raced, and she couldn't stand still, couldn't think. She could almost feel the closing of fingers around her ankle, and she worked blindly, looking only at the water around her. She felt trapped, tethered, until she closed the rappel device back into her suit and began staggering for the nearby shore. The sound of sloshing water filled her ears, no longer filtered through her helmet. It was so loud, so sharp. It made her want to lie down and feel the water lapping against her skin.

But there was somebody in here. She needed to stay alert. She needed to *find* them.

Nothing moved but the shadows racing away from her lamp, and the ripples of the water as she passed. No faces peered out at her from crevices in the rock as she hauled herself from the water. She paced away from the shore, and slowly walked the perimeter of the lake, clambering over smooth outcroppings, skirting the edge.

She checked every niche, every hollow.

She waded into the shallow inlets, searching the bottom of the lake until all that was left were the darker, deeper regions. For those, she would have to dive. The water of the lake beckoned again, but she fought the urge to plunge below. The glowing fungus in the water stopped her.

Even if she could see unimpeded without her faceplate, she could still be contaminated. *Fuck*. What had she done?

She closed her helmet and took several deep, steadying breaths, then bent double, pushing her head below the surface above the darker, deeper reaches. Her light pierced through the water, marrying with the soft glow. She could see everything, and all she could find was rock, huge pillars and worndown boulders.

She was alone.

Gyre hauled herself back out onto land. A low moan built in the back of her throat, and she crawled away from the bank. She tried to feel relief, to feel safe, but there was only numbness there, emptiness. What did it matter, feeling safe, if there had never been a threat to begin with?

Em had been right. Isolation, stress, whatever lingering effects those spores might be having on her brain . . . she couldn't be left on her own, unmonitored. She was compromised. What had she been thinking? That Em would be disgusted with her, would hate her, would abandon her. That, given proof of Gyre's weakness, she'd leave.

And now Gyre was alone anyway. Alone, foolish, and humiliated.

Gyre pulled up the communications settings, face burning. It rankled, crawling back apologetic for her broken brain, but this wasn't a day's descent. This wasn't *easy*. This wasn't something she could do by herself, no matter how much she wanted to.

She tried to close the silent comm line.

It refused.

# CHAPTER EIGHTEEN

Gyre was not a technician.

She'd always cared more about the physical part of caving. The burn of her muscles as she free-climbed out of a deep slot canyon, the dehydration, the burst of energy, the sheer skill involved in smearing up an almost featureless wall. She'd thought of and prepared for the suit as a necessary evil, and she'd avoided learning everything about it that she safely could.

And she hated herself for it as she cycled through every setting she could find, none of them restoring her link to Em.

She'd tucked herself into a small niche in the stone, a den with two entrances that she could watch from one vantage point. Sometime in the past hour, she'd begun shivering violently, and another ration canister and some water hadn't helped. It had just left her with one less food source.

The silent channel sat open, its little green light burning in the lower right of her vision right next to the recording indicator, still going despite the change in connection. They mocked her. Communications open and preserved for the future, but made of nothing.

She had to try something else. If she kept sitting there, she'd lose what little grip on her sanity she had left. She heaved herself upright, her chest seizing with the effort, her shoulders hunching in protective anticipation.

Nothing moved beyond the ring of stone.

Gyre eased out into the open, legs heavy with exhaustion and nerves. She leaned one hand on the rock as she walked out into the open, trying to take stock. She had to come up with a plan.

Em had given her no signs yet, no injections to calm her, no guiding of her hand. It was as if it wasn't only their voices cut off from each other. But she must still have access to the readouts of Gyre's suit. The comm line was only that—a way to talk. The rest would still function.

Right?

She needed to pose a direct question, then, ask for help. Maybe . . . maybe apologize.

The ground beneath her feet was smooth and hard. There was no dust to write in. The lake, on the other hand, likely had silt at its bottom. With a grimace, Gyre edged toward the still margin of the pool, then waded out ankle-deep into it, watching for the bloom of uncertainty as her sensors picked up roiling silt. There had been silt, right? She stomped and slid her feet, but nothing changed.

She flipped through filters, but they all showed the same thing. The water was clear. She could see straight to the bottom. The only difference was that, when she switched to the beam of her headlamp and looked at the water from an angle, she saw the glow.

The glow. The glow that had convinced her there was a body somewhere in the lake. Of course.

It was the same hue as the growths in the lake by Camp Six, and it was strong. She crouched and ran her fingers over the bottom, then pulled her hand back above the water. Her fingertips glowed. An image of the fungus eating through her suit seized her, but she ignored it and instead plunged both hands into the pool, gathering and scooping until she had a handful of spongy luminescence.

She took it to the nearest flat expanse of rock and hunkered down, mounding her paint beside her work space. What should she write? Start with the apology, or keep it simple? She went back and forth between each option, until she realized that the glow was beginning to fade. The fungi were dying, or already dead, and their light didn't last long.

Gyre pushed it against the stone, scrawling out *PLEASE* on the ground in front of her. She fumbled through her sampling options and took a still image of the message.

And then she realized that she couldn't send it.

Voice communications were down. The video link had gone with them. She didn't know how to upload a photo, so how could she get it in front of Em? She could wait for Em to find it, scraping through all the data from her suit, or she could keep staring at it until she faded, but what if it wasn't enough?

What if communications meant *all* communications between the suit and base?

No. Impossible. Em had closed the line before, and she hadn't lost all ability to contact Gyre. But Gyre had done it through settings she didn't understand, had established a connection with the yawning silence of the empty channel.

What if Em couldn't see anything?

Gyre heard a high-pitched whine, then realized it was coming through her own throat. As if emboldened by the acknowledgment, it grew louder, until she was part of it, keening and dropping her head between her knees.

*You arrogant fuck-up, what have you done?* It was her thought, but she heard it in her dad's voice. Her mother's.

Her mother.

She closed her mouth, swallowed hard. The dossier Em had delivered on her mother was still there in her suit, still beckoning. Em had found her. Had found the planet she lived on.

She was down here to get to her mother. Even if everything else faded away, even if Jennie Mercer and Isolde and all the rest didn't matter anymore, she could cling to that. Had to cling to that.

*Your fault, your fault.*

She wasn't sure who she was addressing.

∨

If she could get back to Camp Four, she knew the way home. And she couldn't sit here and rely on Em to fix the problem from her end. That had become clear as soon as she'd woken up that morning, after a fitful, fearful sleep. If Em hadn't been able to solve the problem in what her suit's clock said was nearly twelve hours since Gyre had jammed the comm line, she might not be able to do it at all. And Gyre certainly had no chance of fixing it herself, though she tried three more times to shut down the open line, to no avail.

So. Camp Four.

If Em had downloaded a map to her suit, Gyre couldn't

find it. That meant no hints as to the locations of caches, no markers except the lake she was at and the waterfall she was headed for. There was no flow of water into the pool that Gyre could see, which ruled out following the stream back to its source. That left her with an unknown distance to cover, sixteen meals and, given the remaining power readout from her current battery, one day plus another one to four on the backup. It all depended on how active she was, how inefficient. She didn't have room to wait, and she didn't have room to make mistakes. Didn't have room to panic. At most, she had five days to get back to Camp Three.

Possible as few as two.

The suit battery giving out was a much bigger problem than the rations, and would kill her far faster. If the suit shut down, she wouldn't be able to move or see. She didn't know if she'd still be able to get air, if the exchange fans would lock open as a safety measure, but she knew she'd eventually starve, if nothing else.

She started walking.

If her suit could generate its own map, she couldn't find the setting, so she marked her path with loose rubble, leaving marker stones by each passage she entered. The first two she found narrowed down to bare slits, and she abandoned them. The third required her to climb through a thin slot, then attach anchors on the far side where the ground dropped off abruptly into a ten-meter-deep shaft. Across the way was another crack, though, and she spidered her way along the wall, driving anchor after anchor, running out meters of line. When she reached the other side, she looked at it, chewing her lip. Was it more important to conserve her resources or make a retreat easy? Save the rope, or save her precious battery power?

Gyre landed on the latter and left the rope behind.

It was very possible, she realized as she eased her way through the crevice and into a longer, still narrow tunnel, that the path to Camp Four through here was closed or collapsed from the same movements of the Tunneler that had taken her this far. If she didn't find the waterfall in the next day, she'd have to ascend that rope and keep walking, and hope to meet up with the Long Drop. Or was it better to commit to one path the whole way? She paused, braced herself against the stone, and let her forehead rest against the pitted wall.

*Why won't Em fix this?*

She pushed the childish, desperate thought aside. She could do this alone. She had done this alone all her life.

And if it came down to it, if her battery got low, she could always try to strip the suit off. It was dangerous to do it in the field, without assistance. The cannula in her stomach was reason enough not to try, not to mention her lack of traditional gear. The air wasn't cold enough to kill her fast, but it would kill her *eventually* if she tried to go on without clothing, without protection. But if the moment came . . .

She'd figure it out *when* it came.

For now, she made herself pay attention to what was in front of her: stacked shelves of rock leading up at a steep angle, with no way to go around them. They led up to the ceiling but didn't quite reach it. She climbed the first without tools, then the second. Her muscles burned as she scaled the wall, her pulse pounding in her skull.

As she reached the top, she could see that there was a gap, and that she could descend the other side. But the other side was much steeper, and she was going to have to put in at least one anchor, run at least five meters of rope to get down safely and leave a way back up. As she considered, she felt the hairs on the back of her neck rise up. She paused, then turned, slowly, looking back over her shoulder.

Hanmei stood in the tunnel she'd entered through.

She was hard to make out, missing details at this distance. Gyre's reconstruction wasn't able to show the expression on her face, or even to differentiate her much from the rock behind her. But Gyre recognized her hairless scalp, her wiry frame. She stood, motionless, staring up at Gyre.

Gyre couldn't breathe. Impossible.

*Impossible!*

And though the fear would have been bad enough, beneath it Gyre ached for the dead woman. Needed her. Even with the missing data, even with the inhuman coloring, she looked so real, so solid, and Gyre struggled not to scream. Not to cry. Seeing another person, a body, taking up space not fifty meters from her, made her want to shout. She wanted to rush down, reach out, hold the other woman.

She wanted to not be alone.

As she watched, Hanmei took a step backward, then another. Fragments of her fell away, eliding into the rock around her as she left Gyre's sonar range. And then she was gone, as impossibly as she had arrived. Gyre was moving before she could stop herself, scrambling down the shelves, racing for the tunnel, chasing better data. She ran and she stared and she waited, waited—

And there was nothing. There was nowhere Hanmei could have gone.

It had been an artifact, a misfired synapse, an over-interpretation of a wavering of a signal. She'd been so afraid of the computer hiding things from her, but was this the alternative? Without Em to help manage the flow of data, would she keep seeing the impossible?

Hanmei had died nineteen years ago. She closed her eyes and tried to imagine Em's voice. *Not real, not real, all of this is normal.* Unless it was real. Em had said she hadn't been affected by the spores at Camp Five. Which meant . . .

No. No, she couldn't believe that, not here, not now.

When she opened her eyes again, everything was still. Everything was silent. The empty channel was still open, status light glowing, speakers offering nothing. She stared at the indicator, her jaw trembling until she clenched it.

If the communication channel was more than speech, if it was the whole connection of the surface computers to her suit, then what was she connected to? What was interpreting her data for her? She lurched forward as she pulled up the communications options screen, tried to force the channel closed again.

Nothing changed. The green light continuing to glow beside its ever-present recording twin.

*No. No.* She didn't have time for this, didn't have the resources to be distracted. She made herself turn away and walk back to the stacked shelves, made herself climb even though, on a different day, in a different place, it would have been too dangerous to ascend without a rope with the way her body trembled. She did it anyway. Twice her foot slipped. A third time her body simply refused to summon the force needed to get up to the next plateau. But she didn't fall. She had some luck left to her; she didn't fall.

She hauled herself to the top and once there, didn't pause more than it took to drive the anchor into the crest and tie into a rope before walking down the smooth side.

There was a sloping passage leading down from the far right side of the chamber, and she followed it, fighting the urge to look over her shoulder every five steps. Her helmet trapped the sound of her breathing, of her snorting phlegm back into her sinuses, of her heart in her ears. She could almost hear words in the noise, words in her own voice. Exhortations, accusations, her thoughts twisting into audible reality.

And then she felt it, that same feeling she'd had back in the Tunneler path. Not quite the feeling of being watched; instead, that feeling of forgetting something, of ignoring something important. A tug, a longing that didn't feel like hers, pulling at her spine. It was like a whisper against her ear, a distant cry that begged her to come back, come home.

She clapped her hands over her ears only to hear them bang off her helmet. *Shit*.

She kept walking, thankful for the gentle slope.

Two hours later, she ducked under an overhang and stepped out to the base of the stacked shelf wall.

The pull lessened.

Gyre didn't cry. She didn't curse. She just slowly, slowly, sank to the ground, took out a ration canister, and plugged it into the port in her side. It was necessary, but it was also another one gone. She sat, unmoving, staring at the shelf. Her stomach cramped and crawled, but the nausea didn't make it up to her throat. She sat and she stared for the next half hour.

It should be simple. One foot in front of the other, mark the paths she checked, and she'd have to find the exit. But what if she'd missed something? What if she'd turned around and somehow hadn't noticed it? Figures in the distance, impossible bodies, were obvious. Distressing, but obvious. But what if there were smaller breaks, subtler failures of her brain? How much had Em been keeping her walking in the right direction?

No. She could do this. She'd done this before, done this without help. She was deeper, and she was in a suit, but she was still just fundamentally in a cave on her own, and she'd spent far more of her life in those circumstances than she had attached to Em.

Gyre stood, paced the length of the room, found the crevice she'd originally entered by, and marked it. Came back and marked the overhang, which she hadn't seen the first time. She climbed up the shelves, then walked herself down the other side. She tried again.

The tunnels weren't straightforward, and the easiest path, the one she'd clung to her first time through, wasn't the only one. Thirty meters in, there was a fork, but the tunnel turned up instead of to the side. She had ignored it. But now she made herself scale the wall, climb up into the shaft, ignoring how her fingers ached and the muscles along her spine trembled. A few meters up, there was a slot. She took it, on her belly, dragging herself through. Again and again, she found new paths, a honeycomb impossible to map without tools. She tried to mark her way, eliminated false starts, pushed onward. She moved blindly through the warren, drawing closer to death with every step, every tick of her battery indicator, and fighting to ignore that fact.

The whole time, the empty channel was silent in her ear. The quiet drew out her thoughts, amplified her breathing, made her think she could hear things in the distance. The music was back, then the humming, and once a *bang* that she realized only after she jerked and twisted around that she hadn't heard at all. It was an overwhelming cacophony, until suddenly it wasn't anything.

The honeycomb drew down, narrowed, until there was only one path. It grew in height, in width, into a sloping hall.

She stumbled out of it, straining forward, listening for the distant crash of water. Instead, she saw only the lake, placid and broken periodically by the stone pillars.

Gyre fell to her knees and cried.

Eight hours, and all she'd done was rule out two options—maybe. All she'd done was run her battery down to twenty-three percent. There were still a few branch-offs in the honeycomb that she hadn't checked. Did she go back? Try the next one? The only thing she couldn't do was stop, and yet she dragged herself across the rock to the same nook she'd spent the previous night in, then hugged her knees to her chest, struggling to breathe.

And thinking of Em.

It made the tears come harder, but she couldn't stop. It was like picking at a scab, or digging a finger into a wound trying to understand it, understand the pain and the extent of the damage. She thought of Em and her voice and her instructions. She'd ended up relying on Em, even when she thought she was pushing against her. The give-and-take, the company, just having her close at hand to double-check Gyre's thinking . . . She'd needed it.

And now, she needed it even more. She craved the sight of Em's face, the sound of her voice. She even wanted the warmth of her touch, too, the solidity of her body curled around Gyre's own. She could practically feel it. Her cheeks burned at the thought, from longing and shame. She wanted to laugh at herself, at her own stupidity.

Longing for Em. Beautiful, selfish, cruel Em—who she needed desperately, who she *relied* on. It was everything she'd never wanted. She'd been weak. She'd traded her independence, the only thing that had kept her safe for so many years, for the company of a monster.

And what would they think of her, the silent, watching dead, who she'd promised she would help, only to witness her back off out of terror?

Would Jennie have understood? Had she felt the same

way, longing for Em's voice as she crawled beneath her shelf to die? Had Adrian Purcell cried out for her while he lay crushed beneath the boulder at Camp Two, wanting more than salvation?

Isolation did this to her. Weeks with only Em's voice in her ear, only Em's face in front of her, her whole life orbiting around her, and now days without anybody at all. She hadn't been able to picture her mother's face in years, but now even her dad's felt different, as did the few people she counted as colleagues, even if she would never call them friends. Em was the only memory left to her, the only real person, and her imagination built a shrine to her.

Em, who had been so afraid of losing her.

She stared at the recording light for what felt like hours. Em had said it would go to a black box, inaccessible until she was above the surface. But oh, what she would have given to be able to access it, to play back all their conversations. If she listened back to Em's confessions at Camp Six, would she still believe them? If she listened to their arguments on the Tunneler path, would she see Em manipulating her, or trying to help her?

She wanted that objectivity. She wanted to be reminded to hate her, or to be forgiven for needing her.

She had nothing.

Gyre settled down onto her side and tried to push away the thought of Em, worried for her, wanting her to come back. But it wouldn't leave—it was now one more figure with her in the cave, haunting her—and she couldn't stop the tears from rolling down her cheeks.

# CHAPTER NINETEEN

### BATTERY LEVEL CRITICAL

The warning had been flashing red on her screen for the last two hours, but Gyre was holding out, waiting until the last minute possible before she swapped to her backup. She was trudging up a passage that was almost a hallway, with an even incline broken only by a few short scrambles. Easy. It was easy. Not so easy as the Tunneler passage, but close. Which meant her suit was using less power to help her traverse it, and which also meant she'd been able to turn off the sonar reconstruction and work by just her headlamp, slowing the inexorable drain just that small fraction.

That morning, she'd thought of turning off the recording. The ghost channel connection still refused to close, but the recording could have been severed easily.

But it was her last link to Em. A useless link, maybe, but turning it off was too close to giving up.

She had just pulled herself up over the edge of a three-meter climb, taken without ropes or anchors, when she saw it: a duffel bag, tucked into a crevice not twenty paces from her. She stopped, staring, then cycled through her various displays. Damn the battery usage; if that was what it looked like, if it was *real*—

And it was. It was real. It was there in every display mode she had. She shouted and stumbled toward it, falling to her knees.

A cache. It was a cache.

That meant this was the route.

That meant she wasn't going in circles anymore.

She wanted to kiss the ground, the ripstop fiber of the bag itself, every ration canister she pulled from it. She unloaded her used canisters from their storage area, setting them up in a careful row at the back of the niche, and then hefted the first fresh one, and carefully fitted it into place.

It locked in, and she could have cried from joy at the feeling of sludge moving through the cannula. *They fit.*

And if the rations fit, the batteries would too. Right? It was an old cache, but not *that* old. She rifled through the bag, pulling out anchors, line, other resources she could use. Finally, at the bottom, she found the hard case that housed the batteries. She pulled it free and hugged it to her chest.

Almost, almost.

She got the latch open on the second try. Inside, nestled in the high-density foam, was only one battery, the other slots empty. This cache had never been restocked since its last use. Understandable. But one was enough; it bought her three more days to get to Camp Three, to *home*.

She picked it up, holding it reverently, and reached back with her free hand to remove her backup from its slot. That slot could run diagnostics, could confirm if it still had charge. She set the backup aside, then moved to shift the fresh battery to her other hand.

As she did, though, her fingers tightened around it, then spasmed. Her hand jerked. Her arm moved as if on its own accord, smashing the battery against the ground. The housing bent and the glass crunched into dust.

Its glow died.

She stared at her hand. She hadn't twitched a single muscle. She hadn't *tried* to do that. Her muscles hadn't seized, she hadn't flinched—it hadn't been her.

But did it matter? Did how it happened matter, with the wreckage at her feet?

Trembling, she regarded her backup. She didn't dare reach for it, even though her charge was running out. She had to swap it out with the dying one, and soon, but as long as she didn't touch it, she couldn't break it as well.

Gyre wedged herself back into the crevice of rock. She couldn't think past the pounding in her skull.

There was a tiny shard of glass on her fingertip, rendered flat green in her display. It had scratched the coating. She'd done that.

*I've killed myself.*

A faint humming filled her helmet, followed by a low crackling. It didn't sound like the drone that she'd heard when the quiet was too much. Desperately hopeful, she looked at the comm line indicator. "Em? Em, is that you?" she whispered.

No response.

The line was open, but when she toggled to settings, it was still stuck on that empty channel. She tried to close it, but it refused, like it had the last ten times she'd tried over the past day. It stayed open, susurrations washing over her eardrums, and she realized that it must be connected to *something*, some computer, somewhere. If somebody was sitting at that computer on the surface, watching her, changing her readouts, couldn't they control her suit? Move her hand?

Em had been able to.

"I can hear you," she said. "Who's there?"

No response.

"Close the line!" she said, almost shouted, and then she bit back a wretched sob. "Leave me alone. Just leave me alone, whoever you are."

No response.

She turned her left hand over, clenched her fist, released it. "Was it you?" she asked. "Did you make me do that?" That was what it had felt like, like when Em had made her grasp the rock, down in the sump, or when she'd locked Gyre's suit at Camp Two. External control. It hadn't been her, hadn't been her at all.

She hadn't killed herself. Whoever it was on the empty channel had.

No. The channel was *empty*. She was hearing feedback now, nothing else. Nobody sat at a desk, somewhere topside, watching her suffer, laughing at her, destroying her chance at life. Locking Em out.

She had to believe it was ridiculous. She had to believe she was on her own.

She had—

Her HUD dinged. Her meal was done. She unscrewed the canister from the port and set it aside with the others, then, trembling, began loading up her suit. She needed to run line on every climb going forward. Needed to be overly secure. If whatever that was happened again, she needed to be clipped in and protected. It didn't matter if it was her or some ghost on the empty channel.

**BATTERY APPROACHING TOTAL SHUTDOWN**
**CAVER, SWAP TO BACKUP**

Her hands stilled, and she stared at the text. It sounded like Em. It sounded like Em, and the thought made her want to laugh. Of course it would sound like Em. No doubt Em had written all the alerts, if she hadn't programmed them in herself.

She nodded. "Right, Em," she murmured to herself. "Whatever you say." It was time, no matter the risk of her spasming again. If she waited, she was dead, the same as if she shattered the battery. Her lamp was already beginning to dim. She could hear her air filter's fans slowing to conserve the charge; without power, she'd suffocate first after all. She used her right hand to lift the backup, cradling it gently. With the suit, it hardly mattered, but topside it was her weaker hand by just a hair. Then, holding her breath, she released her dying battery. Her HUD flashed with a timer, the seconds remaining until she had to put in the fresh one.

She'd done this several times now. She knew the motions. She picked up the replacement, slotted it in.

Her suit restored to full power and the timer disappeared.

She sagged against the rock, drawing her knees up to her chest. She should keep moving, couldn't afford to break down again like she had six hours ago. But she was so tired, and for now she had one hundred percent power. For now, she could pretend it would last all four days.

The whispering static prickled at her eardrums.

She was tired, but her fear outweighed it. She rocked forward on her knees and quickly swapped what remained of her swimming gear with what was in the duffel. And then she was on her feet again, staggering forward.

<br>

She heard the waterfall half an hour before she saw it. At first, it was far enough away to be a distant rumble, and she froze where she was, half over the top edge of a short climb, waiting for the passing of the Tunneler. But it didn't come, and as she hauled herself up onto stable ground and began walking, she made out the rush inside the rumble, the flow of water, heavy and relentless. She followed the sound. When faced with branching paths, she marked the one the sound came from the most loudly, then made for it.

And half an hour later, she turned around a bend and saw it. Great gouts of water surged from a gap high in the facing wall, crashing down to the ground, where it had worn a hole clear through the stone. Gyre stopped where she stood and stared up at it, at the raw force on display. She'd have to climb through that to get home. If the cave hadn't shifted, hadn't flooded the sump by Camp Three, it might have been drier, maybe even just a trickle, but now it was nearly a sump of its own. Her battery readout hovered close to ninety-eight percent full. It should be enough. But her scrubbers would be working overtime to keep up with her oxygen needs on a climb instead of a dive, and her suit would be withstanding a lot more pressure. *She* would be withstanding it.

The bigger problem was that she needed sleep. Continuing forward now was impossible. But she could already tell she was too keyed up, too unsteady in her exhaustion. Sleep would be long in coming, and difficult. Useless, when it came. If only she had Em at hand to figure out the dosage of sedative that was best for the current situation . . .

But she didn't, and that left Gyre to her own devices, and to whatever was lurking on the ghost channel. The static had died down over the last two hours, but with the roar of the waterfall, she couldn't be sure it wasn't still there, soft and omnipresent. If she fell asleep, what might it do to her suit? If somebody *was* on the other line, what could they do to her?

She shuddered, but made herself walk forward anyway, to a spot up along the curvature of the wall that was almost a nook. Almost protected.

She hunkered down, knees tucked tight to her chest.

There was movement in the corner of her eye; she ignored it. More darting shadows. They'd grown more frequent, now that she knew to look for them. The murmurings from the ghost channel, too, had nearly turned to song at some points, and if she paid too much attention to them, they seemed as if they could whisper her name at any moment.

More movement.

She squeezed her eyes shut. Counted her breaths.

She opened her eyes again.

More movement.

Groaning, she gave in and turned her head, brought that corner into full view. Cycled through her display settings.

There was nothing there.

There was never anything there.

It was *always* there.

Slowly, Gyre shifted onto her side, remaining curled up. She locked her suit in place along the bottom edge to provide a couch for herself and dimmed the lights. *Sleep.* She needed sleep. She hadn't slept properly since before the sump. Hadn't slept properly since she'd thrown Em out. Sluggishly, she tabbed through the options on her HUD, looking for the medical readouts.

She found the dossier on her mother first.

Gyre pursed her lips, then paged away. *Not yet.* She didn't want to die down here, suffering and afraid, knowing her mother was happy. She didn't want to be able to imagine the details. Sedatives, that was what she needed. Sedatives, not facts. Not answers.

*There.* She pulled up the medical interface, looking at everything still available to her. The levels hadn't changed since she'd noticed the triple dose of sedatives missing. It brought her fight with Em back in full detail, filling her with a rush of self-loathing.

She wished Em had loaded some kind of antipsychotic into the suit. Maybe then this wouldn't have happened.

She selected the sedative Em had used on her before. Along with an array of information on its chemical makeup and the dosage history, there were terse calculation instructions, as well as a guide of how to administer.

Gyre's fingers hovered in midair, poised to select the options that would knock her out. But she couldn't do it. As she hovered over the dosage information, she tensed, drawing in on herself. Her gaze shifted through the text on her HUD to the room surrounding her. Em sedating her was horrible, but it meant there had been somebody to keep watch over her. If she sedated herself, she was vulnerable. It would be hard to wake up. It might be impossible, for a short period of time. If the ghost channel made a move, or if she had really seen motion down by the lake, or in the shelf chamber . . .

If the Tunneler came . . .

No—no sedatives. Not without Em.

She could have laughed at the irony of it.

She closed the menu, then unlocked her suit to shift her position, curling up tighter. Relocked. Dimmed the lights some more. She went through the motions as if they were a ritual, as if they'd bring sleep all on their own.

But her exhaustion did that for her, finally winning out over her fear.

⌄

She slept, fitfully, but if she dreamed, she couldn't remember it. It was only four hours later when she gave up and checked the time, sitting up and reaching for a meal. Four hours wasn't enough, but her battery was down to ninety-three percent. Five percent in four hours, without her doing a single thing but living. It wasn't faster than it was supposed to be, but now, this time, it felt final. A countdown clock.

An alert flashed on her HUD.

SIGNAL LOST

DOWNLOAD ABORTED

It pulsed purple for a few seconds, then faded to nothing. She stared at where it had been a few breaths longer, then sat bolt upright and pulled up the communications settings. There—the ghost channel was still toggled, but the line showed dead now, like it had when Em had closed voice communication for a time. She filled her cheeks with air, then exhaled sharply, and closed the line.

It closed. It *stayed* closed. And, heart in her throat, she toggled to the line that led to Em and blew it open.

The indicator flicked green. The signal connected. She let

out a broken, half-sobbed laugh and fell backward, stretching out over the hump of equipment on her back. "I'm here," she whispered. "I'm here." Her voice cracked.

At first, she heard nothing. Then the rattle of equipment and furniture. A sharp inhale, a harsh, shaking exhale.

"Gyre?" Em asked.

"Hey," Gyre replied, her voice weak with uncertain relief.

No words, just more rustling, more breathing.

"I'm alive," Gyre offered.

Nothing. Then—"Fuck. *Fuck*. I thought—my computer lost all connection to the suit. I thought something had happened. I thought—" Em's words failed her, and Gyre thought she could hear crying.

Em, crying for *her*.

No. For herself. For her almost failure. It couldn't be for her.

"What happened?" Em managed after only a moment, her voice still clotted with tears. "Are you okay?"

A riot of emotions flashed through her—relief, fear, *anger*—because how could Em not know what had happened? But the one that settled firmly into her chest was shame.

Shame, because, for the first time, hadn't it been *her* who put herself in danger?

She didn't want to admit it, didn't want to cede that little bit of righteous power she'd accumulated. Couldn't handle the thought of Em using it against her, using it to prop up her desire to control everything that happened down in the cave.

"I did what I had to," Gyre said, and sat up a little straighter, lifting her chin. "I wanted to think." *I wanted to hurt you.* "You were telling me I was going crazy, and I needed . . . space." Em's face appeared in her screen. The other woman was leaning in, so close to the camera, as if there were only glass between them. Her hair was wild, her face ashen, her eyes bloodshot.

Gyre's heart thudded in her chest, arrested once again by the humanity of her, and for a moment, she lost her words. Then: "I needed to see for myself that I was alone in there."

"You were alone," Em murmured, but it wasn't a correction. Just a murmur of understanding.

"Yeah. You were right," Gyre conceded, wincing.

"But what happened, Gyre? You severed the connection, I get that, but if that was all you had done, I would have been able to reestablish it," Em said. "At some point in the last two days, my system would have pinged your suit, and it would have responded, and I would have had you back. Instead, you stayed dark." She looked away from the camera, wrapping one arm around herself. "And do you know what else stays dark? Broken suits. Dead cavers."

Gyre went very still. "I suppose you know what that looks like better than most."

"That's not—Gyre—"

"Did you start looking at new applications already?" Her gaze flicked to the recording indicator, still glowing cheerfully. She could push here, claw her fingers into the cracks in Em's self-control and wrench it apart. She imagined the anger pouring out of Em, the confessions, the cold, inhuman distance on full display.

Em choked down words, visibly struggling to control herself. Then she said, "No. I was too terrified I'd lost *you*. Not another caver. *You.*"

Gyre's anger fractured. *I was too terrified I'd lost* you. The pain in Em's voice made Gyre believe Em had feared for her with every inch of her being. Made her *want* to believe.

That was it. The tears tracked heavy and hot down her

own cheeks, and she couldn't stop shaking. She laughed, too, the hysterical laugh of the desperate, the dying, and her hands worked, stretching out into the empty air, spidering along the stone, as if she could take Em's hand in hers. She fought it all, tried to tamp it back down inside of her, but it was useless.

In that moment, more than anything else, she wanted the worst thing she had ever known:

The woman who had waited two long days by her computer, hoping to reestablish a signal with her.

*I'm losing my mind.*

Em waited, patient through her sobs.

"I don't know what happened," Gyre muttered, once she'd dragged herself back together. "I . . . I opened another communications channel. And then I couldn't close it. It just closed on its own a minute ago, said something about an aborted download."

"Shit," Em said. Gyre heard keystrokes, slow at first, then growing frantic. She looked back at Em's image to see her composing herself again, frowning at a screen that wasn't the camera. "Stay put," Em said. "I need to run diagnostics. You must have been within range of one of the nearby concerns. Did you hear anything? Talk to anybody?"

She shivered. *It wasn't my imagination. It wasn't a glitch.* She didn't know if that made her feel relieved, or more terrified. Something had been *downloading* to her suit. Someone else had really been able to control her movements. Her breathing.

*Oh fuck.* She'd been *right.*

"I tried," Gyre said. Her lips felt swollen, heavy. "I heard static. Nobody ever responded."

"You were probably just on the edge of the range," Em replied. "That would explain why you couldn't close the channel. Your suit is designed to not terminate a connection during data transfer, if at all possible, especially transfers of the rough size of a software update. It's a safety feature."

Panic flared in her chest again, racing along the now-familiar pathways of her veins and sinews. "Why would another mining concern try to update my suit?"

"Hopefully it was just an automated process. The system found an unknown suit on its channel, running on a different setup, and was making it conform. I'm not seeing any sign of fragmentary code, though. Hopefully it was a package update, and not piecemeal."

"What happens if it's piecemeal?"

"Your suit could begin malfunctioning. It could error out and lock up. It could—god *damn it.*"

"What? What's wrong?" Gyre sat up straight, fingers splayed on the ground on either side of her, ready to rocket to her feet. The channel must have done something to the suit, changed it, and Em was about to tell her that she was dying, this time for real, this time with no way out. The spasm that had broken the battery was just the first symptom.

Or . . .

Her eyes went to the green light still gleaming on her screen. The recording—she could have spotted the recording, and was realizing what Gyre had been planning on doing. She was going to abandon her again.

What use was weighing one betrayal against another, if one person had all the power?

She closed her eyes, trying to steel herself.

"Your battery," Em said, her voice pained.

At first, Gyre couldn't parse what Em had said. Her battery. *Not the recorder.* Em wasn't about to cut her off. Em still cared. But her relief lived for only the briefest moment, replaced immediately by a horrible thought. "There were—text alerts, about my battery level. I switched out to the backup. That was the suit, right? Not some sick joke?"

Em shook her head. "I'm looking at the log right now. You got dangerously low. You were right to switch. But I don't . . . I don't understand."

"What?"

"You must have passed by the cache. Wasn't it there?"

Gyre sagged back into her suit. From one disaster to another, one shame to another. She was too tired to keep up. "It was."

"Then where is it? There's no way you could've burned through two—"

"The suit broke it."

"What?"

"I was holding it, and the suit spasmed. My hand clenched, then my arm jerked. I threw it down, and it shattered." She swallowed. "I think it was whoever initiated the signal controlling me."

Em grimaced. "It's possible," she said. "A tech could've seen the suit come online, but couldn't make verbal contact, so they tried to establish physical control. But they should've left you alone while you were handing supplies. Or at least seen my imprint on the signal coming through and contacted me. Or stopped the download, at least, and used the limited connection to communicate by text with you. You didn't see anything like that?"

"No. There was nothing except for the static. I thought . . . I thought I was hallucinating. Like I was at the lake. If stress was causing all of that—"

"It wasn't all stress."

"What?" No. No, it had all been stress. It had all been stress, which meant it hadn't been real, and the alternative meant . . .

Isolde. Somewhere in this cave. Impossibly in this cave.

More keystrokes. Then Em said, "I lied."

Gyre's throat went dry, her brow furrowing. "Lied?"

"About the spores. At Camp Six. You were right; I did keep you sedated for a long time. I was giving your body time to purge itself of the spores. You were erratic, highly agitated, and your hormone levels were all over the place. I only let you back up once you'd stabilized." Em looked at the camera again, shame twisting her features. "I didn't want you to panic again, and since everything seemed fine when you woke up . . ."

Gyre should have felt anger. Instead, she felt relief, validation. It hadn't all been stress, but it also hadn't been real. *Isolde wasn't at Camp Five. Some weird system update made me crush the battery.*

*I'm not doing this alone anymore.*

She could trust herself now. Probably.

"I'm sorry. I should have told you," Em said. She lifted a hand, as if to reach out for Gyre. Gyre almost responded in kind.

"And the rations?"

"Really fine. Really uncontaminated."

"Then at the lake—why was I—"

"I do think that was stress. I won't know for sure until you're back topside and the doctors can run more tests, though."

Which meant Em wasn't ruling out lasting damage from the spores. Gyre fought back a wave of nausea. She couldn't think about that, not until she was somewhere safe. Here, now, Gyre just needed another few minutes of quiet. A few more minutes of leaning into the story that Em cared, that they could go forward as equals.

Em let her have the time. Five minutes of them looking at each other, breathing, feeling.

Finally, Em sat back in her seat. "How rested are you?"

"Enough." A lie, but one she was determined to live up to. She didn't want to try to sleep here again, not even with Em watching over her.

"Good," Em said. "You're not going to like this next part. I'm going to have to shut down communications again."

Gyre started forward. The words were a piercing blow, puncturing a lung. She couldn't continue on alone anymore. "What?"

"Talking to you, even video, doesn't take that much power. But it piggybacks off the connection between my computer and your suit. That takes a large portion of your battery. Just reestablishing a signal with me, and talking with me, dropped you five points. Holding it open will keep draining it, although slower."

"But all I have to do is get to Camp Four, then back to Three."

Em winced.

"What? What happened?"

"The waterfall," Em said.

"Yeah?"

"It's your only way to get to Camp Four from here. It's a hard climb in dry weather, but right now, it's going to be a nightmare. It's going to kill your battery charge, between your rebreather running and your suit withstanding the force of the water. By the time you reach Camp Four, you'll be too low to safely dive the sump to Camp Three. You'll be right up against the safety margin, and I've seen enough cavers lose that gamble to allow it to happen again. You're going to have to go down, to Five, and resupply there."

She shook her head. "No. There's no way this climb is going to take me that low. No . . ."

"It might. And once you're through, it will be far, far safer to go to Five instead."

*No.* She couldn't risk the spores getting into her suit. Not again.

"I'll try for Three."

*"You can't,"* Em said. "Are you listening? Your suit can get you through this climb, but the next time you go underwater, it could drop you to critical levels. If your battery dies, you have no backup. Your rebreather will stop working. You'll die."

"And if my suit shuts down on the side of the Long Drop?"

"The chances of that are much, much lower," Em said. "Especially if our communications are off and you use only your headlamp whenever possible. The line is already laid; the route will be faster this time."

"And the spores?"

"Came in through water recirculation, not your air filters."

"Are you *sure* about that?"

"Yes. I'm sure. Gyre, make for Camp Five. Do you understand?" Em's expression had turned cold and impersonal. It *hurt.* Gyre wanted to fight, wanted to argue. Wanted to beg for Em to find a way to stay connected.

But that didn't help anything.

"I want to be done," she whispered.

"I know," Em said. "But you're almost there. I know you can do this. You've faced worse odds." Her voice dropped another few notes. "I *know you*, Gyre."

Gyre tried not to think about how those four words coursed through her, electric. *You don't. You can't.*

She wanted Em to be right.

"I'm uploading maps to your suit," Em continued. "And if you need a dose of adrenaline, the system will walk you through the calculations. Don't be afraid to use it, but use less than you think you'll need. Too much, and you'll be sick." There was a pause. Then: "Gyre."

"What?"

"Keep pushing. I'll be there on the other side."

Gyre kept her eyes fixed on Em's face until the connection cut out and the line went dead, wishing she could keep her, wishing they had something more.

Then the recording light blinked out.

Em had seen it.

She *knew*.

# CHAPTER TWENTY

Gyre stared at the map filling her display. She didn't want to look; she wanted nothing more than to sit and worry about what Em would do now that she knew Gyre had been primed to blackmail her, but the only way to win space enough to do that was to get up and get out. And yet she couldn't make herself care.

How could she trust Em's suggestions? If she knew about the recording, then wasn't it better to lead Gyre to her death? Nobody would question an accident, especially not if it happened while Em, tragically, was unable to monitor her caver's suit.

Or did it make more sense to bring Gyre up, because Em could fight the contents of the black box in court and *win*? Was she even afraid of those recordings? Had Gyre captured enough to hurt her, or just recorded her own erratic paranoia?

She couldn't weigh either side of the scales. She wanted to give up, stop playing Em's game. But she couldn't stop, because if she was going to die, she was going to do it *her* way, doing what she did best: climbing.

And trusting her*self*.

First things first: get up the wall and through the chamber the water was flowing from, without getting caught in the waterfall and being snapped from her line—from there, Camp Five or Three was available to her. Of course, a wrong move and she'd fall down, straight through the gap in the floor that the surge raged through, and from *there*, she could end up anywhere, or simply die, smashed to bits on the way down.

So she would make no wrong moves, and conserve as much battery charge as possible while she was at it.

With a sharp boost, she pushed herself up one body length along the wall, then steadied herself to drive her first bolt, meters from the flow of water. She focused on the mechanism of it, pushing through the fear and exhaustion that nipped at her heels. She'd have to do this automatically, in the roaring chaos. First bolt driven, she clipped in, then wedged a few cams in as well to make sure this point was sturdy. If she fell . . .

She couldn't think like that. Couldn't think like that again for as long as she was underground.

She made her way up the wall, avoiding the waterfall and working up toward the side of the entrance. Halfway there, she turned off the reconstruction, but found the lamp wasn't enough for her to work the bolts safely. Reconstruction it was; she would just have to do this faster to balance out the battery drain.

Hand over hand, she scaled the wall. The edges of her mind were already starting to go hazy with exhaustion, and once her next bolt was in, she took a moment to rest while she keyed in a slow-release dose of adrenaline. The suit guided her through the calculation, and then she triggered half that amount. She still felt it immediately, her heart jumping, her stomach curdling. It made her feel sick, but she'd take sick over vague.

The ground fell away beneath her, and the roar of the water grew louder.

This was a new, special kind of torture, knowing Em was only a gesture away, but that gesture might mean the difference between making it to Camp Five and dying alone in the dark. She was so tired, so scared, so desperate to explain the recording, and the offer of relief, that company, that comfort, was so close at hand. It would be so *easy*. It took so much effort to resist, her willpower already struggling as she climbed up to just to the side of the entrance to the passage. Her display became fuzzier with the spray of water all around her. She could hear it and feel where the pressure of the great gouts of water met her suit, but she couldn't see the droplets beading on her helmet, or feel them running down over her hands.

Gyre's fingers itched inside her carapace. Here, the suit was worse than useless. She needed tactile feedback to do this safely, needed to know by touch and split-second reaction how wet her handholds were, needed to see the small rivulets of water, needed to be able to predict what could go wrong. She was certain that the suit had readouts for that, but numbers on a screen or colored lines weren't the same, especially without long practice and familiarity. She'd have to learn by doing, crash course it head-on.

After securing herself in her current position, she reached out and felt the stone, trying to memorize in an instant a new litany of sensations: the way her suit glove dragged over wetter or drier stone, the way her knuckles flexed dry or underwater. She guessed at each gradation based on the macro-level changes her reconstruction showed.

If only she'd had more battery power, she could have activated a textured film on her fingertips to help her grip. She'd never tried it before, had barely remembered it was an option, but she could see it in the settings now, and her mouth watered.

But she didn't turn it on, and she didn't connect back to Em's computer. With one last glance down at the pit beneath her, she edged around the corner into the above-water portion of the tunnel, smearing herself across the wall, just above the raging torrent.

Below her, the water churned and roiled, moving fast and leaping up where it struck the stubborn edges of rocks that hadn't been worn down as fast as everything around them. Maybe six or seven meters ahead of her the path hooked too far to the left for her to see around the bend. According to the map, there was a section soon that would go straight up, largely underwater, up through the waterfall itself.

Her right calf muscle cramped in protest.

*At least I won't be cold.* If she was doing this without a suit, the water would have been quickly sapping her body heat, making her clumsy. The suit was, for all its abstractions and blocks to her normal methods, the better option. She wriggled her foot until her calf relaxed, then found another toehold, dragging herself along toward the bend.

She'd made it to the midpoint of the turn, and could see the vertical climb coming up, when she paused to place a fresh anchor. She wedged her toes into small gaps in the rock only ten centimeters above the rapids, the water leaping at her heels. She found a crack that spared her the need to use up another bolt; she placed a few cams instead and was just about to clip her rope into it when her calf cramped again. Her foot slipped. She had half a second to shout before she dropped into the churning water and was swept down the tunnel, her side striking an outcropping and knocking the wind from her in a sudden, sharp burst of pain.

Scrabbling, she grabbed hold of her line as it pulled taut, catching against the last anchor. Gyre fought her instinct to hold her breath against the onslaught of tumbling force, and dragged herself along the line back to the wall, struggling to walk on the fins that her suit had extended automatically on contact with the water. She gasped reflexively as her head broke the surface and the fins retracted.

*Right. Do it again.*

She took a moment and tried to quell her rampant shaking. She was lucky; she hadn't hit her head or broken any bones. There would be bruises, yes, and she was on the panic edge of adrenaline instead of the strength side, but she was whole. She found the setting for the automatic extension of the fins and turned it off. Shifting her grip on the wall, she worked her right foot in a small, stretching circle, hoping this time it would stick. Then she crawled, carefully, back to the bolt. Clipped in. She skirted the foaming white head of the current and climbed onward into the crash of water meeting stone.

It surged over and around her, and then she was in it, her entire body slammed by the current. It tried to drag her down into the bowels of the cave. She fought it, hanging back just inside the flow, her vision distorted by the wild spray around her, and stared upward, squinting, looking for a likely path. There wasn't one.

She'd make one, then.

Gyre lifted up each hand in turn, rotating it at the wrist, delaying the inevitable. Each stretch only made her feel more tired, the endless cacophony of the waterfall warping her thoughts, making them repeat in increasingly panicked rounds. The flow of water could short-circuit the suit or slam her head into rock or snap her neck, or, or, or . . .

She wasn't Jennie. She wasn't going to trade technique for speed.

She thought of her mother then, of the dossier still waiting unread, of her mother happy and healthy and so far away from this hell. Then she grabbed the image of emerging onto the surface, walking into the bar closest to her home, bragging and getting her pick of women. And then she pictured Em, pictured herself slapping her or kissing her, anything that might let her imagine herself alive after she was out of this cave.

But all the images boiled away the instant she conjured them, and the more she tried, the more exhausted she felt. They were so far away, untouchable, unobtainable. Her only option was the simplest one. She had to go on because there was no other choice but to lie down and die, and Gyre wouldn't give *anybody* that last bit of satisfaction.

So she rolled her shoulders, took one last look up at the gap in the rock, and then pushed up into the deluge. She clung hard to the stone for the first few breaths, staying utterly still, adjusting to the weight of the water on her shoulders and head. Then, as soon as she had acclimated, she began to climb. The longer she stayed put, the easier it would be to simply let go.

The moment her head reached the enclosed space at the top of the downpour, filled with rushing water and unpredictable outcroppings, overlapping currents and impenetrable visual noise generated by the few pockets of air constantly collapsing and reforming, her reconstruction went from disorienting to useless. No choice—she shut it off. Darkness fell around her, but without her screen dancing and wavering in front of her, she could *see* the shape of the rocks by touch alone. Gyre hauled herself up into the passage proper and groped in the dark, powering up the drill to set another bolt. It wasn't safe, but she had no other option.

Her battery edged another micrometer lower.

If she was lucky, going blind would balance out the power the drill was drawing. She didn't know the math, but it was plausible enough to cling to.

She clipped in, and sought out the next handhold, then the next. With each step, her muscles quavered, her shoulders and head bowing under the force of the waterfall, her thighs and chest tired from day after day of climbing and emotional extremes. The passage itself would have been walkable in places if the water hadn't been there, but with it, she struggled to pull herself forward even along the flat sections. Then she would reach another largely vertical stretch and have to haul herself up instead of forward. The joints in her hands screamed in pain and threatened to lock up on her, and the skin of her fingertips protested from the pressure. Her rebreather whirred loudly, struggling to keep up with her oxygen needs at full exertion.

There *were* some stable pockets of air in the choke, and spots where the walls came close enough together that she could lean her back against them as she fought her way up, steadying herself to put another bolt in. But with every narrowing of the passage and every dry spot, the force of the water became unpredictable, harder to manage. Each shelf she could stand on was also a platform that could break her arm if she fell the wrong way against it. Twice, she lost her grip, her toe slipping or her fingers giving way, and she dangled in the full energy of the current, her heart in her throat as she scrabbled for another hold. And once, as she neared what she thought was the top by a change in the sound of the water, the stone gave way under where she had her left knee jammed into it, and she fell, twisting in the current until she was jerked to a hard stop by her rope. Below her was a rough ledge, only a few centimeters away. If she'd driven her bolt just a hair lower, and if she'd snapped her leg—

*Can't think about falling.*

Another few minutes of blinding effort and her head broke the surface of the surge. She switched her reconstruction back on. There was another climb a short distance from her, and above that, the hole widened out into a larger, less vertical chamber. Water flowed deep and fast over the floor, and where she stood it was waist-deep, but just beside her was a dry pocket. She dragged herself into it. Groaning in relief, she staggered and nearly collapsed in place, but she propped herself against the wall and pulled up the map Em had given her.

If she had been connected to Em's computer topside, she would have been able to see her location as a small blip. As it was, she tried to match each feature she'd climbed over against the model of the cave, and decided that, given where she likely was, she'd reached the branch-off point Em had marked for her. She didn't need to climb all the way to the top. This alcove, if it was the one she thought it was, would open onto another, drier path. She turned off the map and looked around.

*There.*

There was a narrow slit in the rock, low to the floor and small enough that she'd have to wiggle through on her belly or her back. If the map was right.

But if she was wrong, it could take her—anywhere. Back to the start, like the paths she'd wandered the day before? She shuddered. *I can do this. I can do this.*

Then she made the mistake of looking at her battery indicator. The remaining charge dropped sharply, impossibly, down past forty percent. The climb had used up over half her battery all on its own.

Her gaze went to the communications settings reflexively, her lips tingling as she imagined blowing out the command that would connect her to Em, just for a moment. To confirm, to console.

But once again she stopped herself. She'd check in when she reached Camp Five. No sooner. She couldn't risk the battery usage, and she wasn't ready to face Em now that she knew about the recording. There would be no consolation, no gentleness. She might not even answer.

The thought almost broke her.

She shook off that feeling. *Just a little farther.* The battery would hold. Em's math had predicted this. Now that she was out of the water, the drain on her power would slow again.

After detaching herself from her rope, Gyre knelt down before the gap, then rolled onto her back, letting her spine arch over the bulk of her shell. She pushed herself along the ground just far enough to get her head in, and she looked around, letting her sonar map out the space. The slot continued. It would be a tight fit, and an awkward one, but it looked doable. She pulled out, then flipped onto her stomach and began to crawl.

The roar of the waterfall was still making her bones vibrate, but it began to fall away as she wiggled the first meter into the slot. She'd made it up the first awkward, slithering climb—just a few paces of gain, but she had to take it as if she were a lizard, pressed flat to a warm stone—when the sound grew again. Except now it sounded different, no doubt distorted by the stone around her. It sounded like a low rumble, a throbbing—

*Oh fuck.*

261

Her whole body spasmed with fear, the narrow slot suddenly too claustrophobic, too tight. Images of Halian's body, crushed to a pulpy slime, crashed over her mind, and she was blind from them, hyperventilating and trying to back out on instinct. If a Tunneler was close, if it found her, she'd be dead. Em would never know what had happened, and—

The rumble stopped.

Gyre sagged down. If it was a rumble, if it wasn't a deep-bone throb, if it stopped, that meant it wasn't close. Right? She was surrounded by stone, more than she'd been anywhere else in the cave. If it moved through stone, if the sound was carried through stone, of course she would hear it better here.

She was fine. She'd be fine.

Still, she quickened her pace as she slithered through the gaps and clawed her way up awkward rises, crawling ever closer to Camp Four. When the passage finally opened up again, she staggered out with the feeling of a prisoner released. Calling up her map, she saw she was only half an hour's easy walk from Camp Four, and she had to pause and wait for her relieved sobs to pass.

From here there was only the Long Drop left, and then she'd replace her batteries and restock everything and just . . . climb out. She'd be done. She'd be on familiar ground, and the hallucinations and sleepless nights would ease or go away entirely. And if they were wrong about the spores, if Gyre had truly seen something at Camp Five, if Isolde was somehow still alive—maybe she had followed her through the sump. Maybe she had died in the great sump behind her.

And if she *hadn't*, if that feeling she'd had in the lake chamber had been real, there was no way Isolde could make it through the waterfall without gear.

*Fuck her, either way.*

262

She staggered toward Camp Four, then stopped short when she saw her battery.

It hovered at thirty percent.

The power drain had slowed, but not enough. Her battery was failing fast. Too fast? Or was this still what Em had calculated—and why she had been so firm about not swimming to Camp Three? She had to keep going, but the fresh panic was too much after the climb, too much after everything that had happened.

She stood there, caught on the thought that maybe she wasn't going to make it, and the panic grew, only to fade again as she waited through it. She turned the recording feature back on. She licked her dry lips, cleared her throat.

"Em," she said, "I made it to Camp Four." As she spoke, her voice rasping against her throat, she could feel every burnt-out nerve ending in her body, every knotted muscle. "I'm almost there, anyway. I'm going to strike for Camp Five immediately. I heard a Tunneler a while ago, but I think it's gone now. But my battery is low. I might have fucked up, in the climb, and I just . . . I just wanted to tell you, in case I don't get to talk to you again—" *In case I don't get to talk to anybody ever again—*

That what? *I'm sorry for taking steps to protect myself and keep you from doing this to somebody else? I've been fantasizing about you, I hate what you've done to me, but I can't stop needing you, I'm so angry, I'm so sorry, I wish we'd met some other way, I wish you weren't crazy, I wish I wasn't an idiot?*

"Just give my money to my dad, tell him where my mother is, and send her a nasty letter about how I died trying to get to her, okay? And then throw me a huge party up on the surface and move on. I know you think it isn't that simple, but . . . fuck, Em. Just move on. At least give us that much respect."

# CHAPTER TWENTY-ONE

She spent almost half an hour in Camp Four, sitting down to rest her aching body and check her suit. Her battery stabilized at twenty-six percent, its drain slowing back to its normal rate of a little under one percent an hour. She should have turned off the reconstruction and headlamp, but she selfishly kept the lights on, unwilling to face the darkness again before there was no other choice. The sump was too dangerous to risk, but the trip down to Camp Five shouldn't take more than five hours.

She gave herself another meal, her leg jittering as she waited for the flow to stop, skin prickling as she felt phantom eyes on her. Her gaze darted around the chamber incessantly. Her head spun, the adrenaline beginning to wear off. It left her heavy and stupid, muddied even beyond what the lack of sleep and the stress were doing to her.

Understanding that didn't make it easier to bear, though.

When the canister was spent and stowed, Gyre stood up, then swore as her rubbery legs gave out from under her.

She should rest, trust the battery. But if she rested here, she'd sleep. She'd lose track of time, blow past the safety window.

And sleeping was five percent she didn't have.

Momentum. She needed to keep her momentum going. *You're hitting your limit*, the tired, exhausted part of her whispered in retort. *You're only human.*

Fuck that.

With a concerted effort, she stood again, this time making it all the way up and staying there, trembling, until her legs remembered how to function. Then she took one careful step after another, wary of her ankle rolling, or her body otherwise making an executive decision to shut down without her input.

She was halfway across the room when she heard it again: a low rumble, distinct and undeniable. She froze in place, looking around. The walls seemed stable, the reconstruction solid. It couldn't be too close, then. And nothing had changed since her climb down. Well, nothing *physical*, nothing external to her.

It must just be in the area. The new tunnel on the Long Drop had already indicated as much. But the rumble didn't stop, didn't become fainter or louder.

What was it *doing*?

She stared at the cavern ceiling, willing her sensors to see past the stone and show her where the Tunneler was, but the rock remained impenetrable. Giving herself a firm shake, she looked around the camp. Right. The best thing to do, if it was on the move, was to get on the move as well.

She eased herself down the ledge where Jennie Mercer had crawled away to die, and had gone a few steps away from it when she frowned and turned on her heel. It was as if she could *feel* Jennie's body, a gravity well pulling her back.

Her throat felt tight and dry. The guilt broke through the heavy layers of personal, immediate fear, of shame at her own weakness. Jennie Mercer didn't know Gyre had promised to stop Em for her.

Yet Gyre couldn't help but tremble.

From here, Gyre could see Jennie's boots, identical to her own. She stepped closer and crouched down, her hand hovering over the other woman's ankle. *You have to protect yourself,* she thought. *Jennie was only down here for herself. You don't owe her anything.*

But Gyre couldn't stop looking at the carbon plating, the tread of the boot. They were identical. They were . . .

Her breath caught.

Face burning with shame, she reached out and took hold of Jennie's ankle. Carbon fiber screeched over stone as she dragged out Jennie's broken suit, the legs still rigid even now that its inhabitant was dead.

The model of suit *was* identical to Gyre's. And that meant that Jennie's suit had used the same batteries.

Maybe she didn't have to go to Camp Five at all.

She rolled the body over and checked the battery that was actively loaded. Dead; it must have powered the suit after Jennie died, Em unable to bring herself to turn it off. But there was a backup. It might also be drained, if Jennie had been making for Camp Four's cache to resupply, but . . .

Gyre pushed the eject button.

It didn't move.

*Great.* The fall that had left Jennie a corpse in a dented exoskeleton must have jarred some of the mechanisms inside the suit. She hesitated only a moment, then brought her fist down on the suit casing near the backup storage area. The suit was rigid enough on the outside that she didn't hear bone crack, but her mind conjured the sound in horrific detail. This would be her, if she didn't get down to Camp Five in time. Locked in, unable to move, her suit a sarcophagus. She struck the carbon panel again, and again, then tried the eject button, fingers fumbling over the release.

Nothing. It was totally jammed.

Gyre crouched there unmoving for a moment, then steeled herself and rolled Jennie onto her back again. She touched her hand to the front of Jennie's helmet. Luckily, she couldn't see inside with the reconstruction overlay running; the transparent plastic was just a flat color to her.

"I'm sorry," she said. "You don't deserve this." This was a far cry from bringing Jennie justice and respect, but even a half-drained, months-old battery might get Gyre through the sump to Camp Three, might let her bypass the Long Drop and those tumorous mushrooms, the memory of Isolde.

She found the button to open the suit, set in under Jennie's jaw, and pressed it. The click of the plates unlocking was audible, but without a functioning battery in the main port, Gyre had to wriggle her fingertips between the plates to pry them off. She started at Jennie's sides and belly, cracking open the suit like a nutshell. From one armpit to the other, down along her ribs and across her belly, she freed the plates from each other. Then she grabbed Jennie's shoulders and hauled her upright, peeling her off the part of the suit that contained the backup. Her body was somewhat preserved, feedback film desiccated and husk-like around her, but it and the flesh gave way when Gyre touched her, pulling apart across her back as she leaned the woman against her chest.

Gyre sat there, breathing hard and staring at the tubes and

electrodes running from the suit to Jennie's torn flesh. This was her, beneath the suit. Wired in, plugged in, part of the technology. In some ways, she was just the brain inside of it, the fine-motor control. Her stomach roiled. She wanted out of her own suit, but she could picture her own skin sloughing off, the tubing tugging, rupturing, her body a bag filled with fluid and blood and bile, punctured and leaking out onto the cavern floor. Vomit rose in her throat, and she let go of Jennie, falling back onto her ass and staring at the corpse, which sat upright on its own, braced by the remains of the suit, hunched forward.

Air. She needed air. But as she opened the front plate of her helmet, she could smell meat, and the faint smell of rot. She twisted, turning herself over as her stomach heaved. Her cannula ached in protest as her gut contracted, and she coughed, hacking, bending close down to the rock.

Nothing came up. The nausea receded, and she sucked in great gulps of air. It was clean enough. It would have to do.

The battery. She needed the battery. She didn't have time for this.

Her stomach lurched as she turned back to Jennie's body and crawled around to the back of her. She wished she'd cared more about the construction of her own suit, had paid attention to it before she put it on. The internal structure and its connections to Jennie's spine were dizzyingly complex. Most didn't pierce the skin itself, but she didn't want to dislodge the leads and rip Jennie's skin open along with them when the film cracked and pulled away. She slid her hands into the thicket as gently as she could, searching. She reached the other side of the battery storage area, and breathed a sigh of relief as her thumb grazed a release catch.

The back of the battery storage area wasn't jammed, and

the door came up easily. She worked quickly, pulling out the battery, weaving it out through the tangle of wires. Once it was in her hands, she sat back on her heels and looked at the path of Jennie's spine. She'd dislodged a few leads despite the care she'd taken, and Jennie's skin looked like it was covered in weeping sores.

It was grotesque.

She didn't deserve to be preserved in the suit, contained and inhuman. But Gyre didn't have time for a funeral, didn't have a way to carry her out. All she could do was lay Jennie back down, gently, into the shell of her suit, and open up her helmet.

Inside, her face was sunken and strange, her eyes just pits. Gyre made herself look. "I'm sorry," she whispered again. "I really did try to stop her."

Jennie didn't respond.

Slowly, she turned away and reached behind herself to swap the new battery into her backup slot so that her suit could measure its remaining charge. Maybe she hadn't owed Jennie anything before, but if this battery worked . . .

She fumbled it, her fingers clumsy. It took five tries, twisting and turning the thing, until she could slide it partway in.

And then it stopped.

The same damage that had made it unable to eject made it unable to be fully seated.

She swore, watching the readouts. Its power levels fluctuated wildly. It had enough charge left to help, but to use it, she'd have to hold it in place, and even then it might not work efficiently, or reliably.

It would be useless for climbing, much less attempting the sump to Camp Three.

She looked back down at Jennie, grimacing. "I'm so sorry,"

she whispered, then closed her faceplate. She pulled the battery out of the backup slot, and stashed it in her side compartment, then turned and struck out from Camp Four.

All that, and possibly for nothing.

She needed to get down the Long Drop, and fast.

She could still hear the Tunneler.

# CHAPTER TWENTY-TWO

It was only a half hour's walk and scramble to the Long Drop, but by the time she reached it, her battery was hovering just over critical state. She stood at the edge of the drop and considered her options.

She was going to go fast; going *down* would be easier than going forward, at least as far as needing to see went. The headlamp should be enough, and switching would slow the drain on her battery. But it would be a long, long descent, and the thought of doing it almost blind made her throat close up.

Better her throat than her suit, though. She didn't want to be a statue, frozen and slowly starving to death, hanging from a rope and hoping that it wouldn't—or maybe that it *would*—break and send her falling to her death.

The indicator ticked down again.

### 23% CHARGE REMAINING

It was all the impetus she needed, so she clipped onto the rope and began her descent, waiting until she passed the second bolt and was comfortable on the cliffside before she turned off the reconstruction and clicked on her small, dim headlamp.

Cutting through the darkness, Gyre rappelled down in smooth, even leaps. The bolts held. She made good time by trusting them, forcing aside any thoughts of falling. It wouldn't happen. It couldn't. They were *her* bolts, and the bolts held, and the yawning darkness welcomed her into it.

She covered the first day's descent in a little under two hours, and when she realized she'd reached the small ledge she'd fallen from a week ago, she was surprised by how relieved she felt. She navigated it more carefully this time and swung down toward the larger ledge and Tunneler path below. The telltale thrum in her bones grew more and more distant the farther down she went, freeing up her lungs for deeper breaths, and her heart from its terrified racing.

Camp Five wasn't far. She could do this. Get to the raft, haul up the battery box, and then she'd be good. She'd be safe.

She touched down on the deep ledge with a relieved groan, her legs quaking in protest as she made them properly take her weight. Her whole body felt impossibly heavy now that she'd stopped descending, and she considered pausing here, taking a nap. A quick look at her battery indicator proved that was out of the question, but she could at least stop to eat.

She walked a short circuit around the ledge first, stretching her legs out, thinking, remembering. The video, the sedation . . . *I should have turned back here.* But even now, with context and distance, she knew she could never have made that choice. She'd already come too far.

Given up too much.

Was she always bound to end up here?

Dwelling was pointless, though, and she stepped out of the tunnel mouth and back onto the ledge proper.

Isolde's face stared back at her.

She shouted in panic and fumbled with the rope, desperately trying to clip in. She had to get away. She had to—

*Not real.*

She stopped, panting, her eyes fixed on the apparition. Isolde's pale face was drawn and exhausted; she was older, perhaps, than she had been in the video. She was also hard to see, doused in shadows. Gyre stared at her, waiting for her to vanish like Hanmei had, but she remained solid. Real. Impossibly real.

Gyre reached out.

Isolde retreated, backing away, away. Past where the ledge should have given out.

And then Gyre blinked, and there was nothing.

Gyre scrambled to the far end of the ledge, switching back to her reconstruction and peering over the rim. Nothing. There was nothing at all.

Except for a bolt, turning yellow as she stared at it. Unsafe. Unknown. There was rope, leading down. It was taut, as if there was a weight on the other end.

Gyre fumbled with her settings, then turned on the external speakers she hadn't used since Camp Five. "Hello?" she asked.

It echoed back from the domed ceiling a few seconds later. "Isolde?"

The cache at Camp Four. The face at Camp Five.

*Em was wrong. There's somebody here.*

*It was never the spores.*

She reached out with one trembling hand and touched the rope.

If she cut it, Isolde—or whoever it was; Isolde was dead by now, couldn't have survived all these years—would fall to their death. Would be *gone*. The threat would be gone.

But fuck, if it really *was* Isolde . . .

She backed away from the ledge and turned off her external speakers. She could feel it again too, the rumble in her breast. The Tunneler was making another pass, circling this section of cave again. It was close—she was certain of that now.

She couldn't move forward until she made a decision. Trembling, she sat down against the far wall of the ledge and set up her feeding. Her eyes never left the bolt, still glowing a faint yellow just past where the ground fell off. Cut or leave? Trust Em or herself?

With a flex of her fingers, her rope-cutter extended from her right wrist. She had to cut it. If she really was hallucinating, it made no difference. If she wasn't, it might save her life.

*Isolde, Isolde, Isolde.* Isolde was impossible. She couldn't make her decisions based on that, and Em would never know. She would never, ever know.

Stomach still crawling from the sludge that was coating it, Gyre shuffled forward on her knees, over to the edge. She stared down into the gray and black rendering of the cave structure around her, at the emptiness. There was no sign of Isolde, only the taut rope, the bolt.

With one jerking motion, she slashed across the line. It gave way, and aside from a quiet slither as it passed through the air close to her, there was no noise at all. Even two minutes later, Gyre holding her breath nearly the whole time, there was no thud of a body hitting the ground.

She couldn't keep waiting, and she clipped into her own line, forcing herself to look ahead. As she switched back to her headlamp, her fevered brain conjured eyes on the far wall looking back at her, shining against the blackness.

Her grimace turned to a violent snarl, and the eyes blinked back in surprise. She released her hold on the wall, taking the next step down in a long, wide, graceful arc. Her muscles protested, but she ignored them.

A few more hours, and she'd have light. She'd have food. She'd have Em back, and a massive computer at her beck and call to monitor everything around her.

Those hours passed in agonizing slowness, her limbs growing tired, her fingers nearly useless. The eyes were gone the next time she looked over her shoulder, but then again, her vision was getting so blurry that she couldn't be sure if they were there or not. She never did hear a body strike the ground far below her, but she always heard the Tunneler, constant rumbling at a distance. It wasn't in her bones yet. She had time.

She took the descent at breakneck speed, so fast that as she returned to the cliffside once, she struck at an angle, banging the arm she'd injured on her first descent. The pain flared to life, briefly eclipsing the ache in her thighs, the pounding of her head. Her jaw hurt from how much she'd clenched it, but she didn't stop, didn't slow.

The battery indicator ticked down.

18% CHARGE REMAINING

Gyre wondered how much of her sanity remained.

# CHAPTER TWENTY-THREE

Camp Five floated motionless on the surface of the sump, covered in a fine layer of spores. By her headlamp, Gyre could see the faint glow and the puckered texture of the powder on the surface of the water. Taunting her.

### 16% CHARGE REMAINING

The alert hovered in her view, joining in the mockery. She grinned, though, fiercely. She'd done it, and she'd done it expertly.

But at such a cost.

Her hands were shaking as she placed an anchor at the rim of the pool, her knuckles brushing one of the fleshy growths of fungus that were clustered so tightly, so close to the water. It flexed slightly, and seemed as if it wouldn't give, but then exploded in a burst of pale, glowing spores.

They settled thick on her hands and she flinched, but kept working.

Bolt set, she tied in, checked her line. *Just a few more minutes.* And then she could rest and hear Em's voice and *go home.* She stepped out into the open air above the water and walked herself down. The light of her lamp bobbed against the darkness, flashing across the smoothed walls of the pit, skittering across the tumorous masses.

Catching the edge of what looked like a face, which darted away again as Gyre looked down at her hands.

*Easy, easy.* She took each step carefully, concentrating on the movements of her hands and feet. She couldn't afford to fall into the water. Her rebreather would turn on, the buoyancy would activate on its own, and how horrible would it be to get so close, only to be trapped, frozen, under the surface?

She paused to put in another bolt, just in case.

At last, she touched down on the raft. It distorted under her weight, rivulets of water sliding over her boot. She stayed tied in, taking up her slack once she'd sat down. Then she grabbed up the rope to one of the boxes and hauled. The heavy crate rocketed up through the water, and then it was in her hands, and she was fumbling at the latch. She opened it. Ropes. A drill. The box of gear, not the one she needed. She closed it, pushed it out of her lap, hauled up the next one.

This one jerked, then twisted, the feel on the line all wrong. It was hard to see beneath the water with the glare of her headlamp on the surface, through the film of spores. Breathless, she kept pulling.

The box broke the surface—open.

Empty.

*Empty.*

No ration canisters, no batteries.

Empty.

She held the box in her hands, staring in disbelief, transfixed. Then, heart pounding, she tossed it aside. It crashed into the surface of the water, throwing glowing spray back at her, but she was already at the edge of the raft, loosening her line, jumping in. Her lamp lit only a small circle in front of her, and she switched back to her reconstruction, battery charge be damned.

Down at the bottom of the cenote, below the tunnel that led to Camp Six, ration canisters and batteries littered the silty floor. They were arranged into concentric circles, a monument to her impending death. She kicked, hard, and was jerked back by her line. Cursing, Gyre cut it and plunged deeper. Her hand closed around the first battery. She reached for another, another, and then pushed up to the surface, three held tight to her breast.

Breaking the surface, she kicked awkwardly for the raft, one hand outstretched while the others cradled her prize. As she reached the platform, she stretched, pushing them onto the raft, then following herself. She ignored the water sheeting from her suit and shoved the first one into the backup port.

It didn't have a charge.

She tried the second, and the third, but they were the same. Cold. Dead. Had the water shorted them? Em must have built them better than that. Must have. Except she'd said, at Camp Three, that the batteries needed waterproof containers to cross the sumps. No. *No.* She dove back into the water, pulled another three up to the surface. Deposited them. This time, she tried to wait for them to dry. She took the rope behind her and shoved it into the backup port, hoping it was absorbent enough to make a difference.

14% CHARGE REMAINING

"Please, please," she whispered.

She picked up one of the batteries and shook it, dislodging the last few droplets. Holding her breath, she reached back and slotted it in.

No charge.

Gyre howled. She howled in pain, in anger, and in hatred. Hatred for whoever had desecrated the box. Hatred for herself.

Because who else was down here, really?

Only her.

She'd been hallucinating from the spores. She'd been panicked. She'd closed the box and thrown it into the sump, and she hadn't latched it right.

She hadn't even noticed it spilling its contents out across the silty bottom as she dove.

Her bellow wavered, fell apart into a sob, and she beat her fists against the wall. The raft shifted under her, the batteries rolling, falling back into the water. "Your fault, your fault!" she hissed, tears burning in her eyes, not sure if she meant her fault or the fault of her mother, abandoning her to the obsessive fate that had dragged her this far.

And then she heard it, faint, like a dream. A whisper.

*Caver, continue.*

Em's voice, there for a moment, and then gone. She stilled, save for the shaking of her shoulders, the trembling in her chest.

"Caver, continue," Gyre repeated. Her lips felt numb. Her head hurt.

She stared at the water.

Camp Six was a long swim away, but it was straight. It was easy. She'd done it alone before.

*Not alone*, she thought. Em had been gone, but the

computer had been there, no doubt assisting. Now, she'd have to monitor everything herself. Buoyancy. Remaining capacity of the filtration canisters in her rebreather. And she'd have to do it without the reconstruction that was even now burning through her remaining battery power.

But it was the only chance she had left. Camp Three was too far away. Camp Four was empty. Camp Five was ruined.

Gyre took a deep breath, then switched to her headlamp. Stared a moment at the glowing film on the surface of the cenote, broken in places, dull and swirled. Then, without another look up at the cave above, without looking for more faces in the dark, she dove.

∨∨

The first minute was agony. The water was dark and her headlamp didn't pierce far into the gloom, and she made her way slowly, fingers trailing along the wall of the pit. Her toes struck one of the ration canisters and she spasmed away from the sudden contact, twisting in the blackness to find only the dull reflected shape she'd come to rely on. All she needed was to find the line she'd put down the first time, but she needed to do it fast. The urgency made her clumsy and slow-witted, made her forget at first that she had put reflective markers on the line. She swung her head wide, when she remembered, until her lamp glinted off the first one.

She kicked for it, reaching out her hand. Shadows darted across her vision, fleeing the light of her lamp. *Fish,* she reminded herself. Tiny things, insignificant life. But she was shaking all the same when her hand touched stone, when she slid her fingers down and bumped against the line itself. She grabbed hold of it, pulling herself tight against the rock. She was close to hyperventilating again, and she forced herself to slow her breathing. Her suit worked best when she was in control. She had to stay in control.

When she'd passed through before, there had been only small, sluggish currents, only the passage, and she'd been able to keep herself calm. But the mother of all sumps had changed her. Her isolation had changed her. Her fading battery had changed her. As she moved hand over hand along the line, she trembled uncontrollably, and it took all her willpower to uncurl her fingers each time. The light bobbed ahead of her, giving her nothing, showing only the small branch-offs and obstructing formations that she knew led nowhere, but feared were her only way out.

### 13% CHARGE REMAINING

She turned her lamp off.

She was plunged into blackness, weightlessness, the only sensations the suit against her flesh, the slight drag of gravity against her, and the tension of the line in her hands. Could she do this without added buoyancy? She dragged herself forward again, felt herself sagging away from the line. What if she let go? No, she needed to be neutral. A single-time inflation had to cost less energy than keeping her light on.

Right?

She made the decision, fumbled with the controls. The sacs spread along as her suit inflated, sharply, too much. She felt herself lift. Swearing, she tried to release the air in small, controlled bursts. She overshot.

Tears stung her eyes, but she tried again. Again. On the third time, the calibrations were just right.

She didn't have time.

She reached farther along the line, into the abyss, and hauled herself forward. Hand over hand; it was the only way she could do it. Hand over hand, flinching every time she brushed against the side of the wall or jostled the line between her fingers, biting down a scream the first few times she reached a directional arrow, not expecting the hard plastic.

Finally, after what seemed like an eternity, her fingers closed around a larger arrow, pointing up. *The bell.* She was more than halfway there, and more than anything, she wanted to surface into it, pretend that she was safe in its little pocket of air. Bathe in the faint glow of its lichen. But she couldn't afford to stop and restart the rebreathers.

She coaxed her knuckles open around the line and dragged herself away from the bell.

Her readout, darkened to conserve power, blinked red.

6% CHARGE REMAINING
BATTERY LIFE REMAINING LESS THAN ONE HOUR AT
CURRENT ACTIVITY LEVELS

"Just a little farther," she whispered, and swam on.

# CHAPTER TWENTY-FOUR

Gyre reached the sloping bank with ten minutes remaining on her readout.

**BATTERY APPROACHING TOTAL SHUTDOWN**
**CAVER, SWAP TO BACKUP**

The words glowed in bright red across her screen, the only thing she could see with her lamp and reconstruction off. She didn't waste time trying to dim the alert, didn't dare use her limited power to turn on her light. She clawed her way up onto the wide bank of stone by touch alone.

As she turned off her limited buoyancy and her rebreather, the time estimate jumped back up to twelve minutes.

*Not enough*, she thought, and staggered for Camp Six.

Hands out in front of her, she felt for the pillars. She lifted her feet carefully to avoid catches in the stone. But she was going too slowly and she couldn't find the way, not without a line. The chamber was too chaotic and too unfamiliar. Getting lost was as much a death sentence as her light.

Cursing, she turned her lamp on. The number fell again: six minutes. Without taking the time to orient herself, she broke into a full run. Her brain struggled to catch up, overstimulated by the shadows after two hours in absolute darkness. She made herself stare straight ahead, refusing to look between the pillars for ghostly faces in the gloom.

Her thighs burned as she sprinted, straining against her weight, which seemed to be growing with every footfall. She slowed meter by meter, struggling forward as if she were sloshing through the lake, as if she were trapped in hardening resin. Her suit was growing sluggish, and each step took more effort than the last.

Gyre clenched her jaw and surged forward, gaining precious speed. She could see the barrier wall that protected Camp Six, there at the far edge of the light from her lamp. But she was clumsy, lurching. Her foot refused to lift more than a few centimeters from the stone, and her toe caught on a ridge. She tripped, sprawling forward, cursing, clawing to get herself back upright.

The suit fought her.

Her lamp went out. The alert disappeared, leaving only the timer, ticking down toward zero.

*No.*

She only had a few hundred meters left to go—even fighting against her suit, only another minute at most. She swore and reached for the equipment hump, but it was like moving under a lead blanket. Her muscles were too weak, her suit too heavy. All she could hear was her own breath, rasping from her throat, and the pounding of her pulse. The film across her skin tightened, pulling at her flesh, suctioning it to the polymer around her.

The suit was dying, and trapping her inside it.

But she was on dry land.

She could use Jennie's battery.

It took all her strength to force her hand back far enough to brush her hip. Without enough charge, the servos that powered the suit and allowed it to respond to her movements were shutting down, locking in place joint by joint. The same mechanism that had supported her on her long climbs, that had given her the sheer strength to climb into a waterfall, was now turned against her. She twisted her shoulder, grimacing in pain as she pushed herself against the exoskeleton. Her fingertips caught the latch to the storage compartment.

The mobility of the fingers on her suit was still comparatively high, even if the arms and legs could barely move, even if her head was frozen in position. She felt for the backup battery, her fingers tangling in rope, displacing bolts.

Something moved on her left.

Gyre's head jerked up, banging into the inside of her suit as the helmet didn't move with her. There was nothing in front of her, but the motion had been to her left. She tried to turn her head.

She couldn't.

Beyond the glow of the lichen, there was only pitch blackness. No faces. No bodies.

*You don't have time for this.* She twitched her fingers, felt something spin. Another twitch. The battery rolled into her hand. *Please let this work, please, please.*

More movement in the corner of her eye. She instinctively

tried to face it but couldn't move except to close her fingers around the backup battery. She dragged her arm back, reaching for the port. It was like pushing against a wall, unmoving, unyielding. She moved so slowly, she couldn't be sure it wasn't a hallucination.

More movement, shadows fluttering to her right now.

She shouted, loud enough to make her ears ring, and jerked her arm. She could hear the suit groaning in protest. She'd really moved, and now she could feel the plane of her back, and she fumbled for the eject button with her thumb, other fingers clenched tight around the battery.

The button depressed. She heard the dead battery clatter to the ground, spent. She screamed as she shoved the backup battery in, and in an instant her headlamp came back on, and she spasmed, her prison loosening. Her free hand clawed against the ground, and she drew her knees up under her, then took off in a lurching sprint for Camp Six.

### BATTERY APPROACHING TOTAL SHUTDOWN
### CAVER, SWAP TO BACKUP

The alert blinded her. She shook her head, puffed out air, tried to clear it. It refused, and she slowed by a hair, fumbling with the controls.

The light in her headlamp sputtered.

The battery wasn't going to be enough.

Gyre surged forward into the red of the alert, the darkness of the cave. Her light flickered again, and then her left knee locked up for just a millisecond, just long enough to throw off her stride. Her shoulder struck a pillar and she spun to one side, nearly losing her footing.

She reached the barrier wall, one last short climb between

her and safety. She jumped, hitting the edge with her stomach, grunting and letting go of the backup for the half second she needed to stabilize herself and sling one leg over. Her lights dimmed, then cut out.

The backup battery began to fall. She cried out, reaching back, grasping it just as she pulled herself onto the top of the shelf. She forced it back in. Her light came back on.

Her suit refused to move.

*No. No.*

The suit wasn't displaying the remaining charge of the backup battery. Was it too low, or not seated? Whichever it was, she couldn't fix it. She couldn't move. Her gaze fixed on the stone that filled her vision. She couldn't move, and soon she wouldn't be able to breathe.

She was so close.

"Fuck!" she shouted. It did nothing. Tears tracked down her cheeks, but they also did nothing. Nothing, *nothing.* She was going to die, ten meters from batteries, from salvation. If she had just closed that box at Camp Five properly, she would have lived. If she had just run faster. If she'd avoided the columns, if she hadn't tripped. She held her breath, cheeks expanding, until, with a shuddering sob, she began puffing through her options.

*Morphine.* Morphine could end this quickly, gently. She didn't want to starve, didn't want to suffocate, didn't want to know which would come first with her broken battery. But she couldn't summon the medical panel, her thoughts racing too fast. Did her suit even have enough power left to inject her? Different settings flickered in front of her. Was the display dimming? How much longer did she have?

The communications setting screen flowed into her vision. She paused, staring at it.

*Em.*

She'd initiated contact before she had consciously decided. She watched as the link established, whispering, "Please, please," like a litany. Her suit still refused to move, and she was pinned to the stone like a splayed, dissected animal as she waited. Waited.

The indicator turned green.

"Gyre?"

"Em," she said, gasping. "Em, fuck."

"What's happened? You're not moving. Are you hurt? Are you—oh shit."

"Yeah," Gyre whispered. "Yeah. I don't know how much time I've got left, but the suit isn't moving. So it can't be long, right?"

"You're getting some power, but the connection is fucked." There was a pause, and then Em's face appeared, filling her screen. "The battery isn't seated right."

"Can't be. Took it from Jennie's suit. It's broken."

Em frowned, her attention laser-focused on her screen. She looked so controlled, Gyre wanted to cry. Wanted to shelter under her for dear life.

"I wanted to say goodbye," Gyre said, her voice thick. "I wanted—I wanted to apologize, the recording, I know you saw it—"

"Do you trust me?"

She stared at the screen.

"Gyre, do you trust me?"

"What are you going to do?" Administer the morphine? Cut the oxygen? Displace with helium? How would Em kill her? She was shaking now, unsure if she was relieved or terrified.

"There's no time, Gyre. Yes or no?"

The answer was terrifyingly easy. "Yes!"

"Don't worry about the recording; I understood. And I'm sorry," Em said, glancing at the camera.

Gyre's chest tightened. Her heart stopped.

And then her screen went black.

At first she heard nothing beyond her heart and her breath, and then she realized what that meant. The air exchange fans had stopped. The fans that had slowed in her climb to the waterfall had gone still at last, ceased exchanging her depleted air for fresh. She didn't have a day before they failed and she suffocated—it was going to happen now.

Her lungs began to ache as each breath took in less oxygen. She panicked, gulping in a huge lungful of depleted air and holding it, holding it, her eyes feeling as if they would burst. Then, seconds later, her arms jerked. Her legs remained rigid, but her hands flexed, one pushing the battery back into its slot. The lights didn't come back on, though, and neither did the air filter. Her skin crawled as the film against it lost something, turned to slime. Everything felt wrong, and her lungs burned, her eyes hurt. Her head swam.

Her free hand reached out. Grabbed what felt like stone.

And dragged.

The whine of polymer pulling over rock filled her awareness as she let out the breath she'd been holding, sobbed as she tried to take another. Tried not to hyperventilate. Her suit inched forward. Em was dragging her to the batteries. All she had to do was hang on. All she had to do was not die.

Her legs were fixed in an awkward position, and it hurt as Em pulled her across the uneven floor, her knee catching on small outcroppings, her hip falling into depressions. But she was moving. She was moving, and just when her thoughts were spiraling apart from lack of air, the filters turned on for five seconds. She couldn't hear them over the pounding in her ears, but she could taste the stale air, and she gasped for it, sucking it down. Then it went away again.

Her hand brushed something. Her arm curled around it. She felt herself lift, pulled up into a sitting position. She could hear her hand, clumsy, not hers anymore, fumbling with a latch.

Her fingers wrapped around something. Her arm pulled back. She closed her eyes. *Em, Em, please*, she thought. What if, when the backup was removed, Em couldn't get the new battery in? What if the connection to her computer, the only thing allowing Gyre to move, gave when there was no direct power? Fuck. *Fuck.* She was crying again, fingers spasming inside her suit, having no effect on how Em eased the backup from the slot.

"Please, please," she prayed.

Her hand holding the fresh battery jerked, slammed the battery home.

Her systems came on full blast in an instant, the reconstruction of the room brilliant and nearly blinding on her screen, her helmet blaring alarms as the air filters started up again. Her vision, blurred and foggy, resolved again as oxygen filled her lungs. She was hunched against the battery box, and she moaned, reaching for another of the glowing rods and fitting it into the slot for a backup.

She was alive.

"Gyre, can you hear me?"

"Yeah." She swallowed. "Yeah, I can hear you."

"Thank god," Em whispered, her voice cracking. The video feed sprang back to life. Em was slumped back into her chair, her shoulders hunched forward, her arms wrapped around herself. "Thank god," she repeated, and closed her eyes.

"Good to see you again," Gyre managed. *Safe, safe, you're safe,* she repeated to herself. Em was there. Em hadn't left her to die. Em had *fought for her.*

She clung to that fact. Slowly, she pushed up to her knees. Her legs were weak, and they hurt from where they'd been badly jarred. And she was tired, so tired, but at the same time, she wasn't sure she could ever sleep again.

*Safe, you're safe.*

The tears came again, ignoring her protests, ignoring the way she wrapped her arms around herself. She waited for the rush of medication, a soothing chemical lullaby to quiet her panic, but none came. Instead, she felt the arms of her suit shift. Gyre stiffened, then sagged forward into the mechanical embrace Em seemed to give her, her suit flexing and moving to support her. Gently, Em eased her down into a curled position that was almost comfortable.

"I need air," Gyre whispered.

At first, nothing happened. Then the reconstruction feed disappeared from her HUD and the faceplate of her helmet released, eased up and out of the way. Cool, damp air curled against her lips, her nose, her eyes.

She vomited.

The bile burned her tongue and throat, stung her eyes, and stank as it spread on the rock beneath her. It was the first thing she'd tasted besides filtered water in weeks, and it was horrible and wonderful. She retched again, bringing up nothing but thin, pale liquid, the result of her sludge diet.

Groaning, she crawled away from it, wiped her mouth with the back of her hand, nearly cutting her lip on the carapace of the suit and savoring the sensation.

"I'm here," Em said, when Gyre's stomach had quieted and her chest had stopped seizing. The suit shifted again, just a little, just enough that it felt as if there was a hand on her shoulder. Without her faceplate, Gyre couldn't see her, but it didn't matter. The sight of her meant almost nothing compared to the feeling, undeniable and real, that she was there, at Camp Six, holding Gyre. It didn't matter that she was using Gyre's prison to do it, or that Gyre's skin remained untouched, or that Gyre still had to climb out. There, in that moment, the most important fact was that Em was with her.

She held on to the feeling tightly, too afraid to relax into it and rest, too afraid it would evaporate if she didn't focus her whole attention on it. After days on her own, terrified she was about to die, she needed that feeling more than she had realized.

It was the only thing that would be able to carry her out.

She curled her fingers inside her gloves, wishing she could feel Em's hand beneath her own. Her shoulders quaked with her quiet crying, and Em said nothing, demanded nothing. Gyre listened to the splashing of her tears against the stone below her, and it felt real. She existed outside the suit, and the suit wasn't just a mechanical cage. It was Em. No matter what, as long as her computer remained linked to the suit, Gyre wasn't doing this alone.

A week ago, the idea would have terrified her. She would have hated Em for taking control of the suit. Now, though, part of her wished that Em could simply walk her out. If Gyre could only sleep, and Em pilot her body out, back to the surface . . .

No. She didn't want it that way. She took a deep, chilled breath, the cold air shocking her lungs and making her feel more alert, more herself. While she appreciated Em's rescue, the more Gyre calmed down, the more she hated the idea of being a puppet. She'd get *herself* home.

Slowly, Gyre tried to sit up. Her suit obeyed her. Em was either watching closely, or had relinquished direct control some time ago. Gyre got to her knees, then shuffled to the crates and eased them apart, settling in between them with her back to the stone wall.

"I'm good," she whispered. "I'm okay." Her voice sounded strange, echoing against the rock. It all sounded strange now. More real, or less real—one of the two.

"Thank you," Em said.

Gyre laughed weakly. "For what?"

"For not dying. For—letting me do that."

"Letting you save me."

"Mm. I—had to cut out your air filters."

"I noticed." Her chest still ached. Her head did too. Gyre reached for the other storage box and began rifling through it, keeping her hands busy to keep her mind from spiraling again. She loaded up on rations.

*Thank you* was what she wanted to say. Ached to say. *Thank you for saving my life, thank you for not abandoning me, thank you for having such a beautiful voice, thank you for . . .*

For putting her down here in the first place.

Her headache spiked. She grimaced, then realized she *could* rub at her temples. She shook as she lifted one hand and gently touched her suited fingers to her forehead. It felt strange. Wrong. Wrong, but perfect. She groaned, rubbing small circles, then let her hand fall away. The cool cave air swept over her skin again, and she reluctantly eased her faceplate back into place, her fingers trembling against the screen.

Em's face reappeared, small, in the bottom corner of her screen. Her eyes were fixed on her displays, and she'd drawn her knees up onto her chair. She looked confused. "You're at Camp Six. Again."

*Right.*

"I keep doing that," she tried to joke, but it hurt. "I fucked up at Five," she confessed instead, bowing her head. "Shorted the batteries last time I was there. I didn't seal the case right. Wasn't . . . wasn't thinking straight, I guess."

"If your power had failed in the sump—"

"I didn't have any other choice." She glanced at the video feed.

Em looked stricken.

"You could have gone to Camp Three," Em whispered.

"Yeah." She sucked at her teeth. "But we didn't know that."

"You had a better sense of what you could do than I did."

"No, I didn't. I was being stubborn. Being right was an accident." She didn't want to talk about any of this. She wanted to be sitting out under the sun, out of this suit, maybe with Em. She wanted to feel the press of a crowd around her, a mass of humanity, for the first time in her life.

"If I'd lost you," Em whispered, "I don't know that I could have gone on."

Gyre stared at the small image of her. "Oh."

"I don't want you to feel sorry for me," Em said quickly. "I know it's too little, too late, and I should have felt this way about the first person I sent down there. I know."

"Yeah," she said. "You're right."

But *I don't know that I could have gone on* wrapped itself around her heart, nestled in her chest. She meant something. She *was* different from the other cavers. The warmth she felt was part rage on those other cavers' accounts, but a lot of it was simply happiness at being seen. At being wanted.

She was pathetic. They both were.

They sat in silence a while longer, Em slowly uncurling in

her chair, Gyre slowly relaxing into her suit, muscle cramps easing.

Then Em frowned. "Gyre, can you feel that?"

"Feel what?" But then she did. She couldn't hear it, not quite, but she could feel the rumbling spreading through her legs where they were pressed to the ground, up into her chest.

"Shit."

Em was still for a moment. Then her face contorted into a demonic snarl, and she slammed her hands down on her desk. "This can't be happening!" she shouted, then clawed her hands through her hair. Her face was ruddy with fury, with panic.

Gyre said nothing, just letting her head fall back against the wall behind her.

"I've been hearing it since the waterfall," Gyre said after a few quiet moments, her voice flat, numb. "It went away while I was in the sump. Not sure when it came back. How close is it?"

"Close," Em said. "Your sensors aren't picking up any movements from the rock besides vibrations. Nothing's fractured yet. But it's close. Can you move everything to the center of the room? There's a bolt, just behind the boxes, you should be able to unhook them."

The second to last thing she wanted to do was move, but the *last* thing she wanted was to die, so she hauled herself up. She pushed her hands behind the boxes, her knuckles vibrating where they brushed the stone. *There.* She unclipped the boxes from their anchor and grabbed the handles, heaving them back across the uneven floor. Her shoulders screamed in pain. She shut it out. The vibrations of the boxes dragging over stone replaced the Tunneler's call, radiating up through her arms, into her gut.

When she reached the middle of the floor, she dropped the

boxes and sank to her knees, panting. "There," she whispered, her arms gone momentarily numb. She held her breath, waiting for feeling to return, hoping all the thrumming would be gone.

It wasn't.

"I opened my helmet," Gyre said, staring up at the ceiling, watching for the first sign of its crumbling. "At Camp Four, and just now. That must be it."

*You don't know that. Nobody knows that.* Em would say that, would try to convince her it would be fine.

Em grunted. "That's almost certainly it. I shouldn't have let you."

Gyre bit back a sob. "What do we do? I can't get in the sump, I can't leave, I'm too tired—"

"You should do your best to be totally still," Em said. "I'll do another systems check of your suit, make sure something else isn't venting strangely after everything it's been through. Can you sleep?"

"Not without help."

"Do you want it?"

She shuddered. "If you sedate me, and the ceiling starts coming down, I won't be able to get out in time."

"I can control your suit, if that happens. It might injure you if I move it wrong, though. It's—it's a risk."

"Is it my choice?" Gyre asked.

Em looked away, biting her lip. Then her shoulders sagged. "Yes. It's your choice."

But it really wasn't a choice. Gyre wanted to get out, and she also wanted to sleep. She wasn't willing to bargain away one or the other, not anymore. "In case of an emergency, that's fine," she said.

"All right. Are you comfortable?"

She laughed bitterly, but shifted in her suit and locked parts of it until she wasn't horribly *un*comfortable. "Yeah," she said, letting her head fall back the few millimeters into the gel cushion inside her helmet. "Go ahead."

She just had to pretend Em was tucking her into a warm, soft bed. Just had to pretend it was all going to be okay.

"Administering sedative. I'll see you in the morning, Gyre."

*Please, let that be true.*

# CHAPTER TWENTY-FIVE

The Tunneler was still close when she opened her eyes again.

She'd been out for ten hours. She checked, remembering with sickened dread the lost time she hadn't noticed when she'd last slept at Camp Six. The readout said ten hours, one dose of sedative; Em had been honest this time.

She would have felt relieved, except that she could still feel the vibrations in her chest. She didn't think they were stronger or weaker, and as she squinted and looked around the cavern, she didn't see any sign of structural collapse.

It was as if the ten hours hadn't happened at all.

"Em?"

"I'm here." Em yawned. "I'm here."

"You haven't slept."

"I was keeping an eye on you."

Warmth bloomed in her chest, pushing back the dread

for a moment's relief. Em had sat vigil. Em had made sure she was safe.

But Em couldn't make the Tunneler leave.

"It's still here," Gyre said, and unlocked her suit. Gingerly, she rolled onto her stomach and pushed herself up onto her knees. Her body was sore, but the kind of sore that meant healing. The kind of stiff that meant ten hours really had passed. She hissed through her teeth as she rocked her hips back, trying to loosen her legs up.

Em's video turned on. She looked horrible—drawn, worn-out, almost disoriented. "Yes," she said, her voice not as clipped and controlled as usual, "but it must be circling. I haven't been able to pinpoint its location, but the vibrations do change minutely, in a cycle."

"What's it waiting for?"

"I don't know." Em sighed. "How are you feeling?"

"Stiff," Gyre said, standing. She stretched her arms over her head, then flinched and brought them back down as a muscle spasmed below one rib, set off by the tremors coming from the ground. "Fuck, let's just get out of here."

"If you're in the sump and it passes too close—"

"If I'm *here* and it passes too close, I'm screwed."

"We could wait it out. It doesn't seem to be above you, just under. The chance of a cavern collapse is low."

Gyre grimaced.

"At least sit and eat," Em said. Yawned again.

"And wait for you to get a nap?"

"It would be appreciated," Em admitted with a bleak smile. She glanced momentarily at the camera, then back to her screen, falling silent. Staring. Her jaw was tense, her brow slightly furrowed.

Something about the set of her shoulders looked ... guilty.

"What's wrong?" Gyre asked, patting at her suit reflexively. "Did you find something while I slept? Is there something wrong with my suit that needs fixing?" Was this going to be the spores all over again?

"I ... I want you to wait at Camp Six," Em said.

A non-answer.

Panic rose in Gyre's throat. The feeling was well practiced now, but horrible all the same. "I want to climb out. Tell me what's wrong."

"You'll hate me."

"Is there something wrong with my suit?" she demanded. "Or with me? What's going on?"

"You're at Camp Six," Em said, as if that explained it all. She wrapped her arms tightly around her middle, refusing to look at the camera.

It didn't click at first, but then she turned and looked at the sump entrance. *No.* Not after all this. Not after she'd cared so much if Gyre lived or died. She couldn't.

And yet ...

This was Em. It had always been Em.

"You want me to go back in," Gyre whispered.

Em nodded. "I'm sorry," she said. "But I couldn't forgive myself if we didn't try. Just one last time. You're there, and once the Tunneler goes away—I trust you. I want to finish this with you."

Her words twisted between Gyre's ribs, prying them apart. Leave it to Em to pair her best instincts with her most heinous.

"What happened to, 'If I'd lost you, I don't know that I could have gone on'?" Gyre snapped. Em's tone had been so soft, so small, but the violence of her words pierced into her like a thousand red-hot needles. She was going to come apart at the seams.

After everything Gyre had gone through . . . No. No, Em couldn't mean it.

But of course she did. Because this was Em.

Em flinched. "They're both true," she whispered. "But we're so close. We're *so* close, and we have the supplies, and now we might know which direction to go—"

Gyre couldn't believe this. She couldn't *conceive* of this. A few days ago, maybe, *maybe* she would have been able to imagine Em being so selfish, so horrible, but here, now—after everything Gyre had suffered through, after everything *Em* had suffered through—

She felt sick again. Her hands rose to the base of her helmet, and she stood there, breathing hard, trying to fight down the nausea. She couldn't open her faceplate again, couldn't risk it, but what she really wanted was to rip off her helmet, tear out her hair, and scream until the cave *did* collapse on her.

"Just one more try, after you rest," Em said. "Just one more. I know you can do it."

"Fuck you," Gyre whispered.

"I know it's not fair," Em said. "But please, if you do it, I'll give you anything. I'll give you *everything*. I can't just leave, not now that we're this close. I thought I'd never see Camp Six again, and it was hard enough, turning away, but now that we're here, now that *you're there*—"

"Shut up!"

Em did.

"You said you understood why I was running that recording. Did you? Did you *really*?"

"You wanted proof of what was happening." Em swallowed. "I assume to blackmail me into—something. More money."

301

"Screw your money! I was recording to *stop this*," Gyre hissed. "To make sure there wasn't going to be another me, ever again. And then I thought, well, I'm at Camp Six, I might as well try, the most effective way to stop her is to *finish this*, but that was a mistake. I almost died.

"And I thought . . . I thought you got it, then. That you couldn't do it again, even if I didn't fix everything for you. That you couldn't bear this anymore. I thought I didn't need the recording, because you'd stop on your own.

"But you're never going to stop, are you?"

Em didn't respond.

"I'm not going back down there, Em. *Ever.* Even ignoring the Tunneler, what happens if I'm swept back to that tunnel? What happens if I'm taken somewhere *else*? And if I get through, what then? What if I can't get out?" The nausea wasn't receding. She felt rotten, stabbed and left with a festering wound.

She'd wanted so badly for Em to finally be on her side.

"If you want it so much, come down here yourself," she said. "Die for it yourself."

"I don't want you to die. I won't let you." Em leaned forward, then looked at the camera again and reached for it. Grasped it, from the blurry shadow that covered the edge of the feed. "You are the strongest, bravest woman I know. I know you can do this, and come out alive. I wouldn't ask you if I didn't believe that."

"Fuck, listen to yourself, Em! It's like you're two different people, one who gives a shit about all of us, and one who can't stop looking back at something that isn't even your fault!"

"I—"

"If you can't decide which one you want to be . . ." Gyre trailed off, bile tickling at the back of her throat. Then she saw the case by her ankle. Realized the power she still held. If words wouldn't work on Em, if even Gyre's near-death hadn't been enough to make her choose, then maybe what she needed was for Gyre to choose for her.

"Then I'll tell you who you are."

Gyre moved quickly. She crouched and flipped the case open and pulled out the remaining batteries. Took one out of the foam and set it aside.

And then she smashed the rest into the ground.

Em shouted as Gyre stood and brought her booted foot down on the batteries over and over again, until they were only twisted fragments of broken glass, distorted polymer and metal, all wreathed in goo that quickly lost its charge as it was exposed to the air.

She waited for retaliation.

None came.

"No more," Gyre said. "No more, after me. You'll kill us. You'll kill yourself. Yesterday, you thought you'd lost me forever, but you didn't. You were given a chance to make amends for my death, straight to my face. So live it. Commit. You couldn't stand the thought of me dying, so don't you dare ever put anybody else where I am right now."

Em stared down at her lap, unresponsive.

"Or," Gyre spat, "I suppose you can spend a year or two trying to restock this point so you can kill the next me. Doesn't sound so great, though, does it?"

"No," she whispered.

"Doesn't sound like you, either." Gyre swallowed. "Not anymore."

"If you need those batteries—"

"I have two fresh ones in my suit and saved a third. If I can't get to Three on that, maybe I deserve to—"

"Don't even joke about that," Em snapped, but at the last word her voice broke. She sagged in her seat, then looked away and pressed a hand to her face to cover what looked like tears. She was a quiet crier, not ugly and heaving like Gyre, but her face was twisted into brutal pain. Pain, and exhaustion. Gyre hadn't seen it before, but she could see it now. Bloodshot eyes, dark bags, a trembling in her shoulders . . . how long had it been since Em had slept?

She couldn't be thinking straight. Gyre swallowed, wanting to say something. But did Em deserve that? The benefit of the doubt, the trust that she hadn't really meant it?

Em twitched again, then looked up, her expression hurt. Tired. "Fine. No more. I'm . . . I'm done. I give up."

Gyre should have felt vindicated as she checked her suit over and prepared to leave Camp Six. But she didn't. She felt only sick. Betrayed. Angry. Angry that Em wasn't understanding, angry that Em was surrendering instead of being freed.

Angry that after all this, Gyre wanted desperately for Em to have been a better person.

"It's not giving up," Gyre said finally. "You're not giving up. You're moving forward. You're succeeding where your mother failed."

"Shut up," Em said. "Don't talk about my mother like that."

"Oh, come on! Be angry! Be pissed! You can love her and hate her at the same time, believe me!"

"I don't want to!"

"So what, then? Where does that leave us?"

"I don't know," Em whispered. Gyre focused on Em's image, and Em looked back into the camera, chin tilted up defiantly even as her suffering was written large across her features. "All I know," Em said, "is that I'm getting you out. I can do that, at least."

"Good," Gyre said, around a sudden lump in her throat. She wanted an apology, wanted, more, that the conversation could be taken back. She wished she'd never known what Em wanted of her.

She wished she'd never known that Em had deluded herself so far that she could believe another attempt wouldn't kill Gyre.

"I'm leaving for Camp Five," Gyre said, her voice clipped, curt. "You should get some rest."

"I'm not leaving you," Em said.

Gyre rolled her eyes as she crouched and picked up the one battery she hadn't smashed. She stashed it in one of her suit compartments, then went through the rest of them, checking how much gear she had left, reloading line, reloading bolts. "Get some fucking sleep, Em. I can't talk to you like this."

*I don't know if I can ever talk to you again.*

$$\vee$$

The video feed was closed, and Em hadn't said a word in the hour it had taken for Gyre to finish prepping her suit and having breakfast, but Gyre was left with no illusions. It was probable—likely, even—that Em was simply sitting there, watching her, instead of actually sleeping. Losing what little remained of her sanity and her self-control.

How quickly everything seemed to change down here, when, at the same time, nothing seemed to change at all. From the exaltation of reconnecting with Em at the waterfall to the knife in her heart from Em's request . . . had it been even a full day?

She almost envied the other cavers, dead without understanding what was happening to them.

*"If I'd lost you, I don't know that I could have gone on."*

The words hurt, but she couldn't stop repeating them. Couldn't stop feeling Em embracing her through the suit, couldn't stop thinking of how Em had clawed her way to Gyre's safety. How had it come down to this? Gyre wanted to scream, wanted to shake Em, wanted to demand that somehow, some way, she be better than she was.

But people didn't change, not that deeply. Isolde had broken Em, and Em would always be trapped down here, just like her parents' corpses. Just like Jennie Mercer.

Just like Gyre, if she didn't get moving.

Final check complete and spent ration canister swapped for a fresh one, Gyre headed for the banks of the sump to Camp Five.

"Diving," she said.

Em didn't reply.

Her chest tightened. She didn't *want* to do this alone. She stared at the water, wishing Em had somebody else up there with her. Wishing she wasn't frightened by just the dark blue sheet of unbroken water on her screen. The swim was easy. She had a line to follow. And this time, she'd have light.

But she could also remember the ticking percentage of her battery life, the blackness, crawling forward using only touch. It hadn't been long enough for her to forget.

*It will never be long enough.*

She held her breath and walked into the water up to her hips.

She couldn't feel the cold or the damp. She couldn't feel any motion except for the relentless throb of the Tunneler, endlessly circling. She wanted, desperately, to open her helmet and splash her face with the frigid water, to feel something *real*, but she resisted.

And then she felt it—a prickling between her shoulder

306

blades, a soundless keening. She turned back, looking over her shoulder toward Camp Six. It was as if she could hear them, somehow, Hanmei and Laurent and the rest.

She was going to abandon them. She was going to make Em abandon them.

Swallowing against a surge of unease, she opened up her external speakers and said, "I'm sorry I can't get you out."

Then she shut them down and dove beneath the surface.

$$\vee$$

In the full light of her reconstruction, the sump was just a huge tunnel, endless, broken by familiar outcroppings and almost-diversions. It wasn't an old Tunneler path; the cross section wasn't uniform, and the walls weren't smooth. But it didn't have the chambers of the sump below Camp Six, or the currents. She floated, kicking gently, taking hold of the line and gliding forward.

Swim the sump, climb the Long Drop, perhaps rest at Camp Four. Keep going to Three, then Two, then One, and finally reach the surface. It was easy, from here on out. Easy, except for the throb in her chest, which seemed louder, stronger, below the surface.

She'd reached the bell when she heard Em clear her throat.

"Welcome back," Gyre said.

"You're already on your way to Camp Five?"

"Nearly halfway," she said. "Did you sleep?" She hadn't sat there pouting, at least. Otherwise, she would have known exactly where Gyre was.

She stopped swimming and bobbed in the water, rubbing at her chest. Her reconstruction was fuzzy. The vibrations of the Tunneler were dislodging a fine layer of silt, shaking it up throughout the chamber.

"I did, yes. I—does that feel stronger?"

"Yeah, I think it's the water."

Em's fingers tapped keys. "No, it's stronger. And it's growing."

Gyre cursed and kicked, her fingers skimming along her line as she shot through the water. "How close is it?"

"Very. Gyre—"

"Don't have time to talk." She kicked harder, then let go of the line entirely so that she could swim with both arms. The vibration *was* growing stronger, as if it had heard them talking about it. *No, you're panicking. Keep moving.*

She inhaled, desperate for air as her muscles burned.

Her chest spasmed, knocked out of rhythm by the thrumming. It was everywhere. It was in her head, in her bones, in her stomach. *Panic, it's just panic, keep breathing, keep breathing—*

The roar was immense, all-consuming, all-possessing, and her entire body thrummed with it. Bone, blood, flesh, all hummed in tune, even as she felt herself give way to it.

"I have to dampen your suit!" Em shouted. The words were barely audible and didn't make sense. "Or it could kill you! You're in a fluid—the sound waves are transmitting *through* you!"

It wasn't beautiful, wasn't horrible—it only was, and it was all around her, inside of her. She didn't have room for terror or for panic or for anger. It was just the roar, the thrum, the throb, the pulsing vibration that was shattering her apart.

"You won't be able to see or feel or hear anything, but I'm here! I'm here, okay? Gyre!"

"Okay," she said, gasping. The sound barely left her lungs.

Then everything went quiet.

It was a strange sort of quiet, not entirely soundless but

something far worse. She could still hear her blood in her ears, but it was faint, far away. At first, she heard ringing. Then, her breathing. Then, nothing. Nothing registered. Her screen was black, and she floated in a void, neither warm nor cold, here nor there. Her first instinct was to thrash in revolt, but though she could feel her muscles shift, she couldn't feel herself move. There was no sense of an outside, of anything beyond herself. And that, too, was terrifying. Locked. Moving but to no purpose.

And then she felt one, single thing: suction.

The walls of the sump must have broken. The water was moving, draining, taking her with it.

She felt the sudden tug in one direction, and then nothingness again. But she knew she was moving, flowing, being stolen away. She curled up, instinctively, and waited for her bones to strike rock, but impact didn't come.

"Em?"

Nothing. Blankness. She couldn't feel anything beyond herself. Not water, not movement, not the vibrations of the Tunneler. There was only herself.

Then her screen turned back on.

And then she felt the buoyancy of her air sacs.

And then she heard Em's voice.

"Okay. Okay. Gyre, can you hear me?"

Around her, there was only water, too much water, filled with overlaid current lines. She knew this. "Oh fuck, we're back in the hell sump," Gyre whispered.

"No. No, I don't think so."

"This wasn't supposed to happen! We're lost, we're—"

"Shh, calm. Hang on. Let me look."

"Fuck," Gyre whispered. "Fuck! Are you happy now? I'm back down here, I'm—"

"Gyre, listen to me," Em said. "You haven't gone far. Those currents you're seeing are stabilizing; they're not that strong. From what I can tell, the Tunneler passed under the sump, close enough to weaken the rock. It broke through because of the weight of the water, and the water took you with it, but you haven't gone far. We'll get you out."

"I can't keep doing this." Her voice came out as a whine.

"I know. I know. Hang on. Breathe."

She sounded so calm, so confident, so in control, like she could only function when Gyre's life was at risk. Gyre wanted to shout at her, wanted to beat her fists against Em's chest. But she made herself cling to Em's words, her voice. The anger, the panic, all fell away.

She'd done this before. She'd do it again. Even if the thought brought her to tears.

"I just ran an inventory of your suit. Everything looks fine. Somehow."

"I'm a lucky one," Gyre managed, desperately trying to sound light and easy. "Is your computer showing if I can swim back up?"

"You should be able to. The currents you're seeing are very weak. There's even a chance the rest of the sump will be empty now, if this space is big enough. You'll be able to walk right out. You might have to climb to get all the way up there, though."

"Of course." She took a deep, steadying breath. *Just climbing. You're good at that; you can do that.* "The universe has owed me for a while now," she said, and slowly, slowly uncurled, lifted her head. She looked around her as the reconstruction filled her screen.

Then she frowned, closed her eyes, opened them again.

What she was seeing didn't make any sense.

It was a hallucination. Otherwise, Em would have said something by now. Would have screamed. Gyre licked her lips. "Are you seeing this?"

"Am I seeing wh—*fuck*."

It wasn't a hallucination.

Just in front of her was a body, floating, weightless, perfectly preserved in an old-fashioned wetsuit, its mouthpiece dislodged, the face bare. She was close enough that she could reach out and touch him, and close enough to make out his features, even rendered gray by her sonar.

She recognized the line of his nose, of his jaw.

It was Laurent. It was Em's father.

"That's . . . that's not possible," Em said, her voice cracking. "That's not—Gyre, get away from him. Get—oh shit. Oh—"

"What is it?" Gyre asked, tearing her gaze away, kicking back from the corpse instinctively. And then she saw them. Other bodies—three of them. One wore a wetsuit. The other two were in suits that looked exactly like her own, cavers who had descended before her. Em's dead floated all around her, scattered throughout the waterlogged chamber.

She'd been dragged back here, as if she could no more abandon them than Em could.

As if the cave wanted her to join them.

Em let out a broken sob, and Gyre heard her retch and then softly whimper, *"Dad."*

Gyre looked back at Laurent. It had been almost twenty years since he'd died, but he looked almost as if he were sleeping. He wasn't withered. He wasn't bloated. He was whole, and so were the others. His skin no longer looked like skin, but like smooth volcanic glass, but she couldn't be sure that wasn't an effect of the reconstruction. She'd never really looked at flesh with it before, aside from the impossible specters of Isolde and

Hanmei, and those weren't real enough to trust. Sonar or not, though, she could see he hadn't decayed.

"Em, is it the water? The—the chemical composition of it, is it the same as that one tunnel? *Is* it water? Am I in water?"

"I can't do this," Em said, gasping over the line. "I—*fuck*, find a way out. Please, Gyre. Go back. Climb out. I can't do this. *Please.*"

The pain in Em's voice cut through to her, through her numb horror, and she swam away from Laurent. She twisted, intending to swim up and back toward the sump to Camp Five, but then she was face-to-face with the other figure in a wetsuit. She could make out the curve of breasts, and even though the mouthpiece obscured the lower half of the body's face, she could still recognize her.

Hanmei.

Em's muffled sobs filled her helmet. Where was the exit? She kicked out, into the heart of the chamber, and spun around, watching as her sonar filled in the rest of the shapes. She watched for the telltale blue sheet effect. There—a possible surface. Maybe just an air bubble, but it could also be the way back up to the original sump passage. She kicked toward it, hoping, desperately, that she was right. Her head broke the surface. Her screen quickly brightened, displaying a full model of the surrounding room. There was even a bank nearby, the opening widening quickly at the water's surface.

It wasn't the way back to Camp Five, or even the lake at Six. But with Hanmei and Laurent so close, could that mean . . .

"Em," she said.

Nothing.

"Em, I'm going to climb out of the water." She waited for a protest, for another outcry of pain, but none came. Em didn't respond. Her sobbing had stopped. As Gyre watched, the voice line shut off.

Em had run away.

Shaking, she went through the menus and confirmed that her suit was still connected to the surface. Em had simply left, and it felt like a blow, even though Gyre could understand.

This was the chamber where everything had fallen apart.

She hauled herself from the sump, her legs trembling as she tried to remember how to stand. She looked at the high ceiling, the gaps in the wall over to her left. It certainly looked like the chamber Isolde had described. And it made sense that only a small bit of rock separated the hell sump from the sump to Camp Five, with the nearby lake the original team had entered through so close to both. She made for the platform near the center of the room, and as she got closer, she could see the scattered shapes of what looked like equipment. Staggering, she reached the edge and hauled herself up onto it.

There was a tipped-over camp stove, several dry bags that hadn't been sealed before they'd been abandoned. And a body.

*Julian.*

He was little more than a skeleton, some gear, and a dark stain on the rock mottled with the imprint of long-gone fungus. His remains looked far more real than the eerie preserved bodies in the sump. She turned to a duffel and dug through it until she found a sleeping bag, still packed tight after so many years. It must have been an extra set of gear that they'd ferried in, that they couldn't take with them when they ran. Or maybe it had been Halian's.

She unrolled the bag and settled it over the bones.

And then she settled in to wait for Em to come back.

# CHAPTER TWENTY-SIX

Em didn't come back.

Her voice line remained closed, and Gyre's suit hadn't moved outside of Gyre's control for hours. She'd checked the uplink again and again, the fear that their connection had been fully severed still lurking at the back of her mind. But it was always there, always steady.

Em was just a coward.

Here Gyre was, at the end. At the goal. At everything Em had worked toward for nearly ten years. This was what Em would have had Gyre break herself for.

And Em had run away.

Gyre paced the perimeter of the cavern, her eyes always drawn back to the small lump of Julian's bones beneath the sleeping bag, and to the blue-slate of the surface of the sump. She could just leave. Em had gotten what she wanted—she'd seen them. She'd been ready to stop before this, and now had no reason to continue. And if Em wasn't going to come back, Gyre had no reason to wait. She could swim out, start the climb. Move on.

But she didn't want to go back in the water. Not yet.

What if it took her somewhere *else*? What if the cave wasn't ready to let her go?

So instead, she sat down, her back propped up against the platform wall. She fed herself, wincing as the paste began to flow. The side of her abdomen itched where the cannula went in. That was new, and unsettling. How long had she been down here? How long until her feeding tube gave out? How long until she could no longer live in this suit, powered or not?

The itch spread over her skin, and she fought down the urge to take her helmet off. She couldn't risk it. She had called the Tunneler before, and if she called it again, here, in *this* cave . . . she knew how bad it could be.

What she needed was a distraction. Her body was benefiting from the additional rest Em's absence was imposing, and it was only her mind that was on fire.

She tried to read her mother's dossier, but she still couldn't bring herself to open it. It felt too much like inviting a piece of Em's madness into her, letting herself be drawn into a cycle like Em's search for Isolde. She wanted to find her mother, she did, but just how far was she willing to go?

If she looked at that file, what would it ask of her?

But beyond the dossier, what did she have left? Music that would just become background noise as soon as she started it. Readouts of her own body, possible proof that something was going wrong. Her skin crawled at the thought, shimmied inside its gel coating that didn't feel quite right anymore. Ever since it had gone slack without power, it had re-formed strangely around her flesh. It felt worn. Used. It had seeped

315

into the braided knots of her hair, making her scalp a web of sensations that shouldn't be there.

She couldn't look at the medical panel.

That left only the videos of Isolde's team.

She didn't want to witness their pain, but before the disasters, before it had all played out, they had seemed . . . happy. They had trusted one another. She wanted that. Craved it, now.

Gyre started a random video about a third of the way through the expedition and settled in. Isolde, whole and healthy, filled her screen.

⌄

It was like tasting water for the first time in days, water that was too hot and burned her mouth, but water she sucked down despite the pain. All she could think about was her parched throat, her scorched heart. All she wanted was more.

*Fuck.* This had been exactly what she'd wanted, but she hadn't realized it would *hurt.* Even knowing what was coming for them, she wanted to be there, with them, the urge crawling down her spine and squeezing at her lungs. She wanted to explore the cave without a suit, like she had as a girl. She wanted to walk with another person, to hear their breathing at night as they slept on their bedroll, close enough that she could reach out and touch them. Jealousy crashed over her, bringing her close to tears.

She shut the vids off, too weak to continue through the pain.

But the ghosts of Isolde's team refused to leave her. It wasn't fair. It wasn't fair that they'd had one another, and she had only herself and Em . . . and now even Em was gone. She would have given anything to swap places with one of them,

316

even knowing it meant certain death. She'd face the Tunneler again, give it all up, because at least then she would be dying with all of them rather than dying by herself.

They wouldn't have abandoned her, not like Em. They wouldn't have had the choice.

That sealed it.

She looked at the blue surface of the sump and hauled herself to her feet.

She had to get them out.

It wasn't about Em when she waded back out into the water. It wasn't about giving them a funeral so that Em could be at peace, or about stopping Em from sending somebody else down here, now that she knew how to find this place. It was because she needed to see their faces, and because she needed to take them out of the purgatory that the foul, twisted sump had become. The solid blue slate of the surface covering her boots made the panic rise in the back of her throat, but she pushed it away.

It was just water.

They were just bodies.

Her suit would keep her safe.

She touched the surface with her fingertips, hesitating for just a moment. And then she pushed out into the sump and dove under.

Her reconstruction lit the chamber in bright, unreal shapes, a few whispers of color here and there laying out the currents. She went around them, working methodically, placing bolts and line just in case. She made her way to Laurent first, then paused, floating, staring at him.

However he had died, he looked peaceful now, and like not a single day had passed. Whatever was in the water, it was a powerful preservative. Grimacing, she wrapped one arm around him and swam back along her line, then hauled him out of the water and laid him out by Julian's bones.

Three to go.

Hanmei took half an hour. The other cavers took longer. Their suits were rigid and locked, and they were heavy with all the gear packed into them. But one by one, she dragged them from the water and arranged them on the platform. She removed Hanmei's mouthpiece, opened the two cavers' helmets. Her battery ticked down as she worked, ten percent lost in her rescue efforts. Her chest tightened, until she felt for the two extras she was carrying. She had time; she could do this for them.

Kneeling at their feet, she pulled up the files Em had given her as a sign of trust weeks back. She needed their names.

One was Michael Doren. The other was Jensen Liao. Absent was Eli Abramsson, the young man who'd come in just before her, who'd been swept away in the currents at the start of the hell sump and lost contact with Em entirely. She mouthed their names to herself until she had them memorized. It didn't take long.

And then she looked at the side tunnels.

She wanted to assume that there was nothing left of Halian, but Isolde's interview had been specific. She'd described how the rock had closed on him, and all they could see were his legs. But if that were true, if he hadn't just been crushed into paste, if there was still something of him left, wouldn't Isolde and Hanmei have brought him out?

But why should they have? It would have been horrible to leave him, but abominable to bring him back.

He would be only bones now. Gyre stood and left the platform. She almost pulled up the interview video to check that it had been the northeast tunnel that had collapsed, but she couldn't bring herself to. She could never open that one again.

She decided she'd been correct when she saw the tunnel blocked off by solid, smooth stone, an unlikely formation in a tunnel like this, a formation that was distressingly familiar now. And there, at its base, were a pair of shoes and the long bones of his shins. There were his kneecaps, discarded, loose against the rock, and then—

And then his femurs, sheared off halfway up.

There were scraps of clothing left too, and she bundled all the pieces together, trembling as her armored fingers touched his bone. He was exposed, eaten, but didn't that make him free? He and Julian had been released from this cave long ago. She gathered his remains into her arms and walked them back out to the platform. She settled the pile of him by the others, and then sat down at their feet once more, staring at the long row.

*We're all here together now.*

"I've run the calculations," said Em.

# CHAPTER TWENTY-SEVEN

Gyre stiffened. Em's words were an intrusion, and so was the video feed that opened in the bottom corner of her screen. Em looked more awake, but so solemn. Gyre stared at her.

Em kept talking, as if she had no idea that the bodies were just in front of Gyre. "I finished a full-detail model based on the data your suit sent to me. The Tunneler passed between the sump to Camp Five and the chamber you washed into. The weight of the water broke the stone on either side. You can get out, easily, the way you came in. Your suit is still stable, and the Tunneler has, as far as I can tell, moved on. It must have been leaving the area when you left Camp Six. Maybe whatever was calling it lasted until you touched water."

The relief that flooded her at knowing she was safe was short-lived, erased by Em's recitation of theories. Gyre said nothing.

"I apologize for my absence," Em said. Her throat worked. "It was . . . unprofessional."

"No shit."

"Are you prepared to keep moving?"

Gyre scowled. "What about them?"

Em was silent. Her gaze left the camera, went to some other screen. Her fingers moved, tapping filling the space between them.

"Ah," she said at last.

"The least you could do is say goodbye," Gyre said.

No response.

"You got what you wanted," Gyre prodded.

"I know," she conceded. Her voice broke, and she cleared her throat. "But if you want me to keep my shit together, I can't do this."

Gyre debated. Em, functional, was far more helpful than Em, grieving. And she didn't owe anything to Em. She'd only ever wanted to help Em to stop the deaths.

Mission accomplished.

But here, now, Gyre wanted Em to witness the people who had died.

"Then don't keep your shit together."

Em gasped, as if Gyre had struck her, her head dropping forward, chin to chest. Gyre shifted, rising up on her knees and locking her suit there, staring at the row of the dead from high enough up that she could see their faces. Their bodies filled Gyre's screen, and she hoped it was transmitting directly to Em.

"She wasn't down there," Em said. At first, Gyre couldn't think of who *she* was, but then it clicked. There was so much pain in her voice, so much bone-deep weariness, Gyre nearly collapsed under the weight of it.

*Isolde.*

"No, she wasn't."

"And my father was."

Gyre swallowed, unsure of where Em was going with this. "Yes."

"That means—" She cut off, hiccupping. "That means she never got this far when she went back down. If she'd gotten this far, she would be dead with him, or she would have pulled his body out, like you did. She wouldn't have just left him."

"I'm sorry."

"And that means I'll never find her."

Gyre flinched. "Because I'm the last one."

"No," Em said. "No. Because if her body was still down here to be found, it would be here, or I would have found it years ago. This was the last place. This was my last chance of finding her. She's not here. She's just . . . gone."

She thought of Isolde by Camp Five. Isolde on the ledge.

Isolde, her body missing all these years.

*Concentrate on the present.* "That's why you ran, when you saw the bodies."

"That's why I ran," Em agreed. "I know it's pathetic. I know you needed me. But I saw my father and I saw the others and I didn't see her and I knew. I knew." Her throat bobbed as she choked down tears.

Gyre couldn't find the words to make Em understand how afraid she'd been, how angry, how overwhelmed. And it wasn't even understanding, really. She was sure Em already understood.

It's just the rest of her pain got in the way of her being able to care enough. To prioritize.

*This* always took the lead.

So this was what they had, together. Gyre licked her chapped lips, then asked, "Do you know why she left?"

Em's shoulders tensed, drawing up toward her head reflexively. "She wanted to see my father again," Em said. "She was trying to—to do what I'm doing, but she wouldn't let anybody else die." Her lips contorted into a thin smile. "She would have hated the woman I grew into."

*Probably.* Gyre didn't say it. "So she went down herself?"

"Not even that, at first. It was just endless R&D, endless meetings and looking for more investors and running this business that was only helping her creep toward her goal. She wanted better gear, gear that would protect her from everything down there. Then she got tired of waiting. Just like you got tired of waiting for your mother, and butchered yourself so you could take this job, even though you knew it was a huge risk. She just . . . went back in. She told me she was going on a research trip. She didn't tell me where. I found the note on her computer the same day the news report came out, that she'd been last seen—well, you read it. We used it for the obituary.

"And in nine years I've never seen a trace of her."

"She's really gone," Gyre whispered.

She had died down here, in some secret place, or some place that no longer existed. Perhaps she'd fallen down a shaft, perhaps she'd been crushed to paste. Gyre remembered her face, hovering at the edge of Camp Five. The missing cache. Fuck, if only it could be true. If only Isolde was somewhere here, alive, scavenging, scraping for survival.

And Em, Em must have been clinging to that too when she hadn't found the body. But now, with the row of corpses in front of them, there was no way of avoiding it.

The end of this all was sad and wretched and pointless.

There had never been any chance of finding Isolde, and that had been all Em had ever really wanted—the chance.

*And I destroyed that.*

"She tried to be good," Em said softly. "She was so broken, but she tried. She wanted me to feel safer than she did, wanted me to not miss him as much as she did, but she couldn't move on. She cried most nights. Some nights, she was so angry. Days, too. The anger could come at any time. You—you watched the interview with her; you know how damaged she was. You could see it, right? It never faded, really. She just got better at hiding it."

Gyre said nothing, caught between wanting to comfort, and knowing with unsettling certainty that when this was all over, that would be her own fate. Broken, never quite moving on, damaged by this cave. By these deaths.

"She never got to see my father again," Em whispered. "After all that, she never got to see him."

Gyre swallowed around the tightness in her throat. "But *you* did," she said, wanting to comfort Em despite herself. "You've gotten to where she wanted to be."

"And killed so many people to get there. She had the right idea," Em said, shaking her head. "It should have died with her. That's why she walked in alone. And there I was, unable to move forward, but instead of being brave like her, I didn't go into the cave myself. I didn't end it. Instead, I sat up here, watching you all march to your deaths for the dream of some cash. It's—I'm disgusting."

"You're a monster," Gyre agreed. Em's flinch brought her no joy, no vindication. "But a human monster. People are selfish. You are. I am. Humans are selfish. It's what we do. You loaded the gun, but Jennie Mercer, Michael Doren, me—we all pulled the trigger. We all decided the risk was worth it. You never forced us."

She remembered standing in Camp Six, looking at the sump entrance, thinking these exact thoughts. It felt different now, returning to this logic. Then, all she'd wanted was for Em to stop.

Now she wanted Em to move on.

"No," Em said, fisting one hand in her hair. "I didn't force you; you're right. I just took advantage of how this world drives people to do horrible things just to survive. I just—played the game, from the winner's chair. Gyre, I thought I was smart. I thought I was *brilliant*, that I was perfectly using my resources to chase this goal, and I never—the goal was the problem, wasn't it? I solved the question as best I could, but I never stopped to ask myself if I *should* solve it."

"Well, now you have. And now you know the answer."

"I won," Em said, her voice soft and thin. "I beat this sick game. I found the person who could take me to them. And I've destroyed you."

Gyre snorted, on the edge of tears but refusing to give in. "Not yet. I'm still alive, last time I checked."

"I do remember all of them," Em said, leaning forward in her chair, large brown eyes open again, gaze boring into the screen. "All of *you*. I do. Maybe not their names, but I remember how it felt every time, listening to them die, watching their stats dive, finally severing the connection between my computer and their suits. Some of them cursed me, in their last moments, and I couldn't—I couldn't apologize. Because I didn't want them to think I wanted their forgiveness. That's not what I deserved, or desired. It wouldn't have made any difference. What made a difference was me making sure their families got their payouts. The few times the next of kin could pay enough to sue me, even though my contract was airtight and I would have won, I settled. I just—couldn't argue it. Legally, they made their own choices. But I killed them. For . . . this."

"You got what you wanted."

"Yeah. I . . . Fuck. I did all this for nothing. I killed them all for nothing. I lost you for *nothing*. There was never any chance of finding her at all."

Gyre's heart tightened in her chest as she unlocked her suit and sank back down to the ground. She looked around her for a moment, helpless, then saw the gear bags left behind by the old crew. Slowly, limbs heavy and thoughts full and sluggish, she went to one, and began rifling through it.

"What are you doing?"

"Looking for a way to give them a funeral," Gyre said.

Em's breath caught, the same way it had back at Camp Two. "I don't want a way to feel less guilty."

"It's not *for* you," she said. Her hand closed around a small, cylindrical pack, and she drew it out. Rolled it between her fingers. It felt right. She sat back and pulled open the drawstring, then fished out the folded-up camp stove.

Perfect.

"I'm sorry," Em whispered.

"I know," Gyre said. The lighter packet with it still worked. She primed the fuel bottle, then hooked it up to the stove.

"Wait—don't light that."

"Why? Because the Tunneler might come?"

"Exactly."

"I'll take the risk, for them. For this." She turned on the flow of gas and lit it, watched it burn for a few seconds, ignored Em's weak noise that could have been fear or pain or surprise.

Then she turned it off and carried the apparatus to the other side of the platform, and set it down above Hanmei's head, where she lay in the center of the row.

Returning to the duffel, she found a pot, bits of clothing, unopened MREs, climbing rope she could tear pieces off of, degraded from decades of cave moisture. She worked quietly, and Em said nothing, but she was there, always there in the corner of her screen. She had her chin in her hands, her fingers clawed against the seam of her lips.

"I watched all the videos," Gyre said softly. "So . . . I need this too. For me. For them."

Em squeezed her eyes shut. "Leave it to you to care more about them than I do." She laughed bitterly.

"I haven't had the time for the pain to be familiar," Gyre pointed out. "And I—I promised them. Back at Camp Six, the first time, I promised them I would stick around to end this. I meant to end the expeditions, but they deserve to be put to rest too. Them, not the ghosts in your head." She swallowed, then cleared her throat. "Plus, they gave me something. Watching all those videos . . . I needed to see people being happy. To hear other voices. To remember what it's like."

"To not be alone?"

"And to be out of this suit." She lifted her hand and pressed it to her side, over her feeding port. Her stomach gave a dull, answering ache. She hadn't been thinking, when she'd vomited the day before. She hadn't had a choice. But ever since, her port had felt—strange.

Her last feeding had been uneventful, however, and what could Em even do? So Gyre said nothing, letting her hand drop. She went back to the little burner and knelt before it, filling it with the scraps, the offerings.

"I opened Michael's and Jensen's masks," she added, even

327

though she was sure Em had noticed. "When I opened Jennie's suit, when I was getting her backup . . . she had barely begun to rot. It didn't seem right."

"The suit does preserve," Em admitted. "It makes extraction easier, but it's mostly a side effect of being a closed system. As the wearer dies, the suit stops exchanging oxygen, and—"

"I don't want to know this," Gyre interrupted, grimacing.

"Right. Sorry. I'm sorry."

"They just seem trapped. Just like Laurent and Hanmei. That they're not rotted means . . ."

"Means they're stuck down here forever," Em said.

Gyre lit the stove. It would take a while for the first wisps of smoke to rise from the pot, but she watched for them anyway. "I know I asked back at the start, but do you want me to carry them out?"

She hazarded a glance at the screen. But Em wasn't chewing her lip in divided thought, and she didn't look as pained.

"No," Em said. "I think . . . I think this will be enough. This is enough."

"And you don't want to ask me to do more."

"I don't want you to *do* more. It isn't about the asking." She leaned in, staring at the camera. "Gyre, I don't know how to apologize enough. Or to thank you enough. But I'm . . . I want to stop running. I think I can stop running now."

"There's not much left to run from."

"There's you."

Gyre frowned and sat back on her heels, her gaze switching from the now-smoking offerings to Em's face. "What do you mean?"

"I was serious when I said that I don't know how I'll go on, if you don't make it out of there."

"If I die."

Em winced at the word. "If you die. I didn't lie; I didn't exaggerate. And that feeling, it's . . . it's hard to manage. But if the time does come, if something does go wrong—"

"I still don't want to talk about this," Gyre said.

"I know, but I want you to hear me. It'd be the easy path to turn off my computer and walk away, but I will be here. I will be here, and I will fight like hell to keep you alive, and if I fail, I'll be here then, too. And you can curse me and hate me and you'll be right to do so. But I don't want you to feel like you're alone, not ever again. You have me."

Gyre looked away. She didn't want to think about *any* of that, and especially not about how it made her feel warm, nervous, *seen*.

She'd trusted Em to protect her, at Camp Six. She knew how that had ended. How it had ended every time.

"You put me down here."

"I know. When this is over, I'll buy you anything you want. I'll do anything I can to make it up to you. Maybe it'll never work, but—"

"When this is over," Gyre cut her off, "you need to apologize. To my face."

"Whatever you want," Em said. She was smiling faintly. She looked—thrilled. Alive. Beaten down, but beginning to glow beneath the bruises. "Thank you. For all of this. I'm glad you took the job. I'm sorry the job exists, but I'm glad it's you here with me. I know that's selfish, but—"

"We're all selfish," Gyre said. "Just take a moment. Look at them, not me. Say goodbye."

## CHAPTER TWENTY-EIGHT

An hour later, the contents of the bowl had burned as much as they were going to without direct flame, and the fuel canister was nearly empty. Gyre shut down the rig, then, hesitantly, took the bowl and scattered the contents over their chests. Halian, Julian, Laurent, Hanmei, Michael, Jensen. She looked at what was left of them, whispered a goodbye, and then turned back to the sump.

"Any sign of the Tunneler?" she asked.

"No," Em said. Her eyes were red-rimmed and puffy from crying, crying that she had tried to hide by turning away and muffling herself. But she hadn't left. Gyre wasn't sure how she felt about that. It had been a private moment, one she hadn't wanted to be party to, but it had felt honest. And she was glad to know Em hadn't simply walked out of the room to avoid looking at the bodies.

Gyre regarded the sump, then closed her eyes as her stomach lurched.

*You did this a few hours ago*, she reminded herself. Em was there, and that should have made this *easier*. But something about the weight of Em's attention made her more aware of her own nerves, and she took a step back from the sump. She sat down, running her hand over her calf.

Her calf responded with a hot itch and a dull, deep throb.

"Gyre?"

She frowned, flexing her toes. There—that itch again. A nascent blister, in a place it shouldn't be.

She wasn't supposed to get hot spots. The gel coating her skin was supposed to prevent that. "There's something wrong with my suit," she said, and tried not to shiver.

Em's brow furrowed on the screen, her gaze directed somewhere off to the right. "It's the contact film," Em said. "Some of it flowed out of place while your suit legs were un-powered. It should stabilize soon, but I recommend resting here a little longer to let it work."

*Should stabilize.* Gyre sagged in relief, pressing her palms to her faceplate. The discomfort during her feedings was likely the same thing; nothing to worry about, to dwell on. A feeding tube had to be able to withstand contractions of the stomach, right?

"A rest sounds good." It was a welcome respite from the sump.

Em nodded, then pursed her lips in thought. Gyre watched her, trying to imagine what Em would have been like if Isolde had stayed with her, or if she'd been able to get to this chamber on her first expedition, her second. Gyre wanted desperately to have met that version of her instead. Beautiful, brilliant arrogance balanced with real ability. Functional. Not dangerous.

"I want to do something for you, too," Em said finally. She glanced at the camera. "I know I can't adequately repay you, with money or otherwise, but . . . but that dossier."

Gyre stiffened. "I haven't looked at it."

"I know. But maybe now is a good time. You're almost back to the surface; you'll need a plan. I still want to help you find her, if you'll let me."

"Then make the plans for me," Gyre said. "You read it. Fuck, didn't you *write* it?"

"I didn't, no. I had some of my employees construct it. All I know are the basics. It didn't feel—right to read more than the summary my team provided me. Especially with how you felt about me at the time." Em winced. "Not that I expect that's changed much."

It had. But Gyre didn't really know how to describe it, or if she even wanted to tell Em. "Well, bring it up, then," Gyre said, pushing past the awkwardness.

Her screen went white, and then was filled with a page of text and a single image. A photograph of her mother. She was older, but though she had a few more wrinkles around her eyes, her skin looked softer than Gyre remembered it. Her hair was glossy and long, pulled back in a well-ordered braid that draped over her shoulder. She wore understated jewelry that looked expensive, well chosen. Whoever she'd married was obviously in an entirely different class from Gyre's dad.

From her.

She'd expected to feel, at worst, annoyance. At best, relief and giddiness, excitement to finally have what she'd been seeking for so long.

Instead, she felt pain.

Gyre stared at that image for what felt like an eternity, nauseated. For all she'd dreamed of finding her one day, she realized that she'd actually spent her life thinking of her mother as ultimately gone. Maybe not dead, but unreachable. A fantasy, a ghost story, a fairy tale. Just like Em's dream of finding Isolde. And just like seeing the reality of her father's corpse had broken Em, seeing her mother alive, and different from how Gyre had known her, was going to break *her*. Her heart twisted in her chest with jealousy and rage, but her mother's eyes didn't change. They just looked at the camera, unseeing.

Gyre dragged her eyes away from the photograph and over to the dossier's text. It was as if she'd forgotten how to read. Her eyes skimmed over her mother's address, the name of her mother's husband, the names of her mother's children. None of them pierced through the pounding fog filling her head.

But a few words made their way in. Under her professional credentials, the dossier said that she was a well-known economist. A respected academic.

Maybe it was the absurdity that helped the words punch through, but suddenly, she was devouring it all. She read the rest of the dossier, read her mother's CV, read half of one of her publications before her head and her heart hurt too much to continue. Her mother, well before she'd moved to Cassandra-V and had a little girl named Gyre—a little girl who was barely a footnote, because while medical and legal records did make their way off-planet, they didn't count for much in the wider galactic arena—had published several monographs on the impact of trade routes and resource extraction on the migrant colonial populations that were being settled on marginal worlds. More specifically, on their purchasing habits. Their consumer preferences. Their utter uselessness in the interplanetary market, because they rarely traveled from their new planets or brought the rest of their relatives to join them in their new, shitty homes, rarely bought much beyond food that was imported in, relying instead on locally produced goods and services. And then her mother had come to Cassandra-V on an assignment for one of the mining concerns, apparently to get a ground view of just what—aside from crushing poverty and lack of education and jobs—was causing money to dead-end in a few pockets on their planet. By the time her research had wrapped up, ending in a report that received little fanfare and had next to no economic impact, Peregrine Price was already pregnant. And so she'd stayed and stayed and stagnated and rotted in place, until finally . . .

She'd done what she had recommended in that last paper. She'd left.

Gyre sat in stunned silence long after she'd finished reading, unable to stop the single, echoing thought in her head:

*I wasn't good enough for my own mother to take me with her.*

It was different, knowing it with certainty instead of assuming it. It cut deeper. Knowing that the letter had always been just a taunt, that her mother could easily have given an itinerary, and instead had chosen to give them a useless fiction. A dare. *Are you worthy of the real me?*

Gyre pulled up her mother's portrait again and searched her face for anything of the woman who had raised her, or the woman who could abandon her own child. She found neither. That woman was as dead and gone as Hanmei, as Laurent, as Isolde. The woman wearing her mother's face, her mother's name, was a woman who had never met Gyre. She had, perhaps, suffered a momentary lapse in her identity, in her good sense. She'd had an—

Indiscretion.

Gyre only realized she was crying when her suit's environmental controls hummed to life, trying to dry her tears. She swore and tried to wipe them away herself, forgetting her helmet until her fist bumped into it. In response, she shook her head violently, sobbing.

"Gyre?" Em asked, softly. "Gyre, are you okay?"

"I shouldn't have looked. What am I even doing down here?"

All her anger and rage were layered meters thick over the pain. It was an old song, an old scar. But it was there and she could feel it now, her bleeding soul and bludgeoned heart. The pain had followed her this far, walking in the outline of the hole her mother had carved in her when she left. When her mother looked around herself and saw that she didn't want this life, that she deserved better, that she'd give up everything else to be comfortable again.

A horrible certainty settled over her.

"I'm her," Gyre whispered.

"Who? Your mother?"

"All I wanted to do was leave. All I wanted to do was get out. I don't have a child to abandon, but I still have a dad, and I fully intended to just . . . leave. I'm no better."

Em shook her head, sitting forward, her brow creasing in confusion. No doubt she had no clue what to do now, how to make this better. She couldn't make this better. "That's a false equivalence," Em said, trying anyway. "You don't intend to ignore everything that happened here once you're gone. Right? You will always be the woman who reached the bottom of this cave system, who faced down the Tunneler and lived. That will always be you."

Gyre shuddered. "And it'll always just be what happened before. I'll be able to forget it, after a time."

"Do you really believe that?"

No, she didn't. She expected to be deeply scarred by this, too. She already was. But if anything, that was worse. She'd seen what it had done to Isolde.

"If you and your father were dying of thirst," Em said gently, "and you found only enough water for one of you, it wouldn't be wrong for you to be the one to drink it. We all prioritize our own survival. We have to. We can't help others if we don't."

"So is that the answer? Is that how this feels better? I give him money? I take him with me?"

"Do you want to do either of those things?"

*No.* "It's not that simple."

"Do you know what you want?"

She flinched. *Get off-world, find my mother.* That was it. That was all there was. It had meant she didn't need to care about anything else, could always just claw her way toward the horizon. If she hadn't gotten this job, she would have thrown herself into caves again and again, until it likely killed her. She hadn't needed to plan anything beyond this moment, here.

She hadn't planned, because her goal hadn't been in the future. It had always been behind her, pulling her back, pulling her down.

There was no future beyond her mother.

What was left to her, then? Open the suit? Let hypothermia take her, or starve? Neither was fast, but both were permanent. Would going back down into the depths end this? She couldn't picture going forward, couldn't see anything growing from the pain she was carrying in her breast.

She didn't want to become Em.

Maybe Isolde had been right. Walking into the cave alone ended the cycle. Staying topside held them captive to it.

"Gyre," Em murmured. "Look at me."

Gyre looked back at the video feed, well-trained now.

"Tell me what you want."

Without her mother, without the promise of some vindication, what *did* she want? Comfort? Independence? It all felt so far away, so distant.

The cave didn't feel distant, though. The cave was her whole world, her past and her future. She pictured herself walking back down to Camp Six, diving in, severing her connection to Em and just giving in.

*No.* No, that wasn't what she wanted. Even if she couldn't think of a single thing she desired, she knew what she *didn't* want. She didn't want to be alone. She didn't want to be dead. She didn't want to be lost and forgotten.

Gyre stuffed the dark impulse to follow Isolde back into the far reaches of her heart that it had crept from, blossoming out of the wreckage like fungus out of Adrian Purcell's suit.

She knew what she wanted.

"I want to be out of this cave. I want to see the sun."

⌄

Gyre waded back into the water, then dove beneath the surface, and swam.

She followed the line she had laid while retrieving the bodies up to where Laurent had once floated, and then she rotated up and faced the puncture in the dome of the chamber. The Tunneler had passed directly above it, and directly below the sump that led away from Camp Five, boring a hole wide enough that it first cracked the dome, then left enough of a gap below the thinned bottom of the Camp Five sump that the weight of the water had broken through. The Tunneler passage had filled with water, and if the Tunneler had shifted left or down or any direction but *up*, the current would have taken Gyre far away from the funeral chamber.

But the Tunneler had gone up, and Camp Five's sump had drained almost entirely into its path, then stabilized. She could swim the whole way up to the collapsed floor of the Camp Five sump, then haul herself into the now-dry pathway.

It was going to be easy.

Her battery indicator glowed. She had days left on this one, and two fresh batteries left after that. She had enough food for a week. She had no more surprises ahead of her.

She swam up, abandoning her line.

"Gyre," Em said.

"I know where I'm going."

"You should still—"

"I'm almost there."

She dragged her confidence around her like armor, shooting through the open, still water, heading for the blue plate of the surface meters above her. If she could have felt the rush of water over her cheeks, the slide of chill against her heated muscles, it would have been perfect. It would have made her feel truly, inarguably *real* outside the ghost of her mother. This was close, though, and she fought the urge to close her eyes as she rocketed up, up, and finally broke the surface into open air.

The sump to Camp Five looked *wrong*, drained of nearly all its water. She recognized the walls from her reconstruction, but they felt fake as she hauled herself over the edge of the break in the stone, a set built more from memory than reality. Standing in the ankle-deep water, she shivered. Her knowledge of the space was dictated by how she had moved through it.

At least she couldn't drown down here anymore.

"Time to climb back up," she said, and began walking.

Em blinked. Frowned. "What?"

"Climbing up. To the surface?"

"That's not what you said."

Gyre stopped, listening to the water sliding from her suit, pattering against the shallow pool she stood in. "Of course it is. What else would I have said?"

"You said time to climb back *down*."

She went very still, the siren call of Isolde's fate echoing in her mind. No. No, she had rejected that for what it was—the fevered exhaustion of a desperate heart.

"Yeah, no," Gyre said, then barked a laugh. It was forced. "Not what I said."

"A slip of the tongue—"

"I didn't say it." She had heard herself speak; she was trapped with herself in her helmet. She knew what she'd said. "Maybe the signal cut out a little. Maybe you misheard."

Em said nothing for a few seconds, then nodded. "You're probably right. I'll check the connection strength."

Gyre managed a thin smile as she began sloshing up the tunnel.

"Other direction," Em said.

Gyre froze. Swallowed. Turned on her heel, remembering that strange pull she'd felt before diving into this sump, the call of the dead. But the dead were just below her, not back toward Camp Six. The dead had been laid to rest.

She pasted on a grim, tight smile. "Right, just got turned around for a second."

*What's happening to me?*

# CHAPTER TWENTY-NINE

She still felt disoriented as she stood at the base of the Long Drop, staring up at her line. It hung, motionless, color-coded by her reconstruction. All the bolts within range were flagged green. Safe. Strong.

The ascender was meant for situations like this. It attached to the front of her suit just like the rappel rack, and it would do the hard work of pulling her weight up the rope. Except for maneuvering around where the rope was still clipped into bolts, it would be like rappelling in reverse, walking up the cliffside.

Her calf burned at the thought. The blister wasn't healing; if anything it was spreading.

And what if the ascender malfunctioned? Worse, what if the line above her snapped? It shouldn't be possible, but then she thought of cutting that rope on the other side of the ledge. No matter if she'd hallucinated that face or not, the fact remained that the cache had gone missing somehow. If there really was something else in this cave beside her, it could drop her just as easily as she'd severed that rope.

Spores from Camp Five glowed up at her from her boots and hands, whispering to her, asking how she could ever trust her own judgment again. She tried to wipe them off, her suit scraping loudly against itself.

"Gyre?"

"Sorry—just stretching out. That's as good as it'll get, I suppose," she mumbled, and went back to the rope. "Time to let the equipment do the work, huh?"

Em hummed agreement, and Gyre stepped up to the wall. She fiddled with the ascender, checking its connection with the suit for the fifth time. She'd been afraid like this before, but not *anxious*. Not this check and double-check, afraid to rely on herself to do simple things like *go up*. She made herself grab the rope and feed it through the slots. Then she fed it through a last-chance brake. It would protect her from all falls short of her rope being cut. It was also more insurance than she usually climbed with and would slow her down.

Em didn't comment.

Finally, Gyre started the ascender, hearing its faint whine as it lifted her from the ground. She reached out, grabbing her first handholds, planting her boots against the wall.

It was going to take about five hours to get to the top, barring any problems, according to Em's calculations. That meant she could probably do it in one push. Get up, get out. As soon as she saw Camp Four again, things would be better.

∨

Camp Four didn't help.

The chamber was just how she'd left it, Jennie's body lying

341

in its cracked-open suit near the entrance. Gyre flinched when she saw her, the wreckage standing out stark against the stone. She heard Em make a noise, wordless and pained.

"She looks—more fragile than I expected," Em said softly.

"She'd look better if I hadn't torn her suit open," Gyre said, unable to walk by. Had she truly left her this way? In her memory, she'd laid Jennie down gently into her suit, opened her faceplate, given her dignity. But the reality was less neat, less kind. With the suit pulled apart at the seams, Jennie's form was broken up by jagged, man-made angles. Her belly, visible now where the suit gave way, had distended. It pressed against the polymer, seeming close to bursting. Small tendrils snaked around the edges of the plates, nascent fungi already making their homes in her flesh like they had in Adrian Purcell. And her face, her face had lost the last traces of humanity. It wasn't just the eyes that had sunken and decayed now. Her cheeks had caved in, her mouth hung open, her tongue was swollen.

*Better than being trapped in there*, Gyre told herself, but the thought was hollow. It had been so clear to her at the time, that this was dignity.

She thought she'd at least arranged the body. But the legs were still stiff and locked, spread apart from how Gyre had dragged her from beneath the shelf. Her arms were splayed at her sides. She'd done the bare minimum. All she'd done was scavenge what she needed and moved on.

It had been necessary. It had saved her life. She turned away.

"You should make camp," Em said softly. "Sit down. Eat. Rest."

Gyre nodded. She moved mechanically to the far side of the chamber, to where she'd slept that first night, a safe distance away from where the cache should have been. Its absence still made her skin crawl, and she eyed that patch as she sat down, looking for drag marks, for any sign of what had taken it. There was nothing there, nothing she hadn't seen before. Her gaze drifted then, to the stone that obscured Jennie's body. To the shaft above, with its glint of remaining, unusable bolts. To nothing.

*Focus.* She needed to eat, to recuperate, to plan.

But her stomach cramped at the thought of food. The blister on her leg had gotten worse even during the climb; what if her stomach hadn't improved either? Weeks of irritation at the cannula site as she moved and stretched and climbed couldn't account for this; the surgery was finely honed to guard against that.

But could vomiting do this? Or was it a consequence of her first surgery? A surgeon willing to fake a suit-hookup colostomy and feeding line could just as easily fuck it up. Her hand went to her side, hovering, unsure.

Wouldn't that just be perfect, if she couldn't climb back out, not because of Em or the sump or her own mind—but her stomach?

*No.* She couldn't afford to think like this, not even so close to the surface. *Especially* so close to the surface. Two more days, and she was out. Two more days, and she could figure out what came next.

Two more days, and *then* she could let herself fall apart.

"How long is the hospital stay going to be, after?" she asked to distract herself.

Em considered. "A week at most, I think. Immediate aftercare, followed by surgical reversal in your gut, then recovery and evaluation. Longer if you'd be more comfortable that way."

Gyre plugged in a ration canister, and clenched her teeth, fighting to ignore the cramping, burning pain as the paste shunted into her gut. "Good. This is starting to hurt," she said, when her willpower failed.

"The suit?"

"The feedings," Gyre said. "Since I threw up at Camp Six. I think I jarred something."

"It's very possible." Em tapped a few keys, let out a soft, unhappy noise. "Yes, it does look like it's been pulled out a few millimeters. Not enough to cause damage on its own, but your stomach is raw again, like when it was first installed. And with the previous scar tissue from your first surgery, it could tear more before you're out. How's your leg?"

"Doesn't feel great, but it's just a blister." A blister she couldn't dry out. A blister she couldn't treat. Could it become infected? Had the failure of the contact film broken a sterile seal?

"Right. This is a full rest stop, then," Em said, arresting her panic spiral. "Eight or ten hours will give me time to tweak things, get you patched up enough to be comfortable."

"No sedatives," she said preemptively. There had been no trace of the Tunneler's rumble in the past several hours. Small mercies.

"Of course not," Em replied.

The feeding finished, and she stowed the canister. Slowly, eyeing the rock that hid Jennie from sight, Gyre eased herself down onto her good side, opposite the port. It meant her back was to the chamber, and a sudden burst of terror nearly made her sit straight up.

She waited it out. Em could see all around her. "Don't leave," she said. "Keep watch. Just . . . just in case."

Em's breath whispered over the comm line. "Of course."

"We never did find that cache," Gyre pointed out, grimacing. "We still don't know what took it. *Who* took it."

"I know," Em said. "But as far as I can tell, you're alone, and have been the whole time. I'll stay here, though. I'll stay here the whole night."

"Good," she said. "I need you there."

# CHAPTER THIRTY

She woke up trapped in her suit.

Her first fumbling attempts to move it failed, her limbs leaden inside the carapace, lips too numb to trigger commands. Her body refused to obey her, refused to so much as twitch.

"Em?" Her voice came out as a hoarse whisper.

Nothing. Panic rose, pooling beneath her sternum. She tried to control her breathing, tried to wiggle her fingers, her toes. Every twitch took an eternity, as if she were being crushed, as if each gesture had to push up through a meter of stone. She could see only a fraction of the cave surrounding her, and she couldn't be sure it was Camp Four. Camp Four wasn't a maw of stone fangs. Camp Four didn't glow faintly.

But Camp Five did.

Her pulse quickened. Had she turned back, somehow? Had she hallucinated the climb up the Long Drop? Dread pooled in her gut and she tried again to lift her hand, but the suit refused to cooperate. Had Em locked her in place to keep her from pushing still further into the bowels of the cave?

*There*—a fingertip budged. But she could sense something, out beyond her helmet. Out in the darkness she couldn't see. It was close. It was coming closer. Jennie? Or the cache thief? *Isolde.* She could almost see her against the glow, pale and desperate, and rushing, rushing—

She woke up again, sitting straight up, the familiar vault of Camp Four above her.

"Em!"

Movement on the other end of the line. "Gyre—is something wrong?" Em asked, concerned, a little confused.

Gyre hunched forward, her hand on her chest, willing her pulse to slow. She was safe. *Safe.* Right where she'd left herself. "Where were you?" she growled.

"Right here," Em said, then yawned. "The whole time."

"Awake?"

"Awake. It's only been an hour."

Gyre checked her clock; it matched what Em was saying. She'd only managed an hour.

"Sorry. Bad dreams," she muttered.

She shoved herself to her feet, rolling her shoulders, trying to forget that terror. She hadn't wanted to ever feel that helplessness again, but it had been just like the fear she'd felt hanging over the lake, and at Camp Six when she couldn't breathe. It was the panic of being near death.

Her brain was conjuring it in her nightmares.

"You should go back to sleep," Em said. "An hour isn't nearly enough."

Em was right, but the thought of lying back down, closing her eyes, made her sweat. "Can't sleep," Gyre said. "Not here."

Grimacing, she paced the chamber, trying not to look at Jennie's flowering corpse. There was no sign of anybody else, no sign that anybody had been there since she had passed through. The cavern was still.

She was safe.

But she knew she wouldn't do any better if she tried to close her eyes again. If it wasn't a nightmare about being trapped down below, it would be a nightmare of drowning, or of the cache thief stealing up on her while she slept. She could ask Em to drug her, but her skin crawled at the thought. No, no sleep. Sleep wasn't an option.

She had to keep going.

She could get to the next camp on an hour of sleep. It wouldn't be comfortable, but she could do it. Just rappel down into the small sump, swim it, get into that tight, protected nook she'd bedded down in before . . .

"I'm heading to Camp Three."

After a second's hesitation, Em said, "Sounds good." She brought up the marker, and Gyre set off, favoring her bad calf. Her pacing had taken her almost to the Long Drop, and she hugged the far wall of the chamber as she walked back around toward the path to Camp Three, desperate to avoid seeing Jennie one last time.

"Wait."

Gyre drew up short, body coiling, ready to react. Her eyes darted across her screen, searching for movement, before she realized Em probably only needed to adjust her suit. Her calf was burning still, whatever reparative process Em had started while she slept unfinished.

But Em didn't say anything else. She just typed, quickly at first, then slowly. Hesitantly.

"What the *fuck* is that?" Em finally whispered.

"Where?" Gyre asked, shuddering as she twisted, searching for whatever it was Em had spotted. "Where are you—"

"Up," Em said.

Gyre looked up.

There, tucked into a narrow crevice two body lengths above her was Jennie.

*No.*

There was no way. Jennie was under the shelf, was behind her. It couldn't be Jennie.

Chest tightening, she made herself step back, far enough to get a better look at the body curled up, crumpled, shoved into a gap in the stone that didn't extend more than a meter into the wall.

No, not a body.

A *suit.*

As she stared, transfixed, she realized the helmet was in pieces scattered around it, only the back curve of the head still in place, bowed forward enough to obscure the missing face-plate. The seams at the shoulders and along the sides had been opened too. She could see the chaos of wires and tubes that had connected whoever had worn it to its interface.

"That's—" She couldn't finish the thought.

"That's not possible," Em whispered.

"An empty suit." *Somebody else in the cave.* Gyre took a step back, twisted, looked over her shoulder. But she saw nothing. No naked form dashing from the shadows, no face hovering at the edge of her reconstruction.

But this meant it could all have been *real.* There could have been somebody down here. Isolde? No, it couldn't be. And yet—and yet—

349

"Gyre, look."

A green light appeared on her screen. It was just behind the suit, but she couldn't see it from where she stood. She returned to the wall and clawed her fingers into the stone, boosting herself up to the bottom of the crevice. This close, she could see the cracked armor matched hers detail for detail, just like Jennie's did. She couldn't bring herself to touch it, to move it out of her way.

But she could see what was behind it now.

It was a box.

It was a cache.

"Camp Four," Gyre whispered.

*"Fuck."*

"Why didn't we see this last time? Why didn't we see the box?" She looked around the cavern; she'd walked this way *herself* on that long night, reading the dossiers.

"It wasn't here," Em said, voice strangled with pain. "I scanned the cavern. It wasn't here."

Gyre's pulse pounded in her ears. It hadn't been here, which meant someone had taken it and then *brought it back*, someone in one of Em's suits.

They had been here recently.

Where had they gone? All she could think about was pale faces in the darkness, motion in the corner of her eye, a figure haunting her up and down the Long Drop and to the rim of Camp Five.

A brief, sharp whine snaked from Em's throat.

"Em, who was this?" Gyre whispered, muscles trembling as she held herself perched on the rim of the crack.

"The serial number," Em managed, voice high and thin. She was terrified. No, horrified. Imagining one of her cavers dying alone, not connected to her computer, not able to hear her voice.

"Read me the serial number. Back of the neck, base of the skull," Em said. "But the timing . . . That model of suit . . . *Shit.*"

Gyre finally pushed herself up into the gap, shuddering as she nudged the motionless husk to the side. It felt light. Wrong. The discarded skin of some deep cavern arthropod.

The serial number was invisible in the light of her reconstruction. It was printed, low relief at best. She switched to her headlamp.

"Serial number ends in HX047," Gyre said.

"It's him," Em whispered. "Shit, it *is* him."

"Who?" Gyre toggled back to her reconstruction, sagging with relief as the room sprang back to full light and was blessedly, blessedly empty.

"Eli Abramsson," Em said. Gyre stiffened at the name, remembering the funeral cavern, the missing body. "He went in nine weeks before you."

"You lost him in the sump," Gyre said. *And I never found him when I found the others.*

Em nodded. "His signal started degrading, and the last I saw, he'd been caught up in a current. Swept away. I assumed—I assumed the signal had cut out, finally, because the suit had—I thought he was dead. He had to be dead. Back snapped like the others, or—or—oh fuck."

Gyre rocked back on her heels and hugged her knees to her chest, staring at the empty husk. "He didn't die," she whispered. "He was just cut off from you, like I was. Washed up, like I did. Climbed back here, like I did. But why? Why not just climb out?"

"Maybe he couldn't," Em said. "I don't know. He was suspicious of me by Camp Five, almost as much as you were, but I hadn't told him anything, and he hadn't seen the bodies. Maybe when he came back up, he saw Jennie. Maybe he thought I'd sabotaged his suit. He got back up here, thinking I'd tried to kill him. He took the cache and tried to find another way out, one I wasn't looking for."

"Em," she whispered. "Em, when did you lose contact with his suit?"

"Five weeks ago."

*Oh god.* "How long would the cache have lasted him?" she asked, not wanting to know the answer, fearing she already did. The cache had been gone when she first reached Camp Four, and now it was back.

"Five weeks," Em said. "If he kept the suit in low power mode, five weeks. He'd fully stocked it at Six."

Gyre trembled, staring at the suit and at the cache behind it. "He was here. Em, he was *here*." When she'd felt like she was being watched, was this why? Had he been there, somehow? But no, he couldn't have been. Not beyond the sump. The events didn't line up, didn't *add* up, and some of it had been the spores, had been her own exhausted mind.

Right?

Em bit back a weak noise. "Check the cache."

"No. No. I need to get moving."

"Check it."

Gyre reached behind the suit, but despite her care, she jarred it loose from the crevice. It collapsed below her, its polymer plates clattering against the ground. She opened the supply box, nudged its lid up.

The battery kit had one remaining ampule. The ration kit had more.

"He didn't use it all." But there had been that overlap. He had passed through here. The rope on the side of the Long Drop—

"It's possible his suit was going unresponsive," Em said.

Whispered. "The same issue that made me lose contact. And then, when it wasn't working, he came back this way, but his suit was failing. He clawed his way out, stashed it out of the way so you wouldn't find him. So *I* wouldn't find him. Tried to get out on foot. But with the ambient temperature at seven Celsius . . ."

"Hypothermia."

Em hummed assent. "Probably within a day. Much faster after swimming the sump, if it had already filled by then. And he would have had to rig a harness for himself, for the climbs."

Gyre stared at the husk. Em's story didn't make sense, but the only other explanation Gyre could invent was worse. Maybe he hadn't tried the sump at all. Instead, he'd felt a tug, a feeling of forgetting something, and he'd turned back toward Camp Five.

On the ledge on the Long Drop, she'd seen rope attached to a bolt that she didn't think had been there before. A face, in the darkness. What if it hadn't been Isolde at all?

What if she'd killed him?

She shuddered, forced the thought aside. She'd never seen the body. She'd never heard it hit the ground.

"I should keep moving," Gyre said, and tried to ease herself back down the wall.

She couldn't.

Her muscles were louder than the shouting of her panic, or maybe they were in on it. She couldn't move.

"He's why the Tunneler came," Em said, her voice wondering and horrified. "The Tunneler sensed him up here in Camp Four, when he took the cache, and it came up, close enough to breach the side of the Long Drop. But then it left again. Something must have happened. He's gone."

Pain twisted her words, and Gyre closed her eyes, trying to feel that pain, trying to let it goad her.

*You can't be him; you have to keep moving.*

There—it was enough, and she could push off the stone, drop down beside the wreckage of Eli's abandoned suit.

And then she ran, refusing to look over her shoulder in case she saw the half-frozen, starved, ravaged man staggering down the tunnel behind her.

# CHAPTER THIRTY-ONE

Gyre stood at the top of the cliff that had taken her four pitches to climb, the last cliff that had led where they'd expected, the last marker of normalcy she'd seen in weeks. The anchor bolt that she'd placed at the top edge was still there, her line hanging down from it just as she'd left it. She knelt to check it, and found it was still secure. Professionally done, unaltered.

She clipped in, and made quick work down to the bottom, slowing only to navigate each bolt her line was clipped to, and to give Em's computers time to work their magic. Her display remained clear, and there were no sounds or movement above or below her.

*He's dead. He's dead, somewhere in the cave, and you don't need to find him.*

If that meant he was lying dead at the bottom of the Long

Drop, so be it. If that was the reality she needed to believe to keep moving, she would relive it over and over again.

She broke the surface with a splash, sinking quickly down. There was no waiting thrum below the water, no vibrations pushing through her suit and becoming part of her.

No Eli.

Silt bloomed around her as her feet touched the bottom, and she waited for it to settle, keeping an eye out for the guideline she'd run that first dive. It appeared out of the murky water, wavering in the sonar reconstruction, and her suit flagged it with glowing green light. She floated up, buoyancy smoothly adjusting to just above neutral for the few seconds needed to bring her level with the path, then stabilizing as she grabbed hold of the line.

Easy. This was easy. Even the tightness around her lungs and heart was easy to ignore, now that she was down here, now that nothing was out of the ordinary.

"Any sign of new currents?" she asked.

"None," Em said. "No obstructions, either. Everything is just like we left it."

Em was thinking what she was thinking, then. They were both scared.

She half expected to find Eli's body floating in the sump as she rounded the bottom of the bend. When he wasn't there, and when she could see the curve that led to the surface was totally empty, she finally began to relax. It was still just a small U-bend that had flooded too early, and she had an easier time of the dive than that first attempt, now that she had more experience at moving weightlessly. It took the pressure off her swollen calf, too. It was like coming down from high altitude, everything moving faster and more smoothly than it had before.

There was no trace of the Tunneler, or the dead. As she

pulled herself from the other side of the sump, fear gave way to the first itching of hope. Two days, and she'd be out. Two days, both easier than any she'd faced down in a long while.

⌄

Gyre was nearly back to Camp Three when she heard the sound of footsteps.

"Em," she whispered, shoulders drawing up defensively.

"What is it?"

"Can you hear that?"

Em's image appeared on her screen as she tapped out a few commands and cocked her head. "No, I didn't hear anything. What was it?"

Gyre swallowed, suddenly afraid to speak. If Em hadn't heard, did that mean Gyre hadn't either? Was this the hum all over again? But she hunched forward, straining to listen as she crept along the passage, and could still make them out.

"I hear footsteps," she whispered, cold terror wrapping around her chest and squeezing.

This was real. This was happening.

*Eli.* She hadn't killed him after all. He was coming.

"Are you still hearing them?" Em asked, concern finally registering in her voice.

"Yes," she said. They were clear, faint but echoing. It was the sound of boots on rocks.

Em pursed her lips. "Gyre," she said hesitantly, her brow furrowing. "Are you sure you haven't just noticed your *own* footsteps?"

"*No.*" She crouched down where she was, a few meters from where the tunnel would let out onto Camp Three. She needed to be ready. Eli would be disoriented, starving, unpredictable. As she waited, she strained to hear something, anything.

She heard nothing.

*Boots on rock . . .* Eli had left his entire suit behind.

Eli didn't have boots anymore.

"It . . . might have been," she conceded, her face burning. No, no, but she'd *heard* them. This wasn't like the humming. This was the rope at the ledge on the Long Drop. This was the pale face in the darkness. Whoever it was must have stopped walking. That was all.

They were waiting for her.

Frantic, Gyre keyed up the map of Camp Three, trying to remember the layout. There was the side tunnel she was in, which was barely a slot at the exit. There was the path back to Camp Two, a broad avenue by comparison. Here was the nook that the cache had been left in, off to the side of where the avenue to Camp Two turned into a narrower ledge that circled the edge of the chamber. And there was the chaotic left side of the cavern, where there were piles of fallen rock from an earlier cave-in that were scattered amid crushed stalagmites and sudden drops and rises in the cavern floor.

She could try to squeeze her way through the jumble, but if she made a single sound, whoever it was could hear her, rush her, pin her down. If they were in the nook, she could try to sneak along the rim, then sprint up the avenue.

But what if it *was* Eli? If it was him, didn't she have to try to help? Try to get him out? How he hadn't died of hypothermia after swimming the sump, she couldn't imagine, but if it *was* him, she could save him. She could save one person.

Em could really, truly try to make amends.

She swapped her view from the map to what was in front of her. For a brief second, as her screen changed over, she expected to see Eli's face staring at her, gaunt and broken. But he wasn't there; it was just her, crouched in the passage.

She still couldn't hear the footsteps.

Her certainty wavered. Maybe Em *was* right. It was the easiest explanation. Swimming the sump meant she hadn't heard her own footsteps in almost an hour. Back on land, she had noticed them, started to panic. Spiraled, like she had dangling above the lake, fueled by the husk of Eli's suit, his body lost somewhere in the cave, just like Isolde's.

"How are you feeling?" Em asked gently.

She was on fire, shame kindled and crackling in her chest. "Embarrassed," Gyre admitted. "Ready to keep moving."

Em looked worried, but turned off the video feed, as if to give her privacy. Gyre appreciated the illusion and stood up. She walked slowly to the slot exit of the passageway. The footsteps *were* her footsteps. Eli, wherever he was, was dead. He'd died at least a week ago, if not longer. Definitely longer.

And if not, he was dead at the bottom of the Long Drop. He was a corpse, either way, naked and forgotten.

She turned sideways and eased herself through the slot into the Camp Three chamber. On the other side, she leaned her back and head against the rock wall, gazing out at the room.

There was a shape in the jumble of collapsed stone.

*It's not there.* She looked upward, counting to ten. Her brain was playing tricks on her. It was the same weakness, the same madness. Shadows at the edges of her vision, over-interpretation of stimuli. She hadn't been sleeping enough; it was to be expected. There could even be lingering effects from the spores. Em was here and could see everything.

Em wasn't afraid.

She looked back down. The shape was still there, indistinct, hunched. She willed it away, waiting. Couldn't Em say something? Couldn't Em nudge her forward?

And then the shape shifted, straightened. Turned around.

And Gyre could see, now, exactly who it was. She could see the cleft chin, the gently curling blond hair. The piercing, haunted eyes.

Isolde stared back at her across the cavern.

She was real.

She was alive.

*Don't see it, don't see her.* She waited for Em to react. She waited for the wail, the scream, the anger, the pain.

"Everything okay?" Em said instead. "You're good to proceed."

Em didn't see her.

*Why* didn't she see her? Gyre couldn't move, her gaze locked on Isolde. The other woman looked back at her for a long moment, then began to pick her way across the talus pile. She was real. She moved like a real person; she looked solid. She wasn't a darting shadow, a stress-induced hallucination. She wasn't an over-interpretation by Gyre's fevered brain.

She was *real*.

Could Em not see her? Was something broken in her computer algorithms that shielded Isolde from her daughter?

"Gyre, what's wrong?"

If she told Em, Em would lose it. She would fall apart. But if it was really Isolde, she couldn't just leave her here. She moaned, low in her throat.

"Gyre, are you seeing something?"

She had to tell her.

"Isolde," she whispered.

Em didn't respond.

"It's her, Em," Gyre whispered. "She looks just like she did in that interview video." *Just like the day she left and walked down here.* The cave had kept her alive. The cave had—

"Gyre, I can't see anything," Em said gently, but her voice wavered.

"It's her. It looks just like her."

"Like the video."

"*Yes.*"

Em made a small, pained sound. When she spoke, her voice was even, measured. Controlled. "The videos are from almost twenty years ago. She would have aged. That's not counting *nine years* down here on her own. She wouldn't look the same, Gyre. She's not real."

"She could have come up for supplies. Gone to the outpost. Maybe this isn't her first time down here, maybe—"

"She's dead, Gyre."

"You never found her body! If Eli survived for weeks without you, what says she couldn't have managed years?"

"You're seeing things! Look! *Look.*"

Her display shifted, flying through the different options. Sonar reconstruction, infrared, finally headlamp. And through it all, Isolde was there. Isolde was there, and as Gyre watched, she continued to move. She hauled herself up onto the plateau Gyre stood on, then straightened up. Leaned forward. Peered curiously at Gyre's impassive helmet.

"I have to try to talk to her," Gyre said, and fumbled for the release for her faceplate.

"Gyre, don't!"

"Em, your computers are *wrong.* I can see her. I *can still see her.*"

Her headlamp switched off, her reconstruction springing to life. Nothing changed, Isolde still approaching in full detail, her clothes old, worn.

"Can you see her now?" Em whispered. She sounded like she was in agony, like she was fighting for every word.

She was beginning to hope.

"*Yes,*" Gyre said.

"Gyre, I'm showing you a recording of the last time you were in Camp Three. You're hallucinating."

No. *No.* It wasn't possible. Gyre shook her head, then opened her face mask, turned her headlamp back on. Chilled air slammed into her cheeks, her nose, but despite the switch from video to darkness illuminated only by her lamp, nothing changed. Isolde was only a few steps away now, and Gyre took a step toward her.

Her suit locked.

*Em.* She snarled, then took a deep breath. Isolde had stopped, was frowning at her. As Gyre watched, her eyes widened. Recognized her as another person.

"Isolde," Gyre said, her voice echoing out into the cavern. "Isolde, I'm—I'm a friend of your daughter's."

"Gyre!" Em cried.

"I can get you out. You're not far from the surface now." She tried to lift her hand and reach out to Isolde, but Em wouldn't let her. "Please, say something. Your daughter—she can't see you. Tell her you're here."

"Gyre, we're leaving," Em said. Her suit jerked. Em lifted her right foot and extended it, placed it down ahead of her. Away from Isolde. Toward Camp Two. "Don't make me do this."

Hot tears stung her eyes, in sharp contrast to the cool, still air of the cavern. "Em, she's *right here.* Tell her, Isolde! Tell her."

Isolde said nothing. Gyre's faceplate slid closed, Em's image appearing instead in the lower left corner. "No! Open the mask, or the speakers. Let me talk to her. We can't leave her!" Gyre pleaded. "I don't know why she's not responding, but—"

"We have to! Gyre, breathe. Breathe. *Listen.*"

And then she heard it: not Isolde's speech, or even her exhale, but a rumbling. It grew swiftly, louder and louder. The very walls were shaking, and the air in her lungs was beginning to echo it.

*Air.* Isolde's chest wasn't rising and falling. No steam plumed from her nose or mouth. But it was cool enough down here that Gyre's own breath had steamed faintly in front of her eyes. If Isolde was breathing, there'd have to be—

Steam curled from Isolde's lips, on cue.

*On cue.*

"You're not real," she said. The sound was swallowed up by her helmet, by the growing roar around her, inside her.

"Gyre, please," Em said, forcing her another step forward. "I can't do this fast enough. I need you to run. Can you run? Please. *Please.*"

She blinked, and Isolde was farther away now, out in the talus field again. She was retreating. She was leaving. Gyre wanted to reach out for her, to call to her, but she couldn't move.

*Not real, it's not real. But the Tunneler is real. The rock is real.*

Small flakes of stone were falling from above her. She focused on them until she came back to herself. "I can run. I can run!" She could barely hear herself as she shouted.

Her suit released.

The roar was all around her, vibrating up her calves, squeezing her heart and shaking her rib cage. She staggered backward, then lurched toward the avenue, breaking into a sprint as she remembered how to move her legs. From behind her, she thought she heard words, Isolde's voice, followed by footsteps.

*Not real, not real,* she thought, fighting against the urge to turn around. Then a man's voice replaced Isolde's. Eli's voice, no doubt, or what her brain conjured in its place. But she couldn't slow, couldn't stop. If she gave in, the cave would keep her, the Tunneler would kill her. Her muscles burned, screamed, seized as she reached the top of the incline. She fell to her hands and knees, but she kept moving, dragging herself forward, forward.

Beneath her hands, the rock was trembling. The rumbling noise left her ears abruptly, and she could barely breathe over how the air in her lungs shook.

"No!" Gyre shouted. *"No!"*

But her words were swallowed up in the roar of the Tunneler as it passed behind her, the broad avenue collapsing. The shock wave knocked her onto her side, and she slid down into the chaos, curling into a tight ball as she slammed into the rocks below. She felt herself screaming but couldn't hear it, couldn't see anything as her sonar went wild.

# CHAPTER THIRTY-TWO

"Left arm has two full breaks as well as severe crush damage from the mid-humerus down. Your cannula has been completely dislodged. There are ruptures in your suit in twelve places that are taking longer than anticipated to close."

"I don't want morphine," Gyre repeated. It had become her litany. It had taken her from Em's panicked shouting, through her begging, to her cold, clinical recitation of every reason that Gyre was going to die. Neither of them had mentioned that the Tunneler was still close enough to hear. Neither of them had mentioned that Gyre had killed herself by opening her face mask to talk to nothing.

*To talk to the cave*, her addled brain corrected. And the cave had heard her, tempted her with Isolde. The cave had brought itself down on her head.

She'd managed to stand up—barely—about five minutes ago. Moving seemed less likely. The collapse had smashed parts of her suit open, her skin visible beneath debris and blood, and the left arm mechanism was too damaged to lock up and protect the bone. The parts that no longer had power were rigid, bracing her wrist and a few of her fingers into awkward positions. The rest of her pulped arm hung limp, screaming in agony. She hadn't looked at any of it yet. Instead, Em had described the damage to her as she'd struggled to extract herself from the few—lucky her—rocks that had fallen on top of her, and on repeating *I don't want morphine* every few minutes.

Her stomach was a blaze of agonizing wrongness, curdled by the adrenaline still storming her bloodstream and by the cannula, now painfully unseated, now allowing her stomach acid to burn through her insides. Infection would follow soon. Blood poisoning, sepsis. It was only a matter of time. Her vision was distorted and wavering, and she couldn't tell if it was from pain or panic or the damage to her suit.

Morphine would be easy, would make everything better, and maybe she'd die less afraid.

She could hear death calling to her, whispering that it could take away the pain, take away the last shreds of what remained to her. It was the urge to walk back into the cave and follow Isolde; it was the fungus growing from Jennie Mercer's face, growing from the rot in her heart where her mother had been. She fought against it out of reflex and stubbornness, struggling to remember what was still dragging her forward.

The surface. The sun. It wasn't enough. It wasn't real anymore. What was sunlight to the desaturated lines of her readout, to the engulfing darkness beyond? What was open air overhead but another threat?

And then she pictured Em, looking at the clinical readouts on her screen, hearing Gyre's agonized cries. Em would sit her vigil, watch her die, watch as they were both chased down by the inevitable at last. Em would watch her die, just like all the others. Except this time, Gyre knew her. Gyre had come so close to saving her.

Gyre's death would destroy her.

And it was that, more than anything else, that broke through to her. *Fight it. Keep pushing. I'm not alone.*

"I don't want morphine," she said, her lips swollen and numb.

She tried flexing her left hand and cried out as the simple motion made her entire mind go blank.

"I don't want morphine," she mumbled again, even though Em hadn't said anything since the last time, or the time before that. She staggered forward, shin bumping into one of the rocks. She struggled to lift her foot up over it, her eyes fixed on the path ahead of her. It was barely a path now. The Tunneler had closed off the way back down to Camp Three, and had passed close enough in front of her that, from what she could see, the path to Camp Two had ceased to exist. It had cut her off from everything, past and future, depths and surface.

The cave had done this to her, using Eli and Isolde against her, trapping her in the labyrinth she had been so sure she could leave. The rumble remained, a constant invitation and threat.

But before she gave up, before she lay down and stopped moving forward like all the others, she had to know that there was no other option. She couldn't give in if there was a way out. Her desperate pride wouldn't let her, even now.

"Em, I don't want morphine," she sobbed.

"I know," Em said. "I won't give you any."

Relief flooded through her, and she laughed, giddy from the stark disparity between the small pebble of relief in her stomach versus the great mass of fear and resignation howling in her head. She watched as one of the breaches over her leg knit itself together, the gel fusing with her blood and coating her skin, the polymer shifting, adjusting, extending scaffolding to cover the gap. It wouldn't harden properly, but it was a shield.

She grappled for a hold with her right hand, her fingers struggling to close around the rock. With a groan, she heaved herself up and over.

Her screen was cracked. She could see it now, feel it, the cool, dank air of the cave filtering through. She could smell the air. Taste it. It was like a balm. It was real. With it came the need to have the suit off of her entirely. She wanted to be free of it. If it wasn't on her, maybe she'd be whole again. Maybe she could live, staggering through the dark.

*No.* That was the cave talking to her again, her own self-annihilating impulse. She shut it out.

She stumbled down into a valley of buckled rock, trying to get to the far wall, moving to catch herself with her left arm. It didn't respond, and she overbalanced, falling, her shoulder colliding with the stone. Her vision went white. She couldn't move her arm, could barely maneuver it.

She couldn't climb like this.

"My arm," she whispered.

"It's bad," Em conceded. "But not—not irreversible. There's a chance, once we get you back topside, that they'll be able to restore some of it."

"It's not that, Em. It's not letting me climb. I need to climb!"

"Gyre—"

"It's going to kill me," she said, sinking onto her back,

staring upward at the dancing ceiling. "I'm going to die; it's going to kill me."

"It's not."

"The suit's going to kill me."

"It's going to keep you alive. Gyre, listen to me. This is the shock talking."

"Shock. Shock, that's going to kill me. If the arm dies, I die with it."

"You've still got blood flow," Em said.

"Then I'll bleed out." She couldn't see, and her tears, hot as they were, were cooling quickly, so quickly, from the little tendrils of air that snaked into her suit. "Em, cut it off. Cut it off."

"No. Gyre, I've got you on antibiotics and blood-clotting agents. I can do this. You can do this. If I just give you pain medication, or anxiolytics—"

"No drugs!" she cried. "I want to know when I'm dying. Don't kill me, Em. Don't kill me." A prick of the needle, and she'd fade away. Em could put her down, end her pain, and Gyre would never know. She fought against the pull of her own exhaustion, her own pain. "No drugs."

"Gyre—"

"Just cut it off. I won't need the drugs."

"You're not thinking straight—"

"I don't want to die!"

"If I amputate your arm," Em said, struggling to sound calm and failing, "you might never climb again. The suit will preserve it, but between the existing damage and the amputation, it will be useless. They won't be able to reattach it. A responsive prosthesis, maybe, but—if you just wait, if you breathe through it—"

"Do it! Listen to me! Listen to me, for once!" She fumbled through the options in her helmet desperately. If Em couldn't do this for her, if Em wouldn't, because she was too afraid to make a choice, then Gyre would do it for herself. She'd free herself. She'd stop the pain, and then she'd be able to keep moving, and she wouldn't need the drugs. Em couldn't kill her then.

Her thoughts were jumbled, but she found it. The interface was complex and demanded actual anatomical knowledge that she didn't possess. But she fumbled through it, queued it up.

"This," she said. "This. Do I have it right?"

"Gyre, don't do this. Just let me give you anxiolytics; we can talk this over—"

"*Is it right?*"

Em cried out, frustrated, then went quiet for one heartbeat, two. Gyre's eyes bulged in her skull.

"Yes," she said at last. "But, Gyre, it's going to—"

She triggered the amputation. She felt pain, horrible pain, and sickness. Her stomach rebelled. She rolled over onto her belly, and she felt her left side swing up, weightless, unburdened.

Then she vomited, and lost consciousness.

$$\vee$$

The rumbling of the Tunneler woke her.

She surged up, surrounded by the stink of bile now inside her suit, the weight of her left arm tugging at her shoulder. But when she opened her eyes, she could see it, lying at her side. Still on the ground, unnaturally bent, the rigid wreckage of a limb. Where her left arm had been there was only a stump, covered in a dome of carbon polymer. The suit had sealed the wound completely, as if nothing had ever been there.

She'd done it.

Oh fuck. She'd done it. She'd been so afraid of death that she'd killed an entire piece of herself.

Oh *fuck*. Em should have stopped her.

Her stomach was a pit of agony as she sat up, and she could feel herself sweating. She felt cold, but the only gap remaining in her suit was the crack in her faceplate. She was running a fever. How long had she been out? Minutes? Hours?

"Em?"

"I'm here," Em murmured.

*Why didn't you stop me?*

Gyre couldn't speak. Her throat felt dry and empty.

"How are you feeling?" Em asked.

"It hurts."

"I know," Em said. "Are you ready to get up?"

"I don't know."

"You don't have much time. The cannula rupture isn't responding to treatment the way I'd like. You need a doctor."

Gyre shivered.

"And without that cannula, you can't get any more calories or moisture into your system. With your injuries, you've got . . . you've got a day, tops. And that's at the outside."

"Fuck," Gyre whispered.

"I know. And beyond that, there's your battery. Your ports are jammed. You can't swap out. The amputation and repairs took a lot of power."

Gyre choked back a sob. One day, nowhere to go, waiting to starve or stroke out or be consumed by the hunger of the cave.

"But you bought yourself some time," Em said. She sounded sick to her stomach. Pained. "The amputation was the right choice. Before, you only had four hours, six at the outside. A day's enough. I've got a medical team ready and waiting for when you get out."

Gyre's world slowed to a halt.

*She still thinks I'll get out.*

She latched onto that detail and dragged herself to her feet. She was still in the pile of collapsed rubble, and that rubble was still vibrating beneath her feet, but at full height, she could see the far wall, where the ground was smoother, less disrupted.

Slowly, she began staggering toward it.

"But I should have medicated you beforehand, to lessen the shock and get you moving sooner." Em was angry, viciously angry—at herself.

*Stop. Stop.* If she was angry, she could shut down, she could *leave*. "Why didn't you?"

"You asked me not to."

Gyre paused, closing her eyes at the swell of tangled emotion in her throat. She wanted to scream at Em, wanted to hug her, wanted to lie down in her arms until the life slipped out of her.

*You asked me not to.*

They were ruined. They were broken.

"Is there an exit?" she made herself ask.

"I don't know," Em admitted. "I saw something that's promising over by the far wall, but I can't tell. Can you get there?"

"Keep talking, and I'll see," she heard herself say as she struggled up the first small boulder.

"What would you like me to talk about?" Her voice was so gummed with grief that Gyre could barely make out her words, but it was better than nothing, better than listening to the relentless thrum around her.

"I don't know." She pushed herself into a gap between two rocks, smearing herself against them as she moved upward, sidling closer to their tops. As they spread apart, so did she.

Then she jarred her arm, and she froze with a hiss, arching her back. It didn't help.

"Read a book, or something. Just keep talking. Please."

"I can't read a book," Em said. "Not while—Gyre, I can't."

"Then recite the alphabet. Timetables for the spaceport. Anything. *Anything.*" If she lost that thread, that last hold, she was doomed. She was dead already.

Em was silent for a moment. Gyre paused again in her ascent, bowing her head forward against the rock. She needed Em's voice, needed it more than she could describe. Without Em, she wasn't leaving this cave, alive or otherwise.

And then Em cleared her throat again, and said, haltingly, "Yao Hanmei. Halian Foster. Julian Flores. Laurent Okeke. Guilherme Barbosa. Agnes Reynisdottir."

She kept up the list of the dead as Gyre shouted, forcing herself through the slot and out onto open ground. Beyond that point, she only had to edge around a few more rocks and fractures before she was up at the blocked top of the passage. She set her right hand on it, feeling it. It was still uneven, not like the smooth tunnel walls, but it looked and felt stretched, like the rock had been bowed out and its outcroppings had spread apart.

"—Rose. Michael Doren. Francesca Clark," Em continued.

Gyre looked along the wall to the left, sagging against the stone. Her head spun. It was so hard to keep from drifting, to think. But there—*there.* A crack in the rock, into the bowed-out wall. She staggered toward it and found that it was big enough to get her head through.

She was looking into a Tunneler's abandoned path.

"Em," she said softly as she pulled her head back and sank to her knees.

"Is that . . . ?"

"It's another path," she whispered.

Em laughed helplessly. "This is—you could still—Gyre," Em said, excitement building in her voice. "It heads back toward Camp Four. It might come close enough to connect."

The tears came in a bitter rush, and she collapsed forward, resting her forehead against the rock just by the crevice. She couldn't do it. She couldn't make that climb, not with it leading only to her death. To Jennie Mercer. To the cliffside.

She shook her head, the suit creaking as it dragged across rock. "I can't make it up the shaft," she mumbled.

"No, you can't."

It wasn't an option. It looked like one; she could keep moving forward, the same as always. But it ended at the same place staying here did.

"But, Gyre," Em said softly, "if you can get there, somebody could make it down the shaft. *I* could make it down."

Hope blossomed painfully in her chest, but it couldn't push up through the waves of desolate horror crashing down onto her, or the distant noise, a rumble instead of a throb, audible instead of tangible, that still echoed through her bones.

"I can feel it, Em. The Tunneler is still here. It could collapse the chamber. It might not be navigable, even if I can get there."

"We don't have any other choice. We go fast, Gyre, make it to Camp Four, and I'll get a team and come down and get you. Stay with me. You just have to get to Camp Four."

"How long until sepsis sets in?"

Em was silent.

"You said I had a day on food. A day on the battery. Less, you said probably less. We don't have enough time," Gyre said bitterly. "I'm dead already."

She stared at her arm, too far across the unstable chamber for her to risk going to. But she wanted to. She wanted to hold the first piece of her to die. Apologize to it. To herself.

"This cave *wants* me dead," she whispered.

"Gyre, listen to me," Em said, desperation fracturing her voice. "Your mother. Picture your mother. The company she works for now, they invest in technology like mine. Imagine, walking into a boardroom in your suit. Imagine taking off your helmet. Imagine staring your mother in the eye and *daring* her to say something, say anything. You'd be magnificent. You'd be powerful. And then you could walk away from her, in turn. All you have to do is get to Camp Four. I'll do the rest."

She could see it, but it all felt so far away, so impossible. Gray and wrong and unknowable. She wanted it to be true, so badly, wanted to feel Em at her side, wanted to feel powerful.

But it wasn't enough.

She shook her head, her shoulders trembling.

Em didn't say anything for a moment, and all Gyre could hear was the rumble and her own sniveling, seizing sobs. Then her suit let out a low whine as the servos and supports tried to force her up.

"Get on your feet," Em said low in her ear, her voice cold. "And keep moving. You are going to Camp Four, caver, and I am going to bring you home. You signed a contract, Gyre."

"*Fuck you.*"

"In a life-and-death situation, you agreed to defer to me. So *do it.*"

Em's clinical tone, so familiar but such a contrast to their last week together, broke through her panic. She pushed herself upright again. She forced herself through the crevice and out into the wide passage. She set off at as fast a pace as she could manage, staggering along the gently curving floor.

But she was unsteady on her feet. She pitched from wall to wall, the floor tilting beneath her. She wouldn't make it. Couldn't make it—

"Injecting anti-emetics and a local anesthetic," Em said. She knew exactly what Gyre needed, using the contract to shore up them both. Gyre nodded, and felt the gel around her skin shudder, change, and a tiny bloom of fire flared by the roiling pit that was her gut. She breathed through it until the pain had faded and the tunnel stopped spinning.

"Thank you," she whispered.

Em smiled. "Keep moving, Gyre. Fast as you can."

# CHAPTER THIRTY-THREE

Her lungs and throat burned, and her muscles protested her every move. Her body was slick with sweat, the gel coating her skin too overused and damaged to properly compensate. It gaped from her flesh, allowing blisters to form, bruises to bloom and swell until each step was a struggle. She had been staggering along the smooth passage for hours now, feeling her time tick down, her body break and fall apart. The monotony of the passage was disrupted by her cracked screen, and from a damaged sensor that caused the reconstruction ahead of her to flicker and shift. Reality danced and swam just like her thoughts did. But Em still had access to most of her feeds, and every few minutes, she'd confirm for Gyre that she was moving in the right direction.

That the Tunneler was far enough away that she was safe.

"Gyre, stop. On your right."

She staggered to a halt, then twisted, looking. There was

a crack in the stone wall, like the crack she'd entered through, like the crack above the shallow lake. It was hard to see, and she squinted, then reached out and touched the rock, her hand filling in the details where her display couldn't. It was wide enough to fit her, wider than the break she'd entered through.

"Go through," Em said.

"Are you sure?"

"As sure as I can be. Go."

Gyre bit back a fevered argument. Em was clearer-headed than she was. All Gyre needed to do was follow directions and rely on her body to know how to move.

But she hesitated.

"Gyre?"

"I'm afraid," she whispered.

*So am I.* She could hear Em's voice saying those words, but the real woman hesitated. Gyre crumpled against the wall.

"It's okay," Em said at last, gentler than Gyre could've imagined. "It's okay, I know. Just a little more. Go through, come closer to me."

She dragged herself through the opening, dreaming of Em waiting for her on the other side. Instead, a cavern stretched out before her. To her right was a spit of smooth ground; to her left there was a great expanse of space where the floor dropped out and plunged into nothingness. A great font of water, larger by half than the waterfall on the way to Camp Four, crashed down into it from the far side of the gap, and below the fountain, her undulating readout showed a bare breadth of rock and more fractures in the wall.

Scanning the chamber, she looked for any sign of Camp Four, but nothing looked familiar.

She wanted to scream.

"Are you sure this is it?" she asked instead, shivering with exhaustion.

"Head inside, about five meters, then turn to your right," Em said.

Gyre eased into the cavern. Her gaze darted to every nook in the rock walls, searching for faces, but none presented themselves. Maybe, just maybe, the hallucinations were at an end. Maybe her brain had moved on. Maybe the cave had given up.

To her right was a small opening, just large enough for a child to fit through, but not for her. The gap was between several boulders, not into smooth stone, and a marker Em set up glowed down inside of it.

"I can't fit," she mumbled, her willpower wavering.

"The rocks around it aren't structural. I think. It widens right on the other side; it's just a small collapse. If you could just move them—"

"With one arm?" she bit out through gritted teeth.

"Use your legs. That's the path. The computers don't lie. We're taking it, and we're going to get through it."

*We.* Gyre closed her eyes a moment, choked down a hysterical laugh, then looked around and approached the pile. She stared at the rocks blankly for a moment before she forced herself to concentrate, inspecting how the rocks sat on one another. The top bit she was able to wedge her right shoulder against and heave off, despite the howling pain it triggered in her gut. The stone crashed to the ground, and panic leaped in her chest as she remembered Camp Two and the falling boulder that had nearly killed her. Remembered the grinding roar of the tunnel collapse. She staggered back, the motion sparking a fresh blaze of agony in her stomach, distant through the anesthetic but worrying all the same.

Em said nothing, and so Gyre chose to believe everything was okay. Em was right. She had no other option.

Settling awkwardly onto her back, she placed her feet on the bigger stones at the bottom and pushed.

It took over fifteen minutes of grunting effort, with Em encouraging her every time she flagged, for her to dislodge enough of the rocks for her to get through. When it was done, she remained on her back, staring straight up. Her chest burned. Her belly felt hot and swollen, even if she couldn't feel the pain. How much longer did she have? Hours? Minutes? The chamber was spinning, wavering, and she thought that it couldn't be much farther off.

"Gyre?"

Gyre focused on the sound of her voice. Her low, sweet, shivery voice. It was all she had left. "I need to rest," Gyre mumbled. "Just a little bit. Don't leave. Don't leave."

"I'm here. Just don't fall asleep."

"I won't. Just . . . just keep talking. Read the names again. I need something to listen to that's not me. And can you cut the reconstruction? It's making me feel sick. I can't think straight with it on."

Em made a sympathetic, small sound. "Of course," she said, and the reconstruction blinked out, replaced with the warm, natural glow of her headlamp. She tensed at first, but the darkness welcomed her. It was less to keep track of. Less to think about. She sagged in relief, on the edge of tears.

"The lamp didn't seem to be coordinated with any attacks, so you should be good like that from here forward, if it's easier," Em murmured in her ear. "I'll let you know if I see anything change. Does that sound okay?"

"Thanks," she managed.

Em took a deep breath, and Gyre waited for her to speak.

It sounded like she was working up to something, so Gyre anticipated nothing good. An update on her vitals? An apology, because Gyre was dying even then?

But instead, Em started singing. Gyre couldn't understand the words, but she could understand the tone. It was a nursery song, a lullaby. Her voice was lilting and sweet, even if her rhythm was a bit off, and Gyre sank into it as it curled around her and into the space outside her cracked screen. She turned up the volume to blot out the distant rumble of the Tunneler, still audible, still following. Her right hand fiddled with a crack in the plating along the hip of her suit, and her left arm remained gone, absolutely gone, but still there in a phantom presence. If she closed her eyes, she could almost pretend she was still whole.

She was so tired.

She didn't care if she ever saw her mother, or even if she ever got off-world. All she cared about now was seeing another person, a real person. Seeing Em. Feeling her warmth beneath her hand. Sleeping in her bed.

Out of habit, she tried to roll over, then hissed as her stomach protested, pain bleeding around the edges of her anesthetic. It was a hundred times worse than the morning after her first surgery, when she had lain there, unable to afford pain meds, convinced she'd made the right decision.

"Gyre."

"Sorry, I'm fine," she said, gasping. The throb was getting louder. Gyre turned up the volume again. "Keep singing. It was nice."

"No," Em said almost in a whisper. "It's the vibrations."

She frowned, then sat up, wavering unsteadily. "The Tunneler?"

"It's getting closer. Move. Move, Gyre."

Her heart seized. She couldn't do this again, couldn't go through the roar, the falling. They were so close, if Em could be trusted, and even if she couldn't, Gyre didn't want to die in another attack. She didn't want to die like this.

"Damn it," Gyre swore, staggering up into an awkward crouch. She looked at the gap she'd uncovered. It was too tight, far too tight. If the Tunneler came anywhere near her while she was in it, she'd be Halian all over again. She staggered to the edge of the drop-off instead, the crash of the waterfall across the gap growing louder. Maybe if she put a line in, hung down in the open space, she could—

The throb suddenly became a roar, and Gyre stumbled back, staring, as across the gap a great wormlike *thing* swam out of the rock, stone moving impossibly like water around it. In the open air, it was too big to support itself, and she watched as it writhed up along the wall and into the ceiling, half submerging itself. Its gigantic conical head, if it was a head, swung around to face her. It had no mouth, no eyes, but thousands of slit-like pits covered its skin, pulsing open and closed as if breathing, smelling. In the light of her headlamp, its brilliantly colored scales flashed, iridescent and vibrant.

"Holy *shit*," Gyre whispered, and it shifted toward her, moving sinuously along the ceiling.

"It was the singing, the *singing*—" Em was saying, and then the voice line went dead, its indicator turning solid amber.

Gyre cried out, "Come back, *come back!*"

Em had left her.

But the worm hadn't, and it was surging forward, and Gyre's scream died in her throat. She shuffled back from the lip of the pit, then strained to hold still against her trembling.

The slits pulsed. The head moved, swaying. But the Tunneler stopped its approach.

Slowly, it shifted its head, casting, searching.

Why couldn't it see her anymore?

Words flashed up on her cracked screen.

DON'T SPEAK

Gyre choked down the faint, nascent sound that threatened to leak from her throat.

The words on her screen disappeared, and were replaced with:

IT HEARD THE SINGING. IT DOESN'T LIKE HUMAN VOICES.

The theory sounded laughable, impossible. How could it hear somebody's voice through hundreds of meters of solid stone? But as she read, the Tunneler continued to move. Away, back into the rock. The vault of the ceiling rippled, and where it couldn't compress impossibly on itself, it fractured, sending a cascade of rubble down into the gap, into the pummeling path of the waterfall across the way. In its wake, the Tunneler left strange hollows and outcroppings along the margins of the cavern, and a lessening throb.

Relief made her weak, and her knees threatened to buckle. And then, from the pit of agony in her stomach rose anger. She stared down the beast that had pursued her throughout the cave.

*You killed Halian. You almost killed me.*

No. She couldn't let it just leave.

As if possessed, she took a step toward it, staring up at the behemoth, her lamp playing across its scales. It didn't react to her movement, or the sound of her boots on the rock. She had no weapons, no hope of killing it, but it didn't stop her from sinking to her knees and straightening her back, shuffling to the edge of the gap. She stared up at it.

If she was going to die anyway, she might as well go out screaming.

## GYRE, WHAT ARE YOU DOING?

She opened her faceplate. It resisted, and she fought it, until a large piece cracked off entirely, and the rest retreated into her helmet. The cool air of the cave was ice against her burning skin, seizing the breath in her lungs.

"You took my arm," she said. The sound didn't carry, and the Tunneler didn't turn. It was nearly gone now, submerged in the rock except for a few meters of variegated flesh. "Look at me! Look at me, you piece of shit!"

This time her voice boomed across the space, and the Tunneler reacted. It spasmed, its skin rippling, its pits pulsating wildly where they were exposed to the air. It twisted back on itself, the rock cracking and splitting, raining down into the gap in a thunderous collapse. She fell backward, away from the rubble and pluming rock, and stared as the Tunneler emerged from the ceiling only a few meters in front of her, giant head dropping into the open air, pivoting, facing her.

Groping behind her, she found a loose stone. She threw it with all her strength, and it struck the Tunneler near the front of its conical head. It didn't respond, didn't flinch. Even its slits barely moved, only continuing their rhythmic pulsing.

Em was probably screaming for her, typing frantically. Her faceplate jerked down, trying to slide back into place, but she pressed the heel of her hand against it, holding it back. She was panting for breath, and she didn't have the strength to stand up, to face the beast, but she couldn't take her eyes off it. She couldn't quell her rage.

This cave wasn't going to consume her. She was going to fight until the very end.

"You did this," she said as the falling rocks thinned out, then stopped. Isolde's face as she described Halian's death filled her mind, followed by the sheared-off fragments of bones in her hands, the smoothed-over stone, the sump, the whole team dead or as good as. "You killed them all."

Its slits flared, and the colors on its skin became more vibrant, almost glowing in the light of her lamp. It pushed forward, until its head was over the shelf she was on, until she could have reached out and touched it. More rock fell behind it, around it, around her. It was going to bring the whole room down.

Well, good. It could die with her, then.

*"Come and kill me, too!"*

Her shout echoed through the chamber, and the Tunneler spasmed again, surging forward. But without stone to swim through, it was clumsy, and it was heavy, and as Gyre watched, its flesh began to distort, to distend. It couldn't support its own weight, and it fell, its body crashing through the thin stone left in the ceiling. She rolled onto her side, covering her head with her arm as rock screeched over rock, as boulders gave way, as the ground split. She crawled, falling forward, toward the hole in the wall.

Behind her, she heard a sound, loud, modulating, rising and falling quickly, erratically. It was like the screech of an animal, or a child in pain. It was a howl, a plea, and she could almost make out words in it. She twisted, staring behind her.

It was the Tunneler.

It writhed in the gap, its head on the stone close to her, its tail at the other side of the chamber, twisting desperately, trying to wind itself into the hole the waterfall spilled from. The pressure was too great, though, and it couldn't stabilize itself. Its body sagged into the pit, and it thrashed, twisted, tried to angle itself into the stone beneath her feet.

And then, still screaming, loud enough to hurt, loud enough to become her whole existence, it fell. It slipped from the ground near her, and into the chasm, and then it was gone, the howl echoing up until, finally, there was only a distant, crashing thud, a heavy shake in the stone beneath her.

Everything was still.

Her faceplate jerked and extended, closing over three-quarters of her face but no more.

### NOD IF YOU CAN READ THIS

Gyre nodded, shaking.

### WHAT THE FUCK WERE YOU THINKING

She had no way to respond, so she just laughed weakly and fell back against the boulder.

### YOU JUST FOUGHT A TUNNELER AND LIVED
### I COULD HAVE LOST YOU

But she hadn't.

Not yet.

But even though Gyre had defeated the monster without plunging into the depths with it, that didn't stop her slow, inexorable death. The cool air felt so good on her forehead. Her thoughts were spinning, disjointed, and all she could do was stare out at the chasm, at the wreckage of the ceiling.

She'd killed a Tunneler. She'd lived. But she wasn't going to make it to Camp Four now. It was all for nothing.

STILL SHOULDN'T TALK. OTHER TUN

Gyre looked at the words, confused.

I DIDN'T DESIGN THE SUIT SO YOU COULD TYPE, Em kept writing, and then the words ran off the broken half of her faceplate. It reappeared: WITH ONE-WAY TRANSMISSIONS. YOU NEED TO KEEP—another gap—CAN YOU MOVE?

She wasn't sure, but she tried. She pushed herself up from the rock behind her, and her body obeyed, more or less.

GOOD

A pause. She could picture Em, angry, scared, determined. Trying to be professional. Trying not to waste time crying or begging. Trying to be better than Gyre had been after the collapse.

THIS GAP LEADS TOWARD CAMP FOUR. I DON'T

The text ran off the broken edge, reappeared:

I NEED YOU TO GO THROUGH IT. I NEED YOU TO GET TO CAMP
I'LL GET YOU OUT

The last sentence remained on her screen after all the other text had faded. Gyre exhaled slowly through her nose, then pushed forward, shouldering her way through the passage.

Surrounded by it, she couldn't hear anything but her own breathing and the faint whirring of her air-exchange fans. No thrum, no roar, no song deep in her chest. Everything was silent, like crawling through a tunnel in a pseudocave, like her childhood home when her parents had gone.

A few meters in, the tunnel widened, the ceiling rising, and soon she could stand and stagger forward. It led her out into a small chamber, and she looked around, her headlamp passing over unbroken stone, unbroken stone, unbroken—

THERE. TO YOUR LEFT, SIX METERS. THERE'S—
YOU'RE CLOSE.

Gyre didn't see anything, but she went to it all the same. But there was only a blank wall of unfeeling rock. She pressed her hand to it, clawed her fingers against it.

DOWN. LOOK DOWN.

And there it was, a crack, barely big enough to squirm through where she stood, but widening out to her left. And below it was a cavern. Her lamp didn't illuminate much beyond the crevice, but she could tell it was big. She could feel it yawning below her.

CAMP FOUR, Em wrote. I'M COMING. GET DOWN THERE. WAIT FOR ME

Gyre nodded, shivering.

WAIT FOR ME
WAIT

388

# CHAPTER THIRTY-FOUR

She made herself go slowly.

Without her left arm, she couldn't climb up, but she could set a bolt and rappel down if she was careful. Without her reconstruction, with only her headlamp, she had less information to work with, less handholding for her fevered brain. But she was able to place one last, strong anchor, and tie into it. She could see, as she dropped over the edge, that there was a good foothold. A good first handhold.

It was enough to keep her moving.

She tried to re-create what Camp Four looked like in her mind. A cavern, with a shaft near the center of the ceiling. Branching tunnels, one of which led to the waterfall she'd climbed up. The shelf covering Jennie's rot. The sloping path down to the cliff. This entrance, the slot she'd pushed herself through, must be up in the vault, as impossible to spot as Eli's niche had been.

Halfway down she took a break to orient herself, hanging loose on her rope. She should have placed a bolt, tied in, made sure she couldn't fall if the line snapped farther up, but she was tired. Too tired to think, too tired to move. Too tired to consider that Jennie had died doing exactly the same thing. The damp chill of the air was filling her helmet now, displacing all her fevered heat, wrapping around her face and throat. It had settled into her skin, and she realized she was shivering. Her broken suit wouldn't be able to maintain her body temperature forever. Her stomach was in agony, every movement and every swallow of saliva causing another spike of pain.

But all she had to do was get down and make it a few more hours. Em would be there. Trembling, exhausted, she locked her rappel rack closed. Her head dropped toward the rock.

Em would come for her.

She closed her eyes, drifting half in and out of consciousness. It was so tempting, to let go. But she could see Em's face, hear her voice, her expectant breath. She made herself open her eyes again, squinting at her light reflecting off the rock in front of her. Slowly, she twisted, looking out across the room, her lamp beam not making it to the far wall. She looked down, trying to ignore the foolish hope that Em would already be there, ready to stage her retrieval. Her battery was starting to run low; maybe she'd lost enough time. Gyre could picture it clearly: Em, kitted out in one of her own suits, ready, patient, safe, surrounded by her employees. Maybe former cavers of hers, the few who had gotten out alive, willing to go back in to retrieve the last of their own.

Her light passed over something smooth and round. Gyre frowned, then twisted back, trying to find it again. It hadn't looked like a rock. It had looked like . . .

*Em.*

Em was standing there, in a suit just like Gyre's, her head tilted up at where Gyre clung to the rock. Gyre bit down a broken sob, then tried to move her left arm toward the line again, to begin her descent. She felt it flex, before remembering it wasn't there at all. Her light wavered on Em's helmet, then dipped low enough to see her raise her hand, to reach out for Gyre.

*I'm coming.*

She turned back to the wall, focused on her line. She opened the brake on her rack, and started walking, unsteadily, down the rest of the wall. Em had told the truth. She'd come for her. Tears burned in her eyes, and suddenly she could feel every ache and pain in perfect clarity, perfect detail. Those last meters seemed impossible, her body heavy as she crept downward, her legs unable to take the large, looping jumps she wanted to. She wanted to go faster, was willing to risk the pain, but her body refused.

Her feet touched solid ground at last. Gasping with relief, Gyre fumbled with her equipment, the rattling of her clips loud in the quiet of the cavern. She glanced over her shoulder, into the dark, but couldn't see Em. Em didn't have a light on, was probably using her reconstruction. Any moment now, Em would be here, with her. Em would take her in her arms, lay her down, protect her.

She was on the ground.

When had she fallen? She didn't remember, couldn't tell if she'd tripped, or if her legs had buckled, or if there was somebody with her now, easing her down to rest. But she squinted and turned her head, twisting, writhing. Her light arced through the darkness, illuminating only stone.

Em was gone.

Em had never been there.

Gyre groaned and tried to sit up. One-armed, her stomach taut and swollen with infection, she could only roll onto her side. Her lamp burned against the stone, blinding her. Her battery indicator hovered at twelve percent.

She was going to die.

She'd told Em she wouldn't, couldn't, but her bravado felt false now, laughably wrong. She should have known she couldn't do this, couldn't get out alive where so many others had failed.

Down in the sump, when she'd been caught up in the current that first time, it had happened too fast for her to see the shape of what was coming for her. Even in the cave-in, even as she'd begged Em to amputate her arm, even as she'd felt death so close at hand, there had been a shred of hope. There had been a path forward. But now there was nothing. There was only blackness and pain.

She was going to die.

Her lungs spasmed in terror, terror so much more powerful than what she'd felt as her suit locked up around her at Camp Six. There was nothing left to struggle toward. There was no way forward. There was no chance to speak to Em one last time, to hear another person's voice, to feel their presence. A week ago, a lifetime ago, she would have shrugged it off. Accepted that one day, she would die alone. But that loneliness had never felt more acute. Death came for her, wearing a form she couldn't fight.

It was coming.

She looked at the kill switch, looked at the remaining amounts of every drug Em had loaded into her suit. Her breath juddered from her chest, filling her helmet with moisture. It condensed in the chill, fogging her screen, blurring the words.

All it would take was a single motion. All it would take

was selecting morphine, dialing up the dosage until it used every last drop. That sac was still full, untouched, unused. Em had listened to her, had kept her promise.

She stared at the level indicator.

*Em.*

Gyre licked at her lips, dry and cold and cracked, searching for her strength, for her commitment. All it would take would be to say yes. But to do that would be to lose this trace of Em. Em had intentionally left this untouched, for her. For her life. As a gesture of respect, of trust.

It was as if that level indicator *was* Em.

"You're coming to get me," she mumbled, her swollen lips aching.

Gyre stared at her display, reaching out as if she could touch it. Then, reluctantly, she closed down the interface, staring instead out into the cave. All Gyre had to do was wait.

The darkness settled around her, black and cold. Her stomach burned.

She was alone.

Alone, but not alone. She could feel them close at hand, all the others who Em had watched die in this cave. They were her reflections, all of them: selfish, driven people, strong and foolish, chasing money and glory and success without a care as to why somebody would pay them so much to come on an unknown expedition. What did any of them lack that she possessed? Nothing. Em had been clear: the only thing unique about Gyre was the combination of her failures.

Gyre stared into the blackness. If only she were back at Camp Two. If only Adrian Purcell could bear witness to this, her undoing. His corpse had spoken to her that horrible day when she'd first realized how doomed she was, telling her to turn back, telling her she would wind up just like him. But she had thought it was Em he was warning her about, not the cave.

She hadn't listened.

Movement—at the corner of her eye. She oriented to it, desperate. Her lips formed the shape of *Em*.

And out of the darkness came Jennie.

She approached in a staggering, unnatural gait. The front and back of her suit hung open, jutting from her waist, and Gyre could see the electrodes and tubes strained and taut, jumping with every step. Her body was wreathed in a pale white glow. Fungal tendrils grew from her chest and bloomed from her mouth, and as Gyre watched, their light grew brighter. Brighter.

Jennie stopped only a few steps away, looking down at her.

"You're not real," Gyre mumbled, the words slurred and barely sound at all. "Not again. Won't do it again."

Jennie didn't respond. Instead, she crouched down and grabbed hold of Gyre's ankle.

Gyre stared up at her. "Not real," she slurred again.

Again, Jennie said nothing. She began to pull, and turned away, hauling Gyre behind her as she walked back to the ledge, back toward the Long Drop. Gyre felt herself move, heard the squeal of her suit scraping over stone. She kicked, weakly, but Jennie was relentless. She kept walking, kept walking, until beyond her, Gyre could see another figure clinging to the edge of the cliff, braced along the steep, sloping slab of stone. It was a man, naked and motionless in the darkness. He watched them both with glassy eyes, his body gaunt and haggard, his skin paper-thin. He was pale, so pale, and Gyre remembered him from the cliffside, remembered the face she'd thought had been Isolde's.

Eli.

And there, too, was Isolde. She stood just in front of him, at the edge of the Long Drop, waiting. They were together, the bodies that the cave had swallowed up. The bodies Em had never found.

*Climb down, climb down.* Gyre could hear the call. She could feel it buzzing in the air around her, cold and damp and dark. *Walk into the cave and don't turn back. Stay with us. Stay with all of us. This is where you belong.*

Eli dragged his emaciated body over the lip of the cliff, trailing rope behind him, and joined Isolde. Gyre couldn't follow the motion, couldn't watch him as he moved. She only saw him leave the spot he'd been in and noticed him by Isolde's side, as if Gyre had lost consciousness, only to come to a few seconds later. Jennie was there too, and Gyre was closer, on her knees, crumpled at Isolde's feet.

She looked up, craning her head, her lamp illuminating Isolde's knees, her stomach, her face, all in stark, dancing shadows. All in real, harsh light. Isolde looked older now, older and tired. Real. She crouched down and cupped Gyre's chin in her hands, her fingers bare millimeters from Gyre's skin, separated only by the plate of carbon below her jaw. Gyre wanted that touch, craved it, and she reached up, fumbling with her helmet. The screen flashed warnings.

### 5% CHARGE REMAINING

She didn't care. She found the release. Took the helmet off and cast it aside.

Isolde smiled at her, then held a finger to her lips.

*Don't speak.*

Isolde was right. If she spoke, she'd call the Tunneler back. If she spoke, the cave would collapse, and she wouldn't be able to climb down. If she was quiet, if she crawled to the edge of the cliff, found her line, clipped in, she could join Eli. She could be with Isolde. Then when Em came, she would follow them all. Em would follow her down, desperate to find her, and then they'd be together, all of them, in the heart of the cave. They'd be together in the blackness.

She wanted that. She wanted that more than she'd ever wanted anything, except maybe to feel her skin again, to see her body. She looked down at herself. Her helmet sat beside her, the lamp still on, illuminating the segmented plate of her suit. It wasn't her. None of it was her. She watched Isolde's hands skim over her legs and nodded. She understood.

Jennie had been trapped in her suit when she died, and now she stood, rotting, glowing, unnatural and wrong. But Eli and Isolde, they had died honestly. They had died themselves.

She wanted to be herself, before her battery gave out and locked her in place.

Her fingers followed the path Isolde laid out for her, and she began cracking apart her suit. Without her helmet on, she couldn't trigger its release, and it fought her. But she pried it apart bit by bit, freeing her feet, her calves, her thighs. One shin was covered in warped, diseased flesh, the blister that had been there now infected, the skin swollen and hot against the cool air. It went numb once it was exposed and the chill seeped in. It felt good, but soon she shivered. The gel on her exposed legs cooled quickly, and with it so did her blood. If she could only get the cold up higher, onto her stomach, high enough to numb the pain, then she could take the rope, start to climb down.

She could hear the cave calling to her.

*Down, down, down.*

That was when she saw her. Jennie, splayed open and motionless just a half meter away, so close to the shelf that she had died under. She looked different now, duller, stiller. Gyre crawled to her. She reached out and touched her, nudged her, lifted her chin. The glowing fungus that had already colonized what was left of her eyes swayed. Gyre no longer felt guilt for desecrating Jennie's body, or shame for not having rescued her. They were together now, and all Gyre could feel was relief.

She wasn't alone.

Shaking from cold, from infection, from exhaustion, she curled up next to Jennie, tucking her head against the other woman's shoulder.

Just a moment's rest, and then she'd climb down.

# CHAPTER THIRTY-FIVE

Water.

She smelled it first, the mineral edge in the air, the subtle drop in temperature that followed. She could even taste it, a faint clearness on her tongue that instantly made her throat contract and her lips feel dry, so dry.

The water was coming.

She could hear it now, the distant trickle that grew to a rush that bloomed into a roar. Water, cascading over stone. In the glow of a thousand fungal filaments that grew from her body and Jennie's beside her, twining them together, Gyre watched as the first trickle snaked past her bare legs, her hunched form, growing, growing, until it touched the lip of the Long Drop and sheeted down.

She watched as the Long Drop filled to the lip, buoying up a constellation of glow. And down in the water was

Isolde. She floated at the surface, silent, pale, beckoning, Eli sunken just below her, bound in climbing rope.

It was a final invitation. It was time.

Boots rang out against stone, above the roar.

She shivered, pressing her face against the mass beside her. The scent of cold rot replaced the sharp brightness of water spray. She closed her eyes, then opened them. The water was gone. The glow was gone. There was no fungus on her skin, in her flesh.

She had lost part of herself.

Rope dragged against stone. Something touched down heavily. Then something lighter. The click of carabiners opening and closing.

Footsteps, running footsteps.

Then the lights came on, two of them, two bobbing, burning globes in the darkness. She couldn't see who they were attached to, but she saw them get closer, closer. She saw one draw up short, surprised. Then it moved more quickly, sprinting, and Gyre's heart pounded as it approached, drawn as if by the call of the cave itself.

And then Em was there, backlit by the lamp behind her. Gyre couldn't see her face, but she could see her wide hips, her short legs. She knew. She *knew*.

Gyre's lips parted, trembled.

*She's not real*, whispered her mind.

But Em felt real as she crouched beside her, as her light illuminated Gyre's frigid legs. Em felt real as she beckoned her companion over, as they turned to each other, their heads bent as if talking. But Gyre couldn't hear them.

She made herself sit forward, roll onto her knees. Her stomach was swollen and taut, burning with fever. Something gave, and hot, fetid slime slithered down between the remaining plates of her suit and her skin, marking a path over her hip, onto her exposed thigh.

Em had stopped moving, watching as Gyre crawled to the edge of the Long Drop.

Em was here. Em was really here. Gyre could have sobbed from the relief. She had thought she wasn't strong enough to go on.

But with Em, she could be.

Em followed her, looking back over her shoulder at her companion. Her suit looked strange, badly fitted, ill worn. Wrong, in all the ways that Jennie had once looked wrong. If Em wasn't real—

She reached the cliff's edge and grabbed for the line.

Em knelt at her side, her faceplate sliding up. She reached out to touch Gyre, then stopped, as if afraid. There was barely any light now, but Gyre could make out the curve of her cheek, the glint of reflection from one eye.

"Gyre, I've come to take you home," Em said, and it was her voice in the darkness.

Gyre smiled, relieved, so relieved. "This *is* home," she said.

Em stiffened, drawing back a moment. But then she said, "I can't go on without you," and reached out and took Gyre's hand, tugged it close to her breast. Clasped it tightly. Gyre curled her fingers around Em's.

She understood.

"Come with me," Gyre said. "If we climb down together, we'll never be alone again. They're all down there, Em."

"Gyre—"

"They're waiting. Isolde is waiting. We belong down there, with them."

Em made a small noise of pain, and then her arms were

around Gyre, and she was hauling her away from the edge of the cliff, up to her feet. Gyre gasped and nearly fell, fighting against her suit. But even as she struggled, she felt the faint whir of the remaining servos and filters go quiet, felt her arm lock into place. The batteries had finally given out. She thrashed, eyes burning with tears. If she couldn't move her arm, then how could she climb? Pain spiked up from her belly in a way she couldn't comprehend, couldn't remember ever feeling before, and she felt as if she were falling. She felt the world fracturing around her.

"Em, please," she said, gasping.

"You don't belong down here," Em murmured in her ear. "You never did. Maybe I do, but you deserve the sun. Gyre, please, stay with me."

"I belong with them," Gyre whispered, struggling to stand, to look back. "This is why you couldn't let go. It wasn't your fault. It was never your fault. It was always the cave."

"The cave is just a hole in the ground," Em said. "It never deserved any of you."

Gyre looked at Em, her chest heaving. She was shaking again, shivering violently. She was so cold, and burning up, all at once.

Something was very, very wrong.

"Don't leave me," Gyre whispered.

"I won't," Em said. She smiled, and the light caught her lips enough, or perhaps Gyre was feverish enough, to see that it was a pained smile, a desperate smile. A smile that wanted to be true, very much. "Gyre, if I could give you the world, I would. Never doubt that."

And then the other caver was at her side, helping Em support her, pulling her away from the Long Drop, toward the shaft. The other caver attached a cable from their suit to hers, and the plates around her shoulders loosened once more, drawing power across the tenuous connection.

"We have to find Eli. Find Isolde. They're just a little deeper—we can't leave them—"

Em bowed her forehead to Gyre's. "I am taking you home, and I am sealing this cave. It's time to put the past away."

*Yes.* Em was right, as much as Gyre's heart ached. Yes, Gyre wanted to get out. She wanted the sun. And if the cave remained open, she knew she would walk back in, one day. It was the right decision.

But she struggled, searching for Jennie's body. They held her tight as she tried to twist, tried to reach back.

"Jennie," she said. "You can't leave Jennie."

Her saviors paused.

"Bring her out," Gyre said, with all her remaining strength. "Bring her out, please. At least her. At least. If we won't join the rest, bring her home."

Em leaned in, her breath ghosting over Gyre's cheek, the sensation shattering in its simplicity. "Of course," Em whispered. "Of course."

Gyre closed her eyes, shaking with relief. She felt herself go limp. Felt herself be set down on something long and flat. Heard one of them walk away. Felt the odd, swaying weightlessness as she began to move, up and up.

She felt sunlight on her cheeks.

She slept.

# CHAPTER THIRTY-SIX

"Please state your name and age for the record."

"Gyre Price, twenty-two years old."

"And how long has it been since you were pulled out of cave designation Lethe, location undisclosed?"

"Three weeks. About."

"Please give as exact an answer as you can, Ms. Price."

Gyre met Em's gaze, her lips twisting into a bitter smile. "You already know."

"For the record." Was Gyre imagining the apology in Em's eyes?

"I think it's been nineteen days. I don't know. I've been unconscious for a lot of them."

She had only seen Em a few times over those long weeks, brief meetings overseen by physicians, psychologists. Nobody knew all of what had passed between them, but everybody had seemed afraid to leave them in a room together unsupervised.

Apparently that had changed. Had the doctors given permission, or had Em decided she didn't care?

The room they sat in was stark and clinical, the walls a bare white, the table between them simple and metal. Gyre sat on one side of it, a temporary prosthetic arm strapped to her stump and supported by a sling across her chest, a test to see how quickly she was healing and how soon she could be fitted with the real thing. On the other sat Em, and to her left a mirror hid any number of observers, concealed behind a twisted reflection of Isolde's interview tape.

Em was sweating.

Gyre fixated on the thin beads of moisture dotting her hairline. The detail was so small her helmet's display would have never rendered it, and so honest it made Gyre's pulse speed up. Real. This was real.

How many nightmares had she had in the last nineteen days, where this exact scenario had played out in more monstrous ways?

"And how are you recovering from your injuries?" Em asked, her voice, so familiar, breaking through the brittle glass of Gyre's worries. *Focus on me*, it said, and Gyre listened. She had been well trained.

"Fine," she said, even as her hand went to her side. It hurt. She'd insisted they take her off painkillers for this interview. She hadn't wanted to answer Em's questions while out of her mind on drugs. She'd wanted to face her as her own person.

*Her own person.* Gyre wanted to laugh.

Em must have insisted on the comfortable chair they'd dragged into the room for this interview. It let her lean back slightly, and supported her abdomen, still weak from the rupture of her large intestine and stomach lining, and the ensuing infection. She was swathed in comfortable, easily laundered clothing, and her hair had been carefully combed and retwisted. Now more than ever, she was Em's creature, dragged back to some form of half sanity from the precipice of the Long Drop, packed back into the shape of a woman.

The seconds ticked by, stretching into minutes, and Gyre realized that Em was struggling to find something to say, her eyes darting to the mirror.

Gyre watched as she took several deep breaths, her chest rising and falling beneath the tailored teal fabric of her dress. A thousand emotions flashed over Gyre's brain, stoking her anxiety. She couldn't endure for long, not with an audience. "Let's get this over with."

"Right." Em forced a thin smile. And just like that, she rearranged her features into calm distance. But Gyre knew where to look now, knew where the cracks would show. It was in her breathing, as familiar as Gyre's own. It was in the pursing of her lips, faint but undeniable. "This interview will specifically cover your encounters with the Tunneler, at the request of the biological research arm of Arasgain Technologies, working in cooperation with Oxsua Mining," Em said, nodding to the mirror with only a slight grimace to betray her distaste of working with her mother's employer. "Are you ready to begin?"

"Just the Tunneler?"

"Yes, we don't need to discuss anything outside of that scope. They have a theory, something to do with life cycles, mating displays, and aquifers."

"Good for them."

"They would like to hear about the circumstances leading up to each sighting, from your perspective."

"Then give them your records," Gyre said.

Em recoiled, her self-control fracturing. "Those—"

"Are going to be more accurate than anything I could tell them."

It was the truth; her memories of those last few days belowground were chaotic and twisted, warped by fever and pain and terror. She remembered everything in perfect clarity, and at the same time could only see brilliant, terrible moments, disconnected and overwhelming, when she tried to focus.

Em looked at her for a long time, then touched a button on her side of the table. Shutters slid down over the mirror. The camera aimed at Gyre went dead, its green light blinking out. "Gyre," Em said, "if I give them those records, you'll never climb again. I can't take that option from you."

That was the truth, too. Three days ago, she'd requested access to everything Em's computers had on her, and Em had approved it. Despite her appointed psychologist's best efforts, Gyre had gone through all of it. The recordings weren't continuous and didn't always have the video of what she'd been seeing through her reconstruction, but there had been enough. She'd listened to herself scream for Em to amputate her arm, listened to herself talk to the ghost of Isolde, listened to herself dying.

She'd wanted to understand what had happened to her. She'd failed.

Em was right. Nobody would ever hire her again after listening to that, not even if she successfully integrated with her prosthesis and got over her newfound fear of the dark.

She shook her head. "I don't want to go back down."

*That* was a lie.

She could still see Isolde sometimes when she closed her eyes. She could feel the rot in her stomach and the cool, dank air of the cavern on her face. She could still feel the pull, the relentless tug, the invitation to climb back down and forget the

406

world above, give in and close off all the pain and the struggle and the loneliness.

What would it feel like, to go back in? To find a different crack into the world below the ground? Even in a different cave, would she still hear its call?

What would it be like, to go down with a team of handlers, management, a reasonable plan?

To go down without Em?

"I don't want you to go back down either," Em said, interrupting the spiraling path of her thoughts, bringing her back to the surface. "But I—I can't decide for you, not anymore. If I give them those records, I ruin you."

Gyre laughed sharply. "Like you haven't done that already."

Em recoiled as if struck, and Gyre imagined how it would feel to punch her, to grab her, to hold her down. She shifted in her chair, then covered her face with her remaining hand. Skin against skin. It felt good. It felt like everything she'd wanted when she'd been down in that cave.

She was topside now. She held on to that fact, looking around at the room and its contents: all man-made, nothing out of stone. She felt the anger subside.

"I'm sorry," Em murmured. "I'll never be able to express how sorry I am, but I—look, I'll give them those records if you ask me to, but in return, you need this." She placed a card onto the table between them. "That's your key to get to the black box. It opens in two days. It's yours, all yours. The recordings will cover things my computers didn't keep, and they're unalterable, easily verifiable. You can access them for any purpose without needing permission from me. I'm going to destroy my own key."

Gyre stared at the card, then picked it up, turning it over in her hand. She waited to feel something. Vindication, maybe.

Empowerment. Even shame, whether for recording Em to blackmail her or for being afraid that Em would hate her for it, when it had been her best option.

But she felt hollow. "What do you think I should do with them?" she asked. Because, really, what *could* she do with them? Em had never admitted to breaking any laws, was on record being honest and human and broken, and every contract Eli and Jennie and all the rest had ever signed had been airtight. Legal. The bedrock on which the colony's economy had functioned for almost its entire existence.

All the recordings proved was that she'd never had a chance, that she had signed up to be the plaything of a broken rich girl. And what could she gain from it? Tickets off-world waited for her as soon as she decided where she wanted to go. A fat paycheck sat in her account, transferred in before she ever left the cave. She already had more than she'd dreamed of when she took the job.

It was a useless relic of another time. A reminder of her ultimate powerlessness.

"If you make those files public, if you let everybody hear me explain not only what I did, but why I did it, you'll give my competitors the ability to destroy me," Em said.

*Oh.*

Those recordings would open Em up to criticism, hatred, even mockery for her weakness and madness. It couldn't harm her in court, no, but it didn't need to.

Em would never find an investor again, never hire a caver again. She would likely have to step down from her position in Arasgain. Who would trust her to run a business, when they knew how many lives, how many resources, she'd wasted not for profit but for grief?

A legal remedy paled in comparison.

The card rested like a leash in Gyre's hand, a leash that wrapped around her horrible, beautiful monster's throat. And Em had placed it there willingly.

"What now?" Gyre whispered.

"Whatever you want. I'll buy you your tickets before the box opens so you can make your choice freely. No more playing on a rigged board."

She could leave. Take the money and go. Take the money and destroy Em anyway. She could get off this planet, get away from the siren call of the caves, get away from Isolde forever.

She could find her mother.

The thought stunned her momentarily, and then she said, "Buy two."

"What?"

"Two tickets." Her fractured memory blurred with the recordings. She'd been delirious with fever, and Em had said . . . "The two of us, walking into my mother's boardroom, me in the suit. I want to do that. I want you to be there. I want you to be there at the end."

Em reached across the table and took Gyre's hand, lacing their fingers together. The touch was electric, racing through Gyre's nerves and to her heart, which stammered in her chest. This was *real*.

"It's not the end," Em whispered. "You saw me at mine, and I'm still here. I haven't left."

"We walk back out of the cave," Gyre said slowly.

Em nodded. She rose, circling around the table, sitting on its edge and clasping Gyre's hand with both of hers. "Do you think you can do it? Put the suit on again?" Her eyes searched Gyre's face. "You don't have to. You never have to."

"I can do it, to see the look on her face. Come with me."

Em's hands tightened again.

"Nobody else understands," Gyre said. "Nobody else will ever know what it was like down there, not even if they watch the recordings a thousand times. If we're apart, we're alone. I don't want to be alone."

"I don't want to hurt you again. Ever again," Em whispered.

"Come with me," she repeated. She couldn't articulate the rest of it, how Em leaving would hurt, how her staying would hurt, how there was no way either of them could ever win. But she wanted Em there, with her. She wanted to experience the pain together, to struggle together, to hate each other and need each other, maybe even to love each other when the rubble cleared. She'd thought about it every day since waking up, and so many days before. It was foolish, and dangerous, and the Gyre of two months ago would have hated her for thinking this way about the woman whose obsession had brought them to this moment.

But it was the truest thing she had left. When Gyre had been ready to follow Isolde, Em had been there to carry her back into the sun. When Em had been forced to see the full horror of everything she'd done, Gyre had seen the humanity in her. They had broken each other open down in the dark, and now that their wreckage was splayed out in the light, Gyre recognized every inch of Em, and Em knew every inch of her.

Gyre slipped her hand from Em's, set the card aside, and reached up to cup Em's cheek.

Em slid from the table, going down on her knees in front of Gyre. "I don't know what I'd do without you," she confessed. "But I can't do it again. I can't base my life around an obsession. I can't follow you down into that cave, I can't give up, I can't—"

"I'm not asking you to give up."

Gyre leaned down despite the pain and kissed Em, the

briefest contact, sensation arcing down her spine. This was the woman who'd put her in that suit, who'd sent her down chasing ghosts knowing it would likely end in death, but who also had refused to *let* her die, over and over again. Em had fought for her even though death was Em's thesis, was her conclusion, was the only thing that should have waited for Gyre. Even though the twisted rot that had destroyed so much had already destroyed the both of them, almost to the core.

Gyre could see it, though: a small fleck of humanity, surrounded by a shell of pain that was beginning to crack, beginning to give way.

And she couldn't be certain, when she got down to that point, whether she was thinking of herself or Em. They both had two options: fester and die, or take what they were given and grow.

"I'm asking," Gyre said, pulling back only a few centimeters and meeting Em's gaze, "for you to *try*."

# ACKNOWLEDGMENTS

First and foremost, I want to thank my husband, David Hohl, for going on this journey with me, for reading my drafts, and for keeping me sane. Thank you for encouraging me to send my book out into the world; without your excitement and confidence, I may never have believed my writing was ready to share. And thank you, too, for correcting my climbing errors. Any mistakes remaining are my doing alone.

To Shyela Sanders, my closest friend and my loudest cheerleader. Thank you for the time you spent with me in the trenches of the first draft, helping me brainstorm much of the original structure, and for every time after that I ran to you with plot problems, triumphs, and fears. This book would not exist without you.

To Morgan Azinger, Katie Marsh, Thea Price, Krystal

Loh, and Sarah Hofrichter for believing in me, celebrating the highs with me, and reassuring me through the lows.

To Madeleine Roux, whose feedback and encouragement made it clear that publishing was the path I wanted to take.

To my agent, Caitlin McDonald, for seeing the promise in this little book, and for your patience, your guidance, and your advocacy; as well as to Rae Chang, Kiki Nguyen, and the whole of Donald Maass Literary Agency for championing me and guiding me through this whole process.

To my editor, David Pomerico, for constantly challenging my assumptions. You made me dig deep and think hard, and it's no exaggeration to say that any version of *The Luminous Dead* without your involvement would have been an entirely different beast, and weaker for it. And to the rest of the Harper Voyager team, with specific thanks to Nate Lanman for keeping this engine moving forward and answering so many of my questions.

To my father, David Starling, and my stepmother, Stacey Starling, for always believing in me. To Dave Hohl and Sukey Hohl for accepting me as your own and supporting me from the first day we met. To my aunt, Carolyn Gehret, thank you—despite being a little afraid of the dark, you have shared and amplified my triumphs at every turn. And to my grandfather, Ned Gehret, for always knowing I'd publish a book one day.

And finally, this book could never have existed without my mother, Betsy Starling. You taught me how to write, how to love, and how to grieve. I only wish you were still here so I could share this story with you.

## ABOUT THE AUTHOR

Caitlin Starling is a writer and spreadsheet-wrangler who lives near Portland, Oregon. Equipped with an anthropology degree and an unhealthy interest in the dark and macabre, she writes horror-tinged speculative fiction of all flavors. *The Luminous Dead* is her first novel.